TEL AVIV
RAMALLAH

YOSSI YONAH

The wind does not blow at the ship's whims (Arabic proverb)

CONTENTS

Tel Aviv Ramallah

Yossi Yonah

CHAPTER 1
Hadil

She waited for the taxi that would take her from Ramallah to the Allenby Bridge, desperate to be out of the house. It was early on a Friday morning and the first signs of spring were in the air. Hadil was heading to a hotel on the Jordanian side of the Dead Sea, as moderator of a Jewish-Palestinian workshop. The following day she would travel to Amman, where she would spend the night with her friend Arij. Her husband Hisham took measured sips from his black coffee, while silently fuming. Sensing the charged atmosphere, their children Leila and Nadim, about to be driven to school by their father, wasted no time attending to their breakfasts. Hadil placed her hand on Nadim's forehead again, whether in a caress or to ensure that the fever he'd suffered during the night had abated.

A car horn was heard from the driveway to their home. The honk was sharp yet short and somewhat hesitant, as if to avoid an unnecessary disturbance. It was how their driver Amer always announced his arrival. Hadil leapt from her seat, thankful to be rescued from the tension of the dining area, then quickly planted a kiss on Leila's forehead as her eyes searched for Nadim. She hadn't noticed that Nadim had slipped into the bathroom just moments before and locked the door She pressed her face against the bathroom door and called, "Come on, *habibi*, baby, come say goodbye to your mother before I leave."

"No."

"*Ya ruhi*, my soul, please, open the door."

"No!"

She tried to coax him to open the door over and over before sadly giving up. Hisham looked at her reproachfully. He had been sitting in his chair, silent, the entire time. She marched then to the door, pulling a small black trolley suitcase with squeaky wheels behind her with her left hand and carrying her handbag in the right. Hisham did not accompany her to the waiting taxi or respond to her goodbye. Leila rushed forward to help her mother, opening the front door for her and taking the bag. Hadil reclined comfortably in the back seat and let out a silent sigh of relief.

After driving through the Hijmeh checkpoint, Amer inserted a CD of songs by legendary Iraqi singer Nazem al-Ghazali into the car's player. Before filling the taxi with his enchanting voice, Amer asked if the music was to Hail's liking. She was about to say that she preferred to make the journey in silence, but she shrugged her shoulders instead and said it made no difference to her. The disc was of poor quality, a cheap bootleg. But Amer enjoyed the warm voice of the artist who'd passed away more than five decades earlier. Hadil was very familiar with the songs of course; Nazem al-Ghazali was her husband's favorite. A thought passed through her mind: was there some kind of guiding hand here or was she merely succumbing to the foolish human urge to search for a hidden omen, some obscure meaning, perhaps a coincidence? Amer seemed to read her mind. He smiled and asked if she liked the singer. She replied that she did, adding almost incidentally that his songs are masterpieces. A slight twist hung at the corner of her mouth. This is exactly how Hisham described his songs - *Rwaa' al-Fan*, masterpieces.

"Nowadays no one sings like Nazem al-Ghazali, Allah have mercy on his soul," Amer declared, gently shaking his head for emphasis. "D'you know," he added, "he was very young when he died. Some say his wife killed him."

"Some say," Hadil replied tersely. It wasn't the first time Amer had shared his thoughts on the circumstances of his idol's death. Her laconic response didn't weaken his desire to engage her in conversation. His imagination was especially sparked by the thought that the famous singer's wife was responsible for his death. Despite the many years that had passed, the circumstances of al-Ghazali's death continued to generate interest throughout the Arab world. It turned into a source of rumors and innuendo that always tied the death to mysterious forces and dark conspiracies.

"You know," he went on, "after he died, she stopped singing. Out of sorrow. You understand?" he snorted. "First, she kills him, then...." He paused for a moment then continued: "They say his wife, who was Jewish, did it out of jealousy. She too was a great singer in Iraq, possibly the most famous of her generation. I really don't understand it," Amer shook his head, irritated by what seemed to him completely absurd. "Can you imagine," he went on, "anyone killing her husband because she envies his success? But who knows," he added in resignation, "As the saying goes: Who is your enemy, if not your partner in art? Only Allah knows how true that is! Right?" His eyes met hers in the mirror, awaiting her response.

"It doesn't have to be so," Hadil dismissed it, "but then envy can definitely be harmful."

She imagined Hisham's enraged eyes. She stopped listening to Amer though he continued to engage her. Here was this pleasant man, she thought, enjoying the songs of his long-dead idol, and he's full of joie de vivre. He doesn't view al-Ghazali's music as a cultural asset, allowing him to look down on others, those who seemingly lack the delicacy to appreciate quality music, those who can't tell a masterpiece from trash. The bitterness that spoiled Hisham's interest in old Arab music and poetry unsettled and distressed her. Where once she had been able to keep up and match his enthusiasm, in recent years her interest in the subject had begun to wane. It was as if they were moving along separate tracks in opposite directions, destined never to meet again. The more he ensconced himself within Arabic poetry and music – while delivering harangues and diatribes bemoaning the lack of respect for high culture, the growing materialism, and other cultural affronts in Palestinian society - the less she was able to share in his tastes. They increasingly bore the weight of Hisham's sullenness and dashed hopes for making a mark in the field of poetry. Yet this art also signaled her own frustrations with him. Developments in the electronic media had further intensified the estrangement between them. While he spent long hours watching YouTube videos featuring old Arab music, mainly that of the greatest, long-dead Iraqi singers, she was incapable of sympathizing with these songs and the profound sadness within them. The technological advances that were supposed to take the world into the future also furnished Hisham with the means to retreat into the past and escape into an isolated inner realm.

Hadil's face took on a thoughtful and slightly tormented look. Her gaze became trapped in the hilly landscape beyond the car window. The road that led from the eastern slopes of Ramallah to the Jordan Valley, covered most of the year with a yellowish undergrowth, now had a green down. The thought crossed her mind that these are the days of grace for these poor hills, coming as they do once a year for a brief period. Noticing her sad mood, Amer switched off the music and the two travelled in silence. The taxi drove past sad-looking Bedouin encampments that appeared as if they had been scattered along the roadsides, answering some obscure logic not comprehended by a stranger's eyes. She noticed a Bedouin girl in a black gown carrying a shepherd's staff. The girl's eyes wandered away from the herd of white sheep currently grazing on some sparse weeds in the rocky ground. She was looking at the cars that flashed past her, as if sketching in the far-off destinations to which they made their way - places her feet would probably never tread.

For better or worse, Hadil saw her relationship with Hisham as being bound to music and poetry. The ups and downs of their relationship, the highs and lows, were woven in the images, colors, sounds, and sights from that world. It was the desert landscape and roadside encampments that transported her to Hisham's tales of ancient Arab romantic poetry. The desert life, as he had explained to her long ago, provided the inspiration for these poems, and he used one of Umm Kulthum's revered songs as an illustration. They were lying on his narrow bed in the small apartment in Bir Zeit, only minutes after making love. He was on his back, she beside him, her head on his chest, with a thin blanket covering them. A few weeks before, they'd made love for the first time, and were not yet free of the discomfiture of revealing their naked bodies to each other. Hisham went on to tell her about Umm Kulthum and her song *Al-Atlal*, the Ruins of Love.

"You know," he said, proudly showcasing his erudition, "the writer of that song was actually a physician who wrote poetry. They said of him, derisively, that he was the best poet among the doctors and the best doctor among the poets."

Hadil gave him a gentle prod in the ribs and protested: "Don't! It's not kind. It's cruel to say that!"

"It's not me," Hisham smiled sheepishly and moved his body away from her elbow. "It was the critics, it's what they said." He went on to remark that many of the songs in olden times began with a description of the remains of an encampment in which the poet's beloved had once lived. The remains, he explained, implied the regrettable ending of their love story. The story had come to an end when the various tribes, including those of the poet and his beloved, left the oasis and proceeded on their separate travels, each tribe following its own destiny. Hisham then went on to recite the last line of a song by Umm Kulthum: And then we both went our separate ways – don't say we wished it; say fate wished it.

"So what," she retorted focusing her bewildered eyes on him, "you're telling me that we're doomed, that your love for me, the love you are constantly declaring, will perish in the end? That our separation is inevitable?"

"*A'aoz beAllah, habibti*; God forbid, my love," he said, horrified. "I'll always love you. You're the love of my life."

"So why do these songs have such a hold on you?" she asked inquisitively.

He looked at her and whispered tenderly, "My soul has been tied to hers even before we were created."

"Is this also from that Umm Kulthum song?"

"No," he replied, "this was written by the poet Jamil al Ud'ri. He lived a long time ago. He wrote about *hub ud'ri*, virgin love. It is said of him that he was a shahid of love, a martyr of love, that he died from love, virgin love, unconsummated love."

"A shahid of love?" Hadil repeated incredulously.

"Ah, ah, *hec*, exactly! A shahid of love!" Hisham said emphatically and recited a line from Al-Ud'ri: "They say to me, Ya Jamil, brace for jihad! But the only jihad I wish is the one waged on behalf of their smiles when they utter a *hadith*. Only then am I willing to be a shahid."

"Seems to me," she teased him, "that for you love is always tied to an ending, to death."

He freed his chest and turned to look at her. He shook his head, smiled, and said, "I swear Hadil, you're *msiba*,trouble." She giggled in gratification.

"We've arrived," Amer cut short her reveries. A self-satisfied smile was spread across his face as if he'd accomplished a grand mission. The journey from Ramallah to the Allenby Bridge had lasted about an hour. On the way they had passed through two more checkpoints with no discomfort or unnecessary holdups: the Jab'a checkpoint east of Kalandia as well as the Musa Alami checkpoint at the southern entrance to Jericho, near the deserted casino once believed to be a sign of long-due rapprochement between Palestinians and Israelis. Hadil thanked him, paid, and added a generous tip. They confirmed that he would come to pick her up at the Allenby Bridge on her way back to Ramallah.

She threw a glance at the disappearing taxi and its back window covered with stickers – *Salli ala al-Nabi*: Bless the Prophet, and *Al hijab ya ochti*: Don't forget the hijab, my sister.

All Hadil had to do now was get through border control on the Israeli side and then on the Jordanian one. It was times like this that she agonized over her refusal to obtain a VIP pass that provided special treatment for senior employees of the Palestinian Authority and their families. Once when Arij whispered to her that her husband Bashir "knew people" with ties to the Palestinian Authority and the Jordanian Royal Court and could obtain such a pass for her, Hadil declined the offer, saying that she'd feel uncomfortable.

"What's your problem?" Arij scolded her. "Anyone who can, gets one.

".*Saha alihom*, good for them!" Hadil shrugged as if to say no.

The transit between the two border points was quick and smooth, devoid of any distressing interrogations. She boarded the bus that picked up the workshop's participants from the West Bank towns and arrived at her hotel.

CHAPTER 2
Yoav

The traffic was sparse on Friday afternoons at the checkpoint between Ramallah and Bir Nabala. Dressed in their ceramic vests and protective helmets, the soldiers threw perfunctory looks at the passing cars. The weather was between seasons per usual yet still felt jarring, as if all the seasons of the year had been pushed into a single day. The morning had begun under a veil of grey clouds, the air thickening as it rose into hesitant light showers. The temperatures started to climb towards noon as a heavy mist made itself felt. Coolness filled the air once the evening dispersed the heat of the day. The sharply-shifting weather provided a suitable background to the political climate. As the religious holidays drew near, hopes for peace initiatives were sparingly rekindled, followed by warnings of potential terrorist attacks and attempts to abduct soldiers.

"You should be prepared for a hot spring," their commanding officers told them repeatedly. Yoav had just finished talking with his parents. They called him daily and, when they heard of any disturbance in the occupied Palestinian territories, however minor, they would call several times a day, wanting to be reassured that he was safe.

He looked around indifferently. There was nothing in the hilly landscape that was exciting or appealing. He was doing his shift at the Rafat checkpoint, known as the Fabric of Life checkpoint. It was situated on a sharp-edged asphalt road, carved under the main highway connecting the cities of Jerusalem and Modi'in. Rafat had been established to provide the villages of Bir Nabala, al-Judeira, Al-Jib, and the ancient Beit Hanina, which otherwise found themselves encircled on all sides by a massive high wall, direct access to Ramallah. Tall piles of wrecked vehicles - likely awaiting recycling - and the stone quarries belonging to the Um-Shuriet village, which spread over the slopes to the north of Rafat, gave the location a decidedly charmless aspect. This horizon far beyond the village was adorned with high-rise residential buildings standing in the middle of Ramallah. To the south rose the tall buildings of Kafr 'Aqab. It stood a short distance from the checkpoint, barely touching an indistinct point at the top of the hill from which the road had been carved. Various vehicles made their way up the road toward Bir Nabala before vanishing from view the minute they crossed the horizon, as if they'd fallen into some waiting abyss. To the west meanwhile, the village of Rafat was hidden from sight by tall dirt ramparts. Yoav's army reserve unit had begun to man the checkpoint only a few days earlier.

"Just another place," he announced as he scrutinized the distant landscapes unfolding in front of his eyes.

His friend Alon, who was sharing the shift, nodded in agreement. "Yeah, it's boring as hell here."

"Boring's good. Let's just hope it continues like that. Three more weeks and we're going home."

He had made the same comment to Tali before leaving for this tour of reserve service. They sat facing each other across the kitchen table in their apartment on Chen Boulevard, not far from Tel Aviv's Habima Theater. Tali was visibly distressed. He stroked her forearm gently. "Why the long face?" he asked in an attempt to raise her spirits. "It's not like I'm being sent to some commando unit with orders to raid the kasbah in Nablus. They're sure to send me to one of the checkpoints like last time. I'll be back in no time." Tali was not to be placated, expressing her chagrin that he hadn't tried to cancel the reserve duty, hadn't come up with some excuse. "We've discussed this already," Yoav replied impatiently, picking up his kitbag, into which he'd shoved underwear, toiletries, laptop, and a few books: *The Ethnic Challenge of Iraq* and two novels in English. "Well, I've got to go," he announced with an air of inevitability. "I'll call in the evening." Then he hugged her, gave her a peck on the lips, and left. Now, standing with Alon at the checkpoint, Yoav expressed the same vacant optimism.

One Friday night more than a year earlier, he had told his family of his desire to continue his studies in America. With the plate in front of him piled with a selection of traditional Sabbath delicacies, he casually announced his intentions. He was well-aware that the news would not be welcomed lightly, especially by his mother. His desire to pursue an academic career had always met with his family's full support, but leaving the country for several years – that was something else altogether. Here, in one of the pictures from his BA graduation ceremony, the pride in his family's eyes was easy to discern. They were all there: his father Shaul, his mother Nava, his sister Merav who was two years older, his younger sister Sivan, Grandpa Shmuel, and Grandma Camilla. They were all crowded into the photograph, standing happily around him in their best clothes, beaming. Their pride knew no bounds when his name was called among the students graduating summa cum laude. Shaul was in a summer suit with a red-and-blue striped silk tie, Nava beside him, her hair specially styled for the occasion. Their necks were extended, their eyes fixed on the stage, watching him with admiration as he delivered the valedictory speech. They supported their son eagerly when he expressed the wish to take up academic research toward the end of his undergraduate studies. He would be the first PhD in their family – Dr. Yoav Yarkoni! But now, as he expressed his desire to take his studies further afield, emotions were stirred up.

"*Madlik*, cool!" Merav rejoiced. "Now we'll have a brother in

America. We'll be able to visit and stay at your place for a few weeks. The Yarkoni family trailblazer in the land of opportunity."

His sister Sivan, who was close to completing her compulsory military service, was also visibly excited by the prospect. "Please," she simpered, "won't you take me with you?"

His father threw his sisters a reproachful glance. "Enough, stop talking nonsense." He turned his eyes to Nava, obviously wary of her response. "America?" he asked, trying to adopt a more impartial and businesslike tone. "Why there, of all places? Where did you get this idea from?"

Yoav said that his mentor, Professor Na'aman, believed he had a good chance of being accepted into one of the prestigious universities specializing in Middle Eastern Studies. Yoav's research on the ethnic and religious rifts in Iraq during the British Mandate gave him an edge over other candidates.

"Iraq is a very hot topic these days," he pleaded, glancing briefly at his mother, who remained silent while starting to fidget in her seat, like an animal trying to escape a trap. Any minute now the signs of distress on her face would intensify, becoming more decisive; unbridled rage was about to erupt. He knew her well.

"Why does it have to be America?" she protested, trying hard, like his father, to stay calm, to keep her composure and appear indifferent. "You know how proud we are of you and how much we support you, and we're eager for you to succeed… but come on, are there no good universities here that specialize in your subject? Does it make sense to you to move thousands of miles away from me, from the Middle East, in order to specialize in what? The Middle East! Don't you think it's strange that you want to move there to conduct research on things that are happening in Iraq? Can't you do it here in Israel?"

Later that night he told Tali what happened. "It drives me insane when she says you're leaving me, you're flying away from me. It makes me crazy. It's always about her. Leaving her, moving away from her, causing her… she's always the victim. She says she wants to protect us, but she's only concerned with herself. It all comes down to the trauma she went through a million years ago. Enough!" he went on as if to his mother: "Get over it!"

"What do you mean, 'get over it'?" Tali replied crossly. "It's not that easy to get over it, you know?"

"Tell me," he assumed an amused tone, "whose side are you on, mine or hers?"

She didn't reply. He tried again to fathom what was upsetting her. "Tali, what's the matter? What's going on?" She stared at him for a long while, as if struggling to come up with a suitable response, then said dryly: "Drop it. I don't feel like talking." He wondered where he'd gone wrong, what it was that had upset her so much. Then he shrugged and dropped the subject.

Yoav responded with frustration to his mother's chagrin at his desire to further his studies in America. "Mom, what do you mean 'leaving you hundreds of kilometers behind'? I don't plan to stay there forever. I just want…" Nava cut him short. She lost her calm and her eyes flashed. "I don't know," she rebuked him furiously, "according to my logic, if you want to specialize in something, it makes sense to be close to it – not to get further away from it. It's like saying you want to strengthen your relationship with Tali and then move to another city." She immediately fell silent, as if becoming suddenly aware that there is more to this point than a rhetorical ploy, a helpful analogy. "Well," she queried somewhat triumphantly, "if we're already on the subject, what does Tali have to say about this? Does she think it's a good idea? Are you going together? Is she staying here? Have you discussed it?" Yoav replied that the decision to study in America had been made together. "It won't be easy to find a university that will take us both, but we'll try." He added that Tali's parents were quite excited by the prospect of the couple furthering their studies together in America. "I don't care," Nava fumed, "what Tali's parents think."

Indeed, this had been her reaction whenever Yoav embarked upon any activity that made her feel unable to protect him and take good care of him should he be in any danger. It had been the same when he opted to do his compulsory military service in the Paratroopers Brigade, and whenever he set out to travel anywhere in the world once his service was over. Yoav's family was familiar with Nava's tempestuous reactions. "There she goes again," they'd say. "This is how Mom reacts when she feels she's losing control over us."

"Whenever any of us," Yoav once jokingly described his mother's behavior, "drops beneath her radar, she goes wild. But once she'd finally realized she couldn't control us," he added, "she developed the habit of withdrawing inside herself, like a tortoise into its shell. Without saying another word, she would sink into the depths of depression, which my father used to describe as 'melancholy'. It would continue for a day or two."

Sometimes it was impossible to know exactly what triggered Nava's rapid change of mood. She would shut herself in her darkened bedroom and sink into a long slumber. Her children learned that at times such as these, there was no disturbing their mother. When the mood passed, she would emerge from her room and act as if nothing had happened. She would fuss around her children, ordering them to carry out various chores, and devote herself to her work as a schoolteacher of language and literature.

Yoav had first heard the expression 'she's sinking into melancholy' one Friday evening around then. His mother had stayed in bed. His father undertook the task of setting the table for Sabbath and serving the dishes his wife had cooked earlier. "Where's Mom?" asked Merav. "She's unwell," Shaul replied tersely. But later, when his maternal uncle Chezi called and asked to talk with Nava, Shaul suggested he call back later, tomorrow even, adding in a whisper, "Nava has sunk into melancholy again." The expression haunted Yoav for much of his childhood. He didn't understand what it meant, although

21

he could sense its dark and foreboding connotations. He was particularly troubled by the word "sunk." In the way of children, he interpreted the word in the simplest sense, imagining various bodies sinking slowly into some kind of liquid: a ship sinking to the ocean floor, his toy car sinking in bathwater, grains of sugar sinking and dissolving in a cup of tea, and so on. One night, he dreamed that he was seeing his mother sink deep into a large vat of putrid water. She was dressed in a white nightgown, her feet ensconced in slippers. Her legs were upright and close together, her hands spread to her sides, mouth gaping and eyes wide open. Fear and anxiety were manifest on her face. Bubbles rose from her mouth to the surface towards the opposite direction of her body, which dropped very quickly downward. Her black hair rose above her head like a long tail trailing downward after her. He awoke terrified.

His decision to further his studies in America provided his father with a great deal of satisfaction. "We'll miss you," he whispered in Yoav's ear, so his wife would not know that despite his initial misgivings, he had come to acquiesce in his son's wishes. "But never mind," he added, "we can visit you from time to time, and you'll surely visit us as well. Your mother too will eventually get used to the idea. It's not the same as those earlier trips of yours to the Far East and those other hellholes all over the world."

It had always been his father's role to counterbalance his mother. While Nava did everything she could to keep her children close to her and close to home, Shaul would loosen the reins, encourage them to slip out from under her wings, and send them out into the big world so they would develop like everyone else, "like normal children," as he used to say. But at the dinner table Shaul made do with questions that were seemingly noncommittal. He turned to his son and asked, "And what about the money? Where are you going to get the money? It must be pretty expensive to study there."

"Don't tell me," Nava cried, detecting in his voice a sign

of compliance with their son's wishes, "that you think it's a good idea for him to go off to America!" She didn't wait for a response and turned her eyes from Shaul to Yoav, letting her fury intensify. "What's all this stuff about opening your mind and developing?" she shouted. "You've opened your mind enough. You've toured the whole of South America, spent months on end in India and the East. Isn't that enough for you? You went off to see the world, to experience new things, and left us here to eat our hearts out with worry. You say this is a crazy place, but what about all those horror stories we hear every day? One day it's the Hindus killing the Muslims, then it's the Sikhs killing the Hindus. Then there's news of some bus rolling down the side of a mountain in Peru, and this is followed by a ferry overturning off the coast of Thailand. And then there are those people who get mixed up in drugs and return to Israel after losing their minds. You're not a child anymore – you're thirty years old. It's time you started thinking about your future!"

"That's exactly what I'm thinking about, Mom," Yoav pleaded. "I'm not thinking of going to the Amazon, to the jungles of Brazil. I want to study in America and then come back and find work here, in Israel, at some university. What? You don't consider that a future?"

Suddenly he changed his tone to one of appeasement, attempting to open a door into her heart. "Doesn't it thrill you that I'll be specializing in Iraq, the country your parents came to Israel from, where Dad was born? Grandpa Aaron always spoke about *Al-Rafidin*, his Mesopotamia: the history, the culture, the poetry, the landscapes, the Euphrates and the Tigris… he spent all those years teaching Arabic in high schools there as well as here. As you did too, Dad. True, you were a child when you left Iraq, but you still have a strong connection to the place, don't you? Your roots and your culture are both there."

"Roots!" his sister Merav cried, barging into the heated exchange. "Since when are you interested in our Iraqi roots? And who, apart from yourself," she grimaced, "wants to reconnect with these roots? It seems to me watching the news that the Iraqis themselves are dying to get out of there, to break away from their roots."

Amused by her picturesque depiction of the upheaval in Iraq, Yoav smiled at her affably, muttering, "stop exaggerating."

"I'm exaggerating?" she chuckled in disbelief. "Believe me, it'll be the best thing for them to get the hell out of there, before they're wiped out by exploding car bombs in the middle of Baghdad. They'll be amazed to learn," she sneered, "that weirdoes like you, in Israel of all places, are clamoring to reconnect with their Iraqi roots." Merav's wit stirred laughter around the table. But Nava was not amused. She seemed once again to have embarked on a journey to melancholy.

"So, you're a purebred Iraqi," Tali teased him once when he was recounting his family's lineage. He looked at her with some trepidation and fired back, "What do you mean by purebred?"

She smiled wryly. "I mean biologically. Your mother and father are Iraqi, both your grandparents are too. No doubt you can trace your ancestry back to the destruction of the first Temple and the expulsion of the Jews to Babylon. It seems to me," she continued to pester him playfully, "that you should be honoring your family tradition and searching for a woman with an Iraqi background. That way you'd be perpetuating and honoring your family's racial purity."

"Fantastic idea," he sneered. "Got a nice Iraqi girl to introduce me to?"

"Now seriously, you're following in your grandfather Aaron's footsteps, aren't you?"

"Maybe," he shrugged, "but my grandfather was very connected to Arabic culture, especially Iraqi culture, and that isn't my forte. I take more of an interest in the political history of the Middle East. I am fascinated more by Rashid Ali al-Gaylani and less by Nazem al-Ghazali."

She raised an eyebrow. "Al-Gaylani was the man who led

the revolt against the British in Iraq in the early 1940s, and al-Ghazali was an adored Iraqi singer. Whining songs, crying and moaning," he added in obvious distaste. "But they continue to cherish those songs!" he uttered in disbelief. "It beats me why to this day he's so popular with members of my family!"

"What nonsense you are talking. Do you really believe it's possible," Tali rebuked him incredulously, "to study the history of Iraq without connecting with its culture, without knowing something of its music, its poetry? And you of all people believe that?!"

He looked at her and replied defiantly, "It's possible. Of course it's possible!"

CHAPTER 3
Hisham

He made his way to his parents' home in the village of Al-Jib on Friday afternoon. Passing through the checkpoint, he continued to drive through the tunnel, crossing the road that connected the cities of Modi'in and Jerusalem. Passing by the villages of al-Judeira and Bir Nabala, he continued until he reached his home village. The soldiers at the checkpoint casually observed the traffic as it sped by uninterrupted. On this occasion, Hisham, who often took his children on such trips to visit his parents', had chosen to leave them at home. He left his house before his daughter Leila finished her school day. He did not want to burden his son Nadim with the trip and left him with Ranin, Hadil's sister. She lived with her husband Elias and their kids in a spacious home perched above a hill of the prestigious al-Tira neighborhood, on the western outskirts of Ramallah. Hadil's frequent absence from home had been a source of much tension between them lately, but on that day her attendance at the Jewish-Palestinian workshop gave him mixed feelings. He and Mandy, the new American teacher of English literature and poetry, were scheduled to meet the next day. Mandy had begun her work at Ramallah's Friends School about a month ago. She replaced the pregnant Nasrin Khuri, whose doctor had ordered her to maintain complete bed rest. He was looking forward to this meeting with some eagerness.

His visit to Al-Jib was his first in a month. Traveling across the West Bank had become a grueling journey whose consequences could not be foreseen. Except for special events demanding his presence, such as births, weddings, and funerals, he did not travel much. Like many West Bank Palestinians, he adopted the maxim: "Unless you have to, don't drive." Not only had his visits to his parents decreased considerably, but Hadil too, had virtually ceased to accompany him on these visits. After all, parents' natural tendency is to identify with their own children when they see them in distress and to resent those they believe responsible for their misery. Hisham and Hadil tacitly understood that if she joined him, his parents wouldn't be able to restrain themselves from saying something, further exacerbating the rift between them.

While his family readily sensed that things were not good between him and his wife, he was still reluctant to share his marriage problems with them. What could he say? That he found it increasingly difficult to put up with Hadil's frequent absences from home? That he was frustrated with her for neglecting their children and her household duties, for being no longer available to him, oblivious to his needs? More than once, he'd overheard his parents grumbling, whispering, suggesting that a woman's place is in the home, taking care of her children and her husband and that the world has now been turned upside down. It was in this way that they let him know what they thought of his marriage, of the disruption that had occurred in the natural order of things. He knew that his family would be attentive if he were to share his problems with them. But he feared that were he to do so, it could affect the possible rapprochement between him and Hadil, and he still wanted to believe that their marriage could be saved. He smiled contritely as an Egyptian proverb went through his mind: "The sage was asked, 'Where is your homeland?' He replied, 'The place where my wife resides'."

His family was quick to notice the signs of a rift between him and Hadil. "He is obviously not happy," his mother used to lament, "even when he says nothing. I can tell; I'm his mother. He's not the same Hisham we knew. Always brooding, quiet. His head is somewhere else. You cannot cover up the sun with a sieve," she would recite a proverb. "It was a mistake to mix breeds that do not mix. You do not mix the month of Sha'ban with the month of Ramadan. Hadil never became one of us, blood of our blood, flesh of our flesh." As she went on and on, grumbling and bleating, her husband and children listened dolefully, making no comment.

When he arrived at his parents' house, he found his father and mother sitting side by side on sofas in the spacious concrete courtyard at the front of the house. The fragrances of spring filled the air but the weather was somewhat inclement. And yet the two preferred to spend the early afternoon hours in the yard, which over the years had become a veranda engulfed on either side by lush vines, now standing in early bloom, sloping with tiny unripe grape clusters. He greeted his parents, kissed them, and sat down on the bed beside his father. "Why didn't you bring your children?" His mother pleaded. "We miss them so much." At the sound of his voice, his sister Siham rushed into the courtyard. Greeting him, she immediately repeated her mother's grievance, and then added, to his chagrin: "Why isn't Hadil with you? How come we no longer see her?" I knew this was coming, Hisham thought, but he replied casually that Hadil had to go to Jordan. "Work," he added dismissively. His parents exchanged furtive glances, as if to acknowledge that nothing could be done. Everyone was familiar with Siham's outspokenness, a result of her mental sluggishness that her family preferred to call mere innocence. "She's simpleminded, naive," they excused her.

Siham never got married and she never left home. When she was a young girl, her parents, Marwan and Nadia, knew they would have trouble finding her a match. Already in her forties, Siham was a good-natured person and well-versed in housework. But these advantages were not enough to find her a suitable match. Her coarse facial features, excess weight, and mental lethargy heavily compromised her prospects. And so while her parents married off all of their children and were blessed with many grandchildren, Siham remained unwed. In recent years, due to strong encouragement by her brother Sharif, she adopted a strict religious lifestyle. She would awaken just after sunrise to attend morning prayer, perform the daily cleansing ritual, and cover her body with a long-sleeved dress and hijab. Every Friday during the month of Ramadan, she would join travelers to Jerusalem for Friday prayers at the Haram al-Sharif mosque, the Temple Mount. In recent years this practice ceased due to the difficulties facing those who did not carry blue IDs and needed to reach Jerusalem or anywhere else in the West Bank. So Siham diligently attended to the various household chores: cooking, baking pita bread in the tabun oven in the yard, scrubbing the floors, laundering clothes, nursing her parents, and serving them loyally.

A few years ago, one of the village elders expressed his wish to marry her, but she vehemently refused. If this is what awaits me, she announced with sobriety that surprised her parents, I would rather stay home with my parents and take care of them instead of becoming a maid to a strange old man. And so Siham resigned herself to her fate, showing no desire to change. She never expressed envy towards her brothers and sisters and derived great pleasure from the company of her nieces and nephews. But her acquiescence with her lot in life didn't alleviate her brother Hisham's sense of grief whenever he saw her. "I don't know how to understand her behavior," he once shared his feelings with Hadil, "her blank expression. Is it apathy or sorrow?"

"Why don't you consider the possibility," Hadil suggested, "that your sister is at peace with herself? Religion," she added, "gives her something to hold on to." But Hisham found no comfort in Hadil's attempts to console him. "My sister does not exist on a desert island. She's aware. She feels that she doesn't have what others have. She isn't like my brother Sharif, who has a family and children. For him religion is something else. And I also hear how the village people talk about her. Anas – an old spinster! You must remember, when Leila was little, asking me, '*Bab*a, what's *Anas*'? She didn't know what it meant but felt it wasn't a good thing. She must have heard it from her friends, who heard their parents' gossip. What can I say?" He sighed contritely. "Fate was cruel to her, depriving her of what everyone deserves, what everyone has." And so it went. Whenever his sister's somber face crossed his mind, he was overtaken by a deep sadness.

Besides Siham, Hisham had two other older sisters and two younger brothers. He was born a year before the war of '67, after his mother had given birth to Afaf and Siham. Two other brothers followed - Sharif and Fuad - and then the youngest daughter, Abir, was born. Except for Siham, they all got married and had children. Afaf, Sharif, and Fuad lived with their families near his parents' house, while Abir married a village man in the Bethlehem area and moved there with his family.

Hisham's father, Marwan Saada, was usually away from home for days, searching for work. After the June

'67 war, employment in his area became scarce, and new opportunities emerged in Israel. Thus, in his late twenties, Marwan had begun to work for Jewish building contractors in various Israeli cities. Due to the distance of the construction sites from his village, he used to stay there for days on end. Sometimes the construction sites provided additional income, such as when his employers entrusted him with safeguarding the building supplies and equipment. "I belong to a generation of orange IDs," he used to declare wryly. "After the establishment of the Palestinian Authority," he added, "the color of the certificates changed. Now it's green, and it says," he smirked, "*al-Sulta al-Falestinia*, PA. But except for the color of the papers, everything stayed the same, nafs al-hara, same shit."

During the olive harvest, the family would gather and drive to their olive groves. They would pick the olives and put them in their shirts, transfer them into sacks, then produce the olive oil in traditional mills. This used to be the case for many years before the mills were abandoned in favor of small factories, to which the plantation owners carried their crops, producing the oil and giving a tenth of the yield to the factory owners. Once, Hisham's daughter Leila shared with her parents the experience of harvesting olives with her Scout troop in one of the villages near Ramallah. Hisham retorted sardonically that, "Once upon a time, the olive harvest was only an olive harvest. Today the olive harvest acquired national significance, and the olive tree has suddenly become sacred." Hadil gave him a scornful look. Later, when they were on their own, she scolded him: "Why should you dampen the girl's spirits?"

As a child, he'd eagerly anticipated the olive harvest. Fridays were particularly joyful. Unlike other harvest days, on Fridays the women would make traditional stews that required special preparation, serving mansaf and musakhan and afterwards filling the air with song. "*Al-*

zeit amud al-bait, the olive is the pillar of the house," his grandfather Mustafa (who passed away in the late Eighties) would say repeatedly. It was through his grandfather that Hisham inherited his great affection for the Iraqi singer Nazem al-Ghazali, whose hits Mustafa would joyfully sing. And it was through him too that Hisham first heard one of Abu-Firas al-Hamdani's better-known poems, "And the Dove" - delivered in al-Ghazali's enchanting voice.

"You should know," his grandfather declared, as he'd tended to do often on various occasions, "that there is not, and never will be, a singer like Nazem al-Ghazali in the entire Arab world, may Allah have mercy on his soul. Many singers sing maqams, but no one sings them like him. The great poet Al-Mutanabbi once said that 'the wine has meaning, but not the one to be found in the grapes'." Mustafa also told them that Al-Ghazali had visited Palestine in 1948, during the war against the Zionists. He'd come to encourage the Arab Liberation Army commanded by Fawzi al-Qawuqji. "'*Makoo awamer*, there are no instructions to assist you' - this was the response of this supposed hero, al-Qawuqji, to Abd al-Qader al-Husseini, who asked him to help in the war against the Zionists in Jerusalem. A real hero indeed," Mustafa repeated derisively. "*Makoo awamer*, of course," repeated Mustafa, the words in the Iraqi dialect. "What can I tell you; everyone knows what happened in the end to the Liberation Army. We lost Palestine to the Jews, and the Liberation Army could hardly save itself. But that's another thing altogether. At least we had the privilege of hearing Nazem al-Ghazali singing in Palestine. That, too, is something," he smirked, as if he'd had to make do with a few crumbs rather than the whole loaf of bread.

While his grandfather sat and recounted his adolescent years, Hisham would sit by his father, who would embrace him and pat his head lightly with the palm of his coarsened hand. An intense pleasure would chill Hisham's head and, like a cat, he would tuck his head into his father's elbow to intensify the friction between the rough arms, the result of long and arduous labor, and his own scalp. Had it not been for his father, who gently pushed him away so that he could tend to the children or some other task, he would have kept still, wishing his touch to continue indefinitely. Sometimes his father's palm would flutter close to his nose. It smelled of nicotine from his tobacco-stained fingers. He wanted to stick his nose into his father's palm, and sniff more of the acrid odor.

Whenever he pictured his father, it was always with a cigarette in his mouth. Hisham's father used to pull a cigarette from the pack in his pocket, light it with a Zippo, inhale deeply, then push the smoke through his nostrils. Hisham was surprised when he first discovered that this skill was not exclusive to his father, and that it was not associated solely with the Time brand Israeli cigarettes his father favored. Once he saw an elderly village woman exhaling jets of smoke as powerful as his father did. In the early days of the first Intifada, while studying at Bir Zeit University, he tried to persuade his father to stop smoking the Israeli-made cigarettes. He was deeply annoyed when his father refused to comply with the call to boycott Israeli goods. "*Yaba*, you're helping the occupation," Hisham protested. But his father responded with a dismissive wave of the hand; he stayed loyal to Time cigarettes and refused to replace them with cigarettes made in the West Bank, even when the Israeli cigarettes became harder to come by. "*Ya ibni*, my son," he mocked, "if I stop smoking their cigarettes, then the occupation will be over? Is that what you're saying?" Marwan shook his head, expressing astonishment at Hisham's naïveté while continuing to inhale the smoke from the cigarette he held between his stained fingers. "It's all *kalam fadi*, empty words," he said, jerking his head dismissively.

Marwan broke the oppressive silence that followed Siham's insensitive remark concerning Hadil's absence. "The pruning we did to the olive trees a year ago," he reported, "is good for the olives. I think it'll be much better this year, not like last year. We put too much time in collecting them, and all for nothing; it would have been better to leave them to rot on the trees." Hisham glanced at his father as he continued to sit on the bed in the house's courtyard, drawing smoke into his lungs. He'd turned old before his time, Hisham thought. It's all due to the prolonged, debilitating manual labor he had been doing for many years. His eyes wandered to his ragged palms and focused on the nicotine stains. "Those Israeli cigarettes are going to kill you," he scolded him.

"This is what I tell him all the time, *ya ibni*," Hisham's mother backed him up. "He doesn't stop coughing at night because of those cigarettes. But he doesn't listen. Smoking and smoking."

"Everything is God's will," stated Marwan, looking upward as the smoke was sucked into his damaged lungs and then streamed out of his nostrils. "'Say', he began to recite from the Quran, 'only what God has decreed will happen to us. He is our Master: let the believers put their trust in God.'" Marwan noticed his son's eyes rolling in despair and continued to defiantly recite: "Wherever you may be, death will overtake you, even if you should be within towers of lofty construction..." Thus, in the way of believers, Marwan maintained that there was no connection between the logic guiding celestial powers and the one governing earth. If God wishes, he'll continue to smoke as much as he pleases and no misfortune will ever befall him, or if God wishes otherwise, he'll suffer some terminal illness even if he stops smoking. It's in Allah's hands alone. No one can escape his destiny.

Siham came into the yard, bearing a tray with a copper coffee jug and small coffee cups. She put the tray on a small wooden table and sat down on the bed beside her mother.

"In the name of God, ya Hisham," she suddenly declared, "I miss your children very much. I haven't seen them in such a long time." His parents froze. There she goes again, they probably thought, she's going to mention Hadil. They sighed in relief. This time she said nothing about her sister-in-law. Hisham gave his sister a sad look, a bitter smile hanging at the corner of his lips.

CHAPTER 4
Tali

The trip to Jordan was long and exhausting. She left Tel Aviv on Friday morning and was scheduled to reach her destination in the late afternoon. She accepted her classmate Yael's offer to attend a meeting on the east side of the Dead Sea that featured Israeli and Palestinian students. The meeting took place while Yoav was doing his reserve service. She had free time. She had submitted her research thesis several months ago, and all she did now was wait anxiously for answers from the American universities to which she and Yoav had applied. Professor Hoffman, or Galia, as she preferred to be addressed, seemed quite confident that Tali would be accepted into one of them. Galia was th one after all who wrote passionate letters of recommendation for her and maintained close contacts with some of the scholars involved.

Galia herself had successfully completed her studies at one of the top universities in the United States. After several years of teaching and research, she'd returned to Israel. She was then in her mid-forties, a brilliant scholar and a charismatic teacher, and a role model for her students, especially the female ones. A handsome woman with a fashionable wardrobe, she was always dressed in pantsuits, dresses, blouses, skirts, and heels, displaying demure elegance. Her hair was always carefully styled. Galia

Hoffman was unmarried, a fact that attracted endless speculation about real and imagined love affairs she either had in the past or was currently having. Carried away by their admiration, her students entertained the belief that her brilliance put men off, which explained her having no life partner or children – since anyone who considered being with her knew he'd have to live in her shadow. There are not many men, they stated decisively, willing to play second fiddle to a woman like her. Rumors were rife in the department's corridors about failed love affairs spanning oceans and continents, and there was also a stubborn rumor of an affair with a married faculty member in the Faculty of Humanities.

Tali received special attention from Galia, who had already chosen her as a final-year BA student to be her teaching assistant. Sometimes she shared her various views with Tali. "Career and academic life," she would say often, "is not everything. A person should have a well-rounded life, with friends, hobbies, pastimes." Yet she never mentioned romantic liaisons or family. Tali wanted to ask her about these sensitive issues but didn't dare, afraid of crossing the line. Tali, on the other hand, told her mentor that she herself had no intention of relinquishing her dream of raising a family. She hoped that this remark would prompt Galia to share the details of her life. Pensive, Galia gave her a lingering look, as if considering a reply, but finally said nothing. Only later, when they became more intimate, did she allow Tali a deeper look into her private life.

Indeed, Tali's desire to combine her studies and family life had guided her in applying to different US universities. She and Yoav chose academic institutions that answered their respective fields of interest, or at least ones located close enough to one another to allow them to live together. They were under immense pressure in those days, anticipating the admissions or rejections that loomed. When they were busy filling in registration forms, Yoav joked, "We don't look like we're applying to the departments of psychology or Middle Eastern Studies, but to the department of relationships."

"That's exactly what we're doing," Tali replied wryly, leaving him to wonder at her prompt reaction.

She had inherited her looks from her mother rather than her father. Her long dark hair, parted in the middle, was pulled up into a hair band and was in sharp contrast with her pale skin, giving her an exotic look. She was tall, and her shapely figure was quite sturdy. Her weight was a source of constant concern, and whenever she noticed the slightest alteration, usually perceived only by her, she'd make sure to lose anything she'd gained.

They first met four months after her separation from Avi. It was an early afternoon in one of the university's cafeterias. Yoav was carrying a loaded lunch tray, looking for a place to sit. Tali was alone at a table for four. He looked at her inquiringly. "Sure," she replied casually. He sat down, positioning himself diagonally from her. She was wearing a strapless shirt, revealing a delicate gold necklace and a tiny bit of cleavage. Yoav wore jeans and a t-shirt with a faded inscription. They exchanged furtive glances. Once their eyes met, and she smiled diffidently, politely. She liked his looks. He seemed to be struggling to find words, to spark a casual conversation. She gave him an encouraging grin. He affected an aloof look, attempting to display a nonchalant attitude, and asked, "What are you studying?"

"Psychology, MA. And you?"

"Middle Eastern Studies, also master's degree. You're not from Tel Aviv," he wondered, "are you?"

"What?!"

"Originally. You're not from Tel Aviv?"

"Right, I'm from Haifa, from Neve Sha'anan to be exact," she replied, and narrowed her eyes. "Why do you ask?"

"Don't know. There's something different about you, maybe your way of speaking…"

"Should I take this as a compliment?" she asked, tilting her head slightly.

"Of course," Yoav replied promptly, adding a smile as if to support his words.

"So, thank you," she smiled back.

They continued talking, studying each other, learning about each other's interests and sharing experiences from trips they'd taken around the world after their compulsory military service. Tali suddenly glanced at her watch and announced apologetically: "I have to run. I need to go to the library." She had arranged with a friend, she said, to pool efforts towards completing an assignment. As she was about to leave, she added that they would probably meet again on campus.

"Can I have your phone number?" Yoav asked, somewhat timidly.

"Sure," she replied, in a seemingly detached manner, and waited until he entered it in his cell phone. She made her way to the library, galloping over the mowed lawn with big strides. A vague thrill reverberated through her. "I met someone in the cafeteria at Gilman," she apologized for her slight tardiness, adding a sly smile.

"Who is he?" her friend Liat was curious, noticing the glee on Tali's face.

"He's studying in the department of Middle Eastern and African History, a master's student."

"Good for you," Liat exclaimed. "So tell me more," she demanded. "What's his name?"

"Well," Tali snapped her head up as if preparing to make a formal presentation: "His name is Yoav. He's tall and thin, not too—"

"Ectomorph physique," Liat interrupted, volunteering her knowledge in a theatrical tone, "which means he has a long and lean physique. And what else?"

"His features are delicate. He has black eyes, a little sad, and a high forehead. And he has thick black hair. He looks good!"

"And that turns you on, doesn't it?"

"What?"

"The color of his hair."

"No, not really, that's not the point," Tali shrugged. "Most of the men I've been with, and there weren't that many," she chuckled, "were actually white, chalky." She kept silent for a moment, then continued to describe Yoav. "He was wearing jeans and a black t-shirt. The truth is, he needs new clothes."

"You've just met him," Liat teasingly reproached her, "and you already want to change his clothes?"

"Well, you know what I mean," Tali laughed. "Anyway," she went on, "he has such big hands…"

"Big hands?" Liat repeated the words, as if in disbelief.

"Well, you know," Tali began to explain, "when he speaks, he swings his hands and you can't ignore his big palms and long fingers."

"So, like I said," Liat declared, "an ectomorph physique!"

"Whatever. You're the expert on men's bodies," Tali replied and plowed on, eager to recount her impressions of Yoav.

"That's right," Liat giggled, "but it's not just men. It holds true for men and women."

"Anyway, that's what caught my eye, his palms and big fingers. And he's also completely different from Avi. Down-to-earth. And he has a smile," she paused, then continued, "such a sweet, shy smile. He was timid, even a bit awkward, when he asked for my phone number. He was stuttering…"

Yoav called that very evening and asked to see her. She had to complete an assignment, she apologized, and the deadline was three days from now. But Yoav would not relent.

"So how about we get together," he suggested

hesitantly, "the night after you hand in the assignment?" She agreed.

It was her first visit to Jordan. The journey was extremely long. The bus departed from Tel Aviv heading in the direction of Jerusalem. It proceeded to the Jericho junction then continued the long drive to the border crossing at King Hussein Bridge, located in the northern Jordan Valley. It crossed the border and then headed in the opposite direction toward the Dead Sea on the Jordanian side. Tali followed the landscape with interest as it stretched out across the border. Most of the villages and towns they passed looked pitiful to her, even disgraceful. The hotel complex on the eastern shore of the Dead Sea stood in stark contrast to them, as if a parallel universe had been erected in close, eerie proximity. The contrast wasn't apparent immediately. The hotel's humble exterior resembled an old Nabataean village engulfed by a mountainous landscape, revealing nothing of its interior glamour. A silent, astonished gasp escaped her as she entered the lobby. The hotel stretched across vast spaces. Apart from the central multilevel building, the halls, rooms, and exterior wings dangled down a cliff leading to the sea. The winding paths were adorned on either side of the palm trees, ornamental bushes, and ferns. Ponds, water fountains, rock gardens full of exotic flowers and fitted with stone benches, and a natural stream adorned the winding paths. Shades of brown dominated the hotel and its surrounding buildings. The marble floors were covered with large, multicolored oriental rugs. The walls glowed from the wide-framed windows orange curtains that hung down to the floor. The converging point between the ceiling and the wall was adorned with light green double stripes, resembling a sukkah decoration. The rooms were equipped with wide balconies overlooking the arid landscape.

The balconies gave way to a panoramic view of the

Dead Sea, across which Israel could be seen in peaceful rest. The illustrated hotel pamphlet declared proudly that this is the largest and most luxurious spa hotel in the Middle East. Indeed, Tali had never stayed at a hotel so opulent, and so surreal: a kind of eastern Disneyland, an oasis designed to fulfill the exotic fantasy of tourists from all over the world. To complete the picture, the event calendar in the lobby invited hotel guests to "relish the magic of the East," to enjoy evening music and belly dancing by the best dancers in the Arab world. It reminded her of an event she had attended with Yoav at Tel Aviv University's Department of Middle Eastern and African History, celebrating the end of the academic year. The event featured Arabic music, belly dancing, cuisine and traditional costumes worn by some of the guests.

Immediately after settling into their rooms, Israeli and Palestinian participants were asked to convene in one of the hotel's halls and begin their first meeting. Tali did not find the discussions particularly interesting. She felt like they were treading water, covering the same ground over and over. She was expecting something else: intimate encounters where everyone could speak about themselves and bare their experiences and feelings. But to her disappointment, the participants instead exchanged accusations and seemed to compete over which of them had a greater share of suffering and torment in the lingering bloody conflict between Jews and Palestinians.

The tensions intensified as the Palestinians began to discuss the walls, checkpoints, and barriers established by Israel throughout the West Bank, and the harsh behavior of the soldiers manning them. The Israelis, in turn, argued that though unfortunate, these were necessary measures designed to forestall terrorist attacks on innocent civilians. Tali felt ill at ease. Reluctantly joining the heated discussion, she suggested that it was wrong to generalize when talking about the soldiers at the checkpoints.

"There are soldiers, especially reserve soldiers," she

stressed calmly, "who carry out their duties with sensitivity and treat the Palestinians with respect. It's better," she added, "that such soldiers, older and more sensitive, serve at checkpoints than younger soldiers."

The following day, when the tragic event unfolded, she found herself in an extremely delicate situation, especially vis-à-vis the Palestinian moderator. Earlier, during Friday night dinner, Tali and the moderator had held a brief, rather reserved conversation in which Tali repeated her frustration with the nature of the seminar and the hurling of accusations between Israelis and Palestinians.

"I'm sick and tired," she protested, "of listening to both sides blame each other for the political impasse. It's a political matter," she added, "and we have no control over it. I'm not a political activist. I'm more comfortable dealing with the personal side of the conflict - how people feel, how they deal with fears, with anxiety."

The Palestinian moderator seemed unhappy with Tali's attitude, and began to explain - obviously containing her impatience - why the Palestinian participants, unlike the Israelis, wanted to engage mainly with political issues rather than emotions, anxieties, and fears. "It's your prerogative," she stated somewhat irritably, "to confine yourselves to the personal side of the conflict. We are not so privileged - we urgently need political solutions."

Tali replied that in this case she was not sure seminars such as this promoted political solutions in any way. She attempted to steer the conversation in another, more personal direction. The Palestinian woman began to yield, hesitantly at first, but gradually softening to her interlocutor. She appeared to feel affection towards Tali. They were both curious to discover the hidden meanings in their respective names - Tali and Hadil - and shared some basic details about their personal lives and professional pursuits.

Hadil gave Tali her business card, with the name of the organization she headed. *New Horizons - The Center for*

Women's Empowerment was inscribed in Arabic and English above her name: Hadil Saada, Director. Hadil also spoke briefly about her two children and mentioned her husband. Tali for her part told Hadil of her academic studies, her boyfriend Yoav, and even her future plans. She avoided, however, the sensitive matter of Yoav's current whereabouts.

Tali declined Yael's suggestion to join her at the large poolside bar. The long ride, tedious discussions, and overly rich meal had taken their toll, and she felt sluggish. As she passed by the front desk on the way to her room, it occurred to her to check her email. In recent days, she had done this very frequently, apprehensively. The receptionist referred her to a nearby room with Internet access. Tali soon logged into her email and scanned it thoroughly, finding no important messages. She entered Yoav's inbox. Her eyes fixed on a message from Harvard University. She opened it with growing eagerness and read with rapidly roaming eyes: "We are pleased to inform you that the Center for Middle Eastern Studies..." She leapt merrily from her seat and yelled, "Wow! Great! He got accepted!" She continued to read the contents of the message with growing excitement and then called Yoav.

"You're not going to believe this," she whispered. "You've been accepted to Harvard!"

There was silence on the other end. Seconds passed and then he whispered, the incredible having become reality. "I got accepted to Harvard..." The whisper turned into a cheer: "*Yesh!* Great! I got accepted to Harvard!" Briefly quelling his excitement, he asked for more details. She told him he'd been granted a full scholarship for the duration of his studies. The person signing the letter, she added, was a Professor O'Brien.

"Of course, James O'Brien. He might be my doctoral advisor. He's a world-renowned expert on Iraq! I've got his book with me here, *The Ethnic Challenge of Iraq.*"

"That's great!" Tali shared in his enthusiasm. "They've

accepted you and now this man wants to know as soon as possible that you'll be taking him up on it."

"Of course, I'll let him know," Yoav began to say then stopped. Tali also fell silent. A moment later he went on to say: "Well, I don't have to reply immediately. I can do it in a few days. But then," he added, as if holding a dialogue with himself, "I can't wait too long, you know. If I don't tell them soon, they'll choose someone else from the waiting list. And you know the kind of selection processes they go through to accept a candidate." Tali maintained her silence. Yoav stopped his monologue. The initial enthusiasm seemed to have waned.

Tali retired to her room, pulled Philip Roth's *The Human Stain* from her bag, and laid down on the bed. She had bought the original version in English. Her teacher, Galia Hoffman, strongly recommended the book, which deals, so she explained, with the limits of freedom that a person has in shaping and reshaping his personal and collective identity. "It'll also provide you with useful unofficial information about academic life in the US," Galia had said. The plot of the book captivated Tali yet she felt uncomfortable with the crude and blatant sexual language of Roth's protagonists. "'If Clinton had fucked [Monica Lewinsky] in the ass,'" Tali read while recoiling, "'she might have shut her mouth.'" She thought about Galia Hoffman's words: "There's nothing like reading English literature to enrich your vocabulary." Galia certainly didn't have this kind of vocabulary in mind, Tali smirked to herself.

In fact, she and Yoav had a shared interest in original English literature. Recently, a new dimension had been added to this pastime: such novels were very useful for passing the language proficiency tests required by American universities. The couple continued to pursue the activity even after successfully passing the tests. While reading the novels, she and Yoav would highlight unfamiliar words, which they would later write down in the yellow pad and translate. Over the past year, they found themselves memorizing these newly found words and making a hobby of quizzing each other on them.

"What does *ominous* mean?" she would ask. Yoav would reply and then shoot back: "What does *propitious* mean?" This game was met with ridicule by Liat, Tali's childhood friend.

"You'll be playing *Shabetz-Na* in English next," she teased them.

Yoav smiled and retorted, "Oh, you mean Scrabble? We're already doing that."

Tali did not bother to open the book before placing it on the bedside table. She went out onto the porch and watched the distant, flickering lights from the Israeli side of the Dead Sea. She was overcome by an eerie feeling, as she looked over towards the place she had come from, her country, Israel, trying to see it through the eyes of a foreigner. She often felt like this: estranged, placing a disconcerting inner distance between her and her own sense of self. She remained there, letting the desert chill seep through her limbs, watching the dark sky as if trying to decipher some mysterious secret. Was she destined to fill the role of loving and supportive wife, she wondered? Was it her role in life to follow Yoav whither he goeth, as her friend Liat had asked her disapprovingly just a few days ago?

CHAPTER 5
Hadil

She'd been invited to attend the seminar in Jordan thanks to her extensive experience moderating meetings between Israelis and Palestinians. Engaging in such activities over the years had eroded her passion and diminished any hopes that she could bring about real change. "Ever since I began doing this work," she used to say with dry humor, "things have only gotten worse. Maybe I should quit doing it and then things will improve." Hisham had a point, she thought, when he told her that she was wasting her time and energy on futile activities. "But don't forget," she once replied, "it's also a living." He agreed, but added that she could find proper compensation in activities that empower women in Palestinian society.

"Not only will I and our children get to see more of you," he grumbled, "but your livelihood won't suffer either if you direct all your efforts towards Palestinian society. Praise God," he added sarcastically, "the occupation creates a lot of work opportunities in this field."

And indeed, as the years went by, Hadil devoted much of her time to activities within Palestinian society. The NGO she founded and managed - *New Horizons: The Center for Women's Empowerment* - received generous donations from various international foundations. Her association with Quaker communities and branches of the Anglican Church worldwide was extremely valuable to her ability to raise funds. She utilized her training in social work and psychology effectively to prepare and coach individuals who joined the center she'd built from scratch. The center's modest offices were located on Ramallah's main thoroughfare, but the main activities took place in schools and cultural centers in the villages around the city. The closures, restrictions on movement, and dwindling opportunities for a livelihood following the second Intifada had exacerbated the plight of many Palestinian women and girls. They were increasingly becoming scapegoats, and occasional punching bags, for frustrated men.

Already before the afternoon session, she felt that once more she would be partaking in a conversation she described as a dialogue of the deaf. The Palestinians will talk about the occupation and the Israelis about terrorism; the Palestinians will lament the Nakba and the Israelis will raise the trauma of their Holocaust. She felt herself sinking into despondency. The fresh memory of that morning, before she left home, and especially of Nadim closing himself up in the bathroom, tormented her. She wished the seminar was already over. She was not up to small talk with either the Israelis or the Palestinians attending. This is one of the reasons why she was initially reluctant to respond to the desire of the young Israeli woman, Tali, for a light conversation with her at dinner. She recounted the dialogue to herself. "This is a privilege for you," she replied rather impatiently when Tali vented her frustration at how the meeting between the Israelis and Palestinians had gone so far. "Those who live in Tel Aviv don't have the slightest idea what it means for us Palestinians living in the West Bank. We can't put politics aside. The political issues are woven into our daily lives. You Israelis, are everywhere: on my plate, in my home, in my children's schools, at work. Even in my bedroom... We're intimately familiar with your holidays and know exactly when they take place – the day and the hour. You know why? Because when you're celebrating, we're placed under siege, locked in our homes, prisoners." Slowly, however, her tone softened. She wanted to know what Tali's name meant, and the Israeli woman was happy to oblige.

"Those who believe in numerology," she said in a seemingly apologetic tone, "say that anyone with this name, Tali, is practical, thorough, and rational. They also say that Talis don't like to share details of their personal lives with others. They tend to be somewhat introverted, reclusive…"

Hadil was amused. "Rational! Do you see the paradox? Rational people," she stated, laughing, "don't believe in numerology."

"I don't believe in numerology either, but I'm really rational, and I guess somewhat introverted."

Hadil explained the meaning of her name – a dove's coo. They went on talking awhile, sharing more details about their personal lives, families, and interests. "My research," Tali told her, "deals with how boys and girls in youth movements interpret their volunteer activities." Hadil wanted to know more, adding that Leila, her daughter, was a member of the Ramallah Scout Association. "So," she asked, "did you find an interesting difference between boys and girls?"

"Yes," Tali answered jovially, happy to share her findings with Hadil, "big differences. The boys are much more concerned with their egos. Even when they're volunteering, they're always competing, they want to lead. It's important for them to get recognition."

"Well," Hadil laughed lightly, "at least we have something in common." She felt the fatigue spreading through her limbs. She retired to her room soon after, wondering about the Israeli woman with whom she had spent the last hour. She's nice, she thought, but exists in her separate, shielded world. Politically indifferent. Like many Israelis. I don't understand why she bothered to attend this seminar. Hadil called home, wanting to talk with Nadim. Hisham picked up. "Yes, everything is fine," he snapped dryly. "Yes, yes, Nadim feels good." She asked Hisham to put him on the phone, wanting to hear his voice. It seemed that Nadim was reluctant. "Come on," she heard Hisham ordering him, "talk to your mother!" Nadim relented but replied curtly to her affectionate entreaties. "My soul," she pleaded with him. "Mama loves you a lot, you know."

She lay on her back on the spacious bed and stared at the ceiling. Her wretched relationship with Hisham gave her no rest. She and Hisham cannot go on like this, she concluded. Maybe her parents were right after all, she thought. She recited a proverb: "The rupture is too wide, and the patch too small."

The first time she met Hisham was when they made their way from Bir Zeit University to Ramallah in an old Mercedes taxi whose engine sounded like a groaning old man, the worn seats testifying to its age. This was before the first Intifada, before the land shook under their feet, before minibuses replaced taxis as the prime means of transportation in the West Bank. They sat crammed in the back of the cab next to a heavyset passenger. It was late afternoon and Hadil was on her way home from the university. Hisham was on his way to tutor a student at the Friends School in Ramallah. The child, he explained, has difficulty with Arab grammar. He gave these details after he and Hadil had managed some tentative and fragmented opening sentences. His own family, who lives in Al-Jib, helped pay for his education, but it wasn't enough, so he had to find additional sources of income. Hadil said that she noticed he was attending the same modern Arabic poetry course as she was. "Yes," he replied, "I know who you are -- I mean," he immediately rephrased, noticing her slight recoil, "that I also saw you in the class." She said she was returning home. She lived in lower Ramallah near Al-Manara Square. He said that he was heading in the same direction, as the boy he was tutoring lived in her neighborhood. She asked about the name of the child's family to see if she might know them. It turned out she indeed knew the family. They were neighbors of Arij's parents, who was one of her closest friends.

When she told her that evening about her random encounter with Hisham, Arij said she knew him, though not personally. She had heard about him though; the parents of the child he was tutoring never stopped praising him. "They say the student is working miracles with their child and with other children as well. They marvel at his incredible knowledge of Arabic poetry. He knows endless poems by heart, they say in amazement. And he also writes poems himself. He's a shy, humble guy," she added.

After their ride to Ramallah, Hadil and Hisham gradually became close friends. They sat side by side in class, exchanged views on the topics they'd learned, ate together in Bir Zeit's restaurants, joined by their respective friends, and prepared for exams together. Sometimes they met in her parents' house. Hisham even got up the courage to show her some of his own poems, gingerly displaying his romantic sentiments. She liked them. They reminded her, she said, of how poems were written in the past: tight structure and meticulous rhyme. He seemed to detect a disparaging quality in her words, but was afraid to say anything.

"I really like them, I do," she was quick to reassure him.

Some of their meetings were held in the cafés spread around the village of Bir Zeit, since the university's buildings were scattered all over. The cafés carried more-or-less distinct political identities. Some catered to students affiliated with the Fatah movement, including many from the Gaza Strip; others attracted students affiliated with the Popular Front; other students were affiliated with the Communist Party, and so on. But the cafés were also nurturing greenhouses where love affairs sprouted and grew. It was there that Hadil and Hisham's love slowly sprang and flourished. It wasn't love at first sight: it subtly, surreptitiously infiltrated her heart and took firm root in it. Was it Hisham's innocence, his modesty, his passion for poetry, or his agreeable countenance that drew her to him? She couldn't come up with a decisive answer.

He had charcoal-black, slightly curly hair, deep honey-brown eyes with a somewhat dreamy look, and a chiseled nose that matched his elongated face which, except for two thin lines beside his nostrils, remained unwrinkled even past his fortieth year. He was an average–sized, sturdy man. When Hadil wondered at the secret to his physique, he replied that he hated sports and paid little attention to a healthy diet. "It's all a matter of luck," he'd smile, and she didn't know whether he was being defiant or apologizing for the gratuitous gift of his robustness. He used to add to his aphorisms an ironic smile, rendering it difficult to guess his intention. When he was in a rage, his eyebrows would contract, becoming one seamless brow. She found this trait rather amusing and was unable to overlook it even when angry exchanges erupted between them. When she pointed it out to him, Hisham grinned contentedly and said, "So, this is why you want to fight with me all the time?" Even after they drifted apart, Hadil continued to find him handsome, much like the young student she'd met over two decades ago in Bir Zeit. She would also be charmed by the way he recited poems, whether his own or others'. She was not moved by the words themselves, but by the way he recited them – not in hyperbolic exaggeration, as many who recite poetry, and not with broad physical gestures, but with restrained movements and a gentle, tender voice.

She began to be aware of her feelings towards him indirectly, when attempting to explain to herself why she refused all those young men who sought her company. And it was also her close friend Arij, who never held back about Hadil's feelings for Hisham, suggesting that this went beyond mere friendship. If at first Hadil dismissed Arij's comments, telling her "We're just good friends," she gradually recognized the truth. But even when she admitted it to herself, she knew it was up to her to take the first step if she wished to turn their relationship into a full-fledged romance. Hisham, she knew, did not have the audacity to do so. And when she finally bared her heart to him, her words were met eagerly.

A few months later, the first Intifada broke out and things changed radically in Bir Zeit. Studying was no longer the first priority; teachers and students alike took part in protests and demonstrations calling for the end of the occupation. Bir Zeit University became one of the main hubs for political activism and civil uprising. It was there that initiatives to boycott Israeli products and the Israeli job market began, as well as halting tax payments to the Israeli civil administration of the West Bank. In response, the army locked the university's gates and studying had to go underground for five full years.

The political upheaval of those days seemed to add romantic glamour to Hisham and Hadil's budding affair; it seemed as though the Intifada infused their love with additional meaning. There is nothing like love born in the eye of the storm, one that seemed to usher reality into a new epoch. And those momentous days made it easier for Hadil to hide the true nature of her relationship with Hisham from her parents. For most of that period, her parents did not know the details of her schedule, what she was up to, or when she was supposed to return home from the makeshift university. Sometimes she would return the following day, blaming it on the occupation. "The army blocked the way from Bir Zeit to Ramallah," she would say, explaining that she was forced to stay with female friends in the dormitory or in one of the village's apartments. And thus the political revolution also brought a revolution in her own private life. Her parents discovered the truth only three years later, when Hadil and Hisham decided it was high time their families learned of their intention to build a future together. Although she did not expect her parents to be delighted when she broke the news, she underestimated the intensity of their wrath and fierce objections.

When the shock subsided, Hadil's mother was quick to explain to her daughter why the idea was completely insane, believing that Hadil was not fully aware of the implications. She pleaded with her to let go of this ridiculous notion. "You know this is impossible, baby," she implored. "We may not observe our religion very carefully, but we're Christians after all, and his family is Muslim. They have their religion and we have ours. As the proverb says, 'Let each hold to his religion, and God shall help him.' No good comes from mixing. What happened, my dear daughter? Aren't there suitable, educated, wealthy Christian men who'd die to marry you, build you a home, and have children with you? What's gotten into you, mama? Come on, 'steer clear of evil and bid it farewell.' What are we going to tell our uncles and aunts if they hear about this? How will we deal with the shame? You, who sang Christmas hymns in the Friends School choir. You, our pride and joy! And now you want to become Muslim? What got into you? You want to replace the Christmas carols with the fatha, with verses from the Quran? True, the proverb says 'Love is the ally of the blind,' but this is total blindness!"

"Mama," Hadil pleaded with her mother, "it's not that I'm getting someone off the street. Hisham is from a respectable family and he's well-educated. He loves me very much and I dearly love him. You'll love him too, you'll see."

"My daughter," her mother fumed, "respectful or not, I don't care — he's not for you! He's not Christian! And this is a problem, a huge problem. Oh God," she sighed heavily, "I always felt that we'd have problems with him, with this Hisham. 'That which we dreaded has befallen us,'" she cited a proverb. "Hisham, Hisham. All the time you spoke about him. He said this, and did that and the other... how smart and how interesting. I told your father a long time ago, 'I don't like what I hear, and I don't like what I see.' I saw how he looked at you when he visited you here. I saw. And when I asked you what's going on between the two of you: 'We're just friends, just friends.' Sure! Just friends," she shook her head angrily. "And your father," she turned to Salim. "'No reason to worry,' he said. Sure! Hisham spoke with him about politics and poetry, and he drove him to his village once," she added with virulent mockery. "You didn't notice that this Hisham was already plotting to steal your girl from under your nose, like a thief. This *nawari*, this ungrateful gypsy. Of course, ya Salim, no reason to worry. Why?

Because 'Hadil is a smart, clever girl,'" she quoted him derisively. "'We can rely on her. She knows what she's doing.'"

"But I do know what I'm doing, Mom!"

"No, you don't!" Salwa roared with vitriol, completely losing her composure. "And this, this marriage idea, won't happen! Abadan, never! We won't give our daughter to this gypsy. That's it!"

All the while, Hadil's father sat silently. Salim was a man of good temper. He rarely raised his voice. He was the descendant of an aristocratic Greek-Orthodox family that had established itself in Ramallah over two hundred years ago. His ancestors, he proudly used to say, had come to Ramallah during the second half of the eighteenth century from Dayr Aban near Jerusalem, when Ramallah was a tiny, neglected village. His mother, too, was from an old Christian family. But her family had come to Ramallah later, in the mid-nineteenth century, also from the Jerusalem area. Salim enjoyed saying that the house they lived in within lower Ramallah was built on the ruins of his demolished family home and renovated several times to accommodate changing times and evolving needs. Before he was twenty years old, Salim had made his way to the American University of Beirut where he'd studied pharmacology. He returned to Ramallah about a year before the war of '67 broke out, and after a few months married Salwa, his maternal relative, who was eighteen at the time. Salim was six years older than her. A few years later, he opened a pharmacy in the center of town, affording his family a comfortable living.

Salwa was the descendant of a Greek-Orthodox family originally from Jaffa. In 1948 her family had to abandon their home. While Salwa's parents had settled in Bethlehem, her uncles and aunts – on both her parents' sides – settled in Amman. Many of them emigrated over the years to Santiago, Chile, integrating into the city's old Greek Orthodox community in the district of Patronato. This district, whose old buildings still featured arched windows and doors in testament to the heritage of its original Middle Eastern occupants, lay at the foot of a tall hill that overlooked the entire city and was named after San Cristóbal, the patron saint of travelers. Middle Eastern émigrés already began to inhabit the borough in the final stages of the Ottoman Empire, when the Palestinians were Ottoman subjects and held Turkish passports. As a result Christians and Muslims alike were given a derogatory nickname, Turkos, Turks. But in time the hostility and suspicion towards them faded. As befits immigrants who wish to embrace their new homeland, they worked diligently to make use of the opportunities available to them, and successfully integrated within Santiago's economy, politics, and culture. The word "Palestine" became commonplace in Chile thanks to the magnificent Deportivo Palestino Santiago football club, founded by the Palestinian community – which also became a source of pride for Palestinians back in the ancient homeland. Little wonder that over the years Santiago's Greek Orthodox community became a magnet for other Palestinians forced to abandon their homeland, rendering it the largest Palestinian diaspora outside of the Middle East. Yet the homeland was not forgotten, and the cross that hung from women's necks was replaced by a gold relief map of Palestine from the sea to the river.

Hadil visited Santiago on two different occasions. On her first visit she was still a young girl. She'd spent a summer vacation there which left her with especially warm impressions. A few months after, she proudly told her parents that if she'd stayed a few months more in Santiago, she would have gained fluent Spanish. On her second visit she was part of a political delegation conveying to Chilean society the dire reality of the West Bank. She also paid a visit to her sister Mariam, who had emigrated to Santiago with her husband and three children just a few years after their marriage. Hadil's elderly relatives were grateful to the city that had adopted them so generously.

"Santiago opened its heart to us," they repeatedly praised their new country. "And it may have been San Cristóbal," they added, "who had mercy on us and helped us overcome our hardships on the way here from faraway Palestine."

Hadil had two younger sisters, Mariam and Ranin. She herself was born in 1968, a year after the 1967 war. "All my girls," her father used to say, "were born under Israeli occupation and don't know any other reality." Mariam was born a year and a half after Hadil, while Ranin, the youngest, was born two years afterwards. Their parents had wished for a boy but gave up trying after their third daughter. "Let us praise the Lord for what he gave us," Salim sought to encourage his wife, who'd wished to give him a son. Salim and Salwa spared their daughters nothing and were keen for them to receive good educations. All three girls attended the prestigious Friends School, where classes were held in English. Referred to by all as "Friends", the school enjoyed a good reputation throughout the Arab world. Before the 1967 war, it functioned as a boarding school, attracting children of aristocratic families from Arab countries. In contrast to Mariam, who married into money and gave up having a career, Hadil and Ranin acquired educations and professional skills that afforded them more than decent livelihoods. While the center Hadil ran – *New Horizons* – proved to be a good source of income, Ranin and her husband, Ziad, opened a successful travel agency in Ramallah and enjoyed a high standard of living.

The news had struck Salim like a sledgehammer. He sat in his armchair dumbfounded, uttering not a sound, letting his wife do the talking. Hadil knew well that his silence did not mean he endorsed what he heard. It would have been easier, she felt, if he ranted and raved, shouted and exploded, but he was consumed with grief. And so, even though her mother did the talking, yelling, and screaming,

Hadil turned to her father now, pleading with him.

"*Baba*," she beseeched, crying, "Hisham loves me and respects me very much, and he really doesn't place any importance on religious matters." She paused and then continued fiercely. "You yourself never placed much importance on religion, either. You always made fun of our relatives in Beit Jala and Bethlehem for being intolerant fanatics. You always argued that religion is for *jah'lin*, ignorant people, and that it divides Palestinian society rather than uniting it, that it creates more hostility than solidarity. That's why you signed me up for Friends, because of their interfaith tolerance. That's what you said!"

"True, I said those things," Salim replied with a cracked voice, "but this has nothing to do with it. Religion has many negative sides, but we have to take it into consideration when we decide whom to marry, whom we want to raise a family with. We don't ask our daughters to pray at church every Sunday, but it is important for us that they maintain their identity. True, we're secular, not religiously observant, but we are Christian nevertheless. It's not as if you're going to marry a kafer, a heretic, someone with no religion. You want to marry Hisham, and Hisham is a Muslim! It means that you and your children are going to be Muslims. My dear daughter, how do you expect us to give you our blessing? How? You must think very hard before you go down this road, before you do something irreversible. How can we agree? You have to think about this. Love doesn't last forever. You know," he recited a proverb, "'when morning comes the glowing embers of night turn into ashes.'"

Hadil's mother was more resolute. "You have to put an end to this foolish story," she demanded furiously. "You can't do this to your family, your sisters, your uncles; and you can't do it to yourself either. Wake up, wake up from this stupid dream of yours!"

"I'm not stupid," Hadil shouted angrily at her mother, and stormed off to her room. Her parents didn't stop her.

They also preferred to be alone in an attempt to calmly process the situation and consider their options, to think about how to forestall the calamity which was about to befall them. Salwa was furious, finding it impossible to calm down. She confronted her husband and began to reproach him. Hadil could hear her mother's harangues. "It's all because of you. Because of the education you gave her. You constantly brainwashed her with your ideas. You heard what she said," Salwa fumed and began to mimic her daughter: "'Religion doesn't matter; religion is only good for idiots.' Now you tell me, who's the idiot here? Who? My family from Beit Jala and Bethlehem that you make fun of all the time? No! I'll tell you who. You and I are the idiots! Oh God, who's going to save us from this catastrophe?"

Salim looked up at his wife and said, as if repenting for a sin: "I really didn't think about that. And you know how stubborn your daughter is. If she wants something, nothing stops her."

"That's it? You give up?" Salwa stormed. "She'll do what she wants and we'll do nothing, because my daughter is stubborn? I'm stubborn too. It won't happen! G'asban a'nha, over my dead body. She'll not marry Hisham."

"And how are you going to prevent it?" Salim asked sarcastically.

"How? I'll tell you how," Salwa said loud enough for Hadil to hear. "I'll just tell her, unequivocally, that if she insists on marrying him, then she's not our daughter anymore. None of her family will be at her wedding. Not you, not me, not her sisters, not her uncles, and not her aunts. No one! If she insists on marrying him, then she can go ahead. But we're going to break away from her. We impose a *mukata'a* on her, cut her off. Go, go," she continued, as if she was addressing her daughter directly, "and live there, in his village, in Al-Jib, with those gypsies who cover their faces with hijab. Let them adopt and feed you. Let them take care of you. That's what I'll tell her!"

"You don't have to talk about them like that," Salim protested. "You know I don't like it when you use that word, gypsies."

Hadil didn't hear the rest since he lowered his voice but she could guess the gist of it by her mother's response. "I don't care. I told you, I'm more stubborn than she is," Hadil's mother snapped angrily. "As if we didn't suffer enough of a scandal with my brother, and now our daughter is heaping her share of disgrace on us."

"What do these things have to do with each other?" Salim said with exasperation. "What's the connection between this, your daughter, and Kamal?"

"There's a connection," Salwa insisted. "Al-ard w' al-a'rd, the land and family honor. She's damaging our honor and he's betraying our land. And now because of her we won't be able to look people in the eye. If it continues like this, we may have to leave Ramallah, go away. Maybe to Chile, like my family. How many times have they told me, 'Ya Salwa, why don't you persuade Salim to make a decision, and leave Ramallah. He doesn't see that there's no hope left, no future for us in Palestine.' How many times have I tried to convince you to leave and start a new life in Santiago or any other place in the world where we have relatives? By now we could have found our stubborn daughter a nice husband, a Christian. We should have followed the example of the Hadadin" – a Christian tribe that fled Jordan and established Ramallah, not wanting to give their daughters to the son of a Muslim sheikh.

"How many times has my family asked about her, after visiting them in Santiago a few years ago? But you were never willing to hear of it. Every time I said, let's leave Ramallah, let's go there, you gave the same answer: 'We stay in Ramallah.' You may have forgotten that many of your relatives did not stay in Ramallah. But you? No. You won't leave. What's good for others is not good for Salim."

"Oh," Salwa let out a long sigh. "There won't be many

Christians left here soon anyway. Anyone who could, got up and left. And only you, who boasts of his secularism, upholds the duty of sumud, the clinging to the Holy Land. What do you want? You want to fulfill our duty to Christians everywhere, as the bishop said in his sermon? 'Christians have a duty to stay here in the Holy Land, to preserve our holy places.' The bishop's right," Salwa added in bitter mockery, "the real life is here, in the Holy Land." She paused then furiously declared: "Life here is shit. We live between the hammer and the anvil, between the Jews and the Muslims."

"And in Santiago," Salim said hesitantly, "we wouldn't have been referred to as *Turkos*?"

"How dare you compare?" she fumed. "Compared to here, compared to Ramallah, Santiago is Paradise!"

Hadil succumbed to neither her mother's threats nor her father's solicitations. She was determined to tie her future with Hisham's, even at the heavy price her mother threatened to exact from her. And now, lying on the bed in her hotel room in Jordan, she brooded on whether it had all been in vain, whether the marriage could still be saved. Perhaps her parents had been right after all, went a nagging, unsettling thought, when they tried to dissuade her .

CHAPTER 6
Yoav

The reigning calm at the Bir Nabala checkpoint on Friday evening stood in contrast to Yoav's inner turmoil. He first called his mentor, Professor Na'aman, to inform him of his acceptance to Harvard and to thank him for his efforts. Professor Na'aman did not sound surprised; it appeared he was already in the know. They spoke briefly. The professor congratulated Yoav, adding: "You're getting the opportunity of a lifetime." They arranged to meet a few weeks later after Yoav finished his reserve service. Next Yoav called his parents: "I've got wonderful news! I've been accepted to Harvard!" His mother, who'd already given her begrudging blessing to his plan for studying abroad, away from her, whispered: "Yoavi, we're so proud of you!" That's it, he thought, all I need now is for Tali to be accepted into one of Boston's universities and my joy will be complete, perfect. He was in an elated mood for hours, toying with the promising and exciting scenarios that awaited him.

"Yoav!" he heard Alon shouting from across the road, pulling him back to the drab reality of the checkpoint, "how do you say 'incitement' in Arabic?" Alon was engaged in an exchange with the Palestinian passengers of an Audi headed to Ramallah. For a moment Yoav ignored him, figuring that Alon's desire to know the word in

Arabic served no real need. That pyscho's picking on them again, he thought. Nevertheless, he somewhat reluctantly answered Alon. In the meanwhile, a long caravan of vehicles, seeking to make their way to Kalandiya and Ramallah, had built up behind the new Audi.

"What's going on? You caught someone involved in incitement?" Yoav asked mockingly. Glancing at the long caravan of cars, he shouted, "Why don't you just let them through?"

Alon did not respond. But he turned to the Audi's two passengers and yelled contemptuously, "Go already, go."

Yoav's army reserve unit consisted of soldiers of different ages who'd all belonged to various infantry units. They'd served with him previously, manning checkpoints across the West Bank. They too had been drafted a year before during the Second Lebanon War but didn't take part in active fighting. He knew most of them, some more and some less. There was Amir, the company commander; Alon, the youngest soldier in the unit; Yevgeny, Marcelo, Nimrod, Shlomi, Lior, Tedros, Matan who lived in one of the nearby settlements, and various others. Their job was to man the Fabric of Life checkpoint, situated on the main road between Ramallah and the village of Bir Nabala.

"What's unfolding in the Occupied Territories following Hamas's victory at the beginning of last year," their commanders briefed them, "is anarchy. The peacekeepers of yesterday are the brutal terrorists of tomorrow, and vice versa. Fatah and Hamas could easily exchange roles." Amir, the company commander, who was Yoav's age, referred to the reserve service as just a chore they were duty-bound to carry out, devoid of any ideological significance. "Let's do our jobs the best way we can," he demanded, "and we'll go back home safely, each to his wife, girlfriend, and family." Listening to him, Yoav imagined him as a marketing manager planning to introduce a new product into the market. He wasn't trying to infuse them with a sense of mission or political zeal. This approach was to Yoav's liking and consistent with how he himself approached his reserve service, a mandatory duty he performed somewhat perfunctorily.

Alon, Yoav's current shift mate, had finished his compulsory military service a few years ago in Givati, a prestigious infantry brigade. He'd been living with his parents in one of the moshavim, the agricultural communities, in the northern Negev desert near the Bedouin city of Rahat and the Jewish city of Netivot. His parents belonged to the second wave of moshav founders who emigrated to Israel from Libya and Kurdistan in the early Fifties. They had met while taking part in the Moshavim Youth Movement. The youngest of their four children, Alon was a short-tempered young man, a trait exacerbated by the belligerent fervor with which he treated the Palestinians traveling through the checkpoints. "With the Arabs," he used to say, "you cannot make peace. It's a waste of time. No matter how much you give them, they'll ask for more. Acre, Haifa, they want everything." In one of their heated exchanges, Alon angrily roared at Yoav: "For your information, they want your Tel Aviv too. Come and see, come to where I live. Talk to the people there, try to understand what it's like to live in fear, in our own country, not in the territories. Come and see the Bedouins, see how they steal whatever they can lay their hands on - equipment, sprinklers, cables, tractors, everything. Even the police are afraid to deal with them. You should know the next war is no longer here," Alon pointed to the horizon: "it'll be in the Negev, inside Israel. My father and mother," he went on, seething with anger, "rebuilt our farm with ten fingers, after a million crises and disasters. They gave us a love for hard work. Not like these parasites. Living on social security. This is what you leftists don't understand. The Arabs are willing to make peace with us only if we give them everything, everything. Here, we gave them Gaza and what did we get in return? Hamas, Islamic Jihad! That's it, no more concessions!"

He paused briefly, as if to process new thoughts bouncing around his head, then went on: "But their music is something else. I'm serious," he reacted to Yoav's incredulous smile. "I don't speak Arabic. I learned a word here and a word there, from the Bedouins who work on our farm, but I love to hear Arabic music. It's probably because of my dad. He loves their music. But politics," he hurriedly snapped, "is something else! There's no partner for peace!"

But Alon's guarded affection for Arabic music, to his mind, cost him. Yevgeny told him that the first time he saw him he thought he was an Arab, Druze or Bedouin soldier. Alon's face crinkled at a perceived insult. "I hope I didn't offend you," Yevgeny immediately apologized. "It's because of the music," he explained. "You were listening to Arabic or Middle Eastern music - I never could tell the difference. Also your accent, your color, you know. I was sure you weren't Jewish." He paused and added, "Maybe you should wear something on your head... a yarmulke... something to distinguish you from them, you know..."

As the traffic resumed and flowed uninterrupted, Yoav turned to Alon and scolded him. "I don't understand what you meant when you yelled at them go already, go. You're the one who held them up with your stupid questions and caused the traffic jam. Because of you we'll have problems here."

"I have to listen to your bullshit again?" Alon replied furiously. "Why don't you go and live with them if you feel so sorry for them?"

Yoav shook his head and waved his hand dismissively, demonstrating his helplessness. The gestures seemed to fire Alon up. He exploded with rage. "Why don't you find yourself some rich Ashkenazi woman," he shrieked, "someone from Checkpoint Watch? You can join them and preach to us about not losing our humanity and all that bleeding-heart bullshit they talk about. We aren't guarding some mall in Tel Aviv. We're at war here." Yoav didn't respond, which enraged him even more. "You've been accepted to school in America," he lashed out at him, "so why not leave us alone? Go to America, you and all the English books you read. This here isn't a university. It's the Islamic Jihad, Hamas... I don't know how I get stuck on the same shift with you every time... from now on, I'll make sure we don't do shifts together. I've had it with you and your lecturing. Preaching all the time! You're not better than us. What the hell are you doing here anyway?! Come on, make up some excuse, invent something, exempt yourself from reserve service, like all your leftist buddies... "

The question of dodging reserve service had in fact come up several times in his conversations with Tali. His reasons for not getting out of it never satisfied her. "All you said," she laughed angrily, "is that you feel like you can't come up with a good excuse. Why? Because you're a model citizen. Because it's your civic duty and what would happen if everyone else dodged theirs?"

Yoav resented Tali's depiction of him as a *frayer*, a sucker, conformist. "That's not what I said!" he growled, but quickly changed his tone. "Say, how come you, who used to be a Scout instructor encouraging your kids to contribute and enlist, expect me to come up with an excuse to skip reserve service?"

Tali smirked and replied with a touch of exasperation, "Indeed, how come? Maybe because I care about you and worry that something might happen to you?"

"Nothing will happen to me, don't worry. And besides," he added, "I know it may sound stupid to you, but with my family, enlisting in the army and doing reserve service is a civic duty. You don't dodge. I'm not a draft dodger! You have a problem with the policy of the government, whether you're left-wing or right-wing, say it through the ballot. If I refuse to do reserve service because I disagree with the right-wing government's policy, then tomorrow those who oppose the left-wing government will refuse. Where will it end? Anarchy! That's where."

Tali looked at him, tilted her head and went on to tease him: "So you're *frayer*, a sucker."

"Okay, I'm *frayer*," Yoav said irritably. He paused, then mused: "I don't know, maybe it comes from the same place that makes me bother you when you take long showers and let the water run endlessly. This waste of water annoys me. We talked about it once. It's not a matter of money, you know."

"That's what bothers you?" she asked with disbelief. "That I stand in the shower and let the water run?"

"Yes, it seems like a terrible waste of water in a country like ours. Maybe I got it from my father. He used to monitor the water level in the Sea of Galilee like it was the stock market. I know I'm weird about that. I once called the university maintenance department to tell them the flush tank in the toilet was broken and the water was leaking."

Tali frowned and pulled her head back as if listening to sheer nonsense. "Where do you get these ridiculous notions? What's water in the flush tank got to do with any of it? What on earth is the connection?!"

"There is a connection!" Yoav replied angrily. "Both of these things have to do with how I feel. I told you," he grumbled, "it's the sense of responsibility for where I live. It's the same with the Scout movement, isn't it?" he stated reprovingly. "That's what you once said… So where my family's concerned, military service is something that shows you're a part of society, of the state, a contribution that everyone has to make."

Tali looked at him despondently and said in a mocking voice: "I just want you to know that there are lots of people who don't feel that way, who don't think that serving in the army is what secures their rights in society, or that not serving in the army means they don't belong."

"I know, I know, I'm aware of that," Yoav replied

bitterly. "Sometimes I also think the reserve soldiers, who join up whenever they're called, are *frayers*, suckers. But when I'm called, I go. That's all there is to it."

CHAPTER 7
Hisham

He glanced impatiently at his watch. Hisham was not in a hurry and nothing required his immediate attention, yet he already wanted to return home. He couldn't bear his family's compassionate looks, their guarded language, their unspoken words. He called his cousin Nabil, who wanted to ride with him to Ramallah, to hurry up. Nabil was his confidant, his soulmate. In the past they used to talk with each other often about life, worries, problems... but that was no more. Only a few minutes passed before Nabil showed at the door. He greeted everybody, approached Hisham with a smile, and kissed him on both cheeks. "I'm ready when you are!" he declared. "Sorry if I kept you waiting, *Sha'er Al-Jib.*" A slight twitch appeared on Hisham's face when he heard his schooldays nickname, the Al-Jib Poet, but he said nothing. Nabil suggested Hisham join him and his friends when they arrived in Ramallah for a musical event at one of the cultural centers, but he declined.

"Hadil went to Jordan," he apologized, "and I need to be home with the kids."

Nabil never attended high school. At fourteen he'd already been forced to go to work because his large family struggled to make ends meet. He used to accompany

Marwan to work, where he taught him the building trade. As the years went by, however, Nabil and Marwan went their separate ways. He meandered from one Israeli city to another, following job opportunities. When he reached the age of twenty-three, he married Fadia, his mother's relative. They had five children. Until two decades ago, the cousins, Hisham and Nabil, had maintained a strong bond forged in their childhood. But the bond weakened when Hisham attended Bir Zeit University.

"I wonder what would happen," Hadil once told Hisham, "if you and your cousin had to spend an extended period of time together. You no longer have much in common but the past. Maybe you manage to maintain this close bond precisely because you don't see each other that often, and when you do, it isn't for long." Hisham scowled at her. "Just a thought," she said, shrugging. "Nabil loves you very much. He admires you, even reveres you a little."

This had always been the case even when they attended al-Ittihad, Al-Jib's primary school. Hisham was an excellent student. His teachers noticed the unusual talent for memory he possessed, showcased by his ability to recite long, complex poems by heart. On special occasions, he would be asked to climb the concrete stage in the schoolyard and recite familiar poems suitable to the occasion. He even dared, while attending Ibn Khaldun boys' high school, to write a special poem celebrating the release of an Al-Jib man from Israeli prison. Hisham remembered nervously waiting for the principal, Ahmad Awad Al-Shami, to complete his long-winded speech so he could deliver the poem. Al-Shami greeted the released prisoner, a former student of the school, who now attended this ceremony in his honor. Al-Shami lauded the high price the man had paid on behalf of the Palestinian cause and declared that the man epitomized the values that the school strove to instill in its students. He went on to mention the tenacity of the Palestinian people in its struggle against occupation and the special place of Al-Jib

in Palestinian national history. "The inhabitants of Al-Jib,"
he declared, "are the descendants of a Canaanite
population that lived in Al-Jib since 2000 B.C., long before
the Jews arrived in Palestine. We have a kinship with the
original population of Al-Jib since time immemorial! That
is a fact that even the Torah does not dispute," he cried
out.

"And as you know, dear students," he continued, "the
archaeological sites scattered around our village – the rock-
hewn pool, the ancient burial caves where our ancient
ancestors were put to rest, the wine cellars – all testify to this
better than any book or document. And if objective proof is
needed," he roared, "then we have Dr. Gluck, the famous
American archaeologist, who tied his fate with ours, and
visited our village many times. The inhabitants of Al-Jib," he
said with growing fervor, "embody the value of sumud,
attachment to the land, more than any other Palestinian
settlement. More than Al-Quds, more than Haifa, and more
than Jaffa. We are attached to this place like the roots of the
trees to the soil! Our hold on the land is firm! We won't be
uprooted!" he shouted. "We have been here before anybody
else and will stay here after everyone leaves!"

It had been many years since Dr. Gluck met his end
under mysterious circumstances. This unresolved case
occurred in the early 1990s before the signing of the Oslo
Accords. No one knew who shot the archaeologist with
three deadly bullets. Were the Jews responsible for his
death because they were unhappy with his archaeological
findings? Or perhaps the blame for his death rested with
the relatives of his research assistant, the Ramallah woman
with whom he was suspected of carrying on an illicit affair?
These questions never received satisfactory answers, and
Ahmad Awad al-Shami had long since retired. He left a
dubious legacy however; his proclivity for long-winded
speeches infused with bathos made him a laughingstock in
the village of Al-Jib, years after his retirement. Whenever a
person delivered drawn-out speeches or engaged his

companions in tiresome harangues, people would say "Oh God, he talks like al-Shami," or they would sigh in exasperation, "Enough already with al-Shami's speeches!"

On that day after the principal ended his long speech, he invited Hisham to read his poem. The schoolyard crowd greeted him with enthusiastic applause. The hero of the event also shook his hand warmly, kissing him on both cheeks. The poem was based on a simple rhyme and was written with overblown pathos. Each column ended with the refrain you're our symbol, you're our glory, you're our pride, you're our future, bestowing superlatives on the man. Later in life, whenever this poem crossed his mind, Hisham felt deeply embarrassed and pushed it back into oblivion.

He owed his high school and university graduation to his parents. He was the apple of their eye, and they spared no effort or financial resource to ensure his studies continued unimpaired. They were the first to notice his natural gifts. His father was particularly impressed by Hisham's ability to absorb the poems he heard, inscribe them in his memory, and readily recount them. "He's like a clear echo," the father boasted, "rising from the depths of a hollow well. This boy is gifted," he added, grinning with pride. "He's a recording device." And so, while his brothers worked from an early age helping to support the family, Hisham was left to pursue his studies. Except for his brother Sharif, who resented and envied him for it, his siblings learned to accept the special treatment accorded to him by their parents.

Hisham's special gift won him several school contests over the years. He particularly excelled in competitions that required participants to recite a poem starting with the last letter of the previous contestant's poem. The winner was the last man standing. It was then that the nickname *Sha'er Al-Jib*, the Poet of Al-Jib, stuck to him. During his Bir Zeit years, he managed to modestly justify the nickname by having some of his poems published in literary journals. But his creative activity was not widely recognized within Palestinian cultural and intellectual circles. Thus, while his longtime friends and acquaintances continued to call him, with much affection, the Poet of Al-Jib, Hisham felt distressed whenever he heard the nickname thrown out. To his ears it sounded like "failed poet".

He once heard a notable poet lamenting the difficulty of creating anything of worth in the shadow of great poets like Mahmoud Darwish and Fadwa Tuqan. "Darwish," the poet protested, "suppressed my creativity for a long time. I felt as if my poetry was pale, insipid." But that's not the case with me, Hisham conceded to himself. I know good poetry when I see it, but I'll never write like the great poets. Some are meant to write poetry, others to teach it. He tried to reconcile himself to the fact that he belonged to the latter, and gave up writing in favor of teaching Arabic poetry and literature at the Friends School in Ramallah. But on occasion, he still grappled agonizingly with his failed dream. The title "the Poet of Al-Jib" continued to hound him, at once eliciting a profound sense of failure and vague aspiration to still live up to the name. There were times when he flirted with the idea that, once he settled in his teaching job, performing it with less effort, he would have the time and mental space for creating. But he was not able to produce anything of real value. Hadil, with whom he used to share his frustration, tried to cheer him up, noting how esteemed he was by his peers for the wonderful work he does. "Sure, sure," he nodded, as if he did value that esteem but drew insufficient reward from it. "My love," Hadil would plead with him, "this is not the end of the world. When I was a girl, I sang in the Friends School choir. We weren't taught music systematically, and we didn't have the beautiful music institutes we have now – not the Edward Said Conservatory and not the National Music Institute. There was nothing. I thought I had a future in that area. The music teacher, Miss Wilson, believed in me. I was good, but I was not a prodigy. And when she went back to London, my musical career ended. It made me sad. I really wanted to develop my skills, but it was impossible. So I moved on. There are other options. You can't stand still, you've got to move on. Life is trial and error. If you don't succeed in something, try something else. That's what you've done. You've become a highly–esteemed, beloved teacher, so why can't you enjoy what you do best? Not everyone can be a teacher, a good teacher. You have a special gift, and it's a shame you don't enjoy it."

"You must remember," she tried tenderly to reassure him, "what the graduates of 2001 wrote to you. Don't you remember how proud you were, showing me the card they wrote you with the gift?" Hisham remembered. He had kept the card, together with others, in a special binder hidden in his desk drawer. This particular one stood out in the wording. "To our beloved teacher Hisham," it read, "the teacher who taught us to love the written word, who showed us original ways of looking at words, we extend our great love and appreciation. We go out into the big world and don't know what to expect. We face many challenges and don't know how we shall meet them. But we do know that we have a compass in our hands that will help us make the right choices. A heartfelt thanks for the faith, the dedication, and especially the love. Friends School, class of 2001."

At first he didn't find teaching at the school easy. Securing the position thanks to warm recommendations from the parents of students he had tutored, he embarked on it with enthusiasm and awe. "You can't compare Friends School and the schools in Al-Jib," he used to say excitedly, "Friends is like a university. The teaching methods, the students' attitude, the level of education, the material infrastructure, library, everything is different there." The warm appreciation of his peers and students drove him to excel at his work, to prove that he deserved the opportunity he was given. The veterans among the teachers remembered Hadil and her sisters favorably. Initially Hisham was affectionately referred to as Hadil's husband, but as time went by, he managed to be recognized by colleagues and students alike on his own merits. Despite all this, he was never completely at home at Friends School, feeling as if there was some permanent hurdle he couldn't clear, a ceiling he couldn't break through. I'll never become one of them, he brooded miserably. He lacked a certain sophistication, a certain self-confidence, the subtleties interwoven in the way other teachers, parents, and even students carried themselves. There was something in the way they spoke, and perhaps their mastery of foreign languages, which made him perceive them as a privileged elite. Hadil and even Leila commanded those qualities - but not him, not him.

As soon as Nabil crossed the doorstep to his parents' house, Hisham stood up, ready to bid his parents and sister farewell. Before he left, his mother stuffed a large bag with a bottle of olive oil, a jar of homemade olives, zucchini stuffed with yogurt sauce, and stuffed vine leaves. "Take it, my son, take it, they're the blessings of the earth," she urged him. Following the standard ritual, he first voiced mild reluctance then took the offerings.

"How's Hadil?" Nabil said casually as they began the drive to Ramallah. "I haven't seen her in a long time."

"Neither have I," Hisham snapped. He immediately rushed to defuse Nabil's puzzled expression. "I mean I don't see her enough either. She's very busy, and I'm busy too. A lot of work at school... We don't get to spend much time together." But his attempt to mask the resentment of his original reply failed. The crack he had opened invited peering eyes.

"Is everything good?" Nabil gazed intently at his cousin.

"Everything's fine, I told you."

"Let me tell you, ya Hisham," Nabil said, cajoling him into sharing his woes, "you're not the man I used to know, cheerful, energetic...you look worried, upset. What's eating you? I hear people talk..."

"I'm fine," Hisham nipped his cousin's entreaty in the bud. "Everything's fine, *alhamdulillah*, praise God." Focusing his gaze on the asphalt road, he asked: "And what about you? How's life? How's Fadia? The kids?"

Nabil let out a sigh as if giving up on getting his cousin to share, and soon began an extended harangue. "What can I tell you, ya Hisham? I'm tired of this shit. For months I've been trying to get a magnetic card. Without it I can't get an Israeli work permit. I spent hours at the Coordination and Liaison Office filling out all the paperwork over and over. They asked for proof of marriage, I gave it to them. They asked for me and my children's birth certificates, I gave it to them. They wanted a certificate from the police that I don't have a record, I got it. They wanted a letter from my Jewish boss saying I'm urgently needed, he wrote one, and he even paid them some money. And the answer – negative! Why? 'You're *mamnua amni*, denied for security reasons,' that's what they told me. I asked them, what did I do? They say, 'We don't know. You're turned down for security reasons.' *Ein horaot*, they tell me in Hebrew that they've got orders. So nothing can be done!"

"Maybe they denied you because of our family name, Saada," Hisham suggested. "When I studied in Bir Zeit, during the first Intifada, I took part in demonstrations and was arrested once, remember? But it was a long, long time ago. Who can tell? Or maybe," he entertained another notion, "it's because of my brother Sharif the Hamas activist?"

Undaunted by Hisham's interjection, Nabil went on with his rant. "In God's name, I don't know why I'm denied a work permit. So what choice do I have? I work in Israel without a permit and have to pay a big share of the money I make to the smugglers."

"They are Palestinians?"

"Who?"

"The smugglers."

"Of course, you're surprised? Here, Kamal, Hadil's uncle, isn't he one of us, a Palestinian? And he was also…"

"What's one thing got to do with the other?" Hisham fumed.

Nabil took a brief look at him, as if to decipher the reason for Hisham's angry reaction, but quickly went on venting his frustration. "When I'm at work I never sleep quietly. Always scared. The tiniest noise and I say here comes the police. You know," he began, "once I worked in a Jewish settlement here next to our village, in Gibeon. They say that Gibeon is the old name of Al-Jib. And so my employer said to me, like he's joking, 'You, the people of Al-Jib, are our slaves, the same as the ancient people of Al-Jib who used to be our slaves. This is what's written in the Torah,' he said. Damn him!"

Nabil paused then concluded bleakly: "What can I tell you, ya Hisham. By God, that son of a bitch is right. We're their slaves."

They approached the Bir Nabala checkpoint. Normally, the soldiers paid special attention to the vehicles traveling towards the Palestinian enclaves cut off by Highway 443, being less concerned with those moving in the opposite direction towards Ramallah. This time they also stood on the other side of the road, examining the cars going to Ramallah. "What happened?" Hisham speculated facetiously. "Maybe the Islamic Jihad intends to commit terrorist acts in Ramallah, and the Israeli army wants to make sure we don't come to any harm there?"

Hisham recognized the soldiers. They were the same ones who stood in the afternoon on the opposite side of the road leading to the enclave. One of them, the younger of the two, signaled the cars approaching the checkpoint to slow down and took a good look at the passengers. He demanded to see identity cards, licenses, transit certificates, and other documents.

"Hawya, ID card," he shouted in Arabic. Nabil presented him with the card, adding in Hebrew: "Here it is."

"Oh, so you speak Hebrew?" the soldier grumbled.

"Yes," replied Nabil, providing additional details to facilitate smoother passage through the checkpoint. "I worked in Israel before the Intifada in many places, in Tel Aviv, Kfar Saba, Holon, Ness Ziona. I'm a bricklayer. I have many friends in Israel."

"And he," the soldier focused his gaze on Hisham, surveying his meticulous clothing - fashionable khaki trousers and a branded polo shirt - "does he also work in construction or maybe he's a building contractor?"

"No, he's a teacher," Nabil replied.

"No kidding, *achi*, bro?" the soldier reacted with affected appreciation. "A teacher. What does he teach? Ask him," he commanded.

Nabil turned to Hisham and translated the question. Years of working in Israeli construction sites had suddenly become an advantage. Though he never learned to read and write in Hebrew, he maintained a good level of the spoken language.

Hisham suddenly felt despondent, tongue-tied, completely dependent on his cousin. He tilted his head forward, grimaced slightly, and told Nabil, "Tell him... tell him I teach poetry and Arabic literature."

Nabil did as he was asked. "He's a teacher... songs, books... he teaches songs and books."

"Songs, books, really," the soldier shook his head as if to indicate that he wasn't someone who could be easily fooled. He barked at Nabil while keeping his eyes fixed on Hisham, studying him carefully.

"I don't understand what you're saying," Nabil replied.

The soldier shook his head in irritation, called out to the other man who stood behind the concrete antitank cube on the other side of the road, and exchanged heated words with him.

"What does he want from us?" Hisham turned to Nabil, taking advantage of the brief respite while the soldiers talked.

"By God, I don't know," Nabil shrugged helplessly. "He's asking the other soldier something."

"*T'hrid, t'hrid*, incitement," the soldier gestured towards Hisham. "Ask him if that's what he does in school," he turned to Nabil. "He's turning the children against us. He teaches them to become martyrs, terrorists, that's what he does! Songs... books... sure," he snorted contemptuously.

Understanding what the soldier had in mind did little to advance the situation, for there was not much to be done with his veiled allegation. "He doesn't expect us to take this seriously," Nabil said in an angry whisper. "He just wants to pester us." Yet he did as the soldier commanded, and referred the question to Hisham, adding an apologetic look.

Hisham looked at Nabil, shrugged, raised his hands as in prayer and said, "*Shu bidi aa'ulu*, what can I tell him?"

"What do you mean *shudooloo, shudooloo*?" The soldier raised his voice, trying to imitate Hisham. "*Achi*, bro, he knows exactly what I'm talking about. Playing dumb. Songs and books, sure."

They sat frozen in the car, helpless. Then the older soldier began scolding his younger compatriot. He glanced at them contemptuously then waved them on, yelling: "Go already, go!"

"He calls me *achi*, I'm his brother! Can you believe that?!" Nabil sneered bitterly as they made their way to Ramallah. "I'm his brother, that dog, damn him, son of a whore."

"Not everyone's the same," Hisham tried to soothe his cousin's anger. "Some of them are better. You saw, the other soldier, the older one, seems to be a decent man. He does not love us, for sure, but he didn't give us trouble. He's doing his job."

"*Kos ochto*, his sister's cunt, he's doing his job," Nabil said, seething. "Doing his job? Sure! What's his job? Protecting the settlers? Let's invite him to the Mukata'a then so Abu Mazen can give him a medal of honor."

Hisham chose to remain silent. The aftereffects of his visit to his parents, the harassment at the checkpoint, even the company of Nabil, his cousin and childhood friend, all coalesced into a dark mood. When they reached the center of town, Nabil got out of the car and walked to the musical center, while Hisham drove to Ranin's house to collect his children. He reconfirmed with Ranin that Nadim could stay at her place the following evening as they had agreed. He prepared a light dinner for the children and soon after, they showered and went to bed. He watched TV for a while, flipping through the channels erratically. He lay on his bed, slightly abuzz at the thought of the following day's rendezvous with Mandy.

CHAPTER 8
Tali

The possibility that Yoav might renege on his commitment to her came up in her conversation with Liat just days before her trip to Jordan. Tali had angrily dismissed Liat's doubts. But following her last conversation with Yoav she had lost some of that certainty. Doubts began creeping into her mind and were threatening to grow stronger, to sink deeper down, gnawing, unsettling. Maybe Liat knows what she's talking about, Tali brooded apprehensively. After all, the questions she raised didn't seem unfounded, her anxiety somewhat reasonable. What happens, Tali wondered, if I don't get into a university in the US? Would he give up on studying abroad, on Harvard?

It was early afternoon when the two women met days after Yoav had begun his reserve service, settling comfortably into either side of a window table in a café in Masaryk Square. It was then that Liat challenged Tali's unequivocal trust in Yoav, doing so out of genuine concern, a duty forged through years of close friendship. Sometimes it's the role of a true friend, Tali granted, to play devil's advocate rather than rubber stamp one's hopes.

"So where did they station Yoav this time?" Liat was curious to know.

"In the Territories, somewhere between Ramallah and Jerusalem."

"The Territories? Where are they, these territories?" Liat smiled facetiously.

Liat's derisive reaction echoed the attitude of many Tel Avivians her age, who showed no interest whatsoever in what was unfolding 'there', beyond the city limits. The Territories, the West Bank, were to them remote provinces of the metropolis. Liat's countenance, however, turned serious.

"So what," she said, nodding admiringly, "you're flying away soon?"

"I hope so," replied Tali. "We're supposed to get answers from the universities any day now."

"Tell me," Liat wondered, "what would happen if only one of you is accepted? What would happen then? What would happen if you got accepted and he didn't?"

"Well," Tali said emphatically, "we'll continue our studies here."

"You've always been like this," Liat teased her, "having a relationship is all-consuming for you. That's how you were even as a young girl. The only time you didn't have a boyfriend was after you came back from the United States. A whole year! Here in Tel Aviv people change partners every day, but you and Yoav - an island of stability. I'd say," she giggled, "an island of stability in the middle of a stormy ocean."

That was indeed how many of Tali's friends described her. "Tali is in touch with herself," they agreed. "She knows what she wants, she was always into having a stable relationship. 'The stormy seas of Tel Aviv', as Liat described the casual romance scene that drew many of her peers, never appealed to Tali.

"Good for you, this ocean," she replied with a shrug as if to emphasize her lack of interest in this lifestyle. The delights of sexual rapacity were not for her. She enjoyed sex, but to her it was inexorably linked with trust and affection.

"Maybe you're just afraid of losing control," Liat challenged her, laughing.

"You've already said this before," Tali snapped. "True,"

she added, "I'm not as adventurous as you are, but not because I'm afraid of losing control." She paused for a moment, softening her expression as if to compensate for her outburst, and then continued, "I'm almost thirty, and I'd like to have kids at some point. Say, two, three years from now. I don't want to end up an old maid, a bitter academic, like some shriveled carrot forgotten in the fridge drawer."

"Interesting metaphor," Liat smiled slyly. "I wonder how your admired mentor, Professor Galia Hoffman, would react if she heard you now?"

"I told her this!"

"You told her what?!" Liat cried out, startled. "That she's a shrunken carrot left in the fridge?!"

"No," Tali giggled, "I told her that I don't want to give up on marriage and family."

"Well, that will never be a problem for you. Even if you travel alone to the end of the world, you'll instantly meet someone, marry him, and have children." Liat suddenly looked at Tali as if scanning her, then asked: "Tell me, what are you going to do if the opposite happens? I mean, what if Yoav's accepted and you're not?"

"Well?"

"Well," Liat repeated decisively. "Do you believe that he won't go through with it and leave you behind? And if he's accepted and you're not, would you follow him, supporting and loving him, like many wives do?"

Tali ignored the derisive tone and stated affirmatively: "No! He'll stay in Israel too!"

"You say this with such confidence, such certainty," said Liat, and went on relentlessly. "How do you know?"

"I told you already," Tali retorted somewhat impatiently, "Yoav and I have talked about this possibility. In that case we both stay in Israel."

Liat leaned in, touched Tali's hand and said softly: "I hope that you and Yoav end up gracefully growing old together in Haifa."

Tali couldn't tell whether Liat was teasing or being

genuinely affectionate. So she chose not to respond. A silence set in, accentuated by the bustle of the city, the coffeehouse chatter, and the heavy traffic heading towards Rabin Square.

In her youth, Tali had belonged to the Afik Scout troop. They operated out of a wood cabin located in a thick pine grove, not far from her home in Haifa's Neve Sha'anan neighborhood. The troop held its summer activities in Zippori Forest in the Lower Galilee. They built models of castles and mythical beasts from variously sized logs, beams, and boards, draping them in colorful cloths. Tali soon became adept at this. She was elected to represent the troop in speed-building contests, even winning first place on several occasions.

"If you asked me to demonstrate all the knots I learned," she once lightly bragged to Yoav, "like diagonal lashing, square lashing, round lashing, constrictor knot - I could do it in a heartbeat."

Scouting had always been intertwined in her memories with Ronnie and Liat, her close friends since primary school. She often recalled incidents from those days, some eliciting tender smiles, others fleeting gloom. She vividly remembered the time when the troop gathered to debate the supreme values of honor, equality, and fraternity. Liat snuck into Ronnie's unattended bag, took out the sweets he had in there, and passed them around, giggling and exclaiming: "Here, we're all brothers and sisters, sharing everything." Ronnie was furious. He chased them all, staining their foreheads with a red marker and squealing angrily, "The mark of Cain on you! The mark of Cain on you!" Long after the incident the expression was used in jest whenever members of the Afik troop wanted to reprimand each other.

Years later, Tali became a leader in the same troop. Her attention to the children in her care was legendary. "You treated us like a mother treats her children," one of them wrote. "You were always there for us when we needed you," wrote another. When time came for her to join the army, it was only natural that she served as a welfare NCO, offering guidance and assistance to soldiers struggling with personal issues. Asked during placement why she's qualified for this demanding role, her answer was plain and direct: "I care, and I know how to listen." In this sense, she was indeed old beyond her years. To a large extent, her army service dictated her later academic and professional course. The gut-wrenching, one-on-one encounters with soldiers suffering from severe social and emotional problems – poverty, trauma, domestic violence, sexual abuse, loneliness, social alienation, and more – drove her to seek helpful knowledge and effective solutions for treatment.

After returning from a post-army trip to the US she began working for the Scouts in her hometown of Haifa while living with her parents. She would describe it rather dryly as "A year of turning in, of recuperating from my 'American episode'," never sharing any more details about it. During this year, she regularly visited her grandmother, Bracha-Bianca, who lived nearby.

"I needed a haven, a warm place with love, simple love, not romantic love, and with as little talking as possible," she once shared with Yoav. "My grandma speaks almost no Hebrew, and I don't speak Romanian at all. But that wasn't a problem, quite the contrary. These visits gave me strength, they helped me get through this awful time," she added, not specifying what made it so. All she was willing to say was that she was going through a severe emotional crisis. "I didn't know what I wanted and what I should do, even when I continued to work with the Scouts that year. Maybe working there helped after all, because it meant I didn't sever ties with the outside world."

At first Tali thought of combining her work in the Scouts with studying psychology and education at Haifa University, but ultimately decided to give up the Scouts and study at Tel Aviv instead. The decision to move to Tel Aviv was motivated in part by the endless solicitations of Liat and Ronnie who'd already moved there and started university. Although she would have saved money by staying with the Scouts and living with her parents in Haifa, her parents gladly financed her studies in Tel Aviv. "A university education," Tali's father used to say, "is the best economic investment you can make in your children. Education is money! That's what I tell my clients at the bank."

Indeed, Tali's father, Micha, who ran a bank branch in Haifa, was a man who gauged everything by cost-benefit. "What do you get out of it?" he used to ask whenever tackling a major decision. Tali resented her father's pragmatism and what she saw as his narrow view of university education. "With all due respect to cost-benefit calculations," she once told him, "a diploma isn't necessarily the best way to get rich." Micha was not impressed. "That's true in the case of an education degree," he conceded. "What can that get you? You'll end up poor. When you said you wanted to study education, your mother and I said nothing. If that's what you want... but when you changed your mind on it, we were very happy, I've got to admit. Now, psychology, on the other hand..." he declared firmly, "that's different! Psychologists live very well, let me tell you. Some of them have accounts at my branch. They should thank God," he laughed, "for all the nutjobs in the world, especially these days."

"Dad," Tali cried out. "That's not funny!"

If in the beginning of her academic studies she thought that clinical psychology would be most rewarding, most suited to her proclivities and her desire to help those in need, she eventually changed her mind. "I can't be a clinical psychologist," she shared with Yoav. "To do it, you need to be able to detach yourself, not get drawn into the inner lives of your patients, sympathize but not identify. I don't know how to set my own boundaries. My tendency to identify sometimes gets to the point of hurting myself," she emphasized painfully, "really hurting myself."

"What do you mean?" Yoav pressed her for more details. "What do you mean you don't know how to set boundaries?

Can you give me an example?"

The image of Harvey came into Tali's mind. For a moment she thought she might be ready to share with Yoav the horrific experience she'd had with Harvey in New York. But she changed her mind. She never talked about that with any of her friends, nor had the courage to seek professional help. She was good at listening to others, knew how to make them tell their innermost painful secrets, how to make soldiers shed tears telling her about broken homes and drunken fathers, how to have female soldiers open up about violent rape, sexual abuse, horrid incest stories, yet she found it impossible to share with anyone her own terrible, unspeakable secret.

"I can't think of specific examples," she lied to Yoav. "But you can probably imagine what I mean."

Yoav wasn't easily fooled. "No," he replied, "I can't imagine what you mean. Why don't you tell me what you mean?"

Pulling herself together and shelving her secret in the very back of her mind, Tali spoke about the Scout trainees who would call her day and night for advice, about visiting soldiers' homes, sitting down for hours on end with their parents, helping them work through family problems, and about occasions when she gave her own money to needy soldiers. "Even now," she added, "you see how devoted I am to the students, how much prep time I put in. It's my nature, my character. I'm a lost cause! Even Galia said that I overdo it, that I need to let go a little. "

Tali noticed that Yoav was only half-listening, as if to signal that he knew she was dodging the real thing, the unimaginable, the unspeakable. But she went on nonetheless as if by inertia. "Therefore," she said as though concluding a formal argument, "I want to focus less on human pathology and more on everyday behavior, especially gender differences in volunteer work. Men and women approach these activities differently... what?" she said, noticing that Yoav still wore a skeptical expression.

"Nothing," he answered pensively.

CHAPTER 9
Hadil

Although Salim loved all three of his daughters, he reserved special affection for Hadil. It is difficult to admit but parents do not allot equal love to their children. And indeed Salim never admitted it openly, but Hadil could feel it. She was his eldest, his pride and joy. He drew satisfaction not only from her scholastic achievements, but also from her maturity and sincerity. Hadil's sisters noted their father's favoritism, but had learned to accept it, and bore no special grudge. They too loved and admired their big sister.

"She's not as frivolous as her sisters," Salim used to say with gleaming eyes to Salwa, "she has self-discipline, and she's determined. Hadil is *shatra*, clever. We can count on her."

The frequent accolades he heaped on her became a source of bitter derision from Salwa years later when Hadil flattened her parents with her intention to marry Hisham. Though not a stunner, Hadil never wanted for men who were charmed by her and sought her company. Was it her round face and her radiating heartfelt expression that appealed to them? Her animated black eyes, her silky dark hair, high cheekbones, and pretty dimpled chin? At times Hadil would tie a large bandana over her forehead for a fresh, stylish, somewhat defiant look. Gaining some weight in recent years, her curves rounded and softened. She towered slightly over Hisham in high heels.

"If we have beautiful children," Hisham used to tell her, "it will be because they take after you."

"And I hope," Hadil responded, "they'll have your eyes and your long eyelashes. But not your eyebrows," she added teasingly.

She had decent musical talent, characterized by a clear, agile voice in the upper register. When her music teacher, Jane Wilson, noticed Hadil's singing, she implored her parents to explore different options for nurturing and developing it. But in those days there were no real options for musical training in Ramallah. Aside from Miss Wilson's dedicated guidance, which lasted about three years before she returned to England, Hadil did little to develop her musical gift. Yet her parents took pleasure in watching her sing in the school choir, especially when she performed solos. On rare occasions, especially when by herself at home or on long car rides, Hadil would hum songs she used to sing. One song, *Simple Gifts*, often came to mind. Taught to her by Miss Wilson, it embodied the Quaker faith: 'Tis the gift to be simple… 'Tis the gift to be free… and then we will all live together in true love and harmony.

After graduating from Friends School and obtaining her Jordanian-format *al-tawgiyeh* matriculation, Hadil thought at first of applying to prestigious universities in the US or England, but eventually chose to apply to the English Literature department at Bir Zeit University. She had only a vague idea of what she would do with the degree. Teach English literature, perhaps? She was accepted and began her studies in the second half of the 1980s, a year before the first Intifada broke out. She drew great pleasure from her studies, but like many of her friends she felt a growing alienation towards academia with the Intifada's outbreak. "Of what relevance," she would ask in despair, "is English Literature to the political reality engulfing us? How can I study Jane Austen novels and love sonnets when everything around us is on fire?" Hadil's favorite lecturer, she noted to herself, devoted most of her time to the national struggle, becoming one of the main leaders of the Intifada.

"Who cares these days," Hadil would ask rhetorically, "about Austen, Shakespeare, Emerson, Wordsworth?"

Taking after her father, she joined the communist faction on campus, which was broadly supported by the Bir Zeit faculty. Informed by a secular agenda, this faction espoused a two-state solution to the Palestinian-Israeli conflict, and embraced nonviolent struggle against the occupation in the early stages of the Intifada. These activities were consistent with the Quaker worldview that guided the Friends School. This ideological dissonance puzzled her at first: how could heretics, and even self-proclaimed communists, find common ground and harmony with God-fearing believers? Her bewilderment grew further when she discovered that Quakers, like Muslims, emphasize the importance of Shahadat, Testimonies.

"Get it?" she once shared her revelation with Hisham. "The Quakers, like the Muslims, endorse martyrdom – it's just that martyr in English sounds less threatening than shahid. Like our school principal used to say, 'Let your life speak' – meaning that words like peace, equality, integrity, and simplicity are not just words, you have to manifest them in your behavior, your everyday life. So you see," she summed up, fusing sincerity with jest, "now we have bona fide Islamic martyrs, martyrs of virgin love, and Quaker-style martyrs."

The first Intifada seemed to provide her with an opportunity to manifest this worldview, becoming a martyr in her own way, the Quaker way. She participated in the countless demonstrations and sit-ins at Bir Zeit, spoke at various student gatherings of the virtue of nonviolent struggle, and even helped distribute United Headquarters leaflets calling for action in the spirit of those values.

It was during that time that her approach to academic education shifted. Hadil wanted to acquire knowledge that could be of relevance to people's everyday lives, skills that could improve those lives, if only slightly. Thus, she switched to social work and psychology. Although the political upheaval delayed her graduation, she felt that she had found her calling – focusing on women's issues in Palestinian society. Her teachers implored her to consider pursuing a PhD abroad. Hisham was enthralled by the prospect. "I know it would be difficult for me to find something to do there," he said, "but I'd love to leave this crazy place for a few years. Who knows, maybe I could teach Arabic there." Yet Hadil soon decided against it.

"No university in the world," she declared, "can train you like daily experience here."

But this was all in the past, she thought, seemingly unreal, worlds apart from this seminar at a Jordanian Hotel on the shores of the Dead Sea. It was Saturday and the pre-lunch session took place in the shadow of a suicide attack earlier that day at one of the checkpoints surrounding Jerusalem. The attack, perpetrated by a Palestinian activist in the al-Aqsa Martyrs' Brigades, had killed two soldiers. The atmosphere at the seminar shifted radically. If, until that morning, the encounters between Israelis and Palestinians were infused with some strain and suspicion, following the deadly event, tensions ran high. Boundaries, both real and symbolic, that had been cautiously removed were now rigidly reinstated. All it took, as Hadil knew too well, was one tragic event, one horrendous act by either a Palestinian or an Israeli, to undo achievements gained through painstaking effort over months and years. And if this weren't enough, it turned out that the boyfriend of Tali, the Israeli with whom Hadil had conversed the previous evening, was manning one of the checkpoints. Fearing that he might be one of the fatalities, Tali was freaking out. Hadil's feelings were mixed. The checkpoints and the soldiers who ran them prominently represented the humiliating scourge of occupation and rightly drew much of the Palestinians' ire and resentment. Yet Hadil could also identify with the young woman, terrified by the prospect of having lost her beloved in the attack. She must understand now, Hadil pondered ruefully, what it means for us to live under the reality of the occupation, in the fear of constant harassment and sudden death.

Hadil waited impatiently for the seminar to end. The suicide attack had rendered it altogether pointless – regrettably, for if ever dialogue among enemies seeking reconciliation was needed, it was in a moment like this. But then such a thing, she had learned from long experience, was nearly impossible. The shock of fresh violence sent each side crawling into its shell, to grieve over its dead and seek succor among its own. And so it proved again on this occasion. Gathering reluctantly in the seminar room after lunch, members of both groups launched into empty speeches about the importance of continued dialogue, thanking the organizers for the opportunity to participate in the seminar and gain insight on how the other side experiences the conflict. Some even expressed hopes for a follow-up. The two delegations boarded separate buses and started for home, the Israelis heading to Sheikh Hussein Bridge, the Palestinians to Allenby Bridge. Hadil made her way, as planned, to her friend Arij, who had been living in Amman's prestigious Abdoun district.

After dinner, Arij's husband Bashir and their children left the two women alone. Hadil and Arij moved to the living room of the spacious house. It had been their routine ever since Arij moved to Amman. They would sit for hours, sharing intimate details about their lives, children, husbands, work, problems, and concerns, adding juicy gossip about shared acquaintances from childhood, school, and university. The seeds of their friendship had been sown at an early age. Their parents lived next door to each other in lower Ramallah and sent their daughters to the same preschool, operated by the Friends Girls' School. Both Hadil and Arij subsequently attended Friends primary and high school, then Bir Zeit University. Nearly two decades ago, shortly after Hadil got married, Arij married Bashir, a Palestinian graduate of Bir Zeit whose parents had already settled in Amman.

Arij had long since given up her teaching career, devoting herself to her children. She gave some of her free time to charity work, raising money for educational projects in Palestinian refugee camps in Jordan. As she once disclosed to her friend, "Bashir is a very successful real estate businessman, praise God. His income is more than we need, so I don't have to work." Thanks to her husband's ties to Jordanian high officials, Arij managed to become a permanent citizen of the Hashemite Kingdom, bidding farewell to her green temporary resident card.

"We've killed the *G'ula*, the Transjordan ogress, and found the cache," Arij joked once, referring to a well-known Palestinian fairytale. Passed down from mother to daughter, the story told of a Palestinian family's journey to Transjordan in search of a livelihood. Arriving in a ruined town, the family encounters a many-faced, man-eating jinn. They overpower her and seize her cache of grain and oil.

"Praise God," repeated Arij, "we are fortunate. We're doing very well, and Bashir spares no effort and no money in taking care of us, me and our kids."

"You hardly said a word at dinner," Arij told her friend apprehensively as they sprawled on the living room sofa. "You seem down," she added tenderly. "What's up? What's bothering you?"

Hadil sighed, looked her friend in the face, and said as if in confession: "I've lost the joy of living, that's what's happening to me." She paused then added, "Maybe I lost my marriage too."

Jumping back, Arij cried out, "What?! What do you mean, maybe you lost your marriage?!"

"Shhhh... lower your voice."

"Okay, okay," Arij whispered, "but did something happen? Does he have someone?"

"Hisham? No, no," Hadil emphatically dismissed her friend's concern. "That isn't him. I've told you before what the problem is. It's just been getting worse and worse. There's so much anger, frustration... It feels like we're two strangers living in the same house." Shrugging, she added, "I think that if we didn't have kids, we would have split up by now. Yes, yes, I know..." she anticipated her friend's rebuttal, "he's a good man and dedicated father, I can't complain. He gives his heart and soul to the kids. He worries about them, dotes on them. He definitely spends more time with them than I do, because of my work, you know," she added somewhat contritely. "But..."

"See?" Arij interrupted. "Even you say he's a special man. Do you know many other husbands who behave like him? And don't forget how he's always standing by you, supporting you and encouraging you to continue your studies, to develop... There are no husbands like Hisham today! Here: when you work late, when you travel abroad, who stays with the kids? Who cares for them? Look at Bashir, he barely sees his kids. He's always busy working. "

"You're right, you're right," Hadil said, "but he's angry with me because of it, he resents me for it. It's not given freely. You should have seen his face when I left home... he didn't even say goodbye. And the kids - they see everything. They can tell their parents' marriage is going down the drain. We can't hide it from them. And it affects them. They're losing their confidence, their peace of mind. Would you believe," she continued, gloomy-faced, "that Nadim hit a classmate, that Leila misbehaved and was rude to her teachers?"

"Leila?"

"Yes, Leila!"

"I don't know what to say," Arij grimaced and tilted her head, surprised at the seriousness of the situation.

"You told me you were having problems, but I never thought it was that bad. Then again, who doesn't have problems? You have to do everything, everything in your power, to patch it up between you two, especially after you've sacrificed so much to be together."

Hadil replied with a hollow expression, "You're right, we've sacrificed a lot to be together. But you know how it is with marriage. It's like a watermelon," she cited a saying: "you see what's inside only after you buy it. The sacrifices couples make to be together, no matter how large, don't guarantee future happiness. And let me tell you, the fact that couples paid a price to be together shouldn't deter them from saying goodbye if things don't work out. You shouldn't enslave yourself or be a hostage to your past decisions, no matter how heroic or correct, if the present makes you feel miserable."

Arij did not relent. Unwilling to give up, she demanded to know how deep the marital rift was, hoping for details that could prove the marriage wasn't doomed. "Don't tell me you don't love him anymore?" she asked, her tone suggesting that a negative answer would not be accepted.

The question had lately been on Hadil's mind, but a clear answer wasn't in sight. She didn't expect to feel the same towards Hisham as when they first fell in love or even their early marriage. Her father was wrong: the embers of night did not turn into ashes in the morning, at least not so quickly. They'd enjoyed good years of genuine romantic love and mutual affection. But those had drastically waned, dissipated. Even if one can't expect them to last forever, she thought, there are other, more subdued, feelings of warmth, affection - even sex, though it can't be as thrilling as in the beginning. So what about those feelings, those desires? Hadil didn't share the thought with Arij. She looked up at the ceiling, as if searching for a good answer.

"So?" Arij repeated. "You don't love him anymore?"

"I don't know. I don't know what to tell you…"

"What do you mean, 'I don't know'?" Arij protested.

"I don't know," Hadil replied, flustered. "Leave me alone. What do you want me to tell you? I really don't know!"

Smiling mischievously, Arij made one last effort to assess the rift. "You don't...?" she nodded her head suggestively.

Hadil replied, smiling somewhat ruefully, "Truth is, I've already forgotten how to do it."

Chuckling slyly, Arij reassured her: "You might have forgotten, but the body never forgets. As they say, it's like riding a bicycle. The body does its own thing. You don't need your head for that. If anything," she giggled lasciviously, "the head can even be an obstacle."

"I guess you're right," Hadil laughed, but then turned serious again: "Sometimes it's impossible without the head. "It's something I learned from you when we were young women, in Bir Zeit. I remember you told me how in the beginning, you and Bashir did everything, everything, and you were still able to keep your virginity. We tried it, Hisham and I. In the beginning. We failed. "

Arij giggled with satisfaction. "True," she nodded proudly, "we're creative. But you were always different, a rebel. You went straight to the point, without intermediate arrangements, without trust-building measures, straight to the 'permanent status solution'. You should join the Palestinian negotiating team." They both burst into hearty laughter. Then Arij turned serious, giving her friend a long probing glance. "So what are you going to do?" she asked. "What are your plans?"

"My only plan right now is to survive from one day to the next," replied Hadil.

"Okay, okay," Arij said impatiently, "but what's going to happen now?"

"I have no idea," Hadil shrugged her shoulders. "I can only tell you that we can't go on like this."

Their conversation was interrupted by a phone call. It

was Leila. She wanted to meet her friends in downtown Ramallah, but her father forbade her to leave home. They wanted to meet at Rukab's Ice Cream or Stones Cafe near Al-Manara Square. Leila asked Hadil to persuade Hisham. Hadil suggested a compromise: "Why not invite your friends over instead?" She backed Hisham's decision, thinking it would be unfair to undermine his authority while he stayed at home taking care of the kids. His reason, conveyed by Leila, was also compelling: in recent years, many girls in Ramallah had fallen victim to public harassment, especially by young men from nearby villages who came to spend time in the city. Such incidents often required police intervention.

"How ironic," Hadil told Arij, "that Hisham wants to protect Leila from village youth, including ones from his home village of Al-Jib."

Arij's attempt to pick up the conversation from where it had left off was gently but emphatically rebuffed. Hadil felt like a mother trying to carefully wiggle free of a toddler's grip on the hem of her garment. She and Arij were soulmates yet she didn't want to delve into her marital crisis any further. She needed more time on her own to think. Words publicly spoken are like birds spreading their wings and leaving the nest. They acquire a life of their own; they became like public oaths, making it difficult to renege on them. Unspoken thoughts, instead, allow for vacillation. They do not require unmitigated and outright compliance; they afford some leeway before making decisions of monumental significance.

Heeding Hadil's reluctance, Arij let the matter rest. They went on talking for a while about other things – children, work, and common friends, even touching fleetingly on the hopeless political reality in the Occupied Territories. Weariness overtook Hadil's expression. Her eyelids grew heavy. Her body seemed like it was about to dissolve into the deep leather sofa that cradled her.

"Come on, you probably want to sleep," suggested Arij.

"Yes," Hadil replied, "very much."

CHAPTER 10
Yoav

Yoav looked around with disinterest; the traffic through the checkpoint was especially sparse. He had the odd feeling of being stranded on a road leading nowhere through an arid wasteland, augmented by the unending slowness of the shift. His military training had taught him to take in the surroundings with all of his senses. "Take the humidity of Tel Aviv in the summer," he used to say, "and add a bit of stench: that's the smell of Gaza. It's like rotten fruit in a compost heap. And the sewage," he grumbled, "flows openly in the streets. It's like a big dumpsite. I don't know how people live in that fucking place. But the West Bank is different," he stated with more than a modicum of admiration. "When you go there, you can feel that you went up from the lowlands to the highlands, the mountains. It's impossible not to be taken in by those amazing landscapes: the hills of Samaria, the olive groves." If Gaza was linked in his memory with stench, the villages of the West Bank, especially during winter nights, summoned the scent of smoking charcoal and other combustibles used for heating. Yet despite their differences, Gaza and the West Bank shared common features when compared to the settlements that dotted the landscape. They seemed alien to him, erected as architectural enclaves and suburban encampments, drawing their hyper-modern style far from the Middle East: usually straight or curving rows of large, red-shingled, land-attached houses. "Where the Jewish settlement begins," Yoav remarked ironically, "the biblical landscape ends." They were best exemplified by their nocturnal appearance. Where the settlements were easily discerned by the orderly light poles all along their streets, footpaths, and perimeters, the light from Palestinian villages was scattered randomly like arbitrarily flickering stars.

"That's what allowed me to find my way around the Territories during navigation exercises in the army more than a decade ago," he said.

As he paced back and forth, Yoav suddenly focused his gaze on two anthills on the side of the road by the concrete antitank cube. He crouched and watched for a long time as the black ants rushed to and fro as if on an errand. They moved in two long, separate columns, each either hurrying towards its mound or away to some unknown destination.

"What are you looking at?" Yevgeny asked.

"The ants," Yoav replied in amusement, "look at them! Running crazy like someone on speed. Look, what's the distance between the two mounds? Half a meter? But these ants live in separate worlds. They don't mix: they go in and out of their own mound, like there's an unseen border. Sharing the same territory, but worlds apart."

"So what?" Yevgeny asked. "What does it mean, Dr. Yarkoni?"

"I don't know," Yoav mused, ignoring his derisive tone. "You think the ants from the two mounds ever meet? Clash with each other?"

"How should I know? What do I know about ants?" replied Yevgeny. "But anyway," he immediately continued, "I heard once that ants wait for summer to come out of the ground. In winter you never see them. They must get bored down there. You know what?" he teased, "When you go to America, try to find out. Maybe you should research ants instead of the Middle East. They must have a center for that. The Ant Research Center," he laughed, pleased with himself.

The cell phone rang in Yoav's pocket. It was Tali; she was still in Jordan. "I was doing some thinking about this thing, your admission to Harvard," she said in a muffled voice. "Yoav, if you want to tell them 'yes' before I hear back from the universities, then do it. I don't want you to miss out on this opportunity because of me. I don't want you to resent me," she added. "I know how important this is for you, so, if…"

"Everything will be fine," Yoav soothed her, "we don't have to make a decision right now. Let's wait a few more days and see what happens. We'll hear from all the universities soon." He knew it wasn't the answer she had expected. He added: "Write them back for me. Tell them I really want to study at Harvard, but need a few more days before making my final decision, because my girlfriend also applied to universities in the Boston area and hasn't gotten answers yet."

"Your girlfriend?" asked Yevgeny after Yoav tucked the phone back into his pocket.

"Yes."

"The same woman from last year?"

"Yes, the same woman. Her name is Tali."

"Nice name, Tali."

"Yes, I love it."

"Because you love her."

"Probably."

"You probably love her?"

"No, no," Yoav replied impatiently. "I love her, and that's probably why I also like the name."

"Where is she from?"

"She was born in Haifa."

"Originally, I mean…"

"Her parents?"

"Yes."

"Her mother was born in Israel and her father was born in Romania, but her grandparents are from Poland."

"So she's a native Israeli," Yevgeny stated with mild appreciation. "You know, I think I've never dated a native

Israeli," he said, searching his memory to be sure. "And not just me. Most of my Russian friends would tell you the same thing. I once wanted to, but now it's irrelevant… that's it," he shrugged, "I'm married."

"How do you explain it?"

"I really don't know," Yevgeny mused, "maybe because they have a bad opinion of us Russians…but as my Dad always says, every medal has two sides. So maybe this way is better – everyone sticking to their own kind."

"Every coin," Yoav corrected him. "Every coin has two sides."

"In Russian we say medal: the medal has two sides," Yevgeny insisted. After a pause, he added: "But we have differences, too."

"What differences?"

"My family's from Moscow, Russian-Russian. And Katya, my wife, she's from Chernivtsi – that's a small city in Ukraine. The Russians look down at the Ukrainians, you know, especially if they come from some godforsaken place, from the backwoods. And even that's nothing compared to what they think about people from Uzbekistan or Georgia, Asian countries… Russians consider them totally primitive."

"You mean that's how Russians look at the non-Jews of those countries?"

"Jews, non-Jews. It makes no difference to them. They think anyone from those countries is primitive. But my parents are afraid to say things like that when Katya's around. They actually love her, call her Katinka. It's easy to build a good relationship when you have the same culture… the same mentality… when you speak the same language. It's important. In the past, all I wanted was to be Israeli like everyone else. I don't anymore. I'm glad I'm Russian. When our boy was born, we gave him a Russian name, Yuri, not an Israeli name like Itay or Amir. It would sound strange, phony. Even Yoav," Yevgeny smiled.

"I'm okay with that," Yoav laughed. "As far as I'm concerned, you can call him Putin. But you know," he added earnestly, "that might get in the way later. What, you don't want to fit in? You want to stay different? Not be Israeli like everyone else?"

"I fit in," Yevgeny protested. "Language, holidays, army, work, I fit in. But I'm Russian, what can I do? A person should be loyal to his identity. My Dad says people are like trees, they have roots. You can't transplant them without the roots. Without roots they die, they become crooked. Invalids."

"Yes, I do love her." Yoav reflected on his rather laconic answer to Yevgeny. It was about two months after their first meeting that he realized he loved Tali - truly loved her and wasn't just attracted or charmed by her. Far from being a mere mental recognition, it was a revelation, heralded by a throbbing, melting feeling inside, an overwhelming flow of emotion. It was the night of their long walk back to Tali's place after the year-end party at the Department of Middle Eastern and African History. Yoav had completed his second year of graduate school. The party featured a rich spread of local Palestinian cuisine as well as Israeli singers performing music by Arab music legends such as Umm Kulthum, Farid al-Atrash, Fairuz, and Warda Al-Jazairia.

Yoav introduced Tali to his supervisor, Professor Gadi Na'aman, who specialized in the spread of Arab nationalism following World War Two. Professor Na'aman used the opportunity to repeat his earlier suggestion that Yoav focus his research on the role of the British Mandate in shaping ethnic identities in Iraqi society. "It's a very interesting and important topic," he declared, "especially these days." He droned on incessantly, basking in the admiration of graduate students and junior faculty, imparting his wisdom on current events and trends in the Middle East. After all, he was the authority, the one whose face flashed on TV whenever some regional upheaval called for expert analysis. Professor Na'aman had gained national prominence as a daily commentator during the Second Gulf War. Astonishingly, despite being one of those who readily propagated the lie that Iraq had weapons of mass destruction, his reputation remained intact. The invasion of Iraq, he passionately maintained, was designed to remove the threat of nuclear apocalypse that hung over the Middle East and Israel in particular. He remained a sought-after Middle East commentator on TV. His detractors in the department observed, with more than a modicum of envy, that this was owing to the prevailing tempora and mores, citing Cicero. Truth doesn't matter anymore, they claimed. The public don't remember what was said yesterday, and TV channels aren't looking for truth but for telegenic entertainers – which Professor Na'aman was, through and through.

Walking back from the party, Yoav wanted to hear Tali's impressions of the evening. "It seems to me," she began in a low, hesitant voice, "that your professor likes to hear himself talk. He's full of himself, like many academics."

"So, you didn't enjoy yourself?" Yoav asked with a bit of trepidation.

"It was okay…" Tali drew out the words. "But don't you think the event was a little problematic, a little… exotic?"

"You mean Orientalist?"

"Yes, yes. Something like that. Orientalist," she clung to the word.

"I don't know, maybe a little," he conceded. "But they wanted to give it an authentic feel," he reasoned.

"I think they achieved the opposite effect," Tali declared emphatically. "Think about it. First the Arabic cuisine, then Arabic music, and then," she raised her voice incredulously, "red hats! Fezzes! It's like visiting some ethnic reservation for tourists. And I haven't even mentioned the belly dancer."

"You've got a point," Yoav conceded. "Like I told you once, I'm not really into those things, like Arabic music, even though I recognize some of the songs. I used to hear them in my grandparents' house, Grandpa Shmuel and Grandma Camilla." He paused, and then asked if she liked the music at the event. Tali reminded him that she didn't listen to Arabic music. But she did manage to identify one of the songs, Umm Kulthum's *Inta Omri*. A few years before, she had seen a modern dance piece that was set to it: "I think it was Ohad Naharin's dance ensemble," she said. "I don't remember exactly. But that's easy. Who doesn't know *Inta Omri*?" She paused and added that she did like the singer Dikla. When she'd first heard her on the Radio, she was sure it was an Arab person singing in Hebrew. "I like her!" Tali gushed. "You can tell she sings from the gut."

Yoav asked what she meant. "There was a power and a roughness in her voice," she explained. "Her pain felt real, like she was baring her bleeding, wounded heart for us to see. She's a total artist! It reminds me of something," she added, "when we get home, I want to show you something on YouTube. My mother's crazy about Yossi Banai. When I was a kid, she was always listening to his songs, which already," she smirked, "were a bit old-fashioned, nostalgic back then. He covered a lot of French singers, especially Georges Brassens and Jacques Brel. It would drive us nuts, my brother Itamar and me. I think maybe those songs are her way of escaping, of reconnecting with her youth…maybe with the loves she once had, or the love she no longer feels for my dad…I don't know. When Yossi Banai died last year, she took it hard, like a personal loss.

"Anyway, now I really enjoy those songs. Maybe because they remind me of my own childhood in a strange way, my youth. A couple of months ago, when I was visiting my parents, I saw she got a new CD. Songs from the 80s: If We Shall Learn to Love, by Jacques Brel. I saw him on YouTube once singing *Ne Me Quitte Pas* - do not leave me. I think it's his best-known song. The point is," she continued, "the way he sings it, the way he does it… unrepeatable!" she stated emphatically. "That level of devotion, that level of truth, happens only once."

Yoav looked at her intently. "What do you mean, only once?"

"I told you," she replied, imploring him to be patient. "I'll show you when we get home. He completely inhabits the figure of a deserted man, crying, pleading with his woman not to leave him. But you know, he was also an amazing actor. What an artist!"

"So you're saying it's all pretend?"

"Could be," Tali shrugged. "I'm not sure. You see…" she went on explaining Brel. But Yoav was no longer listening, not because of disinterest but its opposite: Tali's words, their content and intensity, her insights, all made his heart overflow. "I love her!" he whispered inaudibly. He put his arm around her and pressed her softly but firmly to his chest, saying nothing. When they arrived at her apartment, Tali's roommate wanted to hear about the party. They gave short answers, eager to be alone. Yoav pulled Tali to the bed, but she gently pushed him away, wanting to show him Brel's unrepeatable rendition.

"We'll watch it later," Yoav begged, grabbing her waist, kissing her face and neck. Tali slipped out of his grip, giggling, and reached the computer. "He won't run away," he implored. "Tomorrow he'll still be pouring his heart out, begging his woman not to leave." But Tali insisted and he finally went along. She sat in his lap and they watched Jacques Brel plead in black-and-white: *Ne me quitte pas.*

"Wow," Yoav exclaimed. A moment later they were intertwined, their lips glued together, teetering towards the bed. Yoav felt this time was different. He felt she was letting him in, free of invisible shackles, of inhibitions and reservations, giving into unrestrained delight. Tali was on her back, facing him. He leaned in, buried his head in the hollow of her neck and whispered: "I love you!"

"What?"

"I love you."

Tali pushed his head tenderly backward and focused her eyes on his. "I love you too," she whispered with glittering eyes, "I love you very much."

The two-way radio rang. Amir, the battalion commander, informed them about the suicide attack at a checkpoint near Bethlehem that had killed two soldiers. The high command had declared a state of alert throughout the West Bank, calling for special vigilance. Amir added that reinforcements were on the way. The serenity of the morning was gone; a long queue of vehicles had begun to build in both directions towards the Bir Nabala enclave and towards Ramallah. Fully absorbed by the commotion at the checkpoint, carefully inspecting the passing cars, Yoav didn't bother with the repeatedly-ringing cell phone in his pocket. Only when things temporarily cooled down did he check it. It was Tali: she had tried to reach him over and over, leaving several frantic messages. Yoav called her at once, figuring she'd heard about the suicide attack. She picked up immediately, even before her phone rang. Hearing Yoav's voice, she burst into a cry of relief.

CHAPTER 11
Hisham

The first time he saw her in the teachers' lounge, he was intrigued. When the principal introduced her to those present, she shook their hands, saying with a diffident smile, "Mandy, Mandy Claxton." She wore a light-blue pantsuit with a white-collar shirt. Long copper hair slid naturally down her back. As Hisham discovered in the following days, her wardrobe usually included long skirts and long dresses with muted colors. Sometimes she wore a top that she removed when the weather got warm. She wore black flats shoes. Her clothes, slightly oversized, wrapped around her body casually as if to hide its curves, and she made sure not to expose her legs and arms. She was a foreign woman, and foreign women staying in Ramallah for long stretches of time did not allow themselves the same liberty that many of the local women exercised in choosing their clothes. They feared they might send the wrong signal and be seen as promiscuous Western women. During one of the afterhours city tours Hisham gave her, he brought up the issue carefully and circuitously.

"Are you religious?" he wondered.

"No. Why do you ask?"

"Your clothes."

Mandy told him that one of her friends who'd been to Ramallah had advised her on the appropriate dress code for foreign women visiting the city. Hisham rushed to defend the city's liberal credentials, claiming that Ramallah was an open-minded and tolerant place, especially compared to other cities in Palestine and the Arab world. Mandy concurred with him and admitted her surprise to find this was indeed the case.

"But it's not just Ramallah," she said. "Don't forget, I'm a Quaker. Regardless of Ramallah's cultural norms, we Quakers uphold the value of modest dress. Anyway," she added, "things are changing in that respect."

It was Hisham who first suggested that they meet in the evening. "If you want," he offered timidly, "I could show you some places around Ramallah." At the time, he was walking Mandy home from a visit to a few local cultural sites, including Sakakini Cultural Center, Al-Kasaba Theatre, and the new Ramallah Cultural Center which commanded a hill in one of the western neighborhoods. After this, they lunched at the famous Zarour restaurant, followed by ice cream at Rukab's.

"You know," he pointed, "the street here is named Rukab street after the owner of this ice cream parlor."

"Interesting," she observed, trying to hide her distaste after taking a small bite.

"You don't like it?" He stared at her anxiously.

"Oh no, I really do," she quickly replied, carefully nibbling at it.

"You know, it's a national symbol," Hisham stated, as if trying to reconcile the ice cream with her palate. "There's Al-Aqsa, the olive tree, and Rukab's ice cream. Really" he smiled slyly. "You know, Israelis take foreign dignitaries to the Wall of Tears, but here Arafat would take them to Rukab's Ice Cream."

"You mean the Wailing Wall?" Mandy suggested.

"Yes, yes, the Wailing Wall. It's the same."

At first, he refused to admit that his interest in Mandy meant anything more than collegial friendship. As a foreigner, she needed someone to show her around, help her navigate marketplaces, banks, restaurants, clinics. But when the thought of suggesting an evening encounter crossed his mind, it dawned on him that he'd taken a liking to her. He reflected on her beguiling smile that emerged whenever she was in conversation. The smile seemed to enlist her entire face, gleefully pouring out of those shimmering blue eyes. Hisham couldn't recall seeing anything like it before. He would glance at her furtively. Once, he watched her reading a book in the school library. She wasn't smiling. She seemed completely absorbed and in a world of her own. Yet whenever he imagined her face, it always wore that tender, charming smile, like an independent image divorced from concrete circumstances.

They had agreed to meet on a Saturday night during Hadil's brief sojourn in Jordan. That day Hisham planned to take the kids to lunch in a restaurant of their choice. Nadim suggested Tomasso's Pizza in Al-Manara Square. Leila vetoed it, saying she'd just eaten there with her friends the night before. Hisham decided on Pronto, also near Al-Manara Square, which catered to his kids' respective tastes. After returning home, Nadim and Leila retired to their rooms. Nadim disappeared into his video games, while Leila listened to music, flipping between Arab and foreign pop idols. Hisham tried to check students' assignments, but he was restless, preoccupied with his upcoming rendezvous with Mandy. What did it hold in store for him? What did she expect from the meeting? Did she feel the same?

In the early evening, Leila informed him that she wanted to go into town with her friends.

"You go nowhere tonight," he snapped at her.

Taken aback by his decisive reaction, she was momentarily speechless. Usually he showed no objection. "Why not?" she asked, recovering her wits. "You should rest," he replied, "it's a school night." He paused and then continued, hitting upon a better argument: "And Ramallah isn't what it used to be. It's not safe for girls your age to walk around at night."

Leila refused to comply with her father's decree. She called her mother. Hadil offered a compromise of sorts, which Leila rejected, peevishly locking herself up in her room. Hisham called Hadil's sister and cancelled a visit by Nadim, who preferred to stay home with his sister. At the scheduled hour, he left to meet Mandy.

She waited for him outside her downtown apartment building, located a stone's throw from some of Ramallah's key cultural and shopping centers. When she saw Hisham her smile appeared instantly. Her fresh scent hit his nostrils. She was wearing a beige dress that extended below her knees, a turquoise top, and a black wool shawl with blue fringes. The shawl had been bought in Ramallah, a homage to the local aesthetic. Mandy's hair was tied with a silver pin, and she wore nondescript black leather shoes, a pair of small gold earrings, and no makeup.

At first he thought of taking her to the centrally-located Ziryab restaurant, a known draw for leftist activists and intellectuals. On second thought however he decided on Vatche, located in the sparser and more remote Al-Masyoun district. They chose a table in a wing that was designed as a home lounge, with dark wood paneling, old photos, and oil paintings that gave it a cozy, intimate atmosphere. At Hisham's suggestion, they both ordered authentic Palestinian cuisine and a bottle of red wine.

He wanted to learn about Mandy's personal life, especially what made her come to Ramallah. To his surprise, she was extremely forthcoming with intimate details. Her parents, she told him, lived in a small town outside Philadelphia. She had a sister, Samantha, who was a few years younger and lived in California with her husband and two kids, a boy and a girl. Mandy and her sister weren't very close, especially since Samantha had moved. She saw her about once a year.

"Once a year?!" Hisham exclaimed.

"Sometimes even less," she shrugged. She went on to tell him she'd been married before but had divorced shortly before coming to Ramallah. She'd first met her ex-husband, James, eight years before. "We got married without a priest, before the congregation and before God," she declared somewhat enigmatically. "No," she anticipated the question, "we don't have children. We thought we would, but we put it off more and more until," she smiled ruefully, "we got divorced." It was through James that Mandy first become acquainted with the Quakers. His family had been part of the community for generations. Mandy herself was from a Nondenominational protestant family, so she had little difficulty in adopting the tenets of the Quaker faith. She liked it a lot, she stressed; it suited her worldview and values. "There's no need for a mediator between us and God," she elucidated. "Simplicity, justice, self-sufficiency, equality, honesty. Those are the values that the Quaker faith espouses."

"Yes, honesty," she smiled ironically, the corner of her mouth twitching. "But it's all behind me now. No, no," she rejoined, noticing Hisham's bewilderment - "I don't mean those values are behind me. I mean life with James. Anyway, he was the one who initiated the divorce. He got involved with someone in his work. He's an engineer. It started as an affair and ended with him choosing her over me." Although they had drifted apart during their last year together, Mandy still struggled with the betrayal. After the breakup she needed a radical change. Browsing through a Quaker website, she saw that the Quaker school in Ramallah was looking for an English language and literature teacher, starting immediately. "I didn't hesitate for one moment," she told Hisham. "I knew this was what I needed to do. It was like a sign from God. So," she smiled again, "here I am." She planned to stay in Ramallah until the end of the following school year. She didn't plan to visit home over the summer vacation. She wanted to use part of it to visit the holy sites, and perhaps travel to nearby countries.

Hisham told her that Ranin and Elias, his wife's sister and her husband, owned a travel agency so he might be able to get her a deal. But he immediately checked himself. That's all I need, he thought. For them to find out.

Mandy wanted to hear about him and his family. "You know everything about me!" she declared. "Now it's your turn!" Hisham was happy to oblige, enthusing about his village and family. Mandy showed great interest, expressing a desire to visit his family in Al-Jib. Gladly, he said, adding that his parents would be happy to meet her too. He paused for a short moment, then added that such a visit could be arranged, also taking Anton the history teacher and Suad the chemistry teacher along. "My parents would love to talk with you," he grinned. She looked at him quizzically. Hisham laughed.

"Like me," he waved his hands around, "talking with hands."

When he described his children, Mandy mentioned that she knew Leila from her English class.

"Her English is very good," she observed with admiration.

"I wish I could speak it like her," Hisham beamed proudly. "As you can see, my English is so-so. Leila's English is from her mother, not from me. You know," he suddenly declared, placing the wine glass on the table, "your name should be *Ibtisam*."

"Oh?" Mandy smiled, wide-eyed.

"Yes, yes, exactly. *Ibtisam*," he repeated, "it means a smile, a laugh, in Arabic." He gazed at her intensely and began to recite, eagerly, in Arabic: "She smiles at me from her balcony above / As a flower from its petals."

"What does it mean?" Mandy asked, curious.

Hisham translated, adding that the poem was by an Iraqi poet. "I don't recall anyone ever reciting a poem for me before," Mandy confessed with some embarrassment. She asked him to repeat the Arabic word for smile.

He did and she tried to pronounce it. "*Itam. Itam.*"

"*Ib, Ib, Ibtisam*" he laughed, amused by her thick American accent. She tried again unsuccessfully.

Suddenly Hisham noticed, in the corner of his eye, an acquaintance of his entering the restaurant: a local lawyer whose children attended Friends School. The man walked past, probably on his way to the restroom. Their eyes met, and the man snuck a wink at Hisham, with a sly smile of male camaraderie, as if to say, "well done". Hisham ignored the innuendo-laden gesture, distressed. He felt like calling after him: "It's not what you think!" But he did nothing.

Mandy and Hisham spent over three hours together, until Leila called, wanting to know when he was coming home. "I'm on my way," he replied, shooting Mandy a quick glance. He tucked the phone into his pocket and said, "It's Leila, my daughter." An awkwardness followed, then he added, as if obeying an order, "I've got to go home."

They drove back in silence. When they reached her apartment building, Hisham cut the engine. He extended his hand to Mandy. She squeezed it warmly, thanking him wholeheartedly for a lovely evening. She leaned in abruptly and pecked him on the cheek. Hisham froze. When he regained his senses and tilted his head to kiss her back, she had already turned her face from him.

"Good night," she whispered, opened the car door, and left. Hisham sat behind the wheel, watching her walk away and disappear into the stairway.

CHAPTER 12
Tali

The ride from Jordan to Tel Aviv was long and exhausting. She withdrew into herself in one of the window seats to the rear of the minibus. To her relief, her riding companions weren't in the mood to talk either. A heavy stillness pervaded the minibus on the ride home. She should have refused Yael's offer to attend the seminar. The day's events unfolded to her once again, still painfully fresh. The panic that engulfed her when she heard about the suicide attack, her discomfort when Yoav's whereabouts were made public, his response when she offered to release him from their mutual commitment for the future. They altogether drove her into melancholy.

She couldn't contain herself when the Palestinian moderator, Hadil, interrupted the discussion to laconically inform them of the attack, which had claimed the lives of the Palestinian perpetrator and two Israeli soldiers. Tali stormed out at once, her anxiety-stricken face impossible to hide from the other participants who watched her, puzzled. Her friend Yael soon followed.

Tali frantically dialed Yoav.

"Come on, come on, answer already, answer," she begged. *"You've reached Yoav. I can't pick up right now. Please leave a message and I'll get back to you as soon as I can."* She tried again and again to no avail. She left him a message in a broken voice, pleading for him to call back as soon as he got it. Restless, she paced back and forth in the hotel lobby. "What should I do? Who should I call?" she asked Yael. She tried desperately, mindlessly, to reach Yoav again. She considered calling his sister Merav.

"What would you say? You'll just cause her to die of worry," Yael warned. Tali decided to dial Liat. "I have to talk to someone," she told Yael. But Liat was unavailable and Yoav still wasn't returning her calls. Tali's anxiety was spiking. She called her parents. "Talush, relax," her father tried to calm her, "nothing happened. You know how many checkpoints there are around Jerusalem? A million!" He paused, then added with hesitation: "And if something bad happened, the army would have immediately notified his parents. I listened to the news. They didn't mention anything..." Tali cut him short. "That means nothing, Dad. It takes time until they report it on the radio. First they have to find and notify the parents. Only then it becomes public." Despite Yael's advice, Tali couldn't resist the urge to call Merav. She won't express outright worry, she promised Yael: she'll casually ask Merav how she is, and gauge by her response whether anything happened. But she knew it wasn't that simple, as they weren't in the habit of calling each other. But Tali's need was stronger than her inhibitions; she dialed the number. Merav sounded surprised to hear from her but required no explanation for the call. She sounded normal; Tali was relieved.

"Tali, is everything okay?" Merav asked, mildly concerned.

"Yes, everything's great. I just felt like calling you," said Tali.

"Well, we should get together. We haven't seen each other in a long time."

Tali was at a loss, back to pacing the lobby in front of Yael when Yoav called. Tali stormed the phone.

"Everything's fine," he assured her. "I saw your

message just now and called you back immediately."

"Are you okay?"

"I'm fine, I'm fine. Sorry I couldn't call before. I was tied up. So, you must have heard the news. It wasn't here, it was a different checkpoint, next to Bethlehem. Tali, are you crying? Everything's fine. I told you. Don't cry. Tali? Tali? Anyway," he said, "I can't talk. They need me here! I've got to go; I'll call you back soon. I love you!"

"Be careful! I love you too."

She washed her face in the ladies' room by the lobby, stared at herself in the mirror for awhile, then returned to the seminar room. The room fell silent with all eyes on her as she took a seat. Tali sat frozen, her eyes downcast. Anxiety gave way to embarrassment specifically towards the Palestinian moderator, Hadil.

A week later during Yoav's furlough, she told him about Hadil. "She was something, this woman," Tali nodded in appreciation, "I was very impressed by her."

"You were *impressed?*" Yoav repeated mockingly.

"What's the problem?" Tali shot back.

"It's a bit condescending, as if you didn't expect to meet a Palestinian woman like her."

"That's not what I meant," she protested.

"It's how it sounds."

"I didn't mean for it to sound like that," Tali said in a mildly apologetic tone. She went on to tell Yoav how his service in the Territories came to light at the seminar.

"So what," he asked, taking umbrage, "you were ashamed of me?"

"Not exactly," Tali shrank, "but I was embarrassed. I told people about you, but 'forgot' to mention it," she said, making air quotes. "That you were serving in the Territories - at a checkpoint, no less! When they found out I felt like an idiot for holding out on it."

Yoav tilted his head with growing indignation. "So you *were* ashamed of me."

"Look," Tali explained, "they kept going on about the barriers and checkpoints, and all the abuse and harassment they go through. I just imagined what would happen if they found out my boyfriend was guarding a checkpoint at that very moment."

"Which is exactly what happened in the end, they found out. It just goes to show, truth is the best lie!" Yoav said sarcastically.

Tali didn't reply. She continued to tell him about Hadil. "She spoke so beautifully... she was very assertive. She didn't make it easy for me. She has a beautiful name too. I don't remember it, but she explained its meaning in English. It means cooing, like the sound a dove makes. By the way," Tali said jokingly, "we can use it when we play Scrabble. I forgot how to say it in Arabic. Hold on," she leapt up and reached for her purse, "I've got her business card. I even sent her an email. Let's see if you know the word. Okay. How do you say 'cooing' in Arabic?" She held the business card to her chest.

"Interesting," he teased, "you know the word in English, but can't remember it in Arabic."

"What do you mean?"

"I mean our memory can't save files with Arabic words in them. They go straight into the recycle bin. It's like we have a bug in our software. Something's screwed up there."

"Nonsense," Tali blurted. She glanced quickly at the business card and asked again: "What sound does a dove make?"

"And what sound does a horse make, and what sound does a camel make? Hmm?" he barked. "Are we back in kindergarten?"

"No," Tali giggled, amused. "It's Scrabble in Arabic."

"Well, I'm sorry," Yoav replied sarcastically, "we haven't reached animal sounds yet in our Arabic lessons."

"And I thought," Tali teased, "your Arabic was superb. Anyway, for your information, the word is *Hadil*, and that's her name. A dove's coo. You know, at first I thought she was wrong when she expressed her opinion on what the goal of the seminar should be. But later I could see her point."

"Which was?"

"That all this talk about fears, anxieties, getting to know each other, and learning how we feel doesn't get us anywhere. That we should talk about politics, not psychology; about what we can do to change reality, not understand it or psychologize it."

"So, she gave you a hard time, this cooing dove?"

"Be serious," Tali smiled. "It was really frustrating." She paused for a short moment and then continued, "well, can I say it? She's an impressive woman!"

"You can say whatever you like. You made me want to meet her," he added jokingly.

"Don't get excited," Tali snapped.

"Why?" Yoav smiled slyly.

"Come on, enough with this nonsense," she said irritably. "And just for your information, she's married with two kids. She talked about them at dinner. I heard her talking with them on the phone."

"Since when do you understand Arabic?" he teased.

"You don't have to understand Arabic, or any other language, to tell when a mother is talking with her kids," she shot back.

"Maybe she was talking to her lover," Yoav suggested, ignoring her rebuke.

"And maybe you're a jerk."

On that interminable ride back from Jordan to Tel Aviv, Tali's moroseness refused to dissipate. She couldn't shake the impressions she was carrying back home. Particularly disturbing was that she was no longer certain she and Yoav could realize their plan. Here I go again, she thought, following the same pattern with men: they go and leave me behind. Ever since she was a young girl, she once told Yoav, all her relationships with guys were long-term. And in most cases, she wasn't the one to break them off. She couldn't explain why. She remembered him focusing his gaze on her and imploring her to think about possible explanations. "You must've thought about something. After all, psychology is your field. From what you've told me," he spurred her gently, offering a possible lead, "you grew up in a loving, supportive family, right?"

"Yeah, more or less," Tali agreed. "Still, I can't think of a good explanation. Maybe it's because Mom stopped breastfeeding me too soon," she smiled. "Or maybe because I'm the eldest and always felt I should be an example for my brother," she served up another obvious cliché. "I don't know." She went on to say that it didn't require a lot of effort to remember all the guys she'd dated. There weren't that many. There was Guy, whom she'd dated from ninth grade until the end of twelfth grade, when his parents moved to the US. "He was my first sexual partner," she said, "and I was his first, too. We lost our virginity together over a year after we started dating." Her classmates used to tease her, she added, calling her and Guy 'the eternal couple'. Her parents weren't happy. They thought something was off about the relationship. "Normally parents don't like seeing their daughters change partners often, but even they were concerned. My mother used to say, 'Talush, don't you think you and Guy are spending too much time together? You're not a married couple!'"

Tali did still wonder once in a while how things would have turned out if Guy's parents hadn't moved to the States. Would she and Guy have stayed together, gotten married, had kids? The possibility didn't strike her as odd.

Her second serious boyfriend was during her military service. They went out for a year and a half, and broke up when he embarked on a year-long tour of South America. Traveling by herself to the United States for a year, Tali almost immediately found herself involved with an Israeli named Nimrod, whom she'd met just a few weeks after arriving. He tried to persuade her to stay with him in the US, but Tali refused: she'd run out of money and was sick of working casual jobs, mainly selling cheap paintings and jewelry 'from the holy land'. "We were conning people, lying to their faces," she later recalled with disgust.

But she didn't return to Israel right away. "I stayed for a bit in New York," she stated blandly. "I knew someone there, an American guy. But it was nothing."

"Nothing?" Opening his eyes, bewildered.

"Just nothing," she repeated, "crazy thing. It wasn't for me."

"What *crazy thing*?" Yoav was curious to know. In the past, he had already tried to coax her to talk about it. Tali wouldn't cooperate. She wouldn't speak about the Unspeakable, the Unimaginable. He scanned her face for a long time, trying to glean some clue, but eventually saw that her resistance was firm. "So, who came after this mysterious American dude?" he asked.

"It took me a while, about two years," she replied, "until I was ready to start a new relationship. At that time I had no interest in having a boyfriend. I came back to Israel and spent all my time working with the Scouts. Then I met Avi, my ex, at the university, I already told you about him. We broke up when he decided to move back to the north. He didn't like Tel Aviv; he grew up in the north, like me. After he got his master's, he set up an anthroposophic school. He wanted me to come too, but I didn't. It wasn't a big love. I wasn't really sure I wanted a future with him, but it wasn't easy to break up. Our parents had met and there were expectations. Although my parents weren't all that thrilled about him, they thought he was a bit flaky. They were probably right; no wonder he went for anthroposophy. But the breakup hurt, I have to admit."

"And since then, you didn't have anybody until we met?" Yoav wondered. "No casual stuff? Pubs? One-night stands? "

"No!" Tali stated emphatically. She noticed Yoav's

puzzlement and stopped him before he continued. "I told you already," she added impatiently, "I don't have any interest in casual relationships, and I don't need to reassure my ego by jumping from one bed to another. I leave that to Liat. And believe me, it doesn't make her happy either. I did it once or twice and it left me feeling empty. Even lonelier than before. I really believe that we – or at least I – need to mourn after a breakup, I mean after ending a meaningful relationship, to be alone and get it out of our system."

"Well," Yoav smiled, "I hope there's nothing clogging your system anymore."

"That depends on you," Tali smiled back coquettishly and thrust out her finger.

The ride back from Jordan came to a merciful end. Entering her apartment, Tali first checked her email. Nothing new. Per Yoav's instructions, she emailed Professor O'Brien from Harvard then called both Yoav and her parents to say she was home safely. Liat called, curious to hear about Tali's adventures in Jordan. Tali told her all about the weekend, omitting, however, Yoav's acceptance to Harvard and her own ensuing doubts. She wasn't in the mood for I-told-you-so. She kicked off her shoes, stripped naked, took a quick shower, and lay on the bed wishing herself a good night's rest. But her gloomy doubts kept her awake and perturbed all night long.

CHAPTER 13
Hadil

As Hisham and Nadim made their way home from school in the early afternoon, Hadil worked to get lunch ready. Leila wasn't coming. She was studying for an exam with her friend next door. The meat patties and potato slices were on separate plates on the kitchen table, ready for frying. Hadil had granted Nadim's request for burger and fries, his and Leila's favorite dish, to their parents' chagrin.

"How can you compare hamburgers," Hisham protested, "to our kebab, made with pine nuts, parsley, garlic, onion, black pepper? These kids don't know anything about food," he added with frustration. "Give them a hamburger, fries, and Coke, and they're happy."

He stood now between the living room and the kitchen, at a loss. Aside from a cursory greeting, he didn't utter a word. He was like this, sullen, ever since Hadil's return from Jordan earlier that week. She knew there was no escape and that they must talk. But she couldn't find the emotional wherewithal for this feat. She called Nadim, who was aimlessly channel-flipping, to the table. "Straight to the TV?" she said angrily. "Why don't you sit with us, tell us what's going on at school, tell us about something new and interesting you learned?" The atmosphere was tense. Hadil tried to dispel it. "So, what do you make of the recent developments?" she turned to Hisham. "You think Fatah and Hamas can hash out a unity government?"

"I don't care one way or the other," he said. But as if forced to answer by some alien power, he added: "One day they're talking about the unity of Palestinian people, and the next day they're killing each other. It's not going to end well. All this infighting... I don't know, maybe it's better to dismantle the Authority. Yes, yes!" he nodded emphatically, noticing Hadil's surprise. "Like those Fatah activists said in their pamphlet, they're right. What do we get out of this Authority? Infighting! But you know what? I don't care," he repeated, regretting offering his opinion in the first place.

It was obvious that Hisham's mind was on more pressing matters but Hadil nevertheless tried to avoid them. She thought she'd share with him her experiences in Jordan: the frustrating encounter between Israelis and Palestinians, the people she met, the surprising email from one of the Israelis, the visit to Arij in Amman. She immediately realized her mistake though as soon as she mentioned Jordan he cut her off: "I don't want to hear about Jordan, or about Arij or Bashir."

I should have known better, Hadil scolded herself. It was like rubbing salt on his wounds. Pretending not to know the answer, she asked apprehensively: "So what is it that you want to talk about?"

"You know what!" Hisham snapped.

"Fine," she sighed with resignation. "But now's not the time. Let's eat. We'll talk after I get back from Biddu."

"I'm not hungry!" Hisham barked. "That's exactly the problem, you always have to be somewhere. You're never home."

Hadil motioned towards Nadim: not in front of the kids. "After I get back from Biddu," she promised.

A short while later she was driving her car to the village of Biddu, south of Ramallah. Riham, a female member of Hadil's *New Horizons* center, was in the passenger seat. It had been scheduled since the Jordan visit which had

125

caused Hadil to miss a meeting with a group of women from Biddu. She had visited the village numerous times and knew the way. This time though she and Riham had to make a long detour, since the road for Palestinians connecting the enclaves containing Bir Nabala and Biddu was under construction. They traveled west as far as the village of Kharbatha al-Misbah, passed under the road connecting Modi'in to Jerusalem, backtracked east through the villages of Beit 'Anan and Al-Qubeiba, and only then reached their destination. The trip took over an hour. In the past, before the wall, it had taken fifteen minutes.

The original plan had been for Amer, the driver, to take them. Hadil had arranged for this in advance en route back from Amman. Ironically however, Amer had fractured his ribs in a car accident near the Hizma checkpoint. Hadil refused to hire another driver, deciding to do it herself. The workshop she was going to moderate was about the rising violence against women. Riham filled her in about the previous session. The women wouldn't cooperate with her, she complained, and were unwilling to address their "unmentionable" experiences. Those who showed measured, indirect willingness to speak followed the familiar and vexing pattern of blaming themselves. But Hadil knew how to get women – battered women, oppressed women, downtrodden women, sexually abused women – to open up about their experiences. This time she had brought a CD of the well-known satirical play "Here's to the Motherland", by the great Syrian comedian Duraid Lahham, famous throughout the Arab world for his character Ghawar al-Toshi. First staged following the Israeli incursion into southern Lebanon in 1982, the play lampooned Arab regimes for failing to stand up to Israel, for failing to secure their people's basic needs, and for their endemic corruption.

Hadil chose to screen the play's seventh act, in which the protagonist, poverty-stricken Ghawar al-Toshi, beats his wife following a loud argument. Appalled by his own violent outburst, Ghawar wails, begging his wife to forgive him. The house is too small, he weeps, the bed too narrow, the shoes too tight, his livelihood too meager. The government beats us, we beat our women, the women beat the children, and the children beat the neighbors' children. Thus the vicious cycle goes on forever. Hadil knew from experience that this classic, universally-loved play normally managed to unlock women's hearts, allowing them to share, give vent to their anguish, perhaps even seek a remedy.

"That's exactly what happened to me," one would say. "That's my husband's excuse after he beats me," another would add.

Hadil's center ran similar workshops in villages and refugee camps around Ramallah, as well as in some of the city's neighborhoods. On the drive back from Biddu, Hadil was lost once more in distressing thoughts about her marriage. Riham noticed her mentor's brooding mood and kept silent. They weren't close friends, and there was an age difference. Riham was ten years younger, about to finish her social work degree at Bir Zeit. She interned at *New Horizons*.

There's no escape, Hadil thought, we'll have to talk. She knew what bothered Hisham but not how to deal with his grievances. It's not just my fault, she grumbled silently, he's responsible too. How long can a person moan over his lost potential? How long can he resent the world for his lack of success? And this affection of his for old music, especially old Iraqi music, drives me nuts. But bickering isn't the answer. The question is what can be done. The question is whether there's still a chance to save our marriage.

Her thoughts wandered back to the workshop that had just ended, and the powerful reactions of the women watching the play. Hadil was pleased with herself. Seeing the positive shift in Hadil's mood, Riham decided to share her thoughts about the workshop. She looked at Hadil admiringly and said she was deeply taken by Hadil's ability to make the women share their intimate, difficult experiences. Riham struggled with the wording, careful not to sound like she was judging her mentor. "It was amazing, what happened there," she finally observed. "I only realized later why you asked Najwa to speak first. She was on the edge of her seat, ready to burst. Like she couldn't wait to talk. I didn't see it. Then after she opened up about her husband, all that beating and cursing, suddenly everyone else couldn't wait to share."

"*Habibti*," Hadil replied with true modesty, "it's just experience. I saw her reaction, her body language, when we watched the video. I could tell all she needed was a tiny little nudge. Then again," she added despondently, "we're dealing with a tough situation. Sometimes I get frustrated knowing that we can't do much to help, and if the political situation doesn't improve, these problems will get even worse." Their brief elation had given way to gloom. Hadil and Riham were exhausted. Workshops like the one in Biddu were emotionally draining. Hadil's previous sympathy for Amer, the driver, was mixed with regret that he wasn't the one driving them now through the dark, bumpy asphalt roads.

Hisham was already waiting in the living room. Nadim was asleep in his room and Leila was still awake in hers. Despite Hadil's promise to Hisham, upon returning from Biddu she wanted nothing more than a quick shower and a long night's sleep. A quick glance at her husband's somber expression sufficed to tell her that this wasn't to be. The dreaded talk, sure to turn acrimonious, could no longer be postponed. She stopped for a moment in Leila's room and took her time changing clothes before joining him downstairs.

"I need coffee," she said. "Would you like some too?" He nodded. She went to the kitchen, returning with a tray with a coffee pot and two cups. She sat on the sofa in front of him, and said, as if bracing for the onslaught: "*Yalla*, come on. Let's talk."

Hisham didn't need much to spur him. He launched immediately into a bitter diatribe – and a well-prepared one, as she soon learned. "I don't know what you're trying to achieve with all these workshops, conferences, and seminars. You spend more time on these useless activities than you do with your children, with your family. In the past two weeks, before you went to Jordan, you worked every day from morning to night. We didn't see you at all. You got up early in the morning and disappeared, even before the kids woke up. Then you came home late every night, exhausted. Straight to bed. 'It's very important,' you said. Sure. No doubt. A UN report on Palestinian women is important. But what about us? Aren't we important? A few days from now you'll be off again. An International conference in Ireland. Of course you have to go," he said sarcastically. "I don't know what to say, I really don't know."

He paused, as if hesitating whether to say what he had in mind. But then he dropped the bomb. "Are you looking to be perfect to make up for what your uncle Kamal did? You want to be *mutakamila*?"

It was a vicious punch to the gut. Hadil was furious. She couldn't believe Hisham's tasteless pun, using poetic license to link her uncle's name with an Arabic word that connoted perfection. "What do you mean?!" she snapped, knowing full well what he meant.

"You should know," Hisham lashed out, "you're the psychologist in this house. But if you want to hear it from me, fine. For the longest time," he said, staring at her, "you've been acting like you're contaminated, like there's a mark of Cain on your forehead and you're desperately trying to rub it off. The thing is, no one sees that mark but you! Nobody but you questions your loyalty to the Palestinian people! No one's doubting your commitment to the national cause. Kamal is one thing, and you're another. There's collaborators under every rock. In every city and town you'll find someone working with the Israelis. True, Kamal's your uncle, but your family's not responsible for him or what he did."

Kamal Khuri, Hadil's maternal uncle, was a well-known land merchant in Ramallah. In the early 1990s, solid suspicions were already circulating that he was involved in mediating the sale of Palestinian lands to the Jews. Then a decade ago Kamal disappeared. It was during a surge in the execution of Palestinian land dealers. Everyone knew the Palestinian Authority's security forces were behind the executions, although the PA vehemently denied any involvement. Kamal's case was different: he had simply vanished. With no reliable information of his whereabouts, rumor and speculation grew rampant. Some suggested he was executed by the security forces and buried in an anonymous grave. But why, others challenged, would the PA hide his killing – unlike other collaborators, whose bodies were dumped on Ramallah's main streets to serve as public warnings? Some said this was to hide human rights abuses from the Americans, who were beginning to take notice.

But there were those who suggested an altogether different account: that the Israelis, not the PA, were behind Kamal's disappearance, and that he was living comfortably in Chile, perhaps in Santiago, under an assumed identity. After all he had many relatives there. This speculation was met with doubt. Everyone knows, declared the critics, that the Jews aren't big on rewarding their collaborators. They were *naqrin al-jamil*, ingrates! If they really helped him escape, how come he doesn't contact his family? After all, his wife and kids still live in Ramallah. Has he no conscience? Those who espoused the South America story countered by suggesting that Kamal did maintain contact with his family – in secret, which would naturally be the best thing for him and them.

"Is that what you think?!" Hadil roared. "That I'm just trying to make up for Kamal?! Rub the 'mark of Cain' from my forehead?! Well, since I'm the 'psychologist in this house', let me tell you, not everything is psychology. You're saying I don't care about the suffering of my children, or Palestinian women, all I care about is myself and my complex with Kamal. That's what you're telling me!"

"It's not what I said," Hisham replied impatiently. "I said you're too preoccupied with it. Halas! Enough!" he shouted. "I'm sorry, but it looks like you've forgotten that you have children. You're never home! We're lucky your sister Ranin is nearby to help when you're not here. But you should know, she isn't a substitute! The kids want their mother." He paused and added: "Plus you and I never get to do things together anymore. Don't we deserve 'new horizons'?"

Hadil ignored his sarcasm. She stared at him wide-eyed and whispered angrily: "I can't believe what I'm hearing. I'm to blame that we don't do things together? You're the one who doesn't want to. You and your Iraqi musicians that no one else cares about." She fixed him with a long glare and went on furiously: "I hope you're not listening to any disgusting rumors."

"What do you mean?" Hisham narrowed his eyes.

"Oh, I hear how people talk," she said. "'He lets his wife travel abroad by herself, leave the kids with him. He feeds them, does the laundry, takes them to school, while she's out gallivanting.' And not just the men. I hear the women saying it too."

"You know I don't care what people say, and I don't listen to gossip," Hisham protested. "That's not what bothers me!"

"What, then?"

"I told you already!" Hisham replied with mounting anger. "And you're dodging the issue, taking the conversation where it's comfortable for you. So I'll tell you again: you need to put down that cross you're carrying, or at least not carry it every single moment of every day. Let it rest a little. I'm not saying, God forbid, that you should stay home. You know that's not what I want! All I'm asking you to do is balance your work and your family. Enough. You can't atone for your uncle. What do you want to do? Die for your nation? Walk to an Israeli checkpoint with a suicide vest, like that man two weeks ago when you were in Jordan?"

Hadil listened in silence. Hisham's explanation for her professional devotion wasn't alien to her; she had contemplated it herself. She was embarrassed about her uncle and the shame he'd brought on her family, cringing whenever his name was mentioned, and yes, feeling herself guilty by proxy. Kamal had come up in past discussions with Hisham, although never, ever in order to fault her. On the contrary Hisham sought to release her from this unfair burden. This was the first time that he laid the issue out so explicitly, like a volley of catapult stones Hadil had no way of dodging. But even this wasn't the whole story, she said to herself. Her dedication to her work had other reasons as well. She stopped short of putting them on the table, merely hinting at them when she accused Hisham of listening to wagging tongues and backward views.

CHAPTER 14
Yoav

The Subaru bearing a yellow Israeli license plate approached the checkpoint. It was early morning. Yoav was on a shift with Marcelo. The car, on its way to Ramallah, aroused their suspicion. They ordered the driver to stop. The car had five passengers: two in front and in the backseat, between two other burly men, a bearded man of about forty, apparently an observant Muslim. His eyes moved frantically and he was clearly scared.

"ID's," the soldiers ordered perfunctorily. The man next to the driver asked permission to step out of the car. He did not act like the Palestinians who routinely passed through the checkpoints. It was evident from his easy body language that he wasn't afraid. Well–dressed, he radiated the confidence of someone in authority. He asked the soldiers to call Captain George from the Shin Bet, the Israeli security agency. He gave them a number to call. "Tell him my name," he requested: "Fadi Abd al-Mu'ataz." Yoav and Marcelo were impressed by his relaxed demeanor. They asked him to tell the driver to park next to the checkpoint until the matter was cleared up. "We should ask Amir," Marcelo suggested. Yoav agreed. He called Amir, their company commander, and gave him the phone number Abd al-Mu'ataz had provided. Amir promised to call back. A few minutes later, Abd al-

Mu'ataz's phone rang. He spoke briefly with someone in Arabic. "He must be talking with Captain George," Marcelo suggested derisively, stressing the obvious pseudonym. A minute later Amir called and ordered them to let the car through.

"I didn't get the whole story," Amir replied impatiently to Yoav's queries. "They're Palestinian Preventive Security, something like that... I don't know exactly... they arrested some extremist Hamas leader from one of the local villages, and now they're taking him to Ramallah."

Yoav was puzzled. "But Hamas and Fatah are negotiating a unity government. Hamas just committed to the *tahdida*, the ceasefire. The Fatah-linked factions like al-Aqsa Martyrs' Brigades – they're the ones initiating terrorist acts. What's going on here?"

"Yoav, I don't know and I don't give a fuck, okay?!" It was Amir's usual response whenever his subordinates challenged the logic of the orders he passed on. Nevertheless he made an effort: "Maybe he's from Izz ad-Din al-Qassam Brigades or the Islamic Jihad. Maybe he's a religious leader inciting suicide attacks. Who knows?"

"I still don't understand the logic of it," Yoav grumbled.

"Enough with this!" Amir barked. "This isn't the university, it's the army. We receive orders and carry them out," he stated with growing annoyance before hanging up.

Marcelo, who had been following the exchange, smiled despondently. "I don't know what on earth," he shrugged, "we're doing here."

"Well, you're in good company," Yoav rejoined. "See, Amir doesn't know, the division commander doesn't know, and the Chief of Staff doesn't know. Nobody has a clue. Everyone's just doing their jobs."

Like others in the company, Yoav had special affection for Marcelo, who emigrated to Israel from Argentina in the late eighties. Marcelo was in his mid-30s, married, with two daughters whose photos he would proudly display at the slightest whiff of interest. "Here's the older one, eight years old, Helena," he would beam. "Beautiful and smart, like her mother. All day she spends on the computer. A little quiet. And this is the little one, Lydia. She's six. The complete opposite of her big sister, a volcano. But very sweet. And this is Jacqueline, I call her Jackita, my beautiful wife. She's also from Argentina, but I met her here in Israel. I was nineteen when I came over with my parents. You see," he grinned, "I had to come to Jerusalem to meet a girl from Buenos Aires. I met her in Hebrew class."

Marcelo and his wife married not long after he'd finished his compulsory military service. They spoke Spanish with each other and with the girls. "It's important that they know the language," he noted, "so they can speak with our families in Argentina." He would go on and on, especially about the girls. His company mates would gently tease him. "You're killing us with all these stories about your kids," Alon joked. "Tell me," he added, "doesn't it bother your wife that you mostly talk about your daughters and not about her?"

"No, she doesn't get jealous," Marcelo replied, smiling. "They're her kids too," he pointed out the obvious. "My children are *mi vida*," he would repeat with radiant eyes, as if reciting a religious mantra.

Moments before the shift ended, Yoav's phone rang. He guessed correctly that it must be Tali. She wasted no time: "I've got good news and bad news," she stated.

"Speak!" he urged her impatiently.

"I'll start with the good news," she said, "I've been accepted to UPenn."

"Great!" Yoav exclaimed. "And the bad news?"

"We both got a no from Princeton, and I got a no from Harvard," she replied with disappointment. "They put me on a waiting list. But it's meaningless. Who in their right mind would give up on a Harvard admission?"

"Okay," Yoav tried to cheer her up. "You haven't heard back from Boston University yet."

"True. And you haven't heard from UPenn yet."

"Right, you're right," he said thoughtlessly.

"Yoav…" Tali whispered in a cracked voice.

"What?"

"Your mind's set on Harvard. You really want to study there, don't you?"

"Sure, I want to study there…"

"But what does it mean for us?"

He paused, struggling to find the right answer. "Well, we haven't heard back from all the universities yet," he said, "but if we have to… listen, I thought it might not be so bad, you know, if we have to live for a year or two in separate cities. We could always meet on weekends…"

"This is what you want?"

"Talush, you know that's not what I want. But if we have no choice…"

"There's a choice. If you get into UPenn, we won't have a problem. If we both get into NYU, we won't have a problem. If we both get into Columbia," she went on in an irritated staccato, "we won't have a problem."

"All right, all right, we don't have to decide now," he replied. "Let's tell UPenn like we told Harvard, that we need a few days before we can decide. Talush, don't worry," he noticed the silence on the other end. "I'm coming home tomorrow. We'll talk. Everything will be fine, you'll see."

He put the phone back in his pocket. He felt restless, troubled. He shared his dilemma with Marcelo. "You see?" Yoav protested. "Even she said no one would give up on a Harvard admission. You don't say no to Harvard unless something really bad happens."

"But something bad might happen if you go to Harvard," Marcelo was quick to reply.

"What do you mean?"

"You know what I mean, you might lose her," Marcelo

nodded his head slowly to highlight the risk.

"Why? She got accepted to Boston University. We can live in Boston together." Yoav went on and on, weighing pros and cons as if Tali was the one listening rather than Marcelo. But he was acutely aware that his arguments for Harvard, under present circumstances, weren't compelling – at least not from where Tali stood. At present, saying yes to Harvard would present her with an unfair choice. Yoav was deep in thought when the phone rang again. "Tali again," he assumed and reached for the phone reluctantly. It was an unfamiliar number.

"Hi, Yoav, how are you?"

A thrill shot through him. It was Einat. It had been two years since he last ran into her, on one of the campus's winding paths.

"What on earth are you doing there? Is this a good time?" Einat asked once she learned where he was

"There's no better time," Yoav laughed, "I have all the time in the world." He moved a short distance away from Marcelo and delved into a long conversation with her. They brought each other up to speed. Einat told him that she had gotten divorced over a year ago, taught Hebrew literature at a high school, and was living in Tel Aviv. Yoav told her about his academic life and about Tali.

"Yes, still together," he replied, and shared their plan to study in the US.

"Sorry I didn't keep in touch," Einat said. "You know what it's like…"

"Yeah, I know," he replied. "I didn't make an effort either."

"Listen," Einat said hesitantly. "I'll be coming to Jerusalem next week for a two-day seminar. I'll be staying in one of the guesthouses there - maybe we can meet before you go far away from me. I miss you."

"It's possible," Yoav replied laconically, trying to hide his resurging, long-dormant feelings. "I need to check first, see if I can take a night off. What day did you have in mind?"

"I'll be staying Tuesday and Wednesday nights, leaving Thursday. Maybe we can meet Tuesday or Wednesday evening. If it's okay with you."

"Let me get back to you."

"Great, I'll wait to hear from you."

Einat's call had stirred up emotions Yoav thought were long gone. That passionate longing for her, that intimacy, that sense of an unbroken cord tying them together. He reflected on her words: "before you go far away from me."

She had been his girlfriend for a short period after they met in their sophomore year. Einat was majoring in Hebrew literature and taking additional courses in Yoav's department and in philosophy. She came from a middle-class family in Holon, south of Tel Aviv. Her preference for the humanities wasn't to the liking of her father, who wanted her to join his expanding construction business. He gave her a hard time at first but generously financed her studies and even showed her off.

"Our intellectual princess," he would declare admiringly, "beautiful and smart."

"My father's a pragmatist," Einat explained. "Once he sees he can't have his way, he immediately cuts his losses. And he actually began to appreciate what I do. Besides, my two younger brothers took after him. One's already helping him run the business and the other one's on the way."

When Yoav first met her she was already in a relationship. And yet he was quickly enchanted with her, eagerly sought her company, and felt growing jealousy at any mention or thought of Einat's boyfriend, Assaf. He felt Einat was drawn to him too, that her feelings for him went beyond shared intellectual interests. When she and Assaf suffered a crisis and took time apart, Yoav stepped in. It was a fervent, carnal love affair. "I love you," Yoav would repeatedly confess. "I love you too," Einat would reply while eagerly unbuckling his belt. He had never met anyone like her before, so sexual and uninhibited, free with her fantasies. He was tantalized by the stark contrast between Einat's ravenous sexuality and her middle-class sensibilities: her semi-religious background, her proper speech, her aversion to cursing, her tasteful dress code. Even now, years after she broke up with him and shattered his heart, he felt a pulsing in his loins whenever he thought back to their sexual adventures. These sometimes included the use of force, with Einat the one encouraging him, prodding him. "What do you want to do to me? Tie me up? Smack my ass? What do you want me to do to you?" she would ask, whispering obscenities into his ear.

Once, as they lay in bed, catching their breath, she told him: "I'm not like this with everyone. I allow myself to be a whore with you because I love you and I trust you - and of course, because I like it a lot. Not all men can handle it," she said suggestively. "Besides," she complimented him, smiling, "I've never felt this physically in tune with anyone. I think we were created for each other." Sometimes she would stick her nose into his armpits and inhale deeply.

"I love your body," she would purr. "Oh, this scent... I'd like to have you dripping with sweat one time, before you shower it off."

"You're nuts!" he said contentedly and went on to sniff her body with his head, wagging like a puppy dog's. "Your lips, your face, your tits, your body. I want to eat you, be inside you, in your cunt, disappear like in that Almodóvar movie, stay like that for hours, days, all the time, all of me." He clung to her body continuously. He used to stay inside of her after orgasm and only slide off and curl up next to her when she gently pulled away from his grasp.

It didn't last. After about four months, Einat got back with Assaf.

"Yes, I still love him," she told Yoav, shifting uncomfortably in her seat as if by way of an apology. She broke it to him in a university cafeteria, during lunch rush. Yoav was speechless and devastated. Afterwards, the memory of his profound gloom against the cheerful commotion of the cafeteria, of the world going on as if nothing had happened, remained with him.

He did his best to hide his feelings. "Okay, okay," he mumbled senselessly, and got up and left with her final words ringing behind him: "I'm sorry, Yoav. I'm really sorry." They didn't see each for several weeks. But as the pain and humiliation subsided, ostensibly relegated to a distant shelf in Yoav's mind, they resumed their friendship.

"We can meet for some coffee and cake," she would suggest, outlining the permissible scope of their meetings henceforth.

If Yoav thought that he'd managed to put a lid on his feelings for Einat, her wedding proved him wrong. He was overwhelmed with grief as he watched her walk down the aisle to the wedding canopy, flanked by her mother and future in-laws. Einat was achingly beautiful; he left immediately after the vows. But the campus had a way of bringing people together, like it or not. Their connection was on again, off again. As his sour feelings waned, they started meeting more often, but lost touch during the last months of her pregnancy. Then, after she gave birth to her daughter, Maayan, their meetings resumed.

Why did he keep seeking her company? What invisible thread drew him to her? Was he still in love? Was it his half-admitted fantasy that, single or not, they could resume their crazy sexual connection? "I'm not like this with everyone, I trust you," she had said. Did he hold out some hazy hope that the special bond which brought them together in the past would do so once more? He noted that Einat took care to maintain contact with him, tactfully platonic though this contact may be. Yoav longed to discover whether she, too, held on to a secret yearning, but the stinging memory of that afternoon in the cafeteria dissuaded him.

Around the time that his relationship with Tali began to flourish, he ran into Einat in one of the cafeterias. He told her excitedly about his new love, adding that Tali was coming to join him there. He wanted Einat to meet her. "I'm sure you'll like each other," he promised as if to pave the way for the possibility. Einat stayed. They exchanged a few words about a movie she'd recently watched about romantic jealousy. When Tali arrived he quickly realized it was a mistake to get them together. The awkwardness was palpable. There was no love lost between the two women and little conversation. Knowing that Einat was Yoav's ex, Tali was openly cold, while Einat was unusually reticent. He was surprised later that evening by an email from Einat. The message was attached as a separate file. Yoav opened it and began to read with growing interest and bewilderment.

"I'm sure you'll be surprised to receive this," she began, "I have to admit I'm surprised that I'm writing it. But I have certain feelings and I need to get them out. Today before Tali came we spoke a little about jealousy and resentment. I said that sometimes we get jealous for someone even though we have no right to, and they didn't do anything to cause it. You're probably wondering where I'm going with this. Well after our meeting I couldn't shake this overwhelming feeling of jealously. It's not your fault, and it's not Tali's fault, but I still felt terrible because of her. When I got home I cried my eyes out. I hate myself for it and I felt so bad for Assaf. He doesn't deserve it either. I just don't understand myself. I know I love him, I do, body and soul. So why do I feel this crazy jealousy? Why can't we be happy with what we've got? Why are we so complicated? Or maybe it's only me with these messed-up thoughts. Or then again, maybe it's a woman thing... I do think it's the woman in me crying out. I was so jealous when I saw that beautiful, attractive woman with you. There I said it! I, who have no claim on you, feel cheated. I chose this poem by Dahlia Ravikovitch to describe how I feel: If I could only get hold of the whole of you / How could I ever get hold of the whole of you / Even more than the most beloved idols / More than mountains quarried whole / More than mines / Of burning coal / Let's say mines of extinguished coal / And the breath of day like a fiery furnace…"

Yoav read the poem closely, paying attention to each word, especially the ones Einat had underlined. The letter went on: "I feel," Einat wrote, "that this poem explains this awful but human feeling of jealousy. It seems we humans have a need to feel loved, to feel that we're desired, that people depend on us. This is how we get control over them. Don't worry, I don't want control over you. God forbid. All I want to say is that we want to be desired by the people we love and appreciate. So when I saw you today with Tali, it felt like a knife through my heart, like I'm losing you. I know, I know it defies logic. But who's to say logic is what makes us tick? Anyway that's all I wanted to say. I don't know if I'll have the courage to send this. If I do please keep it to yourself."

For a moment he thought of waiting to write a reply and sorting out his feelings first. But then he decided to do it right away. What difference does it make how I feel towards her now? he thought. She's married and I'm with Tali. But what to write? She must be waiting on pins and needles. He wrote and deleted several drafts before settling on one: "Einati, I'm really sorry that this is how you feel," he wrote. "Jealousy does defy logic, just like you wrote. And by the way men are jealous too… But then jealousy is a fleeting, transient emotion. We eventually learn to be happy for our close friends. I hope we'll get to see each other soon over some coffee and cake."

Einat replied only a day later. She apologized if her message made him uncomfortable. She was sorry to have bothered him with all that nonsense. "Anyway," she wrote, "I'm over it now. I just had to get it out. I'm really fine now. And I'm really, really happy for you. Tali seems like a very nice woman and I wish you both the best of luck. You deserve it." She promised to be in touch soon for the coffee and cake. But she never did call. Days and weeks passed. They ran into each other a few times on campus, but neither made a genuine effort to make a meeting happen.

"It sounds like you really love her," marveled Marcelo.

"What do you mean?" Yoav narrowed his eyes, lifting one borrow inquisitively.

"That was your girlfriend on the phone, right"?

"No."

"So who was it?"

"Long story."

CHAPTER 15
Hisham

It was Tuesday morning and Hisham was driving to school. He'd dropped Nadim off at the elementary division of Friends School and continued with Leila to the upper division ten minutes away. The previous night's angry exchange with Hadil was still fresh. He replayed it over and over in his mind with growing frustration. True, she listened, but they never reached a conclusion. Maybe there's nothing to do. Maybe divorce is inevitable. His thoughts wandered to Mandy. It had been four days since their evening together. He saw her several times since then, in the school library, the teacher's lounge, the hallway. She was her normal affable self, thanking him warmly for the wonderful evening. Her smile radiated. He told her not to hesitate if she ever needed his help with anything in Ramallah.

He wasn't sure what to make of her. Did her convivial behavior signal anything beyond politeness and sociability? He certainly hoped so, even as he noticed her indiscriminate friendliness towards teachers, children, librarians, secretaries, anyone at school. He wanted to ask her out again. But when? And what to tell Hadil? What would his colleagues say if they saw them together in an intimate setting? Hisham recalled the innuendo-laden wink his acquaintance had shot him at Vatche that night. But he didn't give up. The best time, he decided, would be in two weeks' time when Hadil would be in Ireland.

He should strike while the iron was hot and before the mutual interest faded. He googled cultural events that would take place during Hadil's absence, figuring this was the best lure for Mandy. Right away he found an upcoming show by the Sabrin musical ensemble. He had warm memories of them going back to the time of the first Intifada. Held under the joint aegis of the Al-Kasaba Theater and the Al-Kamandjati music center, their show was to feature – as he later told Mandy – a mélange of classical and contemporary musical traditions both Eastern and Western.

As soon as he reached school that Tuesday morning, he rushed to the library, where Mandy often spent mornings browsing foreign periodicals. She wasn't there. Hisham stood by the bookshelves, eyeing titles by Khalil al-Sakakini, Ghassan Kanafani, Emile Habibi, Ghada Karmi, Raja Shehadeh and others, many of whom he taught in his classes. He leafed through a favorite of his, Shehadeh's Strangers at Home. "Shehadeh," he used to tell his students, "does not spare his sharp criticism from his own society, and doesn't give it a free pass because of the Occupation." But at the moment Hisham didn't really care about the book. He kept looking up from the book to the library entrance.

His agitation didn't go unnoticed by Violet, the veteran librarian, who looked at him baffled. She might suspect something, he worried to himself; he didn't normally come in to browse. She stared at him sternly. Hisham was just about to make his exit when Mandy walked in. She noticed him and came over, smiling. They exchanged customary greetings, followed by silence. As Mandy turned to mind her business, he stopped her with a feeble touch on her arm. Stumbling over the words, he made his offer. Mandy smiled, hesitant. Hisham hurriedly added that it's the best musical ensemble in Ramallah, and that she would have a great time.

"Sure, why not," she finally said. "I'd love to hear some Palestinian music." He wanted to give her more details when his phone rang, shattering the silence of the library and cutting their conversation short. Violet the librarian frowned and loudly cleared her throat.

Hisham quickly declined the call, but before he could continue with Mandy, the phone rang again. He looked at the screen: it was his parents. He excused himself and went outside to take it. Marwan sounded panicked, and Hisham could hear his mother and sister clamoring in the background. His father told him that Sharif had been pulled out of bed that morning by some men who took him away. No one knew where.

"We don't know who took him," Marwan said in a broken voice. "They came after he got back from morning prayer. They didn't say why... didn't say anything. Four men... dragged him out like a dog... put him in the car and drove away. A civilian car. We don't know what to do! Yes, yes," he answered Hisham, "his wife's here with the kids, crying. She doesn't know where to go... I don't know who to talk to. They must be from the *Sulta*, the Authority." Marwan paused and then went on, pleading: "Maybe you can talk to someone in Ramallah, someone from the *Sulta*?"

As people often do upon shocking news, Hisham asked for the same details over and over. "When exactly did this take place? Who were the men who took him? How many? What were they wearing? Army uniforms? Civilian? Did they have weapons? Did they say anything, or just take him?" Marwan tried to answer each repeated question.

"Please do something, please," he begged Hisham. "Talk to someone in the Authority, they can help us."

"*Yaba*," Hisham protested, "how do we know the *Sulta*'s involved? Maybe the Israelis took him."

"*Ya ibni*, my son," Marwan insisted, "they're Palestinians. You must know someone who can help your brother. For the love of God…"

"They must have made a mistake," Hisham tried to calm his father. "Sharif hasn't done anything. All he does is talk. He's not a fighter. They'll let him out in a few hours." But as soon as he hung up, he called Hadil, anxious, to tell her and ask her advice. The best option, they both agreed, was to try and enlist one of their acquaintances who had ties to senior Palestinian officials. Hadil suggested Murad Ismail, their classmate from Bir Zeit, who had just been hired as personal assistant to the new minister of health in the recently formed unity government. The minister himself was a Fatah appointment. Murad's number was soon obtained through the secretary at Friends School, where Murad's two children studied.

"I need to see you," Hisham said, skipping the pleasantries. Murad was surprised to hear from him. They hadn't been in touch for quite some time, chiefly because Hisham had ignored Murad's attempts to keep their friendship alive.

"What's the problem?" Murad asked coolly.

"It's a private matter," said Hisham, apologizing for not being able to say more on the phone. "I'll come to you, just tell me where and when… I can come right now to the Ministry of Health. It's in Al-Bireh, right?… Murad?"

There was a long silence.

"Fine, fine," Murad finally answered, annoyed, but added that he preferred a café for the meeting. Within the hour, they met at Al-Bawadi Café, next to Al-Manara Square. Murad's body language indicated displeasure. He was distant and impatient. They exchanged a few greetings and family updates. Murad ordered black coffee and made it clear that the matter at hand would have to wait until coffee was served. He produced a pack of Marlboros from his jacket pocket, tapped the bottom, pulled out a cigarette, lit the end, and began to sip his coffee slowly with measured elegance. Disgusted by Murad's display of self-importance, Hisham remained meek. This was not the time to tell Murad what he thought of him, and Hisham guessed that Murad's conceit was just a way of getting back at him for past insults.

"So, how can I be of assistance?" Murad asked. Hisham gave him the few details he had of his brother's "kidnapping".

Murad listened, his face sealed. Only after Hisham threw up his hands to indicate this was all he had did Murad speak.

"Hisham," he said sternly, still very calm, "we're talking about Hamas radicals. Your brother's no saint. You know what they do to our people in Gaza? Their election victory is just the beginning."

"I know, I know," Hisham nodded vigorously, "but we're talking about my brother... about my brother Sharif. You know him."

"Of course I know him," Murad said sarcastically. He looked up as if to retrieve details. "As far as I can recall, he's always been a radical Hamas activist."

"What can I say?" Hisham said apologetically. "He's like that... we're talking about my brother... he talks a lot, but he never did anything. He's my brother," he repeated the naked fact as if to trump all other considerations. "I beg you, please, see what you can do."

"Hisham, I don't know who arrested or 'kidnapped' your brother, as you say, and I don't know why they took him. But the Ministry of Health is not the address for matters like this. We don't arrest people - our job is to provide health services, cure people, not kidnap them." He collected his cigarettes and lighter from the table and tucked them into his pocket, leisurely but decisively, indicating that the meeting was over.

"I'll ask around," he shrugged. "Maybe someone saw something, heard something," he added and left.

In contrast to Fuad, who had learned to accept his

parents' special treatment of Hisham, Sharif bitterly resented it. Feeling cheated out of equal opportunity to realize his potential, he constantly felt the need to prove that he could make it, that he could excel with or without the help of his family. Driven by this incurable wound, he made superhuman efforts in high school and college, successfully completing a degree at the Islamic College in Hebron. Later he became a prominent political activist for Hamas in his home village of Al-Jib. He grew a beard in the style of a believer and became piously observant, with a missionary zeal and unbending religious and political views. But success brought no inner tranquility or reconciliation. He continued to compete with his eldest brother for the title of brightest Saada son. If Hisham owed his intellectual standing to knowledge of Arabic poetry and literature, then Sharif owed his to mastery of the Holy Quran.

He missed no opportunity for heated arguments with his brother. "It's like he's trying to pick a fight," Hisham once told Hadil. For his part, Hisham tried to avoid these confrontations, though they were often inescapable. Such was the case a year before, following the election to the legislative council. Hisham was visiting his parents when Sharif, who lived next door with his family, came over. The argument began when Sharif mentioned his work on behalf of a Palestinian youth from a nearby village, a member of the military wing of Hamas, who had been killed by "the Jews". This was Sharif's perspective for everything, reducing the Israeli-Palestinian conflict to its religious dimension. He hardly ever used the word Israelis, as if it didn't exist in his vocabulary. For him, the enemies were the Jews, the infidels, adherents of a defunct religion who coveted Islamic land.

"The Jews demolished the home of the martyr's family," he said. Sharif had taken it upon himself to raise money for them in addition to the financial aid they would receive from Hamas. "Acts of charity, as the Holy Quran says," he reminded his family, "chase away troubles and help triumph over the Jews."

"No doubt," Hisham snapped uncontrollably, "Islam is the answer!"

"Yes indeed," declared Sharif. "Islam is the answer, and Islam guarantees the well-being of the people of the Quran! There is no other solution," he went on, "only jihad, holy war. Everyone is beginning to understand this. We won seventy-four seats out of a hundred and thirty-two in the election to the legislative council. Fatah has forty-five, and your Popular Front," he teased Hisham, "has two, only two seats! The next government will be completely under our control, one hundred percent Hamas."

"Sure," Hisham retorted, "everyone understands. Islam is the solution. Here they even made Yasser Arafat into a shahid now, a martyr. Enough, I don't want to talk about this anymore." He paused and then went on as if compelled. "Once it wasn't like this. Before the first Intifada, someone who died for the Palestinian cause was called a *fidae*. No one uses that word anymore. Today everyone says shahid."

Sharif pounced on his brother's error. "*Fidae* is also a religious word! A *fidae* is someone who sacrifices himself for a holy cause. There's even an organization called *Fada'iyan-e Islam* in Iran."

"Even still," Hisham insisted, "you don't like the word *fidae* because of its national and secular connotations. That's why you never use it. But it's not just you. The al-Aqsa Brigades call themselves *shuhadā*, don't they? Shahids! What's worse, shahid is no longer just religious in its connotation, but specifically Islamic. As if a Christian who died for Palestine can't be a martyr."

"Yes he can," Sharif raised his finger, "but a martyr in this world, not the next. His hereafter isn't like that of a Muslim. It's written in the Quran. Besides," he continued triumphantly, "how many Christians blew themselves up on a bus or in a mall in Tel Aviv crying out 'In the name of the Father, and of the Son, and of the Holy Spirit'?"

Hisham lost his composure. "So what!" he raged. "What does that mean? You know I never thought those violent acts were justified or useful. They're even against Islam, which explicitly forbids harming the innocent. It's haram, forbidden! Where are the imams of the past who decreed that even the bones of the dead are sacred, and that mutilating them is murder? If that's murder, then those acts you commit are haram, despite what your precious leaders say, like Hassan al-Banna, Yusuf al-Qaradawi, Sayyid Qutb. You in Hamas have managed to dig up dead, delusional clerics no one's even heard of, like al-Jawziyya, promising seventy-two virgins to anyone who commits these acts.

"But even if we suppose, just suppose for a minute that those acts are justified," he continued bitterly, "who says this is the only way to die for the homeland? What, when a Christian dies in battle with Israeli soldiers, he doesn't get to be a martyr? It's ridiculous. Too bad you don't listen to what Mahmoud Darwish said. 'We won't fight over the martyrs' share of the land, they're all equal.' What can I say," Hisham exhaled in resignation, "the spread of religious belief has only made our situation much worse. Much worse! No one in the world cares about us. People hear about Palestine and think of bin Laden, Islamic Jihad, Hamas. They probably think Israel's doing them a favor by fighting and killing us, because to them we're all radical Islamists who want to take over the entire world."

"And what about the Jews?!" Sharif exclaimed. "Don't they use their religion for war against us? If Hamas hadn't gotten stronger, would they have let us build an independent state? And if bin Laden didn't do what he did, would the Jews stop stealing our lands, like they do now, all in the name of their religion? Would they stop building settlements? Let's be honest, my brother."

"Not all Jews are the same," Hisham replied, "many of them oppose the settlements. But your actions only help their extremists. It's not just Hamas; those who dream about liberating all of Palestine help them too. I supported armed struggle against the Israelis once, but I learned to appreciate the benefits, the power, of civil disobedience, civil resistance. That's what the first Intifada taught us. You don't understand. The Israelis didn't know how to fight us because we engaged in civil disobedience. Now they use every stupid act of yours as an excuse to expand their settlements. And you don't see it! You don't see that you're helping them! While you're building your fantasy Islamic nation and dream about the virgins you'll get in heaven, the Israelis are building more and more settlements in the real world, on our land."

As the brothers bickered out in the garden, their sister Siham grew increasingly anxious. She worried the argument might get out of hand. She said nothing to them, but kept muttering a recitation from the Quran: "There is no might or power except with God." As usual, she preferred to stay inside, minding her own business. Occasionally she'd come to serve hot drinks and pastries. Nadia also worried things might turn ugly. "Come on, children, enough, enough," she pleaded with them. "You're working your nerves for nothing."

"Your mother's right," Marwan was quick to agree. "Please. It's not good for your health. My son," he told Sharif, "you don't need to be more radical than your leaders. When they take power, they change their tune. That's how it is. Here – one hour after Hamas won the elections last year, your leader declared he was willing to sign a peace treaty with Israel based on the '67 borders. That's how it works. You say different things when you're in power."

Sharif hurried to correct his father. "He never said he'd sign a 'peace treaty' with Israel. A *hudna*, at most. A ceasefire. No peace with the Jews."

"That's right," Marwan smiled. "He said *hudna*. What could he say? He had to save face and appease extremists like you. 'Our ancestors were born here, and we'll die here,'" he mockingly quoted Sharif's own words. "I don't know where the other families in Al-Jib are from, but you should know the Saada family came here from Jordan no more than eighty or a hundred years ago."

Sharif shook his head. "*Yaba*, I'm talking about the Islamic nation. That's what the Holy Quran commands. You don't understand. It's either us or the Jews. That's what they also say."

Hisham raised his hand and let it drop in defeat. "Enough," he said. "I don't want to talk about this anymore. As far as I'm concerned, Hamas can take over everything. Go ahead, set up the government, appoint the president, run the local authorities, run the universities. I don't care. Islam is the solution. We'll see where it gets us."

What else to do? Who else to call? he fretted while driving back to school. Murad had no intention of helping. Anxious, Hisham called Hadil to tell her. "He didn't say anything, just sat there in front of me like a sphinx. Said nothing and promised nothing. Only reminded me that my brother's a radical Hamas activist. Thanks very much! Like I didn't know that. Remember the old Murad? The funny guy with the big heart? He's gone. His face was frozen, like a mask. And the mockery, the mockery! 'Our job is to cure people, not arrest them.' Can you believe it?!"

After he finished venting his frustration Hisham called his parents. His father picked up immediately before the end of the first ring. Hisham told him that he had spoken to someone very important who promised to help.

"Yes, Dad, yes," he replied. "He's from the *Sulta*. I'm sure he's going to do everything in his power to help us. Don't worry, everything will be fine. How's Mom? How are Sharif's wife and kids? Everyone's okay?" He promised to call as soon as he had new information about Sharif.

"God bless you, my son, God's grace on you," Marwan

repeated over and over.

He paced nervously up and down the school hallway when he saw Mandy coming towards him. Sharif's arrest was the talk of the school. She shook Hisham's hand warmly, expressing her deep sympathy and the hope that his brother would come home soon. She wanted to know if she could help and offered to fill in for him if needed.

"It won't hurt your students to have a few extra English lessons," she smiled.

CHAPTER 16
Tali

The last phone call with Yoav had left her distraught. It was clear now that he wasn't going to give up Harvard and didn't rule out living in separate cities. What to do? Should she go to Boston University so they could stay together? As Tali brooded over unsettling questions the phone rang. It was Galia Hoffman, Tali's mentor, calling to tell her that the other reviewer of Tali's thesis liked it very much. Tali took the news with equanimity. She told Galia about UPenn. "That's wonderful!" Galia exclaimed. "UPenn's considered a big name in social and cultural psychology. You'll have a great time there, you'll see." Tali didn't share her other concerns. They agreed to meet in two weeks, after Galia gets back from a conference.

Tali checked her inbox. There were no new messages from universities but there was a surprising reply from Hadil, the Palestinian woman she'd met in Amman. Tali opened the message with interest. It was brief; Hadil wrote that she understood why Tali chose not to share Yoav's whereabouts during the seminar – but that she couldn't ignore the fact that these soldiers, even those who oppose the occupation, serve and legitimize it. It was a note of measured reprimand. She ended the message by wishing Tali and Yoav the best of luck with their future plans and signed it *Yours, Hadil.*

Tali replied immediately. She confessed that she didn't want Yoav to do his reserve service in the Territories and had even suggested that he dodge it. And regarding their plan to study abroad there was increasing doubt whether it could even happen, and things were becoming more and more complicated. She paused for a long moment, staring at the screen, wondering if she wanted to share her more intimate concerns with Hadil. She took a deep breath and plunged forward:

I hope I won't have to make an enormous concession just so we could be together. You know how it is with men. They think their career is more important than ours. Anyway, I do hope we meet again, maybe in the US. Yours, Tali.

"The only thing that matters to us," Tali's parents always said as if reciting an article of faith, "is that you're happy." This universal cliché included the promise of not interfering in her choice of career or life partner, then was invariably followed by Tali's parents clearly stating their preference: "We wish you'd find someone with his head on his shoulders and his feet on the ground." Years before Yoav, when Tali was dating Avi, her parents made their reservations known. "He's not a serious man," they'd say, "he's not in touch with reality." With Yoav it was different. She told them about this "new" boyfriend one Saturday afternoon two years ago, when she and Yoav had already been dating for quite a while. Tali was in her parents' living room after a late breakfast with them, when Yoav called to ask when she was coming back to Tel Aviv. He suggested she leave early to avoid the traffic.

"Don't worry, *chamud*, sweetie," she whispered. "See you soon. Bye."

"Sweetie?" her mother smiled. "Who's sweetie?" she asked airily while trying to mask her burning curiosity.

Although it was unplanned, Tali preferred it this way. No big announcements. "His name's Yoav," she said casually. "He's a graduate student at the department of

Middle Eastern and African History."

"Sounds interesting," Tali's father commented. "What's his last name?"

"Why does that matter?" she asked in a low voice, narrowing her eyes.

"It doesn't," he shrugged, "I just wanted to know, if it's not classified information."

Bracing herself, Tali studied her parents' faces. Then she launched into a barrage of staccato details about Yoav and his background.

"His last name's Yarkoni. From what I understand, it's a Hebraized version of *khadri* or *khudri*, which means green or greenery in Arabic. I can look up the exact meaning. His parents are both from Iraq – his dad's family is from Baghdad, and his mom's family is from another city, the name escapes me. I'll ask him next time we meet. He has two sisters: the older one, Merav, works in a bank, and the younger sister, Sivan, is a high school student. They live in Petah Tikva. His father owns an insurance agency. His mother runs a community center. She used to be a teacher of Hebrew language and literature." Tali turned to her mother: "You'll probably have a lot to talk about." She paused to catch her breath, then stated ceremonially: "Now you know everything about him, his background, his family, everything. Is there anything important I missed?"

An intense hush ensued. Tali's parents, Micha and Rina, exchanged baffled glances. Micha broke the silence.

"Looks like he's from a good family," he nodded in appreciation. "He sounds like a guy with his feet on the ground."

"Well, Iraqis are known to be different," Tali's mother added, believing this to be a display of cultural tolerance and openness.

"Different from *whom*?" Tali fired back at her.

"Other groups," Rina replied, "you know…"

Tali bristled. "No, Mom, I don't know! Maybe you

could explain it to me. Go on, I'm listening!"

Rina looked nervous. "Well, you know…" she offered hesitantly, "different from other Mizrahi Jews who come from Arab countries."

"Great! Beautiful!" Tali fumed. "I knew that's what you were going to say. 'Iraqis aren't like other Mizrahi Jews!'" she mimicked her mother.

"Talush," her father protested. "Where's this sensitivity coming from? What did your mother say? Iraqis really are known for being diligent, hard workers who managed to integrate well, unlike other…"

Tali let out a nervous laugh. "Go on, say it. Unlike who? Unlike other Mizrahi Jews, who lack the skills and motivation to succeed? That's what you were going to say, isn't it? I can't believe I have to hear this shit from my parents. Especially you, Dad. How many times have I heard you rant and rave that Grandpa Yosef and Grandma Hinda thought you weren't good enough for Mom, just because their family is Polish and yours is Romanian?"

"That's totally different," Tali's father replied immediately. But seeing that she was ready to pounce on him, he didn't pursue it. He tried to steer the conversation into safer territory.

"So he studies the Middle East? What's his specialty?"

Tali's face immediately softened. She hated that breaking the news of her new boyfriend had turned into an argument, and was glad for the change. "His research is on ethnic tensions in Iraq during the British Mandate," she smiled.

"Sounds interesting!" her father said sincerely. "Before the Americans went into Iraq, who knew they had ethnic tensions there? We thought everyone was just Iraqi. Now we're hearing about Shiites, Sunnis, Kurds, Yazidis… Yazidis?! Who are they? Well, now we can learn from your new boyfriend about what's going on there, in that crazy place." He paused for a moment then added, "I assume his Arabic's very good. He has to read a lot of texts in Arabic, right?"

"Yes," Tali said proudly, "his Arabic is excellent."

"Well his background is a huge advantage," he said casually.

"Dad!" Tali moaned helplessly. "Again with this! I can't believe you're saying these things."

Her parents looked at each other, struggling to understand what went wrong this time, what landmine Micha had stepped on.

"Talush," Rina grumbled, "I really don't know why you're so upset, what did Dad say? His parents are from Iraq and as far as I know, Iraqis speak Arabic! I do not understand why you're so upset!" she repeated, stressing the words – and her growing despair at Tali's temperamental reactions.

"Why am I upset?" Tali fumed. "For your information, Mom, almost no one of our generation, Iraqi or otherwise, speaks Arabic today. I'm talking about Jewish Israelis. So to learn the language, you have to work your ass off. What gives Yoav an advantage isn't his 'background' but his talent and a lot of hard work. Okay?"

"Talush," her mother shrugged, "I still think you're overreacting."

When Tali returned to Tel Aviv that evening, she didn't share the full conversation with Yoav.

"They were very happy to hear about you," she said before adding, "I think they have some preconceptions about Iraqis."

"What?!"

"Don't worry, positive preconceptions. They think you're not like *others*," she said cryptically.

"What do you mean?" He asked apprehensively.

Imitating her father, she said: "'Looks like he's from a good family. He sounds like a guy with his feet on the ground'. It's a little backhanded compliment about my previous choices in men. They like to season their praise with a pinch of insult," she said sadly. "Anyway, they're dying to see you."

"I'm ready," he replied. "We can go whenever you like."

"But know this!" she raised her finger, smiling: "If they like you too much, I'm going to hate you!"

"What?! Are you out of your mind?"

"No I'm not," she said, still smiling. "If they like you too much, it means they think I'm lucky to find you, because *I'm* not much of a catch."

"Well," he waved it off, "the most important thing is that they're happy. All I need now is to pass their test."

"Don't worry, I think you've already passed it." She pecked him on the lips and added, "Thanks of course to my warm letter of recommendation."

Yoav indeed passed the test. "You can tell he's a serious guy," Tali's father proclaimed on the phone to Tali following Yoav's first visit to Haifa. "He's got a good sense of humor, too."

"And he's handsome," her mother added. "And most importantly, he loves you. I saw how he was looking at you."

CHAPTER 17
Hadil

Two days had passed since Sharif was taken from his home, and his family was still none the wiser as to what had happened to him or where he was. These were not normal times in Ramallah. Despite the current unity government, tensions between Hamas and Fatah were escalating. In the Gaza Strip they had exploded into all out civil war that had claimed lives. Hadil and Hisham were thus devoting all their time and energy to finding Sharif. Hisham's entire family pinned their hopes on them, believing that Hisham and Hadil must know someone who could help.

"Ramallah is the *Sulta*, everyone knows someone," Marwan repeatedly stated, echoing a commonly-held belief in the West Bank that anyone from Ramallah had ties to the Palestinian Authority, or at least knew someone who did.

He called Hisham early in the morning, hoping for news.

"The man I spoke with is looking into it," Hisham lied. "He promised to call me back as soon as possible," he went on, shooting Hadil an apologetic grimace.

"Sharif was kidnapped by them, by the *Sulta*!" Marwan said angrily. "He wasn't arrested by the police! They didn't have any papers or arrest warrants. They didn't take him to court... nothing!"

"Everything will be fine," Hisham reassured his father. "Don't worry, I'll call as soon as I have new information." As he terminated the call he noticed Hadil's reprimanding look. "What can I tell him?" he said. "I've got no choice, I had to lie to give him some hope. Maybe that shithead Murad will come through in the end."

Hadil could see Hisham's genuine care and concern for his brother. Despite the yawning chasm between the brothers, despite their mutual resentment and even hostility, Hisham's filial love was unwavering. It sparked a tenderness towards Hisham that she hadn't felt in a long time.

"I don't think Murad is going to help," she muttered despondently. "We need to come up with other options."

"You may be right," he nodded in despair. "I called him four or five times yesterday, He doesn't return my calls and ignores my messages. I don't know what to do. We don't even know who took Sharif. Could be Preventive Security, could be the Security Services. They might be keeping him in the Mukata'a, or in a prison in Jericho. Or maybe some secret place. Who knows? Maybe they handed him over to the Israelis. We don't know anything!" he concluded, frustrated.

They ruled out the possibility of Israeli forces taking Sharif in the guise of Palestinians. Nadwa, Sharif's wife, was absolutely sure of this.

"She said they were Palestinian," noted Hisham. "Their speech, their faces... she said there's no way they were Israelis."

On the day after the kidnapping, just to cover their bases, they stopped at a Ramallah police station to ask if a Sharif Saada happened to be in custody. Hisham and Hadil considered filing a formal complaint: a man was kidnapped from his home and the police ought to investigate, they told the attending police officer. The officer smiled evasively and said: "He's *Hamsawi*, a Hamas activist? Well, in that case," he rolled his eyes to suggest an obvious unspoken fact, "the address is somewhere else - not here, not the police."

"But where is this 'other place'?" Hisham asked, frustrated. It was obvious to everyone present that the security apparatus did not keep public office hours. "We don't even know where they are," he sighed in frustration. "And suppose we do find out, what are they going to tell us? 'Yes, we're the ones who detained him'? Yes, he's in our custody'? Check basement cell number 17?' It's all secrets with them. They'll never tell us anything!" he lapsed into despair.

Hadil had an idea. She would call Arin Sabbagh, her friend from Bir Zeit, who worked as a senior adviser to the Minister of Information.

"You remember her," she told Hisham. "She was connected to one of the projects at my center. I also know the minister, though not very well. I met him once at a conference. He knows who I am. My father knows him. They were both activists in the communist party. Maybe he can help us."

"Good idea," Hisham agreed, smiling bitterly with his father's words echoing in his mind: "Ramallah is the *Sulta*, everyone knows someone."

Hadil called Arin and filled her in; Arin promised to try and arrange a meeting with the minister, adding however that she couldn't guarantee a meeting nor could be assured that a meeting would yield any results. They waited anxiously by the phone. An hour later, Arin called back and said the minister had agreed to meet Hadil within the hour at the Information Ministry building. As Hadil was getting ready to leave, Arin called again, saying the minister had been summoned to an urgent meeting with the chairman of the PA and other ministers. She suggested Hadil come anyway: Arin might be able to slip her in for a few words with the minister. Hadil arrived in the Mukata'a half an hour before the ministerial meeting.

Arin was waiting for her at the gate. She told Hadil she'd already raised the issue with the minister, adding that the minister remembered meeting Hadil and greatly appreciated the work she did at *New Horizons*.

Encouraged, Hadil followed Arin inside. She sat waiting while Arin went into the minister's bureau. Hadil could hear some whispers. When Arin came out minutes later, she jumped to her feet, ready to meet the minister, but Arin told her that unfortunately he could not see her due to his tight schedule. Staring at the floor with profound embarrassment, Arin apologized, promising to pursue the matter and let Hadil know if they found out anything about her brother-in-law. Hadil sank back into her seat. She stared at the closed door to the bureau as if considering whether to storm inside.

"But is he going to help us or not?" she pleaded with Arin.

"I gave him all the details," Arin said, lightly stroking Hadil's shoulder with growing discomfort, "let's see what he can do."

Hadil felt desperate. This was exactly the answer Murad had given Hisham. Heavy fear set in; perhaps Sharif's fate was already sealed. Perhaps he was already dead. *They've probably killed him by now. That must be why everyone's being so evasive. Sharif probably met the same fate as my uncle, Kamal. So there's nothing more we can do.* Hadil slowly pulled herself out of the chair as if shouldering a tremendous load. Arin walked her out, repeating her hollow promises.

On her way out of the courtyard, Hadil saw a well-known senior security official walk in, surrounded by his bodyguards. She didn't hesitate and walked straight towards him. The guards immediately moved to stop her. Hadil didn't flinch but tried to reach him. Taken aback by her boldness, the man stopped walking and looked at her with surprised amusement.

She's sorry for intruding, she said, but she must talk to him, and would greatly appreciate a moment of his time.

Won over by Hadil's boldness, he smiled and said: "Behold, a true woman of Palestine!"

He invited her to follow him into one of the Mukata'a offices, asking first who she was, where she lived, what her husband did for a living. He then asked how he could be of help.

"It's about my brother-in-law," Hadil said. "He was taken from his home, and we don't have a clue where he is." The man listened impassively as she supplied the remaining details, showing no sign that he knew about or was connected to the kidnapping. He asked an assistant to take down the details of the "missing person" as if filing a routine police report. Hadil recited the details in a monotone, feeling that they were simply giving her the runaround.

"We'll contact you if we find anything," the man promised and walked her to the door. *They're all so formal and laconic,* she thought, *so stingy with information.* What does it all mean? Her gut tightened with sudden certainty. *The man knew what I was talking about - he's involved in Sharif's abduction.* At home she told Hisham about her failed attempts with Arin and the security official, adding her firm suspicion that Sharif was in a *Sulta*'s jail. Dejected, Hisham thanked her for her efforts, "even though Sharif never—"

Hadil cut him short. "It doesn't matter now what your brother said about me, or what he thinks about us."

During her frequent visits to Hisham's parents in Al-Jib, she often heard Sharif recite from Hamas charter. "It is impossible to be triumphant," he declared, "without first curing the ills of Palestinian society. And Islam is the solution to these ills. It's a panacea." He condemned urbanites for straying from the path of Islam and taking up Western practices, and although he didn't look Hadil in the eyes during his harangue, she knew he was talking about her and Hisham.

Sharif would froth at the mouth when talking about the growing vice and depravity in Palestinian society. He was infuriated about alcohol consumption in Ramallah, especially among the younger generations.

"What did the Oslo Accords get us? What did the Palestinian government get us? Taybeh Beer!" he raged. "Is that what we need? A beer factory? Palestinian alcohol so we could get our own children intoxicated?! This culture turns people into wrecks." He often fumed about the permissiveness of women who walked uncovered. Whenever one of his sisters burst into song, even at home, Sharif would scold her, "The Prophet forbade singing!" And hinting quite broadly at his brother's specialty, he also disliked poetry that celebrated romantic love: "It fills young people's minds with illusions and steers them off the righteous path."

He always openly disapproved of Hisham's decision to marry Hadil. "She never became Muslim," he would grumble and grouse. "Never converted. She continues to celebrate Christian holidays and take her children to church. It was to be expected. They had the wedding in a church. I was young then, so I came. Today I would never go to that wedding." Hadil's *New Horizons* center also provoked his ire. "She gets western donations to push our women away from religion. Precisely what the Hamas Charter warns us about. Yes, yes!" he responded to their puzzled looks. "Article seventeen explicitly addresses this issue. These organizations talk about new horizons," he ironically referenced Hadil's center, "but their only horizon is one of demolishing our society. In the name of progress and women's rights, they encourage women to be promiscuous, use birth control, have abortions and kill innocent babies. 'Family planning', they call it!" he added bitterly. On occasion, Sharif would make oblique references to rumors about Hadil's uncle Kamal. In time, she and Hisham reached the tacit agreement not to visit Hisham's parents at the same time as Sharif. It was simply best for everyone.

The *Sulta* was a dead end. Hisham and Hadil decided they would have to come up with new ideas. Hisham suggested reaching out to Al-Haq, the Palestinian human rights organization. "Their offices are close to yours," he said. Though attractive, the idea had serious drawbacks. Once a human rights complaint was lodged, any officials who might somehow be willing to help would get mad and shut them out completely.

"I know how you feel," Hadil gently touched Hisham's arm, "but we shouldn't lose our heads. I know it feels like an eternity since Sharif was taken but it's only been two days. If the PA has him, which is what it looks like, then we can't expect them to release him immediately. Let's give it a few more days before we do something radical."

Hisham agreed before adding, "But if he's not released in few days, I'm going to Al-Haq. If the *Sulta* has something on Sharif, let them come out and say it. Put him on trial! You can't just make people disappear. They're just like the Israelis. Worse. Remember what they did to me and Murad?"

"I remember," Hadil sighed. "Of course I remember."

CHAPTER 18
Yoav

On Thursday afternoon, at the end of two weeks of reserve service, Yoav came home on weekend furlough. Tali was noticeably distant as he hugged and kissed her at the door. He knew why and knew that to put things right, he had to reaffirm his commitment to their plan, to her. He grabbed a quick shower and joined Tali on the sofa, sitting at a small distance from her. He went straight to the point, apologizing for his "idiotic" idea of living in separate cities.

"I was just overwhelmed with the news about the Harvard admission," he explained contritely. "You have to admit, it's quite something. But I know," he came closer and held her hand tenderly, "there's no way I could ever give up on you. I love you so much."

Tali pulled her hand away, refusing to be placated easily. Yet he could tell that his sincerity had a softening effect on her. When he later tried leading her to bed, however, she stopped him. "Not now," she said dryly.

They had dinner with Yoav's sister Merav. It was Tali's idea, following her panicky call to Merav from Jordan the previous week. Yoav suggested they cancel and spend the entire weekend alone together but Tali vetoed this gesture of appeasement. He should not renege on his scheduled plan, she said, to visit his grandmother Camilla the following day with his mother.

"You have to keep promises," she said decisively.

They met Merav at Café Noir, not far from their apartment. After they ordered Merav asked where things stood with their university applications. Before they could answer, she told Yoav: "Dad's been calling everyone he knows to say you got into Harvard. I think he's going to put up a billboard...Well done! Harvard! I'm so proud of you! So you're going to Boston!?"

There was a tense silence. Yoav squirmed. "We've gotten some good news and some not-so-good news," he told her with an apologetic look to Tali. Merav looked puzzled. "We don't know where we'll be yet," he added, "but things will work out eventually." Noticing the corner of Tali's mouth twisting, he quickly changed the subject, asking Merav about her recent breakup.

"I really don't know what went wrong," she shrugged in despair. "I thought with Nadav I could finally have a serious relationship. But he was... He gave me the usual crap – he's not sure what he wants, doesn't know if he's ready to commit... one more guy trying to find himself. I don't know what they're looking for. What the hell did he lose that he needs to find it? I'm tired of this bullshit. The man's thirty-five, if he hasn't found himself by now, it's not going to happen. Seriously though," she said in response to their smiles, "I'm sick of these dead-end affairs. It's better to just be alone and sport-fuck."

She was struggling to make ends meet but despite her parents' entreaties that she join her father in his insurance business and move back in, Merav refused, worried that it might put an end to her efforts at independence. "It's not an easy time," she admitted. "I left the job at the bank and opened my own business." She pulled out a business card and read it out loud. "Merav Yarkoni - Financial Consulting. Nice isn't it?" She spoke passionately about the new business.

"I advise people who don't understand the new capital

markets, pensions, life insurance, health insurance. It's not what it used to be. You can't just stick your savings in a pension fund and have the fund manager take care of it for you. Nowadays people have to manage their own savings. That's what I help them with."

She went on and on until Yoav interrupted her gently, asking how she manages her own financial affairs, rent and other expenses. "My sister," he later told Tali humorously, "can go on indefinitely. She's a *perpetum mobile*, a timeless speech machine. She has inexhaustible energies."

"Mom and Dad are always there for me, even when I don't ask," Merav replied. "They never say no. But every time they help Mom says, 'Why not stay with us till you're on your feet? You've got your own room here. What more do you need? We never ask where you're going. You can come and go as you please.' If it was up to Mom we'd all still be living with her. She could feed us, bathe us, and tuck us in at night. She wants her baby chicks close. What happened is going to haunt her – and affect us – till the day she dies."

Yoav's mother, Nava, was in her early twenties when her first son, Shimi, was born. In the early, excruciating stages of his teething, his parents hardly slept a wink. Despite assurances from Nava's mother and mother-in-law that all parents go through this, the exhaustion was devastating. Night after grueling night, Nava and her husband Shaul took turns getting up.

One night sometime in the wee hours, Shimi was screaming in agony. Shaul was trying to get some sleep. Nava took Shimi from his cradle, held him to her breast, and paced back and forth in the small apartment. It was no use. She made several trips from the kitchen to the cradle, trying different solutions. When a frozen washcloth on his swollen gums didn't help, she tried a baby bottle with chilled fruit puree and a soft rubber nipple for him to chew on. Nava looked at Shimi lethargically, her eyelids heavy, as he lay on his back in the cradle. His pain seemed to have finally abated at least for the moment.

The crying stopped and longed-for silence, blissful silence, suddenly filled the house. She lay on the bed next to the cradle, overwhelmed with fatigue. She wanted to lie down for a moment, just a short moment. She heard a gurgling from the crib, like the satisfied purr of a cat. *He's finally asleep*, she thought. Nava did as well.

Later she awoke and instinctively looked into the crib. Shimi was on his stomach in a sleeping posture. She wanted to feel him, but worried about waking him up again. She hesitated then reached out and brushed him lightly. Anxiety crept into her. Shimi's posture was strange, unnatural. He was too quiet, too motionless. She pressed her hand to his forehead. It was cold. Nava quickly turned the baby on his back. Shimi's face was covered in dried spit–up, his big black eyes open, glazed, voiceless. Nava let out a bestial scream that caused Shaul to leap out of bed and rush over. What he saw in the crib and on her face needed no explanation. Shaul reached out his hand to feel Shimi's forehead and cheeks. It was a soft, gentle touch, like a desperate attempt to overturn the bitter news. The first thing that came to Shaul's mind was to rush their son to the nearby hospital. He immediately began to throw his clothes on, expecting Nava to follow suit. She didn't.

"Hurry up," he said, but she just sat on the bed, one hand holding limply to the crib.

"Where to? What for?" she asked, sobbing bitterly. He watched her for a long moment, silently, as the merciless realization set in: it's no use, it's no use. He bent and wrapped her in his arms. Thus they sat together on the bed, sobbing for a long hour.

Later the doctors couldn't tell them the exact cause of Shimi's death. Did he suffocate on the bottle itself? Was it the fruit puree? Or perhaps their son had a neurological defect? "In many cases like this, the cause of death can't be fully determined," said the doctor on the morning after they lost their first and only child.

The loss of Shimi altered Nava permanently, like an unpardonable crime, and her bottomless grief intertwined with guilt that knew no respite. *I left him unattended. I should have picked him up. I should have burped him like before.* No matter how much Shaul tried she was beyond comfort. "The doctor didn't say that he choked on the fruit puree," he used to remind her.

"And what about me?" he would try another tack. "I was there with you, I'm just as guilty. We have to accept that nothing's going to bring him back to us." But the guilt never left, and when in turn Merav, Yoav, and Sivan came along, Nava became obsessively protective of them, vowing never, ever to slip.

Yoav told Tali about it a few months into their relationship. She'd heard Yoav and his sisters mention "Mom's trauma", "Mom and her chicks", and "Mom's old story". For a while Yoav dodged Tali's requests for details, but one Friday night, after dinner at his parents' house, where Merav had whispered something, he agreed to tell Tali. "It's not a secret," he said, "but it's also not something we tell people."

"I'm people'?" Tali retorted indignantly.

"No, you know what I mean… okay, okay," he sought to appease her and began to share with her his mother's tragedy. "You see," he began hesitatingly, "she doesn't like to talk about it. We had to put it together, and finally my father filled in the gaps." When he was done narrating, he observed with some amazement: "And we came out normal, after all. I think it's thanks to my Dad."

"How so?"

"Whenever she wanted to tighten our leash, he'd step in. She tried to stop us from staying out late with friends, and he'd change her mind. She tried to stop us from going on school field trips, and he'd insist we go. He'd always tell her that we're not babies - which is what Shimi was, of course. He'd tell her not to keep us in a fishbowl but to let us enjoy life."

"Wow, that's harsh," Tali said with compassion. "How'd she take it?"

"She knew he was right," replied Yoav. "She'd argue a bit but then she'd give in. She was especially anxious when we were out late. She wouldn't go to sleep until we got back home, back to the nest. Even now if one of us stays overnight at my parents' house, we get 'The Drill'," Yoav made air quotes.

"What's that?" Tali asked, amused.

"It's like roll call. My sister Merav came up with the name. Say I go out Friday night. Mom stays up until I come home, even if it's 4 AM. The moment she hears the door open she goes: 'Is that you, Yoav?' and I go, 'Yes, Mom, it's me. You can go back to sleep.' Every single time. It would drive me crazy. She knew it but she couldn't help herself. Nowadays when we stay there overnight, she doesn't ask anymore, but we know she still stays up until we're safely home."

"How'd your father take it, this Drill?"

"How could he take it? He got used to it. She'd wake him up to tell him it was 2 AM and Merav wasn't home yet, and he'd tell her to go to sleep and not worry. Then he'd get back to sleep and she'd stay awake. One night Merav was out past 3. My mom was so anxious that she went out to the yard and waited for her on our swing. When she saw Merav coming, she jumped up and ran inside so Merav wouldn't catch her waiting like that. But when Merav saw the swing swaying, she freaked out, because she thought it was some pervert lurking out there for her. She froze and wouldn't go in. My mom couldn't understand what was taking her so long. Eventually she called out to Merav and they both realized what happened."

"And you ended up joining a combat unit," Tali lightly scolded him. "Was it a rebellion against her?"

"Maybe, something like that," Yoav smiled. "It was probably just a quest for autonomy. When I went into the Paratroopers I didn't fully grasp that this was my reason. But yeah, I was pissed off with her for pouncing on me at every turn. I always worried that it would turn me into some kind of mama's boy. I'd be playing with kids down the street and she'd come and drag me home. I remember how the other kids laughed. Once I told her I didn't want her coming along as a chaperone on a school trip. She was so hurt by that."

"So your struggle for independence was successful," Tali concluded dryly.

"I guess so. I joined the Paratroopers even though she was freaking out. This was '95, when the terrorist bombings were everywhere. Just a few months before Rabin was assassinated. The irony was that way more people were being killed in the cities than on the battlefield."

"Your mother's story is horrible," Tali said. "Sounds like she never let go of what happened."

"Absolutely," Yoav replied. "Merav and I talked about this many times. It always reminds me of Joseph Conrad's *Lord Jim*. Ever read it?"

"No."

"It's one of the many books I read thanks to my mom. It's thanks to her that I like reading - there were always books around." He gave Tali his gist of the plot, about a young British seaman named Jim who's hired as first mate on a steamer carrying Muslim pilgrims to a port in the Red Sea. One night the ship's hull scrapes against a hard object. Thinking that it's going to sink, the captain and crew, including Jim, abandon ship. Unfortunately for them the ship doesn't sink and is found a few days later floating aimlessly in the Red Sea.

"It's a huge scandal," Yoav stated emphatically. "Not only were they cowards, but they didn't even try to save the passengers. All they cared about was their own skin.

And Jim, who wanted to think of himself as some swashbuckling, death-defying adventurer, felt like the world's biggest failure. He's wracked with guilt and shame. So now, to avoid anyone who might have heard about the incident, he goes on every far-flung high-risk mission he can find, trying to salvage his self-image. He goes on like this for years and years, haunted by his disgrace, until he dies."

"What a story," Tali sighed, "it's tough how one event can haunt you all your life."

"Exactly," said Yoav. "Over time it became family folklore. Once we grew to understand her trauma, we began to have more empathy. We still lose patience sometimes with her over protectiveness, but we try. And with our dad's help, we go on doing what we want."

CHAPTER 19
Hisham

When Hadil told him about her discouraging visit to the Mukata'a, Hisham was blown away by her courage and her loyalty to family, her total effort to bring Sharif home. Whence such emotional resilience to put aside their marital rift? Whence such equanimity to ignore Sharif's repeated insults to her? But along with this mystifying gratitude, Hisham also felt a pathetic, shameful sense of envy as he once more witnessed Hadil's assertiveness, her confidence, her sense of entitlement. He pictured her marching into the Mukata'a and imperiously demanding answers from any and every official, dismissive of their rank and prestige. He wanted to thank her but she cut him off. "We don't have to talk about it now," she stated.

He'd first witnessed her courage when they were students at Bir Zeit, during the first Intifada. When it came to demonstrations, he used to boast, Hadil was no porcelain doll. She wasn't like those toy protestors who stood at a safe distance from the front line and never confronted the Israeli soldiers. On the other hand she was never one to curse out the Jews; she was levelheaded and brave. Years later, when he reminded her of those days, Hadil would minimize her courage.

"We were young," she said dismissively, and began to mockingly recite: "'Defying tank and gun / daring to put

176

her life on the line/nothing in her hand but a stone / behold the virgin Palestinian girl.'" Hisham stared at her, struggling to catch her drift. "We've talked about it more than once," Hadil said irritably. "Every poet in those days insisted on bringing up our virginity. *Al-Fagar, Al-Adabi,* and all those poetry journals were full of poems of this kind – virginity, virginity, virginity. Any Palestinian woman who took part in the struggle was a 'virgin'. Why did they assume that?" she asked.

"You're right, Hisham grinned slyly, "they had no reason to assume that."

It was during the early days of the first Intifada that Hisham got to know Murad Ismail, who later became an assistant to the Minister of Health. Murad, who studied history at Bir Zeit, was from a village near Bethlehem. Akram, their third roommate, was from a village near Ramallah much like Hisham. The three roommates were bound by their shared rural background, evident in the remnants of rural dialect in their speech, and in the condescending attitude they endured from affluent, sophisticated urban students. The three friends made focused efforts to fit in with their new social milieu: changing their clothing and hairstyles, shaving off their mustaches, refining their speech.

Hisham, especially as he grew more attached to Hadil, gradually embraced the worldview that downplayed the role of religion in his Palestinian identity. "Religion separates, secular nationalism unifies," he would repeat the motto popular in leftist circles. Yet unlike Hadil, he stopped short of joining the Palestinian People's Party and instead joined the campus chapter of George Habash's Popular Front, whose platform combined national liberation with class equality. Later he adopted the slogan that compared Habash to Che Guevara: *al-hakim w'al-hakim* – pointing to the fact that both were doctors by training (*hakim*) and wise men (*hakim*). In presenting his political identity, Hisham made sure to point out that he was neither religious nor a heretic. His father once told him angrily: "We didn't send you to university to be an apostate!"

"I'm not an apostate," Hisham assured him, "but I do believe religion threatens the unity between Muslims and Christians."

Akram died in the first Intifada, shot down by Israeli soldiers in a demonstration at Bir Zeit. The image of Akram just before he collapsed was engraved in Hisham's memory. He could readily summon it: Akram, his head and face wrapped in a *keffiyeh*, standing in a hazy cloud from Israeli smoke grenades. Akram bent down, picked up a billowing grenade from the asphalt road and straightened up, his right hand poised to throw it back at the soldiers. Suddenly he collapsed on the road. The grenade slipped from his hand, the smoke continuing to hiss out. They all rushed to him. On seeing him Hadil shrieked in horror. Akram was on his back, face-up. He had been shot in the chest and died instantly. Both the shooting and the stone-throwing stopped abruptly. They removed the *keffiyeh* from his face. His eyes were open wide as if in disbelief.

"He never saw it coming, never thought it was even possible," Hisham used to say when remembering Akram to friends. "When you're young you think you're immortal. Then again, maybe he was: I can still see him standing there, the same age, in the middle of all that smoke."

Like Akram, Murad also belonged to the campus chapter of the Fatah movement. But politics never stood in the way of the roommates' friendship. They'd cook together in their modest apartment, eat at Sonia's Restaurant, and whenever they felt like treating themselves, visit the fancier Tabash Restaurant in the nearby resort village of Jifna. Tabash was famous for its *musakhan*, a dish of minced chicken in sumac. Nobody could figure out what made the Tabash musakhan so addictively mouthwatering. Was it the way the chicken was prepared? The taboon-baked flatbread it was served on? A secret spice blend?

Following Akram's death, they took in a new roommate from Gaza named Said. Everyone called him *Said al-'Gazawi*: Gazan Said. He studied biology but never completed his studies. He returned to Gaza about a year after the Israeli army shut down Bir Zeit University and locked up the dormitories, suspending academic life indefinitely.

"Biology," he explained, "isn't like literature or history. You can study those subjects at home or in a café, as many students do. It's impossible to study biology without the proper labs and equipment." The interim solution offered by the university – giving science students use of the Friends School labs – was unsatisfactory. Said gave up and returned to Gaza; contact with him gradually dwindled. The last time anyone spoke with him, he was already married with two children.

Like many of his friends, Hisham's affiliation with the Popular Front wasn't translated into armed conflict against the Israeli army. At first, he did support it. "Only armed struggle," he would decree, "will rid us of the Israelis." Gradually however, he came around to the views of his professors, and not least thanks to Hadil's staunch opposition to armed struggle. Eventually Hisham became a true advocate of civil disobedience. He was glad to discover that the Popular Front leadership itself had embraced this position, at least in the early months of the first Intifada. His part in the struggle against occupation consisted of demonstrations, throwing stones, raising banners, and distributing United Headquarters leaflets to the local committees in his home village of Al-Jib and in nearby villages. He paid a heavy price for these activities.

He was standing next to Murad and Hadil at one of the Bir Zeit student demonstrations, where some of them threw stones at the Israeli soldiers. Suddenly the soldiers stormed the protesters, snatched up Hisham and Murad along with two or three others, blindfolded then crammed them into a Border Police jeep and drove them away. On the way to their unknown destination, the soldiers kicked them while shouting at them to provide their personal details. Hisham was terrified. The stench of urine rose from the floor and hit his nose; one of his friends had pissed himself. The Jeep finally reached its destination and they were all dragged out. Hisham's legs shook. He was sure he was going to be summarily executed.

He found out afterwards that they'd been driven to "the beating wall", a spot behind the Al-Khatib carpet shop near Al-Manara Square where demonstrators were regularly taken to be savagely beaten. This practice, Hisham learned years later, was part of a policy by Israel's then-defense minister, Yitzhak Rabin, to break protesters' spirits and warn by example. It was before Rabin embarked on the path of peace, realizing that breaking Palestinian demonstrators' bones did little to break the resistance and that the occupation of the West Bank must end.

The soldiers began to pummel Hisham and the others with wooden batons. When the beating ended the Israelis drove off, leaving them aching, bleeding, and bruised. Hisham and Murad managed to get passing drivers to take them to Ramallah's government hospital. In those days a strong wind of solidarity swept through the cities and villages, and drivers competed with each other for the privilege of ferrying injured protestors. Hisham and Murad made their way back that same day to their apartment in Bir Zeit. Consumed with anxiety, Hadil was waiting for them.

"They broke both our right hands," Hisham told Murad with a mournful smile, "but they should have asked what our dominant hand is. You're right-handed, but I'm left-handed, so why should my right hand pay for what it didn't do?"

The Oslo Accords were kind to Murad. Unlike many local Palestinians who'd been instrumental in the uprising but were sidelined when the Palestinian leadership came in from Tunisia, he managed to work his way up, becoming a senior political aide to various Palestinian ministers. He married a Ramallah girl and had three children. During the Oslo days, Hisham and Murad would get together often, visiting each other's homes with their families. But starting with the Al-Aqsa Intifada their contact lessened, mainly because of Hisham's disapproval of Murad's increased involvement in politics.

"I want nothing to do with politics and politicians," he'd tell Hadil, who herself had chosen to put her efforts into a nongovernmental organization. When Sharif was kidnapped, Hisham's disdain for politics turned into outright loathing for the Palestinian Authority.

"It might be best to dismantle the PA," he repeated. "Let the Israelis come back and reinstate the Civil Administration, at least then we'll be able to tell friend from foe. What can I say? *Hamiha haramiha*," he cited a proverb. "Those who are supposed to protect us are robbing us blind."

CHAPTER 20
Tali

Yoav left in the early morning on Sunday to make his early shift at the checkpoint. The sun was stingy, its rays cutting weakly through the clouds and starving the leaf buds on the branches. Their weekend together hadn't completely eliminated Tali's doubts. They lingered as she dragged herself out of bed, stumbled to the kitchen, and flicked on the kettle. She pulled the coffee and sugar jars from the top cabinet and placed them on the kitchen table. Then she fetched the milk from the fridge and placed it beside them. Dumping a teaspoon of coffee into a mug along with a teaspoon of sugar and a dash of milk, she poured the boiling water over everything. She stirred mechanically then put everything back in place. She headed to the "office" in the corner of their bedroom and sat down in front of the computer. She stared at the dark screen for a long moment, consumed with amorphous, fretful thoughts. Eventually she logged onto her email. There were no new messages. She entered Yoav's email. Nothing new there either.

Tali felt like taking a long bath. She washed off the bathtub and the sink, removing the scum and hair left over from Yoav's morning ablutions. He never bothered to clean after himself. There were other things too. Little things, like the clothes he left scattered everywhere, the underwear, the shoes, the coffee cups left on the kitchen table, the dirty dishes he let rot in the sink despite promising to wash them, the urine stains on the toilet rim, the emptied liquid soap and shampoo bottles that would stay forever in the bathroom if she didn't clear them away. Normally she was able to overlook these things but today she felt acute resentment. She knew it was no coincidence; her irritation was a direct result of the past few days. She recalled Yoav's regular complaints about her long showers. Why should he mind? "There's a water shortage in Israel," he grumbled. Yeah, sure. And why should he care that I take a shower after we make love? she thought.

"Why do you have to do this?" he once asked somewhat reproachfully.

"I don't know," she shrugged. "I just feel the need to wash myself. That's how I've always been. Does it bother you?"

"To be honest, it does," he said. "I want us to stay like this, hug, cuddle... but you instantly run off to the bathroom."

"But what's the problem?" she said, staring at him for a long moment, somewhat bewildered. "I come right back."

"True, but it's not the same anymore," he grumbled.

She enjoyed the solitude now, the prospect of splashing in the bathwater without his sermons. She peeled off her clothes and was about to settle into the steaming tub when she paused to observe herself in the mirror. She discontentedly touched her slight belly fat. She observed her breasts, large but firm with dark-brown areolas. There was no discernible slackness. Tali was pleased. *If things don't work out with Yoav,* she entertained a halfhearted thought, *I'm still attractive enough.* Just as she immersed herself in the bath, the phone rang. She didn't bother to check to see who it was. It was her mother who asked Tali to call back, which she did an hour later. They spoke briefly. Rina wanted to know if there was any news about the universities and also if Tali intended to go to a party that night.

"It's Purim!" she reminded her with affected cheerfulness. In the background Tali could hear familiar music.

"I don't like this holiday," Tali said, "I don't feel like going to a party." Before her mother could reply, she asked: "What's that you're listening to, Mom?"

"Yossi Banai."

"That's what I thought."

"You know Tali, these songs have been with us for many years."

"I know. I like them too."

"Anyway, did Dad talk with you about Grandma Bracha-Bianca?"

"No, why?"

"She keeps complaining that you don't visit - her Talinka, her *draga mea*, her *Fatiţa mea*, her dearest baby," Rina imitated her mother-in-law in Romanian.

"Mom you're awful!" Tali laughed.

"Well, you know I love her. But she's right, you should visit more often. You've always been very special to her. You used to visit her almost every day, remember?"

She also remembered the old, deplorable sport of formulating scales, comparing social rank and cultural refinement between her parents. Micha, Tali's father, never forgot the insult that had been dealt at the first meeting between his and his wife's families. The incident took place at Rina's parents' house. "*Merci,*" Micha's mother Bracha-Bianca responded when Rina's mother Hinda served the coffee. She took the china cup in her right hand. It was too hot to hold so she pulled a handkerchief from her purse, placed it in her left hand, and sipped the coffee with the handkerchief as a coaster. Micha noticed a wry smile on Hinda's lips. He heard her whisper to her husband: "What did they invent saucers for?" The remark would have faded with time if her parents had stopped there. But they continued to make snide comments, raise eyebrows, and exchange glances whenever talk of Micha's Romanian heritage came up. These gestures kept reminding him of that first archetypical incident, making it loom larger in his mind. He never shared the incident with his mother, and for all he knew she hadn't even noticed it, but he still carried the insult on her behalf.

Micha's parents, Bracha-Bianca and Efraim-Pavel Kozikaro, arrived in Israel from the city of Iaşi located in the northeastern Romanian province of Moldavia. Like many Jews their age, they remembered the city with mixed feelings. They'd wax nostalgic about Iaşi's rich history and exquisite architecture, its picturesque churches and monasteries. They'd recall leisurely strolls along the footpaths at Copou Park, under the shade of bitter orange, chestnut, and pine trees, and the way the paths glowed under streetlights in the evenings. They'd remember the silver lime tree where Eminescu, Romania's national poet, wrote his poems. Some could still recite him: *Come now to the forest's spring / Running wrinkling over the stones / To where lush and grassy furrows / Hide away in curving boughs.* On Sunday evenings the air would vibrate with the merry music accompanying the countless dance troupes who came in from the surrounding towns and villages, all dressed in rustic, multicolored garb. At the center of the park was Iaşi's botanical garden, the first in Romania. And how can one forget the Jewish theater which was the first in all of Europe?

And then came the calamity and the Nazi reign of terror. Of that they spoke very little but remembered everything.

Luckily, unlike many of Iaşi's Jews, Tali's family survived. Efraim-Pavel and Bracha-Bianca, Tali's paternal grandparents, arrived in Israel in the early 1950s with their two sons, Reuben and Micha. Some years later they had another son and a daughter, Tali. Her father used to joke that his parents owed their luck to their limited education: to prevent brain drain and maximize its investment in human capital, Romania's communist regime granted exit visas only to those with ten years of education or less. At other times Micha offered a different version, in which his parents *did* have over ten years of schooling but hid this fact in order to leave.

"Can you imagine how crazy it was?" he'd say. "Today, people who want to come here forge diplomas and professional certificates to look *more* educated. But then they had to pretend they're ignorant. My parents shed quite a few school years on the route from Iaşi to Israel."

His parents' first, arduous years there were spent in a transit camp in Kiryat Ata, then a small town northeast of Haifa. After ten years in the camp, like many others they were given a small apartment in a new housing project on the edge of town. Efraim-Pavel found a livelihood as a cloth vendor, setting out each morning with a bulging leather bag, traveling by bus to the nearby towns, and selling fabric door-to-door to housewives who sewed all their own clothing. No one knew where he got his wares: were they local or imported?

He could be seen early every morning on his way to the bus: a tall and robust man in a fedora, jacket, and solid-colored tie as befits a trustworthy salesman. He kept a trademark cigarette perpetually stuck in his mouth as if it had always been there and used to juggle it along his teeth, some of which were gold-plated – an involuntary act that gave him the appearance of a short-tempered man. Although he never managed to fully master the Hebrew language, he shrewdly used his limited vocabulary to get his customers interested. It was easy to tell when Efraim-Pavel had had a good day: the old leather bag would be flat and the merchandise sold out. Soon the bag would bulge again, this time with fresh produce and sundries from the neighborhood shops, marking another victory in the daily struggle for survival. On those days, Efraim-Pavel would come home like a hunter back from the hunt, presenting the day's quarry to his wife, Bracha-Bianca, who rarely left home.

Micha was two when they came to Israel while his older brother Reuben was four. Their sister Leah was two years younger than brother Yosef while three years separated him and the older Micha. To their parents' disappointment not all of them acquired higher educations. Reuben and Yosef ran a successful construction firm, P.B. Ltd., which they named after Pavel and Bracha. Driving around Haifa, Micha would occasionally point out some residential or commercial building to Tali.

"See that?" he'd say. "Your uncles built it." Like Micha, Reuben and Yosef also settled in Haifa. Both lived in spacious houses in one of the city's more affluent neighborhoods. Leah, their youngest sister, studied pharmacology and worked as a drug company executive in Tel Aviv, where she'd moved decades ago with her husband and two kids.

Even when there was no longer any socioeconomic difference between the two families, Micha's in-laws clung to their country of origin and year of arrival in Israel as proof of higher status. Holding fast to their pedigree, they assured themselves that no amount of material success could ever make one the equal of one's born superior. The past was non-negotiable and irreplaceable. They had arrived from Poland in the mid-1930s, during the so-called Fifth Wave of Immigration. "We're actual pioneers," they used to declare: "We helped build the state." When pushed, they did admit that they'd come to Israel not due to Zionist zeal but from more practical constraints. Like many Jewish Israelis, however, they liked to embellish their story with ideological motives.

Yosef and Hinda were from the small Polish town of Lubicz, about a hundred kilometers from Warsaw. They got married in the second half of the 1930s and decided to move to Palestine over their families' objections. At the time they were among the few Jews who saw the terrible writing on the wall. After World War Two they found out that both their families had been herded by the Nazis into the Lubicz ghetto, transferred to the Warsaw Ghetto, and finally exterminated at Treblinka.

When Yosef and Hinda first arrived in Palestine they lived for a short period in one of Haifa's neighborhoods. A few years later they bought a small parcel of land near the village of Ata, which later became the town - and then the city - of Kiryat Ata. In the early decades of the State of Israel, the town was known for the Ata textile factory which manufactured clothes for generations of Israelis, cladding soldiers and schoolchildren in khakis and the general public in characteristically austere, uniform-like fashions. Securing a loan from the Anglo-Palestine Bank, Yosef and Hinda built a farm on their land with two dozen cows and a chicken coop. The farm provided them and their three children with relative prosperity, selling the milk to a regional concern and the small egg yield to individual customers.

None of the children followed in their parents' footsteps: ironically the profits from the farm permitted all three to acquire professional educations. Ze'ev, the eldest, became a successful lawyer. Pinchas became an engineer. And Rina got a bachelor's in mathematics and taught high school for decades until she retired. *Sic transit gloria mundi.* Yosef and Hinda's agricultural legacy began and ended with themselves, from the mid-1930s to the mid-1980s, when they became too old to keep going. The land was sold off, and the farm was torn down to put up parking lots and hardware stores, as part of the ever-sprawling Haifa Bay industrial district.

Yosef and Hinda both died towards the end of the second millennium, after a brief stay in an old age home. Yosef was the first to go, and Hinda joined him three years later. They left a dubious legacy of endless bickering over family superiority. During one Sabbath dinner, seeing her parents at each other's throats again following an offhand remark by Rina about an upcoming traditional Romanian music festival, Tali burst out: "Don't you have more important things to fight about?!"

"Tell your mother!" Micha roared. "She's just like her parents. Until their dying breath they never stopped thinking I'm not good enough and that you can't compare Romania to Poland."

"Well, you really can't," Rina teased. Micha went red, but before he could counter, Tali stopped him: "Enough! Enough already! How long are you going to fight about this stupid shit? Who cares where your parents are from or who has a richer heritage? Grow up!" For a moment she felt sorry for her father, knowing that it was usually her mother who instigated these fights. But the memory of Micha dining intimately with a bank employee in a Haifa restaurant quickly put her sympathy to rest.

CHAPTER 21
Hadil

"I told you," Hadil told Arij, "I've always felt there's something off about this restaurant. The architecture, the menu, the dishes, the cocktails, the jazz... it's all so artificially foreign. More New York than New York. You know I've got nothing against Western culture, you and I grew up around it at Friends School and Bir Zeit. But it feels like someone's trying too hard." She pointed to the dessert in front of her: "Don't you think it's weird that we're having mint-flavored crème brûlée at a restaurant in Amman?" It was early evening and they were at the Blue Fig restaurant in Amman's Abdoun district. Hadil had stopped in Amman en route from Ramallah to Belfast, where she was due to fly the following day.

"You make a good point," agreed Arij. "And it's not just this restaurant. All of Abdoun is an America-wannabe. It's no coincidence they call us West Amman, even though we're in the south of the city."

"But what do you think about it?" Hadil insisted.

"Well, I know we live in a bubble," Arij said apologetically, "but it's so comfortable. You know, Bashir's involved in some of the new construction projects here..." She paused and added: "But it's the same in Ramallah, no? You have to admit, it's not the Ramallah we used to know. Everywhere you go, you see high-rises with international logos. There's an Internet café on every corner, and all those restaurants popping up with foreign names. Pronto, Angelo, Tomasso, Eiffel, Pollo Loco, Chicago Cheese Steak. It's just the way of the world. Isn't Ramallah also a bubble?"

"Not exactly. I still think Ramallah's more grounded, more real. It leaves way more room for local culture. It's true we're cut off from the rest of the West Bank, but that's because of the occupation. That's not over yet, don't forget."

"You're right," Arij nodded emphatically, "the occupation won't end anytime soon, so let's not waste our breath talking about it." She leaned closer across the table and asked softly: "Tell me, how are things between you and Hisham? Any news?"

"I told you, the last days were difficult," said Hadil. "I was thinking of cancelling Belfast because of what happened with Sharif. The situation in Ramallah isn't simple right now... but praise The Lord, Sharif came home. They held him for more than a week but they finally let him go. Hisham and I went to visit him right after - he didn't speak, just stared at us like we weren't there. God knows what they did to him."

She and Hisham were convinced that the PA security forces were behind the abduction but they couldn't know for sure. Thus when Sharif was finally released, they didn't know whom to thank: Did Murad pull strings? Did Arin plead with the Minister of Information? They entertained various speculations as they rushed to Al-Jib on the Friday that Sharif was thrown out of a car outside his house.

"A car stopped by, a Subaru," said Hisham's father Marwan. "Two men in civilian clothes dragged him out and left him on his own doorstep. They said nothing. They said nothing when they took him and nothing when they brought him back."

Hisham repeated his belief that someone must have

interceded on Sharif's behalf. Otherwise it was impossible to explain why he was released. "The PA arrested a whole bunch of Hamas activists recently, and none of them have been released. So why him? Someone must have intervened," he repeated with conviction. "It has to be Murad."

"So call him," Hadil suggested. "Call now and see how he reacts."

"That's good news," Murad said laconically, evincing not the slightest hint of involvement in the matter. But he expressed the hope that Sharif would keep his nose clean from now on. It was obvious he didn't want to stay on the phone for long.

Hisham didn't know how to respond. Thank Murad? Say nothing? The call ended with the same cold pleasantries as before.

It was Hadil's first visit to Al-Jib in a long time. Luckily, no one mentioned it as there were more pressing matters. On entering the crowded drawing room of Sharif's house, Hadil and Hisham were immediately aware of the gloom. There was none of the singing or ululation that normally welcomed people returning from jail, hospital, or a long stay abroad. Hadil later commented that it felt like a funeral. Everyone's faces were lined with grief. Sharif's mother whimpered softly while his father stared into space, stunned.

"I always told him," Sharif's mother lamented, "'Don't get involved in politics. My son, leave politics alone. It's trouble. Politics will destroy you, it will destroy your home. You have a family. You have children. What will happen to them if anything happens to you?' He wouldn't listen. 'Islam is the solution,' he said."

Sitting next to her, Siham quietly recited verses from the Quran's Throne Verse, often invoked for protection in times of trouble. Hisham and Hadil walked past her and located Sharif. He was sunk into an armchair in the corner of the room, his gaze empty and distant as if the commotion had nothing to do with him. Hisham carefully approached his brother and offered his greeting: "Welcome back!" Sharif did not respond. He remained still, lost in the chair. Hadil looked at Nadwa, Sharif's wife, for an explanation. Perhaps Sharif had been told about her role in his release and was resentful, Hadil thought. People hate getting favors from people they dislike. But Nadwa put that possibility to rest.

"He's been like this ever since they brought him back," she wailed. "Doesn't move, doesn't do anything. I feed him like a little boy." She started to cry. "*Allahu Akbar, Allahu Akbar.* I wish God pays them back for what they did to him. Damn the people of the Authority!" she yelled. "What are we going to do now? Who's going to feed our children? God will punish them. God is *Al-Muntaqim*, the avenger! Where should I go? Who should I complain to? *Allahu Akbar, Allahu Akbar.*"

"I don't know what to tell you. I don't feel sorry for those extremists," Arij told Hadil on hearing the story. "Especially this man, with all the shit he gave you, I don't think I'd have helped him if I were in your shoes. He doesn't deserve it. By the way," Arij continued as if to suggest that they'd already spent too much time on Sharif, "I heard there's a demonstration in Ramallah tomorrow against the Minister of Education. What's that about?"

Hadil explained. The minister, a Hamas appointee, had ordered the burning of all copies of the book *Uli Ya-Tir*, "Tell Me, Oh Bird", which contained Palestinian fairytales passed down for many generations from grandmothers to mothers to grandchildren. The book was immoral, the minister claimed, with profanities that children shouldn't hear, like shit, ass, son of a whore, and slut.

"The fairytale you mentioned last time, about the Transjordan *G'ula*, is also in the book," Hadil said. "Remember how the father farts with fear when he sees the ogress?"

"Of course I do!" Arij laughed. "It says he farts up a dust cloud."

"Then you understand," Hadil added, "why such words must never appear in Ministry of Education books, especially should our virtuous mothers and grandmothers use them, God forbid. And don't forget that many of the heroes in those stories are women. They're the ones who killed the *G'ula* in the end, not the cowardly father. Like the Minister of Education said," Hadil assumed a mock-official posture: "'These fairytales do not offer even a single role model for Palestinian students to emulate.'"

"So why should you bend over backwards to help these reactionary assholes, like your brother-in-law?!" Arij said.

"It's not about that."

"What's it about then?"

"He's Hisham's brother," Hadil answered, as if stating an obvious and indisputable reason. "He's family."

"Fine. Leave it for now," said Arij. "How are things with Hisham?"

"Well, this thing with Sharif brought us together. It's strange. I never would imagine that Sharif of all people would bring us closer. And like I told you on the phone, I haven't given up yet. I don't think Hisham has, either. But it's not easy."

"I'm really glad to hear it," Arij said with glowing eyes. "Especially since—"

"Yeah, yeah," Hadil completed her friend's sentence, "especially since we sacrificed so much to be together."

Arij ignored the ironic undertone. "Right," she said, "You can't give up. You have to make every effort."

"I'm willing to make efforts, but I'm just not sure what to do. Really!"

"Talk to him."

"We did talk. After I came back from that seminar. Actually he did most of the talking. I felt his frustration - he even mentioned my uncle Kamal."

"What's that got to do with it?"

"Hisham says I'm overcompensating for what Kamal did and that's how I end up neglecting him and the kids. He's got a point, but it still made me so mad when he said it."

"Well, I don't know about Kamal..." said Arij, "but Hisham's right about spending time at home. We talked about it once, you and I. All those conferences, the fundraising trips, the seminars..."

"I can't believe it!" Hadil snapped. "You sound just like him! Taking his side! And what if it was the other way around?"

"What do you mean?"

"What do I mean?!" Hadil retorted furiously. "Would you have said the same thing if he had to travel for work? Or would it be okay because he's a man?" Hadil shook her head. "Every conference I've been to had more men than women. You think their wives tell them to stay home?"

"I supposed some do," Arij shrugged her shoulders. "Personally, I'd like to see more of Bashir. I want him to spend more time with us."

"Yes but you accept it when he's not. And now you expect me to give up. That's what you were going to say."

"I don't know what to say," she uttered in discomfort. "Really, I don't know."

"You've already said it, *habibti*," said Hadil. "You've said plenty."

Yet the conversation stirred up thoughts, thoughts that Hadil had been trying to keep out. If, in the past her frequent trips abroad were indeed due to work. But lately she stayed away from home mainly to avoid Hisham's suffocating company. She looked forward to wandering the streets of distant cities blending into faceless crowds where no one knew her. She craved the pleasure of total anonymity. Letting herself be carried away by aimless strolling, she'd get lightheaded and happy as if she'd had a glass of her favorite red wine.

"I feel like a bird," she once told Arij dreamily, "hovering in the sky, free of the prying eyes of my family, my friends and neighbors, the whole community. When you walk a foreign city, everything's so simple, so open. No barriers, no nothing... I just walk and walk until my feet hurt."

Early morning the next day Arij drove Hadil to Amman's Queen Alia International Airport. The previous night's conversation hung in the air, with both women saying little during the drive. At the airport Hadil thanked Arij, gave her a brief hug, and entered the humming terminal. Although she had slept badly she was quite alert. She pulled out a copy of Amin Maalouf's memoir *Origins* which her sister Ranin recommended.

"You'll love it," Ranin had assured her: "You'll think he's writing about our own family history." But Hadil couldn't focus on the printed page. She waited several hours at Heathrow for her connection to Belfast, strolling aimlessly through the corridors and stopping with dull disinterest in front of grossly overpriced duty-free and name brand stores. Finally she sat down in a café, pulled out her laptop, and checked her email. There was a message from her 'new Israeli acquaintance' as she sardonically described Tali. It had been sent over a week ago before Sharif was abducted. She read the message and shook her head with a sad smile. All men were the same, she thought, no matter if their name was Hisham, Yoav, Bashir, or Sharif. They're always sure they deserve to be center-stage. She wrote Tali a few words of support then pulled out Maalouf's book again and started to read.

It was her first visit to Belfast. Unlike some other places she'd travelled to for work, Northern Ireland, and especially Belfast, deeply intrigued her. She'd heard about the Catholics' abiding solidarity with the Palestinian national struggle and knew of the past cooperation between the PLO and IRA. The UN-sponsored conference she was attending, The Impact of Military

Conflicts on Women and Girls Within the Family, was held at a sprawling estate an hour's drive from the city. It brought together NGOs, researchers, and activists who worked in violence-stricken regions, including Palestinians and Israelis. Aside from the indoor sessions, presentations, discussions, and debates, they were to visit Belfast's mixed Protestant and Catholic neighborhoods for "the opportunity to learn about Northern Ireland's reconciliation efforts".

Once she had arrived, Hadil found a city in a frenzied state of reconstruction and renewal, a ferocious economic and cultural overhaul to transform it into a tourist destination. She couldn't decide if the attempt was as successful as it looked. Had Belfast managed to bury its past? she thought to herself as she walked with other participants through neighborhoods formerly known for protracted, bloody clashes. Were the locals truly on a viable path to interfaith tolerance, solidarity, and prosperity for all? As if to stoke her doubts, she could sense the mutual suspicion and hostility still lingering under the neighborhoods' calm façade. Would these grudges resurface with renewed acrimony, or would they fade into background noise, like they do in peaceful societies? She saw neighborhoods with narrow streets dividing rows of Catholic homes from rows of Protestant homes, where windows still bore the iron grates and steel chains formerly put in place against dangerous projectiles and flying bags of filth, and where high separating walls were being built with renewed vigor, sometimes sprouting straight out of people's backyards.

Then there were Belfast's famous murals, commemorating the long conflict and each side's landmark events, victims, and heroes. Hadil was stunned to discover that Catholics saw themselves as victims of Protestant racism and that they drew comparisons between their own plight and that of blacks in South Africa and the US. One mural boldly read: "It's All About Black and White". Adding to Hadil's bafflement, a cheery group of fair-skinned, blue-eyed boys and girls asked her to take their photo standing in front of it. Handing their camera back to them, she wondered whether they were Catholic, Protestant, or a bit of both. Who was "black" and who was "white"? Color, she concluded, obviously had nothing to do with it.

She brought it up with two of the other participants at dinner. Anne and Vincent were both Catholic, born and raised in Belfast. "Well, it's a bit complicated," Anne told her. "It's not that we really consider ourselves black, more like a race apart from Protestants."

"So why 'black and white'?" Hadil made air quotes.

"Because we're treated in a racist manner," Anne stated emphatically.

"But there are no race differences between you," Hadil insisted.

Vincent, who'd been listening, chipped in. "I don't think racism is only biological. Just think about where you're from. For God's sake, most Muslims, Jews, and Christians look the same, but you've still got racism between all these groups."

One of the murals Hadil had seen featured a Palestinian boy and girl, dark-skinned, holding the key to the house they'd left behind in Palestine. The boy was on his knees, looking over a wall to where Palestine lay in misty night. The local artist, she noticed, depicted Palestine as a dreamy, exotic land of domed roofs and tall minarets. The girl's face was visible. She stared longingly at the key in her hand, which was covered in a glove bearing the colors of the Palestinian flag. Then there was another mural, celebrating the Palestinian struggle with a slogan in Arabic: "Our Day is Coming". Not so soon, Hadil smirked.

As she examined the mural, the tour guide suggested a group photo in front of it. Hadil found herself standing next to Irish, Israeli, Kurdish, Bosnian, and Palestinian delegates, as if they all belonged to the same happy group like the teens she'd photographed. Embarrassed, she wanted to step out of the frame, but it was too late. The camera clicked. Back at the hotel some hours later, she was better able to decipher her uneasiness. The group photo had underscored the disparity between all those pretty pro-Palestinian activities and the kind of work she'd taken part in decades ago at Bir Zeit. The Palestinian cause had degenerated into a relic, a caricature, completely detached from its actual daily reality.

CHAPTER 22
Yoav

Looking at the map, he was surprised to learn that Einat's guesthouse wasn't that far from the army base. "What's the quickest route there?" he asked Matan, his shift partner at the checkpoint. Matan, who lived in a nearby settlement, was glad to assist.

"I live five minutes from the base," he said, "like those pencil-pushers who live in Tel Aviv and serve at General Staff HQ. Now," he continued, smiling slyly, "how do you want to get there?"

"As quickly as possible," Yoav answered.

"Well," Matan kept smiling, "you have two options: either take the Jewish roads or take the Arab ones straight through the enclaves. The Arab roads are quicker."

"Then that's what I'll do," Yoav said. "The guesthouse is right here, beyond these mountains," he continued, pointing to a green ridge in the southwest. "I'll go from here to Bir Nabala, under Route 45, through Al-Jib towards Biddu, past Al-Qubeiba and then to Greb Umm Lahim and through this passage in the fence. The guesthouse is near there."

"That's a perfect route," Matan grinned, "but you can't take it. I was just joking when I said you have two options. You don't. First of all, it's not safe to drive through the Palestinian enclaves. And second, that passage in the fence is closed off for Arabs and Jews. It's unmanned. The army only opens it in emergencies. You'll have to take the Jewish roads: Route 443, past Giv'at Ze'ev and Ramot Alon, continue towards the Jerusalem exit, then right towards Lifta, get on the road to Tel Aviv, take the Hemed Interchange, go past Abu Gosh, and then take a right. You'll see the sign."

"It's crazy, this detour," Yoav said in disbelief.

"I agree," said Matan with a complacent smile. "We need more Jewish settlements, then we wouldn't have to make these detours anymore."

Yoav set out using the Jewish roads. As he approached the guesthouse, he saw Einat waiting for him in the parking lot. Yoav turned off the car, his heart aflutter. He got out and walked towards her with a smile while trying to hide his excitement. Einat looked lovely, her black hair refashioned in a bob-cut that exposed her slender neck, giving her a mature, feminine look that was amplified by a white pearl necklace. Her clothing was still classically understated. She wore a slim, dark-green skirt that ended just above the knee, a light shawl to protect against the night chill of the Jerusalem Mountains, and stylish black tights and booties rounding out the ensemble.

They embraced lightly and exchanged a kiss on the cheek. Einat's freshly showered scent and the airy fragrance on her neck struck Yoav's nostrils, instantly evoking the past. He was subtly aroused. They gently pushed each other away, sizing each other up for possible changes.

"You haven't changed, you look great," he said with genuine astonishment.

"You haven't changed either," Einat replied, "you look good in uniform. Want to go into the lobby?"

"Whatever suits you," he shrugged.

"It's a bit cold out. Then again maybe we should stay here. I don't want to get people talking. I know some of them. Do you want to walk a bit? It'll warm us up. The sun's down already but the scenery around here is amazing."

They followed the narrow, winding path down from the guesthouse. Thanks to the small number of light poles, the star-studded sky was clearly visible. Yoav and Einat brought each other up to date, talking with reserve as if the pair were afraid to display naked longing.

"You know," Einat said, raising her voice as if suddenly thinking it, "I shouldn't have gone back with Assaf after the first time he and I broke up. I thought I loved him… well, I guess I did. But you know how it is: we fall in love with an image. It took me over a year to know the actual person. I'm not saying he's a bad person," she raised her voice again, "just that he wasn't the man I thought he was. We weren't a good match." She had known it all along, she added, though not with the same clarity she had now that they were divorced. That was the reason she broke up with him that first time. But she went back nonetheless. "It was a mistake," she stated firmly.

The old feelings of repressed passion and longing and humiliation swirled together, assaulting him. And still he shared nothing with Einat. He let her go on, laying out the entire chronology of her relationship with Assaf, as if it had nothing to do with them, with him. Einat was careful to keep the two separate, discussing her life with Assaf as if sharing with an old confidant.

"When I told him I wanted a divorce, he begged me to stay," she said. "But my decision was final. He cried like a little kid, just like the first time we broke up."

Listening to her, Yoav was somewhat annoyed. That day in the cafeteria, when Einat broke up with him, came back in vivid detail. The place was thronged with students coming in and out. He knew some of them. He was so deeply hurt that he couldn't speak - he just got up and left with his tail between his legs, like a dog, humiliated, fighting back the tears. Who knows, he brooded listening to her now, maybe he shouldn't have given up so easily.

But what was he to do? Beg? Fall to his knees in front of the whole cafeteria? Yet he knew he was making excuses. He could have called then, asked her to meet, asked her to reconsider. He could have told her how much he loved her, far more than just the sex. He could say that he was willing to do anything. But he did none of it. I was simply afraid of rejection, he admitted to himself. I was proud, worried she'd choose Assaf over me. Unable to resist, Yoav stopped and said: "So, is that the trick?"

"What do you mean?" she stood still, staring at him inquisitively.

"You know, I also should have begged and cried like a little kid?"

"Who knows," Einat replied, herself wondering. Then she resumed her matter-of-fact account, closing the issue as if shutting a window that had burst open to let in a draft. "I was worried," she said, "because I knew that once he stopped begging and crying, he'd be angry over the rejection. Since I didn't change my mind he felt that he humiliated himself for nothing. That's why he dragged out the divorce, to punish me. Like it was all my fault!" She fell silent then spoke again. "My parents didn't support me. They took his side. They asked me what my problem was. Get it? My problem! 'What do you want? Assaf loves you. He adores you! Good father, steady job...' I told them I'm miserable, I don't love him, he bores me, we have nothing in common. They didn't understand. They thought I'm... I don't know, crazy. 'You don't break up a family for that.' And of course, my mom's unforgettable punch line: 'He's from a good family.' Wow! So impressive!" Einat exclaimed.

"What is this, a Jane Austen novel? So what if he's from a good family? Who cares if Zohar, his grandfather, was one of the founders of Tel Aviv. Israeli Mayflower descendants. Big deal! I admit it impressed me in the beginning. His family and all that shit. But what does it mean, I'm upgrading myself by marrying him? I hated how my mom kowtowed to them. His family loved me. Still do. But I always felt like to them I was some piece of exotic jewelry their son was wearing. Yes, yes," she responded to Yoav's baffled look, "they always said how beautiful I am, with my silky olive skin, my lustrous black hair, and my eyes... I was so sick of hearing it."

Einat went quiet again as if to silence the nagging voices of Assaf's family and her own. Then she launched back into her fiery monologue. "My father," she stated proudly, "is very different from my mother. He's got confidence, style. I think it's because his parents are from Egypt. Even today they speak French at home. They weren't happy when he picked a Yemeni woman. They wanted him to marry an Ashkenazi. My mom's beautiful, but she's dark. Darker than you, and way darker than me. God, the things my grandparents on my dad's side said about her... You saw her once at the graduation ceremony, remember?"

"Yeah," sighed Yoav. "She's really beautiful." He seized the gap in conversation to touch on a more delicate matter. "So what's going on nowadays between you and Assaf? Do you get along, or...?"

"We're okay," Einat replied. "I'm in the apartment that we bought together and he rents a few blocks away. We've got a joint custody agreement. He gets three days a week and every other weekend. It's not easy, it takes a lot of planning, but it works out okay. Maayan has two houses and two bedrooms. It's not easy for her. She keeps asking when her daddy will be home. She's going through a rough time. That's why I thought at first maybe I should patch things up with him. My parents guilt-tripped the shit out of me. 'She needs a father!' ...I guess she does. They're very close, and Assaf would do anything for her. I suggested marriage counseling, but he was dead set against it. He 'doesn't believe in psychology'," Einat snorted. "As if I wanted him to join a cult or some vipassana retreat. I just couldn't take it anymore. You know," she mused, "Maayan's the best thing to come out of that relationship. She'll be four soon. She makes me really happy. She's a great kid. Smart and beautiful."

"Like her mom," Yoav said.

Einat smiled, flattered. She stopped and gazed at Yoav, her hand fluttering on him. "It feels different between us," she said softly. She used to touch his arm or knee like that whenever they sat in a café on campus. He noticed that she was the same with other people, breaking down barriers and creating intimacy: naturally, spontaneously, not with any sexual intent. "Remember?" she continued. "We'd talk for hours. We never got bored." She touched his arm again.

"Yes, I remember," Yoav said laconically, wondering if her gestures carried any added meaning.

"What about you?" she smiled, examining his face. "Are you going away with Tali?"

He didn't answer right away. He chose his words carefully. "You know how it is. Things are becoming more complicated than we thought. I don't know if we can work things out. I mean, our plan to study abroad together." Later that night, on his way back to the base, Yoav felt pangs of guilt about this reply. It had obviously been designed to leave the door open. But open for what? What he was thinking? It wasn't just the hope of sex with Einat, which he certainly wanted. There was more than that.

As they walked side by side, both silently consumed by their own thoughts, he suddenly gripped her hand. Einat returned the grip. Her touch stirred him, igniting a powerful yearning for her. He knew it was all in his hands now. They strolled on for a while like that, holding hands. Then he stopped, turned to her, cupped her face, and kissed her full on the lips. Einat reciprocated immediately, clinging to his chest and holding his waist tightly. He wrapped his arms around her, and for a while they stood still on the mountain path near the guesthouse.

"I'm cold, let's go inside," Einat shuddered, taking him by the hand.

"I missed you," she gasped as they entered her room. "I missed you too," he whispered breathlessly, kissing her. They ripped each other's clothes off. This was not the time for the patient, drawn-out lovemaking of yesteryear. Soon Yoav was on top of her, muttering her name over and over, gripping her body tightly as if to prevent her from moving, as if to bring her under his total domination. Then he looked deep into her eyes and exploded inside her with passion, endless passion, the kind of passion he'd experienced only with her. But this time, the passion was mired with rage.

"That was wild," she said matter-of-factly.

"Yes," he replied, unsure if she had expressed satisfaction or a complaint. He lay on his back next to her, panting. He lifted her head gently and nestled it in the crook of his shoulder.

"Would you come to the United States with me?" he said, staring at the ceiling.

"I wish I could," she said ruefully. "Assaf would never let me take Maayan away, not even for a month. If you decided to stay in Israel, though…" she added hesitantly, "it might be a different story."

"Yes, I know," Yoav sighed heavily. "I know."

They lay like this for a long while, until Yoav began to move his legs and shift his shoulder under Einat's head, as if trying for a more comfortable position. Noticing his disquiet, she said dejectedly, "Well, I guess you need to go."

"Yes, I need to go," he said faintly, complying with the inevitable. He pulled himself out of bed slowly, trying not to disturb anything, and began to put on his uniform with measured, almost furtive movements, while Einat, lying on her side under the white blanket, followed him silently with her eyes. He leaned over, kissed her lightly on her lips and assured her: "I'll call you when my reserve service is finished." He left the room, got into his car, and drove slowly away from the guesthouse, hearing the engine's monotonous hum with strange clarity. He replayed the past two hours over and over, as if trying to piece together a puzzling dream. He turned over various future scenarios in his mind. A ring sounded from his pants pocket. Assuming it was Einat, he quickly pulled the phone out, but it was Tali's name on the screen. He paused before taking the call.

"Hi Tali, what's up?" he asked, trying to sound normal, the blood pounding in his neck. He hoped his voice didn't betray what had just happened.

"I've got news!" Tali declared.

"Good or bad?"

"Both. I got accepted to NYU and Columbia, with scholarships and everything!"

"Wow!" Yoav exclaimed with admiration. "*Yesh*, Great! You're a genius! Wow! That's wonderful!"

"Hold your horses," she responded coldly, and after a brief pause, announced: "You got a rejection from NYU."

"I expected that," he said resignedly. "I'm not critical enough for them, not radical enough. You'll see, I'll get a rejection from Columbia, too. Same reason. Professor Na'aman already told me the chances with them are slim. But at least I tried —"

"So does that leave us in the same place?" She cut him off, voicing her repressed anguish.

"What do you mean?"

"You know what I mean!"

Yoav was moved by the agony in her voice. Or perhaps it was the guilt of what he had just done that made him want to protect Tali, dispel her worries, reassure her. "You're right, you're right," he said with great sincerity, "but don't you worry. I promise you, Tali, everything's going to work out fine, you'll see. No matter what," he fervently restated his commitment, "we are going to live in the same city, whether it's Philadelphia or Boston. I promise." Wishing Tali a good night and pledging his love one more time, he hung up and angrily flung the phone to the seat next to him. He emitted a long and quiet sigh, and scolded himself: "Why did I do it? What did I need that for?"

CHAPTER 23
Hisham

Over half an hour had passed since the soldiers stopped all traffic at the Bir Nabala checkpoint, and there was no sign of reopening anytime soon. Hisham was coming back from a visit to Al-Jib with Leila and Nadim. In front of them was only one car, but behind them was a column stretching back as far as the eye could see. "If only we'd left a few minutes earlier," Hisham moaned.

This time he took his children along with him, responding to his parents' repeated pleas. "And you should visit your brother Sharif," they entreated. "Maybe you can make him talk." He tried. He sat next to Sharif, trying in vain to coax a word or two out of him. Whatever Sharif's ordeal had been, he clearly had not recovered from it. He kept staring at the people who came and went like they were strangers. "He just gapes at us," his wife Nadwa wept. The exact circumstances of his abduction and release remained unknown.

Hisham wanted to know how the family was doing financially. Nadwa informed him that a Hamas representative had stopped by, given her some money, and assured her that the movement would provide them with a monthly allowance. Hisham added a handsome sum of his own then headed to his parents' house to pick up Leila and Nadim. Wishing to spare them the harrowing sight of their uncle, he'd left them with his sister Afaf's children.

Afaf had four kids, including Sharin, who was the same age as Leila, and twin boys, Khalid and Walid, who were Nadim's age. Hisham's children derived little joy from spending time with their cousins and had recently shown less and less enthusiasm about visiting Al-Jib with him. He could tell that despite Leila's efforts, there was a growing chasm between her and her paternal cousins, especially Sharif's children. Nadim was still too young to notice the cultural gap but it was clear that Leila knew. The superior education she received at Friends, her command of the English language, her dress style, and her taste in music all set her apart from her contemporaries in Al-Jib, especially those brought up as devout Muslims. Hisham noticed the awe she inspired in her cousins - the same awe he had felt when he first met Hadil at Bir Zeit. It was this difference in upbringing and cultural capital that still had lingering effects on their marriage. Nor had the cultural disparity between the children escaped Sharif, who had blasted "the corrupt and promiscuous education" given to Leila and Nadim by their parents, especially their mother.

The soldiers didn't bother explaining why they'd stopped traffic, deigning only to say that they had their orders. Perhaps they truly don't know. Hisham was willing to entertain the notion on their behalf but he still checked his watch anxiously. There were still a few hours before his rendezvous with Mandy but who knew how long the delay would last? He still wanted to see her, though his enthusiasm had waned since first suggesting it to her, before Sharif's abduction and Hadil's courageous display of loyalty. Hadil was beset with a sense of guilt, yet he couldn't bring himself to cancel the date. He decided to keep it without a clear purpose in mind – which, he later admitted to himself, was willful evasiveness on his part.

The soldiers manning the checkpoint were the same ones who were there a few days ago when he and Nabil went from Al-Jib to Ramallah. There was the soldier who harassed them as well as the older one. Hisham smiled, recalling Nabil's reaction when he described the older as decent: "Let's invite him to the Mukata'a so Abu Mazen can give him a medal of honor." The amusing reverie didn't last long. He once again saw the young soldier harassing the Palestinian drivers, responding to their pleas with jerks of his hand and rude barks to stay in their cars. Suddenly Hisham heard the same soldier humming along to an Umm Kulthum song that was wafting from one of the Palestinian cars.

"Sing to me softly," the soldier intoned in perfectly acceptable Arabic, "sing to me and capture my eyes." Life brings surprises, Hisham thought. The soldier's parents must be descended from an Arab country. Oh, how wonderfully language and culture bridge people, he thought ironically. He recalled a concert he once attended with Hadil in West Jerusalem.

Dedicated to the rich musical legacy of Umm Kulthum, the event had taken place several months before the outbreak of the second Intifada, when movement between Ramallah and Jewish Jerusalem was still tolerable. It featured three singers: two Jews and an Arab. At first Hadil didn't want to go, saying she didn't want to saddle her parents and sister again with babysitting Leila. The rift between Hadil and Hisham was still in its early, innocuous stages, but already she'd told him she had no wish to "engage in nostalgia and listen to some outdated music." This exchange followed their first serious marriage crisis. After Leila and before Nadim, Hadil had had a second-trimester miscarriage. Hisham couldn't resist suggesting, in so many words, that perhaps the miscarriage had resulted from Hadil's unwillingness to work less. She was furious.

"Instead of supporting me," she lashed at him, "instead of standing by me, you accuse me of losing the baby? What do you want? Do you expect me to stay at home, be your good little housewife?!" Hisham had then insinuated that Hadil's devotion to work might have something to do with her uncle's Kamal's infamous legacy. "I never asked you to stay at home," he defended himself, "I just said you have to slow down. You don't have to make a sacrifice for the Palestinian cause." Hadil suggested that Hisham take a friend to the concert, or perhaps his cousin Nabil. But finally she agreed to go.

Sitting next to them at the concert was an elderly Jewish couple who spoke to each other in Arabic. Their body language was stiff and they avoided turning their heads in Hadil and Hisham's direction. But during intermission Hadil took the initiative and introduced herself to the woman. The woman had a distinctly Arab name: Aziza. Initially reluctant to engage in small talk with Hadil, she gradually warmed up. She asked for Hadil's name, place of residence, occupation, and more. Hadil introduced her husband, expecting Aziza to do so as well. But she didn't, merely mentioning his name later – Anwar – when discussing his love for Arabic music.

Aziza had arrived in Israel from Iraq in the early 1950s with her husband and two young children. "We were taken straight to Jerusalem," told Hadil. "Since then they had had four more children. At home they listened to Arabic music, she said, mainly Iraqi and Egyptian. There was a time, she admitted, when they hardly ever listened to this music with their children still living at home. "You know," she told Hadil, "because they were ashamed." But now the children were all married with families of their own, leaving Aziza and Anwar to enjoy the music of their youth. She mentioned Nazem al-Ghazali as one of their favorite singers.

"I don't know if you know him, but my husband," she nodded in Anwar's direction, "adores him. Al-Ghazali was a wonderful singer, but he's before your time."

"Sure, we know Nazem al-Ghazali!" Hadil said enthusiastically. "My husband is also a great fan of his.

There isn't an al-Ghazali song he doesn't know. He has a whole library of al-Ghazali CDs."

"Did you hear, Anwar?" Aziza elbowed her husband in the ribs. "They know Nazem al-Ghazali." The man's stern countenance showed not the slightest ripple. He kept his gaze fixed on the crimson velvet stage curtain. He nodded slightly as if wholly unimpressed with the information. His response embarrassed his wife, and she pointed at him and said with an air of incredulity: "He's crazy about Umm Kulthum. I came because of him. I don't like her songs. They last forever and she repeats the same lyrics over and over." Aziza was anything but indifferent when the music came on however, enthusiastically clapping and singing along with the rest of the audience.

"To be honest," Hisham declared on the way back to Ramallah, "I was surprised to see all those people. I don't know what I expected. I didn't really think about it. Hard to believe. For a moment I thought I was in Jarash or the Citadel of Damascus... And this old couple next to us, until they spoke in their Iraqi dialect, I thought they were Arab. Then I hear her saying to him, *Ayouni, makoo m'kan*, My eyes, there's no room.' To this Stone Age Saddam Hussein, with that ancient suit and tie of his and that groomed mustache."

Hadil smiled and added: "Did you see how he reacted when his wife told him we know al-Ghazali? Sphinx. Nothing."

"Well, I don't know," Hisham said dryly, spoiling the levity, "everyone has hang-ups." He noticed a twitch in the corner of Hadil's mouth when she realized the comment was meant for her.

"You'd think an event like this would give hope," she sighed, casually ignoring the trap Hisham had laid. But he persisted.

"And then you see it's meaningless. It's a waste of time to try and promote coexistence through culture. 'A bridge to peace'," he smirked. "The Jews, especially those from

Arab countries, love our music, but still want to throw us into the sea."

"Maybe you're right," Hadil said. But then she asked if he enjoyed the concert.

"More or less," he replied. "It's hard to fill Umm Kulthum's shoes. Those who dare usually go at it with holy dread. But the singers were fairly successful. Did you see how excited the crowd was?" He went on to say that the song performed by the Jewish singer – Sing To Me Softly – wasn't just another Umm Kulthum song. There was a rendition of it from 1945 where Umm Kulthum juggles with her voice. "No one can replicate it," Hisham smiled admiringly. "It's full of improvisation. It's Umm Kulthum at her peak. To be honest," he nodded, "what you're hearing is a narcissistic artist who knows her worth." The song's lyricist, Zakaria Ahmed, Hisham continued sharing his knowledge, had composed it especially for her, to let her flaunt her talent.

"Listen to the lyrics," Hisham told Hadil and began to recite slowly, excitedly: "'I swear in the name of the master that I'll charm you with my singing. My song will have all the neighborhood girls dancing on the floor... Let me sing, sing, sing, and show my art to all.'" Hisham did not notice that Hadil was losing interest. "It's unbridled vanity," he continued passionately. "But she still manages to sweep you along into tarab, ecstasy. She's a giant of the art form. A true diva. If you compare her old rendition of the song..." He glanced at Hadil and realized she was no longer listening. Hurt, he said nothing. It wasn't the first time she'd lost interest in what he held dear. There would be many more.

Tensions at the checkpoint were running high. Several drivers had gathered around the checkpoint to vent their frustration at the soldiers. The young soldier kept yelling at them to stay in their cars. "There's no instructions," he kept repeating in Hebrew. One of the drivers, a young

Palestinian man in a fashionable jacket and tie, lashed at him angrily in English. Hisham got out to see what the commotion was.

"You're the animals, not us!" the young Palestinian yelled. "Shame on you for talking to us like that!" The older soldier went over to the angry Palestinian and tried to calm him with a gentle hand on the shoulder, but the man shook it off. "Don't touch me!" he exclaimed. "We can't take it anymore! Categories and classifications! Categories and classifications!" he fumed. "If you live here, you can go through. if you live there, you can't. if you come on Monday you can go through, if you come on Tuesday you can't. You need this kind of identity card and not that one. Categories and classifications! And now we're animals?!"

"He didn't say animals," the older soldier tried to explain the misunderstanding in English. "He said *ein horaot*. It means 'no instructions'. He didn't say *hayot*, 'animals'. I assure you." He then repeated the Arabic equivalent for 'there are no instructions' – *makoo awamer* – and promised the gate would open once instructions came down. The storm abated and moments later instructions indeed came. Hisham now sped through the checkpoint towards Ramallah. He checked his watch again - still on time.

"Did you see?" he told Leila. "The soldier calming everyone down was an Iraqi soldier."

Leila looked at him incredulously. "An Iraqi soldier?"

"Yes! Only Iraqis use *makoo* to say 'there isn't'."

"*Baba*, you're kidding me, right? An Iraqi soldier?"

Hisham went on to explain. When she understood that it wasn't a real Iraqi soldier, "an Iraqi-Iraqi", but merely a Jewish soldier with parents from Iraq, Leila lost interest. Hisham thought about the history of *makoo*, which had cropped up quite a bit for him over the years. The soldier had used the same word as the old Iraqi-Jewish couple years ago at the Umm Kulthum concert and many decades before that, Fawzi al-Qawuqji, commander of the Arab Liberation Army, had used the very same phrase as the Israeli soldier – *makoo awamer*, there are no instructions – in declining to help Abd al-Qadir al-Husayni fight against the Zionists in Jerusalem.

CHAPTER 24
Tali

It was early morning when Tali sat down at the computer for her usual routine – checking her email and then Yoav's. The admissions from NYU and Boston University had eased some of her stress, but she still didn't know how things were going to turn out with Yoav. She shared her concern with Liat, whom she met with more often these days. Tali was glad that Liat didn't shoot down her confidence in Yoav's commitment. On the contrary, Liat was sympathetic, even reassuring, telling Tali that she believed Yoav would keep his word. "You'll end up together in the US without you having to make concessions. Yoav loves you. He'd never give up on you. I mean, who would?!"

She spoke with Yoav regularly on the phone but they'd grown somewhat distant in recent days. She noticed a message from Hadil in her inbox. Hadil wrote that she was on her way to Belfast for a conference, "another one of those things that lead nowhere." She also sought to assuage Tali's fears.

"I'm sure that in the end everything will turn out for the best," she wrote. "But that's how it is with men. They always think their careers are more important than their women and that we should follow them wherever they choose to go. And when they 'allow' us to grow and develop they think they've done something extraordinary and heroic. I have firsthand experience with this. They feel like they've made a great sacrifice and you should thank them for the rest of your life. So, don't give up. If he really loves you he'll be willing to make compromises too. Good luck. Hadil."

The intimacy and encouragement of Hadil's email pleased her. It was clear Hadil bore no grudge from what happened in the seminar. Tali checked Yoav's inbox. There were no new messages from any of the universities, but there was one from Einat. Tali stared at it, unsure whether to read it. She left Yoav's email and surfed the Web halfheartedly. Then she reopened Yoav's inbox and read the message. It was short: "Hi Yoavi, I'd love to see you again before you disappear on me. Einat."

Tali read it over and over. Yoav hadn't mentioned a meeting with Einat. Apparently he'd forgotten to tell her about it. Tali chose to believe that there must be a good explanation and let it go. She returned to her own inbox and wrote a reply to Hadil: "Dear Hadil, thank you for your encouragement and support. I really hope things will work out. But as you know sometimes love is not enough. Anyway I'd love to keep in touch and really hope we can meet again in the future. I hope you enjoy the conference in Belfast even if it doesn't lead anywhere. Tali."

The phone rang. It was Tali's father, wanting to know "where things stood" with the applications. As soon as she was done updating him with the new developments – omitting her lingering concerns – he revealed his true reason for calling.

"You'll be going away soon," he said. "We'll miss you but the US isn't as far as it used to be. You'll come visit, we'll come visit you. But it's different with Grandma Bracha-Bianca. I was thinking... Mom and I are going to visit her next weekend. How'd you like to join us? You haven't been to see her for a while and she misses you terribly. She's always asking about you."

"Mom already told me," Tali said, not agreeing yet.

"Yoav's still doing his reserve service," her father persisted, "and you don't have anything major planned before you leave. Talush, people don't live forever, you know. After you go to the US, who knows if you'll get to see her again?"

"Okay, Dad," Tali said, "I'll go with you."

"Good, good," he said, before immediately hanging up.

Following the death of Pavel-Efraim, his three sons and daughter were at pains to find the best arrangement for Bracha-Bianca. They decided she couldn't stay in the same house. Initially she resisted, saying she wished to die in the house where she'd spent most of her life. "This is your father's house," she lamented in Romanian. "It's where all of you grew up. I don't want to move to a new place." Micha considered moving her in with his family but Rina was dead set against it.

"I'm sorry, but why should we take her on?" she protested. "Your brothers and your sister have big houses. Why shouldn't they make room? Or put her in a nursing home. Why not? I have no problem with us paying our share." Micha rejected the idea out of hand. "It would kill her!" he protested. Finally a compromise was hammered out: they would sell Bracha-Bianca's house and buy her a small apartment near Micha's family. Bracha-Bianca grudgingly agreed.

She used to visit her children's houses by turns on Saturday and holiday eves. Money was not an issue so all her needs were taken care of. Micha and Rina did weekly supermarket shopping for her so she could continue to cook, and occasionally she was spared the effort when Rina sent over plastic boxes full of her own food. It was Tali's job to deliver them two, even three times a week. She and her grandmother didn't speak much during those visits - Bracha-Bianca's poor command of Hebrew and Tali's limited Romanian precluded real conversation. Their exchanges moved in circles, covering the same questions over and over. "How are you today, Grandma? How do you feel? Do you need me to bring you anything? Did you take your medication?" Bracha-Bianca would rejoin with her own mantras: "How's your father? How's your mother? How's school? You study good?" Yet their emotional bond was real. "We felt each other," Tali often recalled.

Bracha-Bianca took a special interest in Tali's love life. On one of Tali's visits, about a month after she got back from the US, Bracha-Bianca brought up the perennial "boyfriend" issue.

"No, Grandma, I don't have boyfriend," Tali smiled.

"Why no friend, *copilă mea*, my child?" Bracha-Bianca protested. "*Tu esti foarte frumoasa*, you're very beautiful!" Tali stared at her grandmother for a long moment and then suddenly burst into bitter tears.

"Bunica, grandma, it wasn't good in America," she sobbed. "It wasn't good in America." She was neither willing nor able to elaborate but it was nevertheless a way of sharing the dreadful experience with someone close. Those few words – "it wasn't good in America" - constituted the only account she ever gave of it.

"*Ce, ce s-a întâmplat, copilă mea, draga mea?* What happened, my child, my dear?" Bracha-Bianca said tenderly. "*Vino aici*, come here." She took Tali into her arms and stroked her head. "*Shhh, copilă mea, shhh…* Gata, *Gata, enough, nu plânge, mama*, don't cry." Releasing Tali from her embrace after a long while, Bracha-Bianca raised her finger and declared: "Nobody love I like you."

"Grandma, what do you mean?" Tali smiled though her tears. "You mean nobody loves you…" she pointed to her grandmother, "like I do?" Then she pointed to herself. "Or that no one loves me… like you do?"

"Da, da, nobody love I like you," Bracha-Bianca repeated. "*Tu Înțelegi*, you understand? Nobody here for long time like you."

"I understand," Tali smiled warmly. "Grandma, you're the most *dolce bunica* in the world, the sweetest grandmother."

Tali used to warm up the food her mother had sent, serve it to Bracha-Bianca, and watch her as she ate, closely studying her wrinkled face and shriveled hands. Then Tali would clear the dishes, wash them, and make some tea, served with a slice of Rina's apple strudel, which Bracha-Bianca loved. Watching her enjoy the strudel, Tali thought sadly that she knew so little about her: about Bracha-Bianca's childhood in Romania, her life, how she thought and felt about things. We never had a real conversation, Tali thought, and we never will. She used to know more about the soldiers in her care when she was in the army than she knew about her own grandmother. Preposterous. The visits always ended with the same entreaties: "When you come visit me again, *copilă mea*? I want you come see me more."

"I'll come, Grandma," Tali would promise. "I'll come."

She pushed Bracha-Bianca out of her thoughts, and returned with growing consternation to Einat's email to Yoav. She read it over and over. It was disturbingly intimate; doubts began to set in her mind. Tali recalled the time when she and Yoav lay naked in bed, and she asked him if he preferred smaller breasts. Releasing a mumbled growl and caressing her breasts with theatrical lust, he replied that he loved breasts just like hers, big. "I especially like your areolas. Like big brown halos around a comet. You're my comet."

"Pervert," she giggled then asked in a serious tone: "Tell me, do you think I need to lose weight?"

"No!" Yoav said emphatically. "I like you just the way you are!"

"Still, if you had to describe me, what would you say?"

Yoav grabbed her waist, buried his mouth in the crook of her neck, and purred: "Real juicy!"

Tali pushed him gently away. "What did you say?"

"Juicy… what's the problem?"

"I thought you said *kussit*," she said, disgusted at this obscenity commonly used to describe attractive women through an explicit vaginal reference.

"No, I said juicy. But what's the problem?"

"I don't like that word."

"Which one, *kussit* or juicy?"

"The first one. But I don't like juicy either. I think you used it instead of saying chubby or fat."

"Not true. You're not chubby or fat. You're juicy, sexy." He paused, then asked casually: "Why does *kussit* put you off?"

"I don't know, I just don't like it," Tali shrugged. She noticed he was slightly annoyed. "What's wrong?".

Yoav paused then opened up about how dirty words turned him on. He told Tali that he was surprised to learn this about himself when he was with one of his old girlfriends. "She'd talk dirty, and I got aroused. Very aroused," he emphasized, nodding his head as if by way of apology.

Tali tensed. She wondered if the girlfriend in question was Einat. She felt a wave of jealousy tingling up her spine. She couldn't resist imagining Yoav and Einat's naked bodies in a passionate tangle, Einat whispering lewd words into Yoav's ear. Tali tried unsuccessfully to push the image away.

"Was it Einat?…" she asked gingerly, hoping he would deny it.

"No, someone else," he said, trying to downplay the matter. "You don't know her. It was a long time ago."

But Tali wasn't mollified. "So who?" she insisted angrily.

"What difference does it make?" Yoav said, annoyed. "The important thing is that you turn me on all the time without those words."

Tali stared at him closely. "The same way she turned you on?"

"Tali, really, enough."

Her last talk with Yoav, her jealousy towards Einat, and doubts about the future all joined to dredge up her memory of her father in a compromising situation. That incident went on to overshadow their relationship, though in time Micha grew confident that Tali wouldn't tell her mother.

Tali was in the eleventh grade then. It was spring and she was visiting Haifa's Carmel center with some of her Scout friends. She couldn't remember why they had the day off from school. She and Liat needed to use the toilet so they went into a café. Suddenly, there was Tali's father, sitting at a table with a young woman of about thirty. Tali thoughtlessly walked over with a smile. "Hi Dad!" she waved. Only then did she notice that Micha was leaning towards the woman with his hand over hers. He turned to Tali with obvious fright, retreating abruptly from the woman as if snake-bit.

"Hey! What a surprise!" he feigned a jovial smile. "What are you doing here? No school today?" he asked, trying to hide his distress. Not waiting for an answer, he went on to introduce the woman, as if it was nothing unusual. "This is Moria," he pointed to the woman. "She works with me in the bank." He pointed to Tali and then introduced her to the woman: "This is my daughter, Tali, and her friend Liat." Awkward silence ensued. "Did you have lunch?" he asked, trying to ease the tension. "Come, sit with us. Grab a bite."

"I can't," Tali shrank. "We're here with friends."

"Are you sure? Your friends will wait for you," Micha insisted, though less adamantly.

"No, I've got to run," Tali murmured and hurried out of the café.

"Bye," Micha called out, and the women added: "Nice to meet you."

"She's hot," Liat commented when they left. Tali was too agitated to answer. She was home when her father returned from work in the late afternoon. Her mother was in the living room, marking papers. Micha went over to Rina and kissed her on the cheek with great intent. "How was your day?" he asked casually.

"Okay, nothing special," Rina shrugged, and continued marking papers.

Tali stood like a coiled spring between the living room and the kitchen. She and her father exchanged a glance. "Did you tell Mom we ran into each other today?" he asked casually yet bracing himself.

"No, I didn't tell her anything," Tali replied, shrugging her shoulders in dismay.

"I was having lunch with a coworker in the Carmel center," he announced, "when out of the blue, in walks Tali with her friend."

"Good for you," Rina replied, half-listening.

Tali's mouth twitched into a derisive, barely-perceptible smile. She could tell her father noticed. But the incident never came up again, and the secret they shared formed a schism that only they knew about. Whenever Micha showed affection towards Rina, caressing her arms or praising her to others, Tali and her father would exchange glances, and he would shift uneasily at the same wry smile.

"Do you think he's cheating on her?" Yoav asked when Tali told him about it.

"I don't think he is now. They seem to be getting along well. But I'm sure he did in the past. At the time I couldn't see it, or maybe I didn't want to admit it. But now it's clear he was having an affair with that woman. Moria! Yes, Moria. I can still remember the name. Unbelievable. I was angry with him for years. Not only because he cheated on my mom, which is bad enough in itself, but also because he forced me to lie for him. I felt like I was lying to her too. But I thought I had to, to keep the family from breaking up. I was just a teenager."

"Did you ever feel like telling her?"

"No!" Tali cried out, terrified at the mere suggestion.

"So why are you telling me now?"

"You're not my mother," Tali shrugged. "And I trust you."

CHAPTER 25
Hadil

The session she'd been assigned to took place on the second day of the conference. Hadil shared it with three other speakers from Sudan, Kosovo, and Afghanistan. There were also attendees from Sri Lanka, Angola, Lebanon, Iraq, Israel, and other conflict-ridden countries. Hadil exchanged a few words with the Israeli delegate but ignored her further friendly overtures. The memory of the seminar in Jordan in addition to the thought of having to grit her teeth through another weepy we're-all-victims speech was enough to cool Hadil entirely towards the woman. Then there was the memory of Tali leaping from her chair when news of the checkpoint incident came in. Yet for whatever reason Hadil had grown to like Tali. Perhaps it was Tali's visceral fear for her man's life or her all-too-familiar relationship troubles. Like Hadil, she had to negotiate between career and personal life, between inner truth and human connection.

But Hadil had other reservations about the conference too. Previously she had more than once found herself unable to articulate what the conflict looked like from the more marginalized Palestinian side without causing her listeners to draw false conclusions and see Palestine in a bad light. She wanted them to know about the dreadful effects of the conflict on families who lost loved ones;

about the hidden anxieties plaguing tough men; about children who suffered from chronic nightmares and bedwetting; about the suppressed aspects of a national struggle that sought to portray Palestinians as valiant freedom fighters, all rallying to the cry of "In spirit and blood we'll redeem you, Palestine!"

Hadil began her talk by discussing the widespread domestic violence in Palestinian society, opening with a quote from Mahmoud Darwish: "We store our sorrows in our jars... Tomorrow, when the place heals, we'll feel its side effects." She related the main findings of the UN report that she'd helped prepare. Domestic violence in Palestinian society, Hadil noted, had intensified due to the closures, encroachments, and restrictions of movement between Palestinian cities and villages following the second Intifada. To illustrate, she gave the story of a girl named Waffa.

Waffa – a pseudonym – grew up in a village near Ramallah. She was only fourteen when, due to desperate financial straits, her parents married her off to a boy who was not yet seventeen. They wanted to marry off her sisters first, but the boy, enthralled by Waffa's beauty, wanted her and none other. The wedding was modest. Not only did the restrictions imposed by the IDF prevent relatives from remote villages returning home before curfew, but an ostentatious display would have been insensitive towards the many families with members in Israeli detention – or worse, members who died in the struggle. This shift in norms, Hadil explained, had begun even before the second Intifada in 2000, but certainly took root following it.

Hadil's own wedding had also been less than grand, albeit for different reasons. Before the ceremonial drive to Hisham's parents' house, while Arij and her paternal aunt Maram fussed over her wedding dress, Hadil burst into tears. Just as her mother had warned, Hadil's extended

family had boycotted the wedding. With the exception of
Maram, they had all severed ties with Hadil at her mother's
behest. "We had a daughter named Hadil who died," she
would say. Although less extreme in their reaction,
Hisham's parents weren't pleased with the marriage either.
From the little that Hisham had shared with her Hadil
knew they were deeply disappointed. They'd expected him
to marry a Muslim girl.

"Take the mud from your native land and smear it on
your cheeks," Hisham's mother used to say, emphasizing
the traditional preference for marrying within one's
extended family or social milieu. "That's how you avoid
problems later on.". They were forced to bow to his
decision but Hisham's parents demanded that the
ceremony be held according to their tradition. At first he
objected, worried that it might hurt Hadil's feelings but
eventually he agreed, especially when she herself pleaded
with him to placate his parents.

"My love," she entreated, "I see no reason why not.
You've already let them down by marrying a non-Muslim,
don't take away their traditional wedding too. Plus if we
don't have a Muslim wedding, I'm worried they might
think it's because of me."

Inevitably some of the wedding rituals traditionally
carried out by the bride's family were conspicuously
absent. Hadil's aunts and female cousins weren't there to
prepare the decorative wedding henna. Nor was there the
custom of *ta'alil*, where the male or female friends of the
bride and groom respectively entertain each of them for a
whole week in their separate houses, singing and dancing
deep into the night. Putting the finishing touches on
Hadil's wedding dress, Arij and Aunt Maram
unconvincingly dismissed her crying as wedding-day
jitters. But as they got into the car that was to take them
to Hisham's parents' house she broke out sobbing again.
This was not how she'd imagined her *tl'at al-arus*, the
bride's farewell procession. Instead of a boisterous

entourage of extended family and friends singing and dancing her to the groom's parents' house, she had to make do with Arij and Maram, who quietly hummed a traditional henna song:

A fawn lowered his eyes / and reached its hoof / thus with henna to be dyed. / Why did his parents allow it? / Oh, my mother, oh my mother, my pillow do tie. / Oh, my father, stop walking, I haven't yet my friends bid farewell. / Oh, my mother, oh my mother, my bed's pillows do tie. / Oh, my father, stop walking, I haven't yet my sisters bid farewell. / Oh, my mother, oh, my mother, my hair do braid. / Oh, my father, stop walking, I haven't yet my youth bid farewell.

"I'm sad," Hadil admitted, trying in vain to stop crying. "I know it's stupid, but I feel like I'm some street urchin, an orphan bride."

The wedding ceremony at Hisham's parents' house was short and to-the-point. The day before, the couple had signed the dowry agreement in front of a Muslim qadi. At the time Hadil teased Hisham: "Now you'll have to think twice before deciding to divorce me, unless you want to hand over your sheep herd and olive grove." Hisham looked at her tenderly and whispered, "I have no such intention, my dear." Hadil tilted her head with a grin. "No intention to hand them over?" she asked mischievously. Hisham smiled broadly. "By God," he sighed affectionately, "you're trouble."

As per tradition, they crossed the threshold to Hisham's parents' house, sipped water together from an earthen jug, and smashed it to ward off the evil eye. A local clergyman, one of the village dignitaries, read *al-Fatiha*, the first surah of the Quran, and then made a short speech. He turned to Hadil and told her she was tying her destiny to one of the most respected and well-established families whose historical roots in the village ran deep. Informed in advance about the absence of Hadil's family, he skirted this sore point and instead spoke in praise of the groom, mentioning his longstanding schooldays nickname of "the Al-Jib poet". He concluded with wishes of happiness and fertility. Finally Hadil and Hisham placed the wedding rings on each other's fingers – a break with tradition that they had both decided on.

Though humble, the wedding festivities continued into the small hours. The men danced the *sja'a* and *dabke* in the open space next to Hisham's parents' house. Nabil, Hisham's cousin, served as *shawash*, head dancer, firing up the other men as he waved a handkerchief over his head and occasionally broke into solo performances. The women watched and cheered the men on with ululations.

A few days after the wedding at Al-Jib, they had a Christian ceremony. Hadil wanted to hold it at the Greek Orthodox church in Ramallah where she and her family always went.

"My daughter," the priest informed her in no uncertain terms, "the church does not hold marriage ceremonies if one of the spouses hasn't been baptized into the faith. He needs to convert to Christianity first, and this does not happen overnight. The man must prove that he is sincere." He regretfully refused her. "It's not for nothing that we're called the Blue Bone," he declared. "We don't compromise on matters like these."

Hadil had to settle for the more tolerant Anglican church who embraced any Christian who sought to worship God, regardless of sectarian affiliation. The priest wasn't happy to perform the ceremony but he agreed to do it. "Nowadays," he said mournfully, "there are many religious sects but little religious spirit. So many religions and so little religiosity. You should know," he added, "that the Greek Orthodox church recognizes the Anglican ordination, so if you ever want to baptize your children in our church, you won't have a problem." The couple dressed casually for the ceremony, drawing the priest's ire

– especially Hisham, who had borrowed a jacket from a friend at the last moment - and afterwards they went with a few close friends to a restaurant.

As promised, Hadil was under a sweeping boycott from her family. It lasted almost two years. She never accepted it as a done deal, hoping that sooner or later her mother would come around, doing what she could to bring rapprochement. She maintained her Greek Orthodox affiliation, but rather than embarrass her family by attending their longstanding church, the Church of Transfiguration, she went to the Greek Orthodox Church of St. George near the village of Bir Zeit. Then whenever she was around Hisham's family, she would remove the cross necklace she'd had around her neck ever since graduating from Friends. Hadil's mother had given it to her. "To remind you of who you are," she had said.

Rather than sit idly by, Hadil used Maram to relay news to her family, especially concerning her loyalty to their values and way of life. Maram, like Salim, was blessed with a mild temper and a good deal of common sense. She knew that parents' coming to terms with their children's choices depended to a great degree on appearances vis-à-vis the extended family and friends. This was particularly true with Salwa who worried more than anything about what to tell Hadil's uncles and aunts. Thus Maram took every opportunity to talk those relatives into a softer position on the matter.

At first the doors seemed permanently sealed. Salwa rebuffed Maram's solicitations, furious at Hadil's willful ingratitude. "What haven't we done for that child?" she fumed. "We gave her everything, and then she up and marries this country bumpkin!" But Maram persisted.

"She's still your daughter, blood of your blood, flesh of your flesh," she pleaded. "How can you turn your back on her like this? Sometimes I think you're angry because she defied you, not because of scandal."

When Hadil got pregnant a little over a year after the

wedding, Salwa still wouldn't budge. Hadil learned later that it was her father who finally took it upon himself to change his wife's mind. "We can't abandon her like this forever," Salim pleaded. "She needs us. She needs her mother, especially when she'll give birth to her first child. She stayed true to our faith. She didn't become Muslim like you worried she would. She attends church more than before even though it's all the way in Bir Zeit."

Salwa dug her heels in. "She should have thought of all that before she married Hisham," she grumbled before angrily citing a proverb: "The one who helped the donkey climb the roof should be the one to help it down!" Yet little by little the buds of reconciliation began to sprout. Noticing signs of change, Hadil's sister would call her in secret, lowering her voice whenever Salwa walked by. Salwa, who noticed the conspiratorial whispering, took her time thawing, and the first encounter between Hadil and her mother took place in the maternity ward of the government hospital in Ramallah, the day after Hadil gave birth to Leila.

Hadil was in her hospital bed with the baby in her lap with Hisham standing beside her. When she saw her relatives peering hesitantly in at the door, she smiled in embarrassed apology. Her father was the first to cross the doorstep, marching firmly towards her. He leaned down, held her shoulder, and kissed her warmly on the forehead, his eyes moist. "How are you, my daughter?" he asked softly, sneaking a long peek at his grandchild, who began to wail. Hadil replied with a nod, tears running down her cheeks. Salim stepped back, clearing the way for his wife, who responded to her daughter's tears with sobbing of her own.

"There's no need to cry," she reassured her. "Everything is fine, everything is fine." She hesitated for the briefest of moments then bent down and kissed Hadil on both cheeks. Hadil handed the baby to her mother as if to seal the bond between mother, daughter, and granddaughter. Salwa pressed Leila to her chest and held her out to look at her. Hadil's sister Ranin approached, crying excitedly. An hour later Hisham's parents arrived, driven to the hospital by Hisham's younger brother Fuad. It was the first time the in-laws met each other. They exchanged greetings befitting the occasion.

Leila's baptism took place in the Church of Transfiguration, as did Nadim's three years later. Hisham showed no objection. "Our children are Muslim and Christian," he used to say, "they celebrate both religions' holidays." Salim and Salwa's appreciation for him grew when they learned he did not impede Hadil's career development, and he once again became a welcome visitor to their house. His visits diminished considerably however when the marriage began to falter. Hadil never shared her relationship difficulties with her parents, nor did she ask for their advice, but she wasn't surprised when they offered it – apparently having been informed.

"You should make every effort necessary to patch it up with Hisham," they told her when she visited. "You've got kids," they stressed, "you're not a young woman anymore." Salwa couldn't resist throwing a barb: "You made a choice and need to face the consequences." Hadil didn't respond, but figured that to Salwa, being divorced at Hadil's age – with two children to boot – was far worse than being married to a Muslim country bumpkin.

Hadil went on with the story.

"She was one of ten siblings," she read from her paper, "three sons and seven daughters. Her father and brother, who sat idly at home because they couldn't find work, regularly bullied and beat her. They accused her of being rebellious and unruly. Waffa hoped that her marriage to the boy from the next village would spare her this abuse and was glad that her parents hadn't given her away to an old man. This was the fate of many young girls," Hadil stressed, "due to the economic conditions following the second

Intifada. Many families married their young girls off to old Arab men from Jordan or Israel for a handsome payment." But Waffa's bliss was short-lived. She found herself at the mercy of a violent and fickle young husband. Restrictions on travel in the West Bank and the frequent curfews imposed on the villages prevented her from seeking relief and help from her family. When it became clear that she was unable to conceive, her husband's violence escalated. Neither he nor anyone in his family thought to have her see a doctor.

Waffa wanted to escape her husband and return to her parents' home, but knew she wasn't welcome there. For nearly two years she tried to cope. When she couldn't bear the abuse any longer, she decided to seek assistance from Hadil's Center for Women's Empowerment, which she had heard about from a woman who attended a seminar there. When Hadil first met her, Waffa was suffering from respiratory problems, eating disorders, and uncontrollable trembling of the hands. Hadil found her a foster home in Ramallah with a well-to-do couple in their mid-sixties. Their three grown children lived abroad and the couple was glad for Waffa's company. Waffa did some manual work at the center for a while and was encouraged by the couple to improve her reading and writing skills. After a year away from her violent husband she showed marked physical and mental improvement.

"But this happy ending is the exception," Hadil concluded. "Most women in abusive situations are much less fortunate."

After the session many of the attendees complimented her on the presentation, with some praising her courage for "describing reality as it is, without embellishment." Hadil was deeply disappointed. Her fear had come true: as on so many past occasions her audience had completely missed the point about the role of the occupation in the spread of domestic violence in Palestinian society.

"This isn't about my courage, dammit!" she thought

while she nodded emptily at the compliments.

CHAPTER 26
Yoav

The monotony of the checkpoint allowed for endless rumination. Yoav thought back to the stylish young man, so incongruous with the drabness of the place, who yelled angrily about "Categories and classifications, categories and classifications". The pair of words kept buzzing in Yoav's ears like a mosquito as if his mind was eliciting where he'd heard them before. By arcane coincidence, music from one of the cars at the checkpoint suddenly gave him the answer. The driver was listening to a catchy, unfamiliar duet by an Arab male singer and an Indian female singer, each singing in their own language, with a chorus that began: "*Nari nari…*". The Indian singer's bell-like voice startled Yoav back to India and back to Ashok, the Mandu guesthouse manager who'd made repeated, obnoxious use of "categories and classifications".

Yoav had visited the small town of Mandu about ten years ago. Set in a green landscape rich with waterways, the town started as a fortress around the sixth century AD. Despite being off the beaten path and rarely mentioned in guidebooks, Mandu had served as the seat of several rulers, and the scene for some of the grandest chapters in Indian history. It owed its current name to a popular tragic love story from the 16th century between prince Baz Bahadur and shepherdess Rani Roopmati. He was Muslim, she was

Hindu. During one of his hunting forays, Bahadur heard the enchanting singing of Roopmati, "the Lady of the Lotus". Mesmerized, he begged her to follow him to his palace and be his wife. Roopmati agreed on condition that he build her a home with a view of her beloved Narmada River. Bahadur built her a charming palace atop a cliff where Roopmati spent hours watching the river flow in the valley below. But their love story ended tragically. Akbar, the greatest Mughal emperor in the history of India, waged war against Bahadur – in order, some say, to win Roopmati. The coward Bahadur fled, leaving Roopmati behind, and rather than fall to her lover's enemy, she poisoned herself. Roopmati's castle, with its delicate lines and elegant turrets, still stands in Mandu as testimony to her beauty and unflinching loyalty, and her name, deeply rooted in Mandu's heritage, lives on in ballads.

Yoav spent two days in Mandu. He arrived there with Anka, a German backpacker he'd met in New Delhi a week before. They'd planned to visit the Taj Mahal but a flare-up between Hindus and Sikhs had disrupted public transportation to Agra, so they took a detour. Yoav later learned that his mother, whom he'd failed to update on the change of plans, was mad with worry. Having not heard from him for four days, she drove his father and sisters into anxiety. She called the Israeli Foreign Ministry, seeking information on any Israelis who might have run into trouble in those areas.

"And if that wasn't enough," Merav told Yoav once he returned home, "Sivan was supposed to go on a school trip, and Mom was like, 'You don't go anywhere! You stay home!' It was creepy, like she was waiting for terrible news."

"She thought I was dead," Yoav said plainly. Merav couldn't resist a bit of dark humor: "She wanted us to be together when the news came, so we could start the shiva" – the seven days of mourning – "together. But Dad

insisted that Sivan go rather than stay home and watch
Mom lose it. We had a few days of this awful melodrama
and then finally you called. What a relief! I thought we
were going to lose both of you: you in some shithole in
India and Mom in a mental home."

Yoav and Anka stayed at the Roopmati Guesthouse,
which like so many local businesses bore the name of the
legendary historical princess. A compensation of sorts,
Yoav thought, for the squalidness of the present day. After
checking in, Yoav and Anka went out to the guesthouse
lawn and ordered a papaya shake at a plastic table in the
shade of a tree. The manager stumbled over, introduced
himself, and asked if the shake was to their liking. They
expressed some satisfaction before mentioning that it
wasn't as cold as promised. "I'm sorry," he smiled, "our
refrigerator is broken." He pulled up a chair, set his frosty
beer bottle on the table, and plopped himself down
between them without asking. His bloodshot eyes and
boozy breath indicated that he'd had a few already. Yoav
and Anka exchanged glances, not knowing how to react.

"Did you know," the man began to address them airily,
rolling his eyes as if presenting a riddle to small children,
"that you're sitting under my tree?" They looked at him
puzzled, ill at ease.

"Well," he lowered his voice as if sharing a secret, "the
name of the tree is Ashoka, which in Hindu means 'never-
knowing-sorrow'. And my name," he smiled contentedly,
"is never-knowing-sorrow. Ashok. It's a long story, I don't
want to bother you with the details. The tree is associated
with Kamadeva, the god of love. The flowers bloom in
early spring. Spectacular blooms, inconceivably beautiful, a
sheer celebration of color: orange, yellow, red... you must
come again in spring. I heard you talk about Mahatma
Gandhi!" He suddenly shifted the topic of his unsolicited
monologue, and fell to denouncing Gandhi's humanism.

"I believe that Gandhi's philosophy is totally wrong!"
he declared. "Gandhi ignored a simple fact. The world is

238

made of categories and classifications. The whole world, you must admit, is divided into different types and species. God ordered it that way, not humans. Like everything else in nature, humans are also different from each other." Ashok went on to stress that humans speak different languages, have different skin color, even have different blood. Yoav didn't take him seriously.

"Drunken idiot," he whispered in Anka's ear. But she was less amused and began to cringe in her seat as the man continued to preach his abhorrent worldview. "The caste system," he declared, "is just a manifestation of the natural order, and it is not unique to India. Wherever you go, you will find classifications, categories, and hierarchies among human beings. You will find the caste system everywhere, even if it is not called by that name. That is how it is in America, that is how it is in Europe, and that is how it is wherever you come from. Every person," Ashok asserted, "was born with a nucleus that determined, already then, to which caste he belongs." He touched his index finger to his thumb to illustrate the size of a tiny grain.

"Yes, yes, we are all born with a nucleus," he responded to the puzzled looks that Anka and Yoav shot each other. Amused at Ashok's lunacy, Yoav asked him with mock-seriousness where the purported nucleus was located and how to find it, but Anka was outraged. "There's no scientific basis whatsoever for what you're talking about!" she protested furiously, "And I'm sure you know people who've made remarkable achievements even though they come from a low caste." Ashok was unfazed. That, he countered inconsistently, was merely proof that Indian society was open enough to recognize talent. He went on to emphasize that according to Hindu philosophy all humans were equal regardless of caste. Anka's jaw dropped. Her hands fell to her lap. "All equal regardless of caste! Really!" she smirked despondently. Finally Ashok got up and left.

"I'm in shock," Anka said, disgusted by the encounter.

"Shocked by Ashok," Yoav joked, trying to lighten the mood.

"It's not funny!" Anka lashed out. Yoav looked bewildered. "It's the same as laughing at a racist joke," she berated him. "Like you agree with him, or at least don't object to what he said."

"I do not agree with that fucking lunatic," Yoav protested indignantly.

"No, he's not a fucking lunatic, he's racist," Anka hissed furiously.

As they lay in bed later, Yoav began to stroke Anka's stomach with his palm. She summarily grabbed his hand and pushed it away as if returning it to where it belonged, away from her.

Yoav now recalled Ashok's take on categories and classifications at the checkpoint. To calm the stylish young man, Yoav had explained that what his fellow soldier said was "instructions", not "animals". But did the arbitrary instructions that decided what went on at the checkpoint really differ that much from Ashok's zoological categories and classifications?

CHAPTER 27
Hisham

As he went to meet Mandy, his thoughts wandered to Hadil. They'd been living together for nearly two decades. He used to share all his experiences with her: good and bad, normal everyday events, things that happened with the kids. But since she began spending so much time on the road, things he wanted to tell her became outdated by the time they met. What was the benefit, he sighed, of staying faithful to her? What did he get for his devotion to Hadil and to the kids? He'd been an exemplary husband, supporting her all the way since her master's from Bir Zeit. He cooked for the children, fed them, dressed them, took them to school and the Scouts. He spent days on end with them while she was away. I've become their father and mother, he thought, and now we've talked and talked, but nothing came of it. It's not like I want to shut her in.

After all he himself taught pro-feminist Arab writers such as Hanan al-Shaykh and Laila al-Othman. He even identified with their heroines, but Hadil took things too far, he grumbled to himself. And there she goes again, traipsing off to Belfast! Patience, patience…how much more patience was he expected to show? He thought of a line from Egyptian poet Ismail Sabri which he used to give his students as a linguistic puzzle. Sabri addresses his beloved, Isma, playing with both their names: "She told me, *Ismail, saber*, patience / And I replied, *ho Isma, sabri* / my patience is about to expire."

But as soon as he met Mandy the nagging qualms were all suspended. He gave himself over to their precious time together. It was a time-zone expunged from his past and future, a realm of willing forgetfulness detached from Hadil, his children, his extended family and friends. Only he and Mandy existed.

He planned to arrive at the Al-Kasaba Theater just before the show, to decrease the chances of running into someone he knew. Luckily he didn't recognize anyone. He and Mandy took their seats. As the concert began, he shot some furtive glances in her direction to check that she was enjoying herself. Occasionally he leaned over to whisper details in her ear about the music. "They're called Sabreen. Some of the band members took part in the student protests at Bir Zeit in the '80s, during the first Intifada," he explained.

The physical proximity to her stirred his blood. Her body's aroma, the scent of her shampoo, and her delicate perfume sparked a desire in Hisham that he hadn't known for a long time. But how does she feel, he wondered anxiously. He could tell she was transfixed by the music. This show was a good choice – or perhaps too good, he thought, since Mandy's attention was given exclusively to the concert. She echoed Hisham's thoughts at the end.

"What a great choice!" she marveled. "That was a lot of fun! Thank you!" she said with a flash of her beguiling smile.

"Yes," Hisham affirmed. "They're widely admired, especially by people with good taste. It's complex music, combining different styles – East and West." Mandy accepted his offer to get drinks but added that she had an early morning the next day. They went to Sangria's, a popular spot not far from the theater, and ordered local Taybeh beer. A famous song played in the background.

"Nice music," Mandy remarked.

"This is a contemporary cover of an old song by my favorite Iraqi singer, Nazem al-Ghazali. He's the greatest singer in the Arab world. He died a long time ago. His songs are masterpieces of Arab music."

Mandy listened with interest, encouraging Hisham to share his knowledge with her. He told her that some of Al-Ghazali's songs were based on classical poems. Al-Ghazali made classical poetry accessible to the masses, he noted, brilliantly marrying folk lyrics and melodies to classical verses within the same songs. No wonder, Hisham added derisively, that today's poets have abandoned this disciplined style in favor of free form.

"No one even tries to write masterpieces like before," he vented his frustration. "It's all prose poetry. Do these people want to write poems or short stories? Where's the rhyming? Where's the meter? There's almost nothing left of poetry."

Mandy defended prose poetry, noting that many American luminaries, such as Allen Ginsberg and Bob Dylan, used it. She even taught their work. But Hisham insisted. He went on to illustrate the beauty of classical Arabic poetry with an example from Abu Firas al-Hamdani which al-Ghazali had put to music. "This is no simple rhyming scheme," he told Mandy, and began to explain the poem's double and triple rhymes, assonances, alliterations, and rhyming root letters – all in Arabic. Finally he recited it:

A dove was cooing nearby.
Oh, neighbor, if you only knew my plight.
Love forbid! You haven't tasted the pain of separation,
and my worries haven't crossed your mind.
Can it be that you carry sorrow in your heart,
whilst resting free on a high tree branch?
Oh, my neighbor, fate didn't mete out justice to us.
Come hither, I'll share with you my miseries;
Come nigh, my spirit is feeble,

startled by a body that tortures my mind.
Shall the prisoner be quiet,
but the free cry out?
Shall the sad fall silent,
but the free lament?
It is more fitting that I shed tears,
but as it is,
my tears are rarely shed.

"I didn't understand a word," Mandy smiled apologetically, "but I could hear the rhythm and the rhyming. It sounds great."

Hisham apologized that he can't translate the poem adequately, but he could tell her, in general, he added, what it's all about. Abu-Firas al-Hamdani, he began, was a 10th-century knight from Mosul in northern Iraq. His cousin Sayf al-Dawla, who ruled a kingdom in Aleppo, appointed al-Hamdani as governor of the city of Manbij, which still exists. Al-Hamdani was captured by the Byzantines and spent four years in prison, where his loneliness and separation from his beloved drove him to pen some of the most beautiful love poems in Arabic. After his release, he gained control of the Syrian city of Al-Hama, but was assassinated soon thereafter. Two of his poems gained popularity when they were sung by two Arab greats: Umm Kulthum and al-Ghazali. This poem he just recited, Hisham explained, describes the poet's longing for his beloved. "He sees a dove sitting on... on the window...," he said.

"You mean the windowsill?" said Mandy.

"Yes, yes," said Hisham. "And the dove is crying."

"Cooing, humming," Mandy suggested.

"Yes, cooing," Hisham agreed, "but the word in Arabic is crying."

He carried on explaining the poem, pleased with Mandy's show of interest. It had been years since he could enthuse about his favorite topic to a woman he liked.

Neither, it seemed, did Mandy shy away from the sexual tension between them. Hisham noticed the flush blossom in her cheeks as he gazed into her eyes and softly whispered the English translation for al-Hamdani: "Come hither, I'll share with you my miseries."

The waiter came and asked if they'd like a refill on their beers. Hisham glanced at Mandy. She didn't object, and he ordered two more. But once they ran low, Mandy said it was time to go. Hisham insisted on paying.

"But you paid last time," she protested.

"Yes," he smiled courteously, "but you're my guest."

When they reached her apartment building she invited him up for a drink. Hisham gladly accepted, climbing to her third-floor apartment with vague anticipation. He was surprised when Mandy offered to make them tea. Though privately he would have preferred for them to continue with the alcohol, he said tersely: "I'll have black coffee." He stood and watched her make it for him. She seemed absorbed in the coffee-making, pulling a stovetop coffee pot from the cupboard by the stove, getting the coffee from a drawer, dumping a heaping teaspoon of it into the pot. She was about to add sugar when he stopped her with a gentle touch on the arm. "I take my coffee without sugar. I like it bitter," he smiled somewhat ruefully. "Anyway, you add the sugar only in the end, after the coffee is boiled." They sat on either side of the kitchen table, sipping their drinks and not saying much. Hisham felt the tension but didn't know what it meant or what to do about it. He wanted to get up and do something, seize her, tell her something. But he didn't.

"My children are waiting for me," he finally said with a note of apology.

Mandy said nothing and made no effort to stop him. She just gave him one of her sweet smiles, thanked him for a wonderful evening, and bid him goodbye. They didn't even kiss on the cheeks this time. Hisham walked downstairs, got into his car, sat still for a long while, turned on the ignition, and drove home. It's better this way, he tried to comfort himself.

In the days following their awkward parting, he saw her often at school. Mandy's face lit up whenever their paths crossed but Hisham no longer found the same elusive magic in it that once beguiled him. Instead he felt a gnawing feeling of embarrassment, mingled with slight humiliation.

CHAPTER 28
Tali

It was Friday afternoon when Tali saw the email from the Boston University department of psychology, telling her she'd been accepted to the PhD program with a full scholarship. She didn't hurry to share the news with Yoav as she would have before: she knew how he'd react. He'd expect her to take the offer so that he could go to Harvard. It would be impossible to convince him now that they should both go to UPenn. She'd be the one who would have to give something up and put his interests first. She recalled Liat's ironic prophecy that Tali would end up as a supportive little wife. She left the house in a funk as she started the short walk to one of the cafés near Habima Theater for a meeting with Galia Hoffman, her thesis supervisor.

Galia looked at her. "You look troubled," she said. "What's the matter?"

Tali gave her the rundown of all the schools she'd been accepted to, adding pensively that she was thinking of taking the Boston offer.

Galia recoiled in surprise. "You're going to pass up UPenn, Columbia, and NYU? Tali, you really need to think this through!"

"You're right," Tali smiled nervously. "But I don't want to give up our relationship... Yoav... I want to have children… I mean, not right away, but…"

"So that's it," Galia smiled, "you're afraid you'll end up like me. A childless old academic crone."

"No, that's not why!" Tali said, startled by Galia's bluntness. She blushed. Did Galia see through to her prejudice against Galia's personal choices? Tali thought of that time she described Galia to Liat as "a shriveled carrot forgotten in the fridge drawer."

"So what's the matter?"

"It's not that I think everyone should marry and have a family," Tali said, "but for me it's important," she emphasized, almost apologizing. After a while she added: "And I don't want to go to the US by myself for who-knows-how-long. I'm not a young woman. I want to go there with a partner, someone from here who'll also want to come back."

"I totally understand you," Galia replied. "I felt the same way myself."

Tali looked puzzled.

Galia nodded. "It may come as a surprise to you, but those things were very important to me once."

Indeed surprised, Tali didn't press her for details. Galia almost never discussed her personal life. She stared at Tali for a while, trying to decide whether she should press ahead. They were on the cusp of a role reversal: the admired mentor about to pour her heart out to the disciple. Finally Galia overcame her reservations. At first she recounted her past in a distant tenor, as if describing another life, but as she went on, the narrative took on a warmer, more personal quality, with measured flashes of vulnerability.

She too had gone to study in the US with a boyfriend, whose name she chose not to mention. For several years they tried to have children but it didn't work out. They didn't know what the problem was. "We tried artificial insemination. I still remember the name of the drug I had to take to make my uterus more receptive," she laughed bitterly. "Clomiphene Citrate. I became a pharmacological expert. The doctor would inject the sperm right into my uterus. My ex hated it - he had go to the hospital and masturbate into a cup with porno magazines. You can imagine what it did to our sex life. Zero spontaneity, constant stress. We tried not to think about the pregnancy thing, but it was always there between us. And in the end it didn't work. I didn't get pregnant.

I may be a good psychologist," she sneered, "but he and I coped with it miserably. But we didn't give up. We tried IVF. We returned to Israel, because it was cheaper here. This was towards the end of my doctorate. But the fertilized eggs failed to attach to the uterine wall. They kept flushing out. I took hormones but nothing helped. We tried for a year, injecting me with all kinds of shit, and finally I gave up. Enough's enough. If we can't have kids, so be it. And then came the surprise. My ex, my hero, sits me down one night and tells me he needs time apart. He broke up with me. So I went back to the States to finish my PhD. I stayed there a few years, and devoted every moment to work - research, publications, teaching. It helped me to move on. That's the end of the story, really. He also went back to the States, married some divorcée, and now he teaches math in some godforsaken place. We haven't been in touch." Galia leaned back, as if to signal that this chapter of her life was over and done with.

An awkward silence descended, and the reason for Galia's burst of intimate sharing suddenly seemed unclear. Tali felt sad for her mentor, the stalwart female professor who – so her fans wanted to believe – dared to place career before family. Tali longed to comfort her but didn't know how; physical touch might be inappropriate given their difference in age and status.

Finally she got up the courage to ask: "If you had to do it all over again, would you have done anything differently?"

"Would I have done anything differently…" Galia rolled the question around in her mouth. "But what could have I done?" she brooded. Suddenly Galia saw Ronen Segal, her colleague and occasional research partner. He looked excited. Ignoring Tali, he marched over and told Galia that he'd just heard back from Psychological Review about the article they'd submitted. Galia said nothing, but there was a tiny smile of satisfaction on her lips.

"The editor says it adds an important contribution to the field but needs some revisions," Ronen said.

"So it hasn't been accepted," Galia made sure.

"True. But I don't need to tell you what revise-and-submit from them means. Here, read it for yourself." He handed Galia his smartphone and turned to Tali: "I understand you're on the way to the US."

"Yes," Tali said, and was about to share more details, but Ronen was no longer listening. He waited impatiently for Galia to finish reading the email. They began discussing how to revise the article, leaving Tali sitting idly and feeling redundant. After a few moments, she got up and asked Galia when it would be convenient to meet again. "We'll talk on the phone," Galia dismissed her. Tali felt that Galia might regret opening up to her. She left and walked home, slightly hurt by the abrupt switch from intimacy to detachment.

Only the following day, on Saturday night, did she phone to tell Yoav about Boston. She noticed how he struggled to hide his joy.

"I knew you'd get in!" he declared. "I mean, if Columbia, NYU, and UPenn say yes, of course Boston would."

"Yes," Tali replied laconically.

"It's with a scholarship and everything?" he said.

"Yes, a scholarship and everything."

"So what are you going to do?"

"What do you think I should do?"

"Well, you know…"

"I don't feel like discussing it now," Tali said. "We'll talk about it tomorrow." She was about to hang up, but then remembered. "Oh," she said nonchalantly, "I saw that you're in contact with Einat."

There was a silence. "Einat?" Yoav said. "What are you talking about?"

"She sent you an email," Tali said.

"What did she... where... what did she write?"

"She wanted you to get in touch with her before you go away."

Yoav sputtered: "Oh yeah, yeah. I didn't tell you. She called me the other day. We talked for a bit... she told me about herself... I told her about us... I told her about our plan."

"How come she contacted you after all this time?"

"I don't know. I was surprised too."

"What's new with her?"

"She lives in Tel Aviv. Still teaches at the same school. The usual. She told me she got divorced. We talked about her daughter."

"Sniffing her options?"

"Come on, Tali. She just called to ask how we're doing."

"Good question."

"Tali, enough with this. Things are working out. A few more months and we'll fly away."

"Good," Tali said thoughtfully. "We'll talk tomorrow."

CHAPTER 29
Hadil

After breakfast on the second day of the conference, Hadil decided to explore the estate's exquisite, spacious garden that had caught her eye on the bus ride in. The mansion itself was a massive building - according to the booklet they'd all been given, it had been built in the Neoclassical style in the late 18th century and was considered a masterpiece of minimal elegance.

Swans glided over the tranquil lake set among carefully-tended topiaries. Hadil wandered slowly over the paths, admiring the flora, much of which she had never seen before. Rounding a bend, she came across a groundskeeper diligently pulling weeds. He looked to be more than seventy years old, his animated, agile movements standing in stark contrast to his hunched posture, wrinkly skin, and age spots. They exchanged nods. Hadil asked if he knew the names of the plants he was tending. The groundskeeper proudly replied that he knew them all. He'd been tending this garden for over forty years.

He studied her curiously and said, "Where are you from, miss, if I may ask?"

"From Ramallah."

"Ramallah?"

"Ramallah. It's in Palestine."

"Ramallah, Palestine. Welcome. Ramallah, Palestine," he repeated, trying to correctly place the information. After a moment, he said casually: "It's tough over there in Palestine."

"Yes, it's tough over there in Palestine," Hadil smiled. Rather concise, she thought. He began plying her with details about the plants they saw. Hadil listened attentively, which encouraged him to go on – glad to share his passion for gardening, which had not waned with time. The estate, he explained, was like a botanical garden.

"It's got everything in it. Trees, ornamental shrubs, plants, flowers. Not all of them indigenous to Ireland, incidentally. Some have been brought from distant lands. There's a good variety of pine, oak, and chestnut. And right there," he raised his calloused hand towards the stone wall encircling the mansion, "you can see a lime cypress, a weeping willow, and a few maples. The maples are from North America. It's where you get maple syrup from."

Hadil was surprised. "I thought most of these plants were native," she smiled.

"You know how it is," the groundskeeper smiled, "the trees have a way of misleading us."

Hadil found out that this comment was part of a personal view resulting from a lifetime spent near plants. People think trees have been in place from time immemorial, the man explained, because their roots seem so strong. "But that's not really the case," he said. "Humans aren't the only ones to migrate. And who knows – maybe the trees began to wander even before humans. There's something deceptive about them. People like saying that a plant or a tree belongs to them, that it symbolizes their identity, or their history, but then someone comes along and shows them that this tree or that plant originally came from a different land altogether. You see? Trees can be rootless too."

Hadil listened with curiosity. "Trees can be rootless too," she silently repeated to herself, then asked him jokingly: "Sir, are you a gardener or a philosopher?"

Later that evening, reading Maalouf's *Origins*, she would think back to the groundskeeper's comments. Maalouf describes his family heritage not as a static cluster of roots, but as a collection of random human beginnings. Roots, he writes, hide in the ground, wallowing in filth and growing in darkness, and the tree is a prisoner from birth, its nourishment based on the threat of dying if he dares to break free.

The groundskeeper answered Hadil quite seriously: "We're all philosophers, miss, if we only take the time to look around. Anyone who takes his work seriously, whatever it is, is bound to become a philosopher. The secrets of the world are everywhere. We just need to look closely."

"Sir, you truly are a philosopher."

"I never took botany at school," he said. "I read about it here and there whenever I've got the time." He added that he learns a great deal from experts from around the world who come to the estate. The property, he said, used to be a school for missionaries who were sent to all four corners of the globe to spread the gospel. Before he could go on, Hadil interrupted him: "Is that a lavender bush?" she pointed.

"It makes sense that you'd recognize it," he smiled. "Lavender comes from the Middle East. I was told the ancient Greeks used to call it *nardus*, after a Jewish city in Iraq, I think. I can't remember the name. Something like Nard, Narda?"

"A Jewish city in Iraq?" Hadil repeated with surprise. "Are you sure? Maybe in Palestine?"

The groundskeeper shook his head. "I don't know, miss. My memory might be playing tricks. But that's what I was told: a Jewish city in Iraq. Anyway, next to the lavender, by the lake there, you might recognize another flower. Those are lupines. Next to them you've got peony tubers, and those there are columbines. Right now all you see is those monstrous tubers, but come springtime they'll turn into spectacular blooms. The columbines are native, by the way. The name comes from columba, which is Latin for dove. They probably thought of them as a symbol of peace."

Hadil thought of sharing the meaning of her own name: a dove's coo. On second thought, she decided it was too intimate and instead said: "Everything here is so beautiful. It's amazing what nature creates!"

"Yes," the groundskeeper nodded, "and we do our bit to help it along. You take care of the plants, feed them, and protect them against pests, and they'll love you back. They bloom, just like people do when you treat them right."

Hadil noticed a small, low-lying cluster of unfamiliar flowers next to the columbine tubers, right on the edge of the lake. "What are these?" she asked.

"Oh, those are rhodoras," said the groundskeeper. "You won't find them in Northern Ireland. They were brought here a few months ago. There was an international flower arrangement event, and one of the American participants brought them along. They grow mainly on the east coast of the United States, near water. The rhodora's related to the azalea," he pointed to lush azalea bushes nearby.

"So that's a rhodora?" Hadil said, her curiosity piqued.

"Are you surprised? You thought it was another flower?"

"No, no. I didn't think it was another flower," said Hadil. "It's just the first time I've seen it. I've only read about it before. I know a poem called *The Rhodora*." She bent down to examine the petals, the stalks, the leaves, as if trying to fathom what had driven Ralph Waldo Emerson to write about this particular flower. The groundskeeper wondered at Hadil's sudden preoccupation, but saw that she was already off in her own world. Thinking back to the English Literature department at Bir Zeit, where she'd first heard the poem, she sat down on a bench and began to recite in a whisper some lines she remembered:

Rhodora! if the sages ask thee why
This charm is wasted on the earth and sky,
Tell them, dear, that if eyes were made for seeing,
Then beauty is its own excuse for being

At Bir Zeit, she and Hisham were fond of sharing poems they'd learned, offering them to one another as tokens of love. While Hisham delivered morsels from Abu Nuwas, Al-Mutanabbi and Abu-Firas al-Hamdani, Hadil would recite Wordsworth, Byron, Shelley, Keats, Emerson. *The Rhodora* struck a deep chord in her. A visiting American lecturer, Professor Ross, explained that Emerson was in a category apart from nineteenth-century romanticism. Emerson, he emphasized, was not a romantic but a transcendentalist. Hadil didn't understand the distinction, and struggled to accept the professor's take on *The Rhodora*.

She courageously challenged him: "I don't know what you mean by 'transcendent'. I think his description of the rhodora is very romantic."

"Transcendentalist," he corrected her with the superior grin of the tenured. "I can see as well as you do how *The Rhodora* might be read as a romantic work. But I'd like you to note the vast difference between Emerson and romantic poets. Emerson offers an approach known as 'mystical realism'."

"What are these words?" Arij whispered to Hadil in frustration. "Transcendentalist, mystical realism... I'm lost. I don't know what he's talking about."

"Me neither," Hadil whispered.

Professor Ross noticed their whispering and correctly guessed what it was about. He clarified: "When Emerson writes about a flower, or a bird, or a stream, he doesn't add anything beyond what he sees, what is there. Now, contrast that with Wordsworth. He sees daffodils fluttering and dancing in the breeze," Professor Ross swayed with the description, flailing his arms. Seeing the paunchy, silver-haired lecturer dancing about, the students giggled nervously. "Daffodils dancing? You won't find anything like that in Emerson!" he said.

As the laughter died down, one of the students asked: "So what does Emerson do?"

Professor Ross turned serious again. "He gives a precise account of nature as it is revealed to the eye," he said. "These facts in and of themselves inspire in him a deep sense of wonder and elation. They bear the stamp of the sublime – the transcendent. Emerson couldn't be more clear about it. He wrote: 'Every natural fact is a symbol of some spiritual fact.' You can see this in the final lines of *The Rhodora*." The professor straightened up, lifted his head, and began to declaim:

Why thou wert there, O rival of the rose!

I never thought to ask; I never knew;

But in my simple ignorance suppose

The self-same power that brought me there, brought you

Hadil thought back to the evening when she'd recited *The Rhodora* to Hisham, over two decades ago. They were at a house in Bir Zeit with some friends, talking poetry. She was so enchanted by the lyrics then that she never bothered to think about the physical flower itself, its color and shape. She had challenged Professor Ross because to her the poem felt in such harmony with her romantic feelings for Hisham.

What are my feelings now? Hadil wondered with a sigh. Is there anything left to salvage, to rekindle?... After all, he must still have some of the qualities that drew me to him. He's handsome, a good family man, a loyal husband. True, he's unbearably grumpy and bitter, but he never really sought to slow me down or curb my development. He's just frustrated that he hasn't lived up to his potential. Maybe there's something to be done about that. Who knows?

She thought about their joint efforts to bring back Sharif, and how they were able to instantly put aside their differences. Sitting on the bench, she was surprised to discover new tenderness towards Hisham. Hopefully not deceptive nostalgia for those bygone Rhodora days, but something from the here-and-now, even if smaller, gentler?

CHAPTER 30
Yoav

As soon as he finished talking with Tali, Yoav phoned Einat. He tried again and again, but she wasn't picking up. He was anxious, worried that she might send other incriminating emails. Einat didn't call back until the following morning, after he spent a sleepless night haunted by worst-case scenarios. Yoav was on shift with Marcelo at the checkpoint when she called. The conversation was brief.

"I saw you called several times," she said cheerfully. "Sorry I wasn't available."

"Yes," Yoav replied distantly. "I got your email. In fact, Tali got it."

"I'm sorry," Einat said, noticing the chill in his voice, "I'm really sorry." Her cheer gone, she said: "So I guess you're going away soon."

"Yes," Yoav said dryly. He wanted to make sure she wouldn't send anymore emails, but couldn't say it outright. She has sense enough to understand it herself, he thought. He briefly filled her in on recent developments, and that he and Tali would likely end up in Boston. "Looks like things worked out in the end," he concluded. There was a loaded silence. Yoav was overcome with remorse, compassion, tenderness, and sadness. He wanted the stressful call to be over, but couldn't bring himself to break the silence. Finally Einat broke it.

"I'm happy for you and wish you and Tali all the best," she said. "Bye!"

"What's the matter? You look down," Marcelo said as Yoav walked back.

"I'm sick of it," Yoav said. "The checkpoint, the reserve service. Fuck all of it!"

"It's not that bad," said Marcelo. "We'll be gone by next Sunday. Until next time."

"There'll be no next time for me."

"Don't tell me you're going to be a conscientious objector?"

"No, but by the time I get back from the US, hopefully I won't be relevant anymore. Or maybe I'll come up with some excuse, like a medical reason."

"So what's up with your plan to study abroad?" said Marcelo.

"It's a done deal," said Yoav. "We'll be in Boston. We talked about it this morning. I'll go to Harvard and she'll go to Boston University."

"Wow, you pulled it off!" said Marcelo. "So why are you *triste, deprimido*?"

"I'm fine," said Yoav. "But I could have made things easier on us."

"Because you weren't willing to give up Harvard?"

"No, not just that."

Yoav's phone rang again. It was his mother, calling to say that his grandmother Camilla was in the hospital. "She felt pressure in her chest, so we rushed her to the ER in Beilinson. They ran all the tests, and the doctor says she might have had a mild heart attack. She's under observation. She's feeling better now. They might let her go tomorrow. Chezi and Ilana are with her now, and I'll sleep there tonight. I don't want to leave her alone."

When Tali asked Yoav once about his grandmother, the one with the English name, he replied, amused, that her original name was Kmala, Arabic for "extra".

"See, her parents only had girls, five or six of them, and really wanted a boy. When she turned out female, they were devastated, so they named her "superfluous". It was very common in that generation for families to call their daughters things like *Za'ela, Hamsa, Basiya, Sabriya*: sorrow, anger, enough, patience. To show disappointment at not getting a boy."

"That's so sad," said Tali. "Can you imagine carrying that name your whole life?"

"Yes, you're absolutely right," he said. "But it's interesting. Even though my Grandma Juliet is from a modern city, and even went to a Jewish school in Baghdad for a few years, my Grandma Camilla is stronger, more independent. She never spent a day in school, and only learned to read and write in her sixties, at the local community center. Grandma Juliet adored her husband and waited on him hand and foot, but Grandma Camilla gave my Grandpa Shmuel a hard time. She's been bossing him around the past few years. She was never satisfied with him. She had a feminist mindset, even though she never read any feminist theory. She got a job outside the house against his wishes, and never enslaved herself to the kids or the grandkids, like cooking or babysitting for them. Some people in my family say she's a cold, hard women. I disagree. They're just not used to a woman of her background being tough or independent. She's not a *frayer*, a sucker, like my Grandma Juliet, who would wait on the family even if she was in a body brace with a high fever. And to think that my dad's family think they're more modern than my mom's family, just because they're from the city."

Only a few days before, during his furlough from reserve service, Yoav had visited Grandma Camilla and Grandpa Shmuel with his mother, Nava. Camilla kissed him on both cheeks, and immediately began to shower him with questions. "Why didn't you bring Tali with you? Tell me, what's new with you and her? When are you getting married?" Grandma Camilla never missed an opportunity. It amused him: always the same questions, and always expecting his visit to include good news.

Yoav had his stock reply: "I don't know, Grandma. We'll see."

"What's there to see, *ibni*, my son?! Tali's a good girl, beautiful, and you love her. What do you need to know? Your mother told me you're living together… so it's time to get married."

"Everything will be fine, Grandma, don't worry," he said laconically, scanning the newspaper that was spread on the table. "Where's Grandpa?"

"He's out," she said, "he'll be back soon."

"He's out, he'll be back soon," Yoav repeated, smiling at his mother.

"Mom," she turned to Camilla, "Yoav's flying to America with Tali soon."

"God should deliver him back safely, him and all the soldiers."

"The soldiers?" Yoav laughed. "Sounds like we need to hit the old reset button on Grandma."

"Yoav!" his mother scolded him, struggling to stifle her smile. She turned to Camilla: "Mom, you didn't hear me. Yoav's going to America, to study. With Tali."

"Good luck, *ibni*," Camilla said thoughtlessly, when she suddenly realized what she'd heard. She looked at him and asked: "And when will you come back? Will I see you before I die?"

"Grandma!" he protested. "That's nonsense."

"*Ibni*, your grandmother is going to Hell," she sighed. "My whole body's sick. I went to see a doctor. He said, 'There's nothing seriously wrong with you.' He wasn't any help to me. He said I need a doctor to look at my bones. But the appointment's three months from now. That's what happened with your uncle Moshe. By the time his appointment came, he was dead already. They called him from the clinic after he died to say they had an earlier appointment. Your aunt told them: 'Good, I'll go to the graveyard and tell him.' That's what's going to happen to me too. By the time my appointment comes up…"

"Fine, fine," Yoav cut her short.

"Let's eat," Nava declared, pointing to the plates of bulgur kubba on the table. "Mom, I can never get my kubba to come out like yours."

"*Saha*, enjoy your meal," Camilla replied in Arabic. "Get some olives from the fridge. Your father made them. Get some vegetables too. There's fresh parsley. Clean. I washed it."

Nava lowered her voice and confessed to Yoav that she'd rather visit her mother every Friday afternoon for kubba than make her own. She openly admitted she couldn't cook like Camilla, even after standing next to her a million times and watching her cook her kubba, okra, meatballs, Iraqi cholent, chicken pilaf, and red rice. Even her cowpea, which was simply boiled in water, came out more delicious. It boggled the mind.

"I've watched her countless times," Nava said. "But when she sees I'm not looking, she slips something in. A secret spice or herb."

Yoav searched her face to see if she was serious. "What are you looking at me like that for?" Nava laughed. "I'm kidding! Anyway, your dad also likes her cooking better than mine. It used to upset me, but I'm okay with it now."

"Wow, this is delicious," Yoav said, slicing the kubba and shoving it into his mouth. "Delicious, delicious!"

"Some tea?" Camilla told him.

"I'll make it, mom," Nava said. "Sit down. Take a rest."

After they ate, Nava and her mother went out to the garden while Yoav returned to the newspaper. Nava came in and asked him to join them. "Grandma wants you to help move some potted plants into the ground. They've gotten too big for the pots. Grandpa Shmuel can't do it himself anymore."

"But Arbor Day was two months ago," Yoav joked. "My birthday, remember?"

"How can I forget?" Nava replied, looking at him tenderly. "February 3rd, 1977, same day as *Tu B'Shevat*" – Jewish Arbor Day. "Last year, 2007, it also fell on your birthday."

"Only a school teacher could know that," he told her.

"Maybe. But the day you were born was one of the happiest days of my life." She caressed his face. "Let's go out and help Grandma, sweetheart."

"No problem," he said, putting down the newspaper.

"While your Grandpa Shmuel spends his mornings at the senior center and his early evenings at the synagogue, she's busy taking care of the garden," Nava said.

Camilla went over to a large bird of paradise plant. "My sister's son Nisim brought this. It drinks water like a camel but gives a lot of flowers. It blooms a few times a year. And this one," she pointed to a sansevieria with hard, sword-like leaves, "has been with us a few years now. It grows good. It doesn't like a lot of water. In winter, what it takes from the air is enough." She pointed to a towering schefflera in a pot: "This one didn't take at first. I don't remember what it's called. Nissim knows. I gave it a lot of water and put all kinds of things in the soil, but nothing happened. It wilted. Then I started, I don't know where I got the idea, to put the tea leaves from the kettle into the soil instead of throwing them out, and it started to grow like crazy."

Yoav was amused. "Must be an Iraqi flower if it reacts so well to tea," he said.

"Who knows, my son, maybe you're right," Camilla said, "but I don't remember that we had a flower like this in Iraq." She went on inundating them with details about the plants in the garden, forgetting why they were there in the first place.

"Grandma," Yoav interrupted her, "where are the plants you wanted me to move?"

"I told you: this one," she pointed to the schefflera. "I want you to take it out and plant it there," she indicated a spot between a date palm tree and a Breynia with pink-and-white leaves. Yoav began to dig while his mother and grandmother watched, as if waiting to see him unearth a treasure.

"Back in the day, your grandparents planted only herbs and vegetables," Nava said. "Now my mother fills her garden with ornamental plants. Who would have thought? Mom," she turned to Camilla, "nowadays everyone's growing medicinal herbs, lemon trees, and grape vines, like you used to, and all you care about now is ornamental plants. Where'd you get the idea to grow all these flowers?"

Nava didn't expect an answer, not because of her mother's poor hearing, but because the affectionate reproach was meant for Yoav's ears. "Look at your grandmother," Nava smiled, "always swimming against the current. Back when she and Grandpa Shmuel first arrived in Israel, everywhere they went, they grew spices, okra, cowpea, and pumpkin, and of course planted a lemon tree and a date palm. Even in the transit camp, when they knew they'd be leaving soon. Iraqis can't live without a date palm in the garden. Nowadays it's trendy. Eco-gardening, they call it," Nava sneered. "Your grandparents did that before the yuppies ever had a name for it."

"It's funny," Yoav said, pausing his digging. "Maybe a year from now she won't even have any sage or Aloysia, with all these flowers."

"Perhaps," said Nava. "The date palm will stay, though. It's got serious roots, and besides, your grandpa would never allow it to go. Maybe if it was a male tree, but a female tree bearing fruit? No way he'd let them uproot it. She always complains about the birds eating the dates and shitting on the laundry. But he's proud of it." Grandpa Shmuel constantly gave date fruits to his children and their families. "This tree's a success, like you," she smiled fondly at Yoav. "Last time they fought about it, I heard him say he'll take this tree to his grave."

Yoav often witnessed this sort of exchange between his grandparents. He recalled sitting on the balcony one summer afternoon, when his grandfather Shmuel stepped down the short flight of steps to the yard, went to the palm tree, and bent to pick up the tiny unripe fruit it had dropped. Returning to the balcony, he opened his palm and proudly displayed the handful of green dates, no bigger than tiny olives. He sat down on a plastic chair and began to eat them.

"They're no good for you!" Camilla scolded him. "You're not a young man anymore. This tree only brings problems. Who grows trees for fruit anymore? You can buy them in the market for pennies!"

Shmuel ignored her, and as he often did, began to share memories of his childhood with Yoav. "When I was a boy in Iraq," he said, "I'd go into the gardens of the Muslims and collect dates from the ground. *Khalal al-tosh*, they called them, small and green; they fell off the tree before they were ripe." He pointed to the dates in his hand: "They weren't like these; they were much better. Here, try." Yoav took one and gave it a tiny nibble, carefully tasting it. It was soft as butter and extremely astringent. Yoav's mouth dried up instantly. He secretly deposited the remainder in his pocket, to be tossed later.

CHAPTER 31
Hisham

Music was blasting from Leila's room. "Ya Leila!" Hisham shouted over it. "Yes, *Baba*?" she replied, descending halfway down the stairs from the upper level.

"Would you turn it down? My head's exploding," he said. "How many times can you hear this *nari nari* song?" He began to mockingly chant the chorus: "His beauty burning fire, burning fire; what's wrong with my heart? Yesterday it was Amr Diab. Because of you I already know his song by heart. *Ya habibi*, light of my eyes; *Ya habibi*, dwelling in my mind. Now it's Hisham Abbas, and tomorrow we'll probably be back to Nancy Ajram and 'I'm in love'. How many times do I have to hear these songs — and at such high volume?"

"But I shut my door so it won't disturb you," said Leila.

"At that volume it can cut through steel."

Leila was about to answer back when Hadil popped out of her study and told Leila to do as her father said. "My head's also bursting," she said. "Why don't you just wear headphones and save us the argument?"

"Fine," Leila grumbled, trudging back up to her room.

"These kids drive me crazy," Hisham said, and began to rant about the loss of values and youths' awful taste in music. "The crap they listen to. Go figure what they see in this music. One day they're volunteering to fight the occupation and work in the villages, and the next day they're listening to this drivel. Nancy Ajram, Ahlam, Haifa Wehbe, Amr Diab. Have you listened to the lyrics? I love you, I want you, I dream of you, I think of you, I can't live without you, I'm nothing without you, and I love you again. Masterpieces! And those singers are all half-naked. It's more striptease than singing! Especially the Lebanese. I don't expect kids to sing *biladi, biladi*, my homeland; but can't they at least listen to quality music? Okay, so not the classics, but what about contemporary artists? Marcel Khalife, Rim Banna, Said Mrad, Sabrin. Something a bit deeper, more sophisticated, more sincere." He stopped and looked at Hadil:

"Remember what we used to sing at university during the first Intifada? We'd sing songs by Mahmoud Darwish, Fadwa Tuqan, Tawfiq Ziad… remember this one?" He began to recite a Tawfiq Ziad poem: "Tell the world, tell the world about a house with a smashed chandelier, a lily cut down, a braid on fire. Tell the world about a sheep that stopped producing milk." He looked at Hadil bitterly: "Who cares about these songs nowadays? What can I tell you. Like ibn al-Mu'tazz said: 'Be an ignoramus or pretend to be / for a great reward shall come to thee.'"

"You're exaggerating," Hadil said. "Things are different now. You expect too much of them. You're forgetting, it takes time and maturity to develop appreciation for artists like Darwish or Khalife. Kids don't have patience, but in time Leila will start appreciating better things. That's how the youth are today. They're interested in new clothing, new films, new music. Every day they fall in love with someone else. You criticize them, but they're saner than we are. They insist on living normally despite the situation. It's the power of children; they find joy even in harsh conditions."

"We weren't like this when we were their age," Hisham said. "Your parents wanted you to learn serious music, quality music. You studied with that British teacher, I forgot her name."

"Jane Wilson," said Hadil. "And that was then. Times have changed. Plus, I realized very quickly that I wasn't as talented as she thought. I sang in the school choir, that's all."

Hisham wasn't listening. He raved on about the lack of appreciation for high culture, which he claimed affected Palestinian society at large. "I'm not just talking about kids. How many adults in the Arab world are familiar with our great poets? Think about it. What's left of the Hamdaniyan poets?" He found it upsetting that people didn't know to associate the district of Al-Hamdaniya in Iraq or Syria's Al-Hamadaniah Stadium with the illustrious al-Hamdani tribe, which ruled over vast territory and produced the greatest of poets. "Ask people in Baghdad today what al-Hamdani means and they'll talk to you about desserts."

"Don't talk nonsense," Hadil peevishly cut him off.

"I'm not talking nonsense," Hisham said resentfully. "They've got a pastry chain called al-Hamdani. That's what they know. Not Abu Muhammad al-Hasan al-Hamdani, not Abu Firas al-Hamdani, but a creampuff!" Next he turned his ire to the Palestinian Authority leaders, who had snatched power from the local leaders responsible for the first Intifada. "How excited we were when Arafat came back from Tunisia. 'Welcome back, Abu Ammar!' we chanted. But what about the real heroes of the revolution?" Hisham's pitch rose, as if to disavow all nostalgia. "Where are all the leaders of the United Headquarters? The Palestinian Authority, they call themselves. But all they care about is their own interests!" He stopped, noticing the growing signs of frustration on Hadil's face. "You're right, you're right," he said. "Maybe I'm exaggerating."

"Yes, my dear, you're exaggerating," she said.

"You're right," he repeated, seeking to appease her, regretting that he'd lapsed into his usual negativity, which ran against the new, optimistic spirit that had lately appeared in the house. He softened his expression and said with a smile: "Check out your daughter's exploits. Remember how her classmates said she gets special treatment because her dad's a teacher at school, and that she was selected to go to Doha because I intervened? Well, listen to how your daughter handled it. She started causing trouble at school…"

"Again?" Hadil sighed.

"Wait, wait," said Hisham. He told her how Leila's teachers complained that she was late for class, misbehaved, and even talked back. After speaking to Leila in private several times and telling her she was very disappointed in her behavior, the chemistry teacher, Suad, had to report her to the principal – who, quite surprised at Leila, called her in and wrote her a warning. "And what did Leila do?" said Hisham, beaming. "She took the written warning put it up on the wall in class, so everyone would see she doesn't get special treatment. And it worked. I only heard about it from Suad, the chemistry teacher. Then I talked to Leila, and she told me why she did it. She's a clever one, your daughter," he said proudly. "Like her mother."

"It runs in the family," Hadil said. "That's what my father always said. 'Hadil's a clever girl' – until I married you, that is," she added, placing her hand on his. Her soft touch gave him a pleasant chill, feeding his hope for better days to come. There's the Hadil I know, he smiled inwardly: sharp-tongued but free of malice.

"You're trouble," he said fondly, as he often did when powerless against her wit. After a while, he leaned in as if to share a secret: "And I've got another story, about Nadim," he said.

"What trouble is he up to now?"

Hisham told Hadil that Nur, the music teacher, had given the class an innovative music appreciation assignment. Each student was to choose a song they liked, in any language, and dance to it in any style whatsoever. Only Nadim refused to cooperate.

"It's not just an exercise," Hisham explained. "They each have to work out the choreography with Nur and perform it at the year-end show in front of the parents. It's the first time they've done this at Friends. Nur asked him why he didn't choose a song like everyone else. You know what our macho man said? He said it was a girl thing. He doesn't want to be laughed at, and prefers to fail class. That's what he told her. 'Fail me! I don't care!' I think we should talk to him. Maybe you can. What do you say?"

"I'll sit that stubborn little man down for a talk," Hadil smiled. "See if I can get him to change his mind. I hope it's not too late."

"Where did he get that stubbornness from, you or me?" Hisham asked.

"Both," said Hadil. "We're both stubborn. Maybe it's because of The Rhodora."

"The what?"

"Emerson's Rhodora. You probably don't remember."

Hisham squinted, scanning his memory. "Emerson's Rhodora…" he rolled the words on his tongue. "Of course, I remember!" he declared. "You read it to me at Bir Zeit. A poem about a flower, right? You knew it by heart."

"Wow, you are something else!" said Hadil, amazed. "You remember everything!"

"Actually, I've only ever heard about this flower from you," he said. "I've never seen it."

"Me neither, until a few days ago."

"Where?"

"In Belfast."

"So what's the flower got to do with stubbornness?"

"There's a connection," Hadil smiled mysteriously. "I'll tell you some day. Sometimes good things can come out of conferences."

Hisham smiled, enjoying the sense of a good omen for

a change.

CHAPTER 32
Tali

Tali shot a glance from her car at the hang gliders that swooped gently over the sea along the shoreline. They moved gaily, propelled by an eastern wind coming from the Red Sea. Unlike the western wind, which agitated the sea into a froth, the eastern wind caressed it, as if soothing a wild slumbering beast. It created placid ripples that turned the seawater into a blue carpet stretching into infinity. Tali imagined herself dipping into the water, floating on her back, closing her eyes and letting the waves cradle her. She felt an urge to stop the car and sit on the deserted beach, letting the ripples wash over her feet. She ignored the urge. Pulling up into the Haifa foothills, she turned right towards Neve Sha'anan and her parents' house. Her phone rang. Yoav wanted to know that she'd arrived safely, and urged her to leave early on the way back the following day to avoid traffic.

"Don't worry, I'll leave early," she assured him. "You're starting to sound like your mother, worrywart."

"Talush!" he scolded her.

"Just teasing. Don't worry, I'll be back early."

"When we think of trauma, we usually think of extreme events, such as the experiences young children have when their parents get divorced; the loss of a loved one; a life-threatening experience; rape, sexual abuse; that kind of thing. But traumas don't have to be that extreme. An experience can be described as traumatic even if it didn't feel extremely painful or shocking at the time that it happened. I urge you to take a journey into your past and see if you can come up with an experience that you would describe as traumatic."

That was how the professor at a psychology course that Tali once took at university introduced the subject of trauma. At the time, she grimaced and whispered to the classmate next to her: "He wants us to go on a 'journey'! Like it's some sort of vacation." But the professor's appeal led her immediately to Harvey, whom she'd met in New York a few months before returning to Israel. There were other experiences, of course, but Harvey overshadowed them all. This event never faded into oblivion; it was always there. Now it emerged with renewed clarity, the clinical language inescapably capturing its sordid nature. Calling it a trauma added an extra dimension, intensifying the horror. She could remember the day and the hour, every single detail clear in her mind: the sights, the sounds, the smells, the weather, everything.

She met Harvey towards the end of her year in New York. He stood on a street corner playing a trumpet, not far from where she lived in the Village. It was afternoon and Tali stood waiting for Osnat, her roommate. She listened to his playing, enchanted. They exchanged glances. He continued to play and shook his head slightly, acknowledging her presence. A few moments later he stopped playing, turned to her and they began to chat. His handsome face shone through a screen of long copper hair. He was a well-built man in his early thirties. She loved how he pronounced her name when she introduced herself, stretching out the first syllable: Taaali. Two days later she saw him again. Noticing her, he smiled broadly. They talked, and he told her he was in a bebop band that played regularly at an East Village pub.

He'd love her to come one night.

She went with Osnat. Harvey noticed her as soon as she came in. Shooting her glances throughout the show, he did his best to flaunt his musical skills. Afterwards he joined their table. He and Tali soon became so engrossed with one another that they forgot Osnat. Only when Osnat, feeling left out, got up to go, did Tali become aware of the awkwardness. She apologized to Harvey, told him they had to go, and gave him her number.

"He's really into you," Osnat said with a touch of jealousy as they made their way back to their apartment.

"He's attractive," Tali said, trying to feign nonchalance. "But I don't need to get involved with someone new two weeks before I go home."

"Just let go," said Osnat. "A little adventure can't hurt. I know a lot of girls who'd love to be in your place."

Like you, Tali thought. "Fine, fine," she smiled. "I'll let go."

Harvey called the next day. They met late at night at the same pub where he played, took a fairly isolated corner table, and ordered beers. Harvey was a good listener. He took an interest in Tali's life, family, army service, interrupting only to ask for details. She couldn't recall receiving such earnest attention from a man before. The few young men she'd dated in the past talked mostly about themselves, either being self-absorbed or trying to impress her or both. When she asked Harvey about his own life and background, he answered frugally, preferring to talk about his passion for music. She tried to follow as he explained the finer points of bebop and how it differed from melodic jazz, but it was tough with her limited English, her scant background in jazz, the noise of the pub, and above all her growing attraction to him. As he spoke, Harvey gently stroked her forearm. His touch stirred her passion, and she squeezed his hand. He complimented her on her looks: her black hair, her green eyes, her "enchanting smile".

"The moment I laid eyes on you, I was hooked," he whispered. The confession thrilled her. After chatting for a couple of hours, he suggested they go to his place, which was just a few blocks from hers. Tali nodded and smiled. Soon afterwards she found herself in his bed, in his arms. She surrendered to the touch of his hands, his lips, and the yearning ache in her body to merge with his.

Entering her apartment early the following afternoon, she was greeted by a wide grin from Osnat. "Looks like you had a rough night," Osnat teased.

"Yes," Tali giggled awkwardly. "And I think I'm going to suffer some more. I've never done anything like this. I barely know him, but I took your advice and let go. It felt so good, so... free. Anyway, in a few days I'm flying home and then it'll be over."

"Makes it easy to seize the moment, then," said Osnat.

"I guess so. It's a story without a future."

Eventually Tali pushed her flight back by a few weeks, but the idyll was short-lived. A few days later, she and Harvey were in bed, Tali on top. He couldn't achieve a full erection, and had trouble penetrating her. She delicately suggested they try missionary, but he insisted on trying with her on top. Struggling desperately in vain, he suddenly pulled her back forcefully by the hair. Tali shrieked with pain. "Sorry, sorry!" he said, "I don't know what came over me, I'm so sorry." A few nights later, having trouble performing, he did it again – this time almost tearing out her scalp. Tali let out a terrible animal howl. Harvey was still clutching her hair. She tried to break loose, but his grip was firm.

"What's wrong with you?! You're crazy!" she wept. "I want to go home! Let me go! I want to go home!" But he didn't seem to listen. Before she could move again, Harvey slapped her full in the face with his left hand, still holding her hair in his right. "You're not going anywhere, you fucking bitch," he hissed. Tali froze, her eyes torn open with helpless fear. A moment later he came to his senses.

His face softened, the familiar features returning. Time to get up and go, Tali thought. Her heart pounded wildly. She began to dress, slowly and carefully, afraid to trigger another outburst from him. She gauged the distance to the door. Would she manage to beat him to it? As she finished putting on her shoes, calculating her next step, Harvey turned to her and said: "Tali, don't go. I'm really sorry."

He began to cry.

"I want to go," she said, her voice quaking. "I have to go, I can't stay here."

"Please, please, Tali, don't go. Please," he sobbed. "I really need you. You have to listen to me. No one understands me, no one knows what I'm going through."

I need to get up and walk away, she thought. This man is crazy. But she stayed; whether out of fear or compassion, she never could decide. She took a long look at Harvey, sitting in bed naked and sobbing. She was still on the edge of the bed, frightened, ready to jump back if he tried to strike again. Harvey began to tell her about the abuse he'd suffered as a child. Whining, he edged towards her as if gaining the trust of a frightened animal. He gently placed his hands on her knees, reverently placing himself at her mercy, reversing their roles. Tali recoiled at his touch but did nothing to push him away. Encouraged, Harvey cradled his head in her lap and continued to cry. He begged her to understand him, not to abandon him, not to leave him alone. "Tali, don't go, please," he said. "Stay with me. I need you. At least tonight."

"You don't need me," Tali said, "you need professional help."

"Are you afraid of me?" he asked

She thoughtlessly said no.

She stayed overnight in his apartment. The following morning he lavished her with affection, tenderly stroking her hair, her shoulders, her hands. He passed his palm over her face and flattered her about her beauty again and again. Neither of them mentioned the previous night.

A few days later came the final, most violent and humiliating attack. Tali went to Harvey's apartment late at night with the vague intention of breaking it off, and left it savagely violated. Osnat heard the key rattle in the door and rose to welcome Tali. Her smile vanished when she saw Tali's bruised and haggard face.

"Oh my god," she said, going pale.

"Someone tried to snatch my purse," Tali said. "I fought back and he hit me in the face."

"He scratched your neck?!" Osnat said, carefully examining Tali. "Look at you, my God! When did this happen? Where?"

"Just now. On the street. On the way over."

"How? Did he get your purse?"

"It's fine... I still have it. He ran when I started screaming."

"We should call the police," said Osnat.

"What are they going to do? He escaped."

"Does Harvey know? Call him. He should come over... God, I can't believe it."

"No," said Tali. "I don't want him involved."

"What do you mean?" said Osnat, perplexed. "He needs to know that..."

"No!" said Tali. "It's over between us. We broke up."

There was silence. Osnat gave her a long, skeptical look. Tali dodged her and treaded wearily to the shower. She slowly undressed, peeling off her blood-stained panties. She stood for a long time under the stream. She got out, wrapped herself in a towel, stumbled to her room, pulled the covers over her head, and began to weep silently, spasms of sharp pain piercing her lower body, and waves of disgust and shame rocking her.

When she told her parents about the decision to study in Boston, they were delighted. It seemed they weren't so much concerned about what school she chose as long as she and Yoav lived there together. Her father said the news deserved a celebration. He made a reservation at El Gaucho, a famous meat restaurant in Haifa and his standby for special occasions.

"Maybe we should wait for Yoav to finish reserve service so he can join us," Tali suggested. "It's not like I'm flying out tomorrow."

"Talush," her father protested, "we want to have a family event, just the four of us. How often do we get a chance for that? This is the perfect opportunity. Don't worry, we'll have a proper farewell bash with Yoav before you go."

From their table by the window, Tali could look out to the port of Haifa and the lighted ships. Far to the north, the lights of Haifa Bay twinkled. "When I have to explain to my friends in Tel Aviv how I feel about Haifa, I tell them about this night view," she said. "I'll miss it."

"What about us? Won't you miss us?" Micha asked only half-jokingly.

"Of course I will," Tali said placatingly. "But as far as a place to live, this is where I want to come back to. The mountains, the sea, the city."

Micha filled their wine glasses and announced: "Before the food comes, a toast to our wonderful, brilliant daughter, and the first doctor-to-be in our family." He raised his glass with a smile of unbounded pride. "Good luck, Talush, or should I say Doctor Tali Nevo." Tali's mother kissed her on both cheeks.

"We're so proud of you," she whispered excitedly. "Who would have thought? Our baby girl."

CHAPTER 33
Hadil

On her way home, Hadil dropped Leila and Nadim off at
the Al-Saraya community center, where the Scouts held
their activities. It was where she and her sisters Mariam
and Ranin had also gone as kids. Be prepared, she recited
the Scout motto. In her day, the World Organization of
the Scout Movement did not recognize the Palestinian
Scouts, since Palestine was not yet a state. Only ten years
ago, after the Oslo Accords, did the Palestinian Scouts
join as full-fledged members. One might even think we
have a state, Hadil smirked. She thought back to the
slogans she and her friends used to sing in the streets:
"The Crescent Scout, the lions' hope... every hour be
prepared... strength and resolve, integrity and faith,
Palestinian scouts... sing it in the lowlands, in the
mountains and the forests, in the Arab homelands."

She thought of Leila, a source of such satisfaction for
her and Hisham. Not only was she an excellent student,
but she displayed unusually mature political awareness and
social responsibility. They were delighted when she told
them she'd been chosen as a delegate to a UN meeting in
Doha. She was usually the first to volunteer for activities
with her Scout troop. Hadil recalled the time Leila shared
her experiences harvesting olives in one of the villages
outside Ramallah.

"We had to climb ladders, pick the olives with a special comb, and collect them into these sacks," she enthusiastically told her parents. "One of the guides taught us a song about the harvest." She giggled and began to sing it: "*Ala dal'una, ala dal'una*, the olives from my village, the green almond, the sage, and the za'atar / How delicious the oven-hot pastries, sprinkled with oil." Their troop leaders praised them, she said, for contributing to the national struggle by picking olives. Hisham couldn't stifle an ironic snort at this hyperbole. Afterwards, Hadil scolded him in private.

"Why do you have always to be so cynical? You have to spoil it for her?" But she knew that despite his grumpiness, Hisham took great pride in their daughter and would do anything to help her flourish. Like many parents of students at Friends, they had no doubt that Leila would go on to university. They were glad when she accepted their suggestion to take the international matriculation exams, which gave graduates a shot at better universities. They both agreed it would be better for Leila to study outside Ramallah, even if it meant she'd be away from home; like Hadil's sister Mariam, who'd emigrated with her husband to Santiago.

"There's a good chance she'll get a scholarship," Hadil told Hisham, "and we'll help her as well." He agreed: "She's got no business staying in Ramallah. She should spread her wings, see the world." Hadil couldn't resist smiling ironically, recalling her mother's repeated claims that there was no future for them in Ramallah, and that they should have left long ago when Hadil and Ranin were small. At the very least, Hadil's mother once said, it would have prevented her from marrying Hisham.

Hadil got home, killed the engine, and sat in the car for a while. Then she got out and slammed the door. She was determined to act immediately, as she had promised herself on the flight back from Belfast. She would talk with

Hisham: not in the evening, or tomorrow, or on the weekend, but now. Suddenly she was anxious. What if it was too late already? She pushed the thought away. He would cooperate, she was sure of it. And if not, then at least she tried. She entered the house and marched to his study. She stopped at the threshold. Hisham shifted his chair around and turned towards her, somewhat surprised, waiting to hear what was on her mind.

"What do you say we drive together, pick up the kids, and eat out? We haven't done that in a while," she said.

She knew her husband well, and noticed his surprise: Hisham looked at her with eyes wide-open before immediately letting them shrink back.

"It's a good idea," he agreed.

"I'm making coffee, do you want some?"

"Yes, please. Good idea," he repeated. "To take a break from work. It never ends. You know how it is."

He tried to act casual about her suggestion, but clearly it was outside their normal routine. He's wary, she thought. They sat on the balcony wordlessly sipping their coffees. Finally Hadil broke the silence: "I've been thinking a lot about us lately, especially after the other day, when you told me how you feel… I don't want to repeat everything we said. The important thing is that we should give ourselves a chance, see what we can do. I hope it's not too late. I guess we should have talked about this thing a long time ago. Or maybe not. We were probably afraid to do this. I know I was afraid of what might happen if we did. But I'm more optimistic now. I don't know if we'll succeed, but I want to try. We need to talk openly. About everything. You know that some of our problems are related to what happens to us at work. Know what I mean? We talked about it once."

Hisham looked up at her and said nothing. She guessed that he comprehended but didn't want to say it. Some truths were too hurtful to get at directly, but she wanted to make sure he understood. "I mean," she said, choosing her words carefully, "that when we're unhappy with our work, or when we think we haven't achieved what we want, it can have a negative effect on the marriage."

To her surprise, Hisham didn't rush to deny or defend himself. On the contrary, he implied that he was aware of it. "We both need to make changes," he said. "We both need to make an effort." He made it clear that he knew some of the responsibility for their marital trouble lay with him. He also went on to casually tell Hadil about new projects he'd started at school. He had the principal's approval to compile a poetry book with poems by the students. He was also taking part in an initiative to hold an open poetry contest for high school students from Ramallah and the surrounding villages. Hadil, on the other hand, told him she'd decided to cut down on her workload so she could be more available to him and the kids.

"I know I've neglected you," she said, "and one of the reasons is that I was unhappy at home."

At the appointed hour they drove to collect Leila and Nadim. The kids were surprised to see their parents together, and even more surprised when they took them to a restaurant. Hadil could tell they were excited, especially Leila. Hadil and Hisham sat at the table and listened attentively as she shared her experiences from school and the Scouts. Kids, Hadil had always thought, were the best seismograph for their parents' marriage, and there was no denying how low her children's spirits had been in recent years. She didn't fool herself: there were tough challenges ahead for her and Hisham. The first challenge came that very night, when they retired to their bedroom. They were both hesitant and tense. Their attempt to rekindle the passion utterly failed. Can't expect to simply jump right back in after all this time, Hadil comforted herself.

Nostalgia was inevitable. She thought back to their wedding night. They were renting a small flat in Ramallah at the time. It wasn't their first time making love, but that night was special. Hisham whispered in her ear: "My love, the church bells were ringing for us today." He got close, grasped both of her hands, and began to softly recite a famous poem about romance between Christians and Muslims, especially Christian women and Muslim men:

Who let the dusky damsel,
kill a Muslim man with her thus enraptured.
Adoring, he brought before her his complaint.
I saw her ringing the bells, and I said:
who taught the maid to ring the bells?
I called after her, Ho, gazelle, may God inspire you,
Come, close the gap towards me, your slave.
She said, No!
I asked her:
Which is the more painful strike?
And I asked myself:
Which is the more painful strike?
The striking of the bells,
or the striking gap
that separates you from me?
Ponder...

"I'm glad we didn't wait," she told him later. "It's a good thing that we came to our wedding night with some experience. This night should be special." Hisham looked at her a long while and said nothing, embarrassed by her openness. With time, their passion waned. As the relationship began to sink, they still gave in to their desires, but sparingly. Even then it usually happened at Hadil's signal. They never discussed the habit they'd developed over the years: she would rub her toes with his. That was the sign. She could tell in advance, most of the time, when he wanted her. But that desire, fueled more by natural instincts and less by the spirit of love, was also finally suppressed. In the beginning, the lack of sex provoked silent protest on both sides. When they went to bed, Hisham turned his back to her, defiantly withdrawing into himself, as if to indulge in a tranquil night's sleep. She lay awake, and could tell by Hisham's endless shifting of positions and normal breathing that he was wide awake as well, seething with frustration.

Now, as she lay on her side recovering from their futile stab at passion, she recalled Arij's recent comment. No, my dear friend, she imagined telling Arij, it's not like riding a bicycle: your head needs to be in it too. But Hadil wasn't too bothered. With a little patience, she thought, things would work out fine. Hisham, on the other hand, was visibly distressed by his failure. He lay on his back and said nothing. Hadil reached out and lightly stroked his head.

CHAPTER 34
Yoav

"Yoavi," his mother asked him on the phone, "don't you think it's high time we invited Tali's parents for dinner? Maybe one Friday night before you and Tali fly away."

"I agree," said Yoav, "you should all meet. Tali thinks so too."

"So, you don't mind?"

"Why should I mind?"

"When I suggested it a few months ago you weren't exactly keen on it. You didn't want to…"

"You're right," he said. "But now it's different. Now we have to do it," he added playfully.

"Do you think her brother should come too?"

"I haven't thought about it," he said. Alon, his shift partner, drew his attention to a teenaged Palestinian boy approaching the checkpoint.

"Mom, I've got to go," Yoav said. "I can't talk. I've got to hang up."

"What happened?!" she asked anxiously.

"Nothing, nothing happened. But I have to hang up. I'll call you later."

The teen covered the remaining distance to the checkpoint running the whole way. Yoav and Alon raised their rifles and aimed, calling at him to stop and lie face-down on the road with his arms out. Though the teen's worn blue jeans and t-shirt indicated that he had nothing on but his clothes, they wanted to make sure he wasn't wearing an explosive belt. They approached him slowly and carefully. A slight movement of his hand toward his torso or waist would have sufficed for them to shoot. The t-shirt was untucked and partly folded up, revealing part of his naked back. They ordered him to stand and began to question him.

He had a delicate face with brown almond eyes showing fear. He carried no identification. Yoav realized that the teenage boy wasn't afraid of them: he had run towards them unarmed. Running from someone Palestinian, Yoav realized. "What's your name? Where do you live? How old are you? Why'd you run to the checkpoint?" Yoav fired questions at him. At first the teen said nothing. He seemed to have trouble answering.

"Maybe he's a collaborator," Alon mused aloud. "He's probably running from the Palestinian police."

"What collaborator? He's a kid," Yoav demurred. "He's barely seventeen. And if he was a collaborator, he'd give us his handler's name, like that guy who made us call the Shin Bet." But as they speculated on the boy's circumstances, he surprised them by speaking in Hebrew.

He understood everything they said. His name, he said, was Nizar Mansour. He gave them the number for a handler named Captain Jimmy, who would help him.

"What's going on here?" Alon said in astonishment. "The other day it was Captain George, now it's Captain Jimmy? It's like the British Mandate never ended."

They radioed their company commander Amir for instructions while the boy sat patiently on a stone near the checkpoint. Amir called back a few minutes later, informing them in an amused voice that "Captain Jimmy" wasn't answering. He added however that someone from Coordination and Liaison or the Shin Bet was going to pick the boy up.

"So this scum's a collaborator after all?" said Alon contemptuously.

"I don't know who he's running from," Yoav replied impatiently. The boy's young age, delicate features, and fragility piqued his curiosity. He went over to talk to him, trying to draw him out. He wanted to know how the teen knew Hebrew. He assumed he must have spent some time among Israelis. Nizar's answers were elusive and incomplete. He confirmed that he'd stayed in different places around Israel, mainly Tel Aviv, and had worked in construction, restaurants, and auto garages. The police caught him and deported him back to the West Bank, where he was forced to live with his family, in Bir Nabala.

"So who are you running from? The Palestinian Authority?" Yoav asked.

Nizar shook his head.

"Your family?"

Nizar stared at the ground. Then it dawned on Yoav: the boy was gay. He recalled a documentary he'd seen on young homosexual men from the West Bank seeking sanctuary in Israel. The Shin Bet must have recruited him, blackmailing him into collaboration by threatening to out him to his village. They probably gave him some money as well. When Yoav delicately broached the possibility, Nizar remained silent, implicitly confirming it. He said he'd smashed his cell phone to avoid being traced. His family, who knew about his proclivities, had threatened to kill him – not intending to do it, he said, but just saying it so he'd leave the village and spare them the disgrace. They thought it better that he live with the Jews, who didn't mind such perversions, so his family thought.

Yoav smiled, wanting to tell the boy that not all Jews were that open minded. As if to prove his point, Alon sneered: "So what, he's not only a collaborator but also a pillow-biter?"

Yoav shook his head in resignation. Arguing with Alon again would be pointless. After their heated exchange the other day, they minimized their interaction and tried to avoid sharing shifts. Amir did his best to accommodate them, but it wasn't always possible. Ironically, as if to punish and defy Yoav, Alon's treatment of the Palestinians had gotten deliberately harsher. In a week, Yoav tried to console himself, it would all be over.

Amir called half an hour later with an update. "Captain Jimmy's still not answering, but an at-risk officer from Coordination and Liaison is coming to get the kid."

"At-risk officer?"

"A guy that deals with people under threat. Anyone in danger from the PA or Hamas. Anyway, the kid's just BI."

"What that?"

"Basic intel. Gives them warnings on simple stuff – riots, stone throwing, road blocking. Things like that."

"What's the at-risk officer going to do with him?" Yoav asked.

"Who cares?" said Amir with exasperation. "Quit breaking my balls with your fucking questions. It's their job, not ours. Maybe they'll get him a place in Tel Aviv. Maybe set him up with an older Jewish gay guy. Anyway, the procedure is that you need to cuff and blindfold him. Otherwise someone going through the checkpoint could spot him as a collaborator."

An hour later the boy was driven away in a military vehicle. "Just what we need, to take in a fag informant," Alon grumbled. "Can't we just toss him to his people and be done with it?"

Yoav ignored Alon, moved away, and called his mother. He knew the last call had left her terrified. "Hi Mom!" he cheerfully shouted into her ear.

"Are you okay?"

"Everything's fine, mom, you've got nothing to worry about," he said in a reassuring tone of voice. "Listen, I thought about that family dinner. Let's have Tali's family over. Merav and Sivan and Tali's brother should all come, too. Maybe not Grandpa Shmuel and Grandma Camilla, though," he added laughingly.

CHAPTER 35
Hisham

It was the first time in a long while that he, Hadil, and the kids had driven together to visit his parents in Al-Jib. Sharif's tragedy had brought everyone closer together, and Hadil's unwavering efforts had earned her the renewed appreciation and affection of Hisham's family. The inexhaustible trove of proverbs and idioms that previously served to criticize Hadil was now turned around to praise her, and she was no longer seen as an interloper but as flesh of their flesh.

"The woman is the crown to her husband's head," said Hisham's mother.

The ride to Al-Jib was giggly and optimistic. Hadil and Hisham tried to contain Leila and Nadim's giddy banter but were secretly delighted. At one point Leila brought up the new substitute English teacher.

"We like her," she said.

"What's her name?" asked Hadil.

"*Al-Mubtasima*," Leila grinned. The smiler.

"What?!" said Hadil.

"It's a joke," Leila replied, "because she's always smiling. Her name's Miss Mandy Norton, but we call her *Al-Mubtasima*. My classmate Imad – you know him, right? – he came up with that name. She's so nice, always helping us with the class materials after school. A few days ago when she came in, Imad said: 'here comes *Al-Mubtasima!*' and we all laughed. She was embarrassed, because she doesn't speak Arabic, but then she understood and smiled. Or maybe she didn't, but she smiled anyway. She's always smiling for no reason."

"Poor woman! That's not nice…" said Hadil. "But it's true, Americans do smile all the time. I never understand them. You tell them something and they smile at you. You can't tell what their smile means, if they agree or disagree, if they're happy or upset… Is it courtesy? Affection? Embarrassment? Impossible to tell."

Hisham cringed, hoping to change the topic. What an idiot I was, he thought: even the kids were able to understand that her smiles are meaningless.

"So what other nicknames do you have for teachers?" he asked aloud.

"Which ones?" said Leila.

"Any teachers."

"Wait," Leila looked to the ceiling trying to recall. "Anton is *Al-Manara*, the lighthouse, because he's tall. Suad, the fat chemistry teacher is *Huta*, whale," she giggled. "And Nuhad…"

"What about me?" said Hisham. "What name have you got for me? Go ahead, it's okay," he urged Leila, noting her hesitation.

"*Rwaa' al-Fan*, Masterpieces," she said quickly, trying to unload the fact like a hot potato.

"What?" Hisham exclaimed.

"Well, you know, Dad…" Leila said hesitantly. "You always use that word. 'These poems are masterpieces of Arabic poetry… Abu Firas Al-Hamdani wrote masterpieces…' So they call you Masterpieces. With love. They say it when I'm around, so they mean it in a nice way."

"It's a good name. Your father's a masterpiece himself, isn't he?" said Hadil. He shot her a quick glance, trying to decipher her meaning, but immediately looked back to the road. As they approached the checkpoint, he noticed it was manned by more soldiers than usual.

"What's this? Are we supposed to be stuck here now?" he fumed at no one in particular. "May God destroy your house," he cursed the soldiers and added a proverb: "We're like the poor at the villain's table."

The column of cars inched forward. Sensing the growing tension, Leila and Nadim fell silent, as did Hisham and Hadil, who looked through the windshield trying to make sense of the extra security. Only the monotonous hum of the engine could be heard. All Hisham wanted was to get through without hassle or agitation. It's all a matter of stupid luck, he thought. The soldiers waved some drivers through but stopped others for inspection. At a soldier's command, Hisham stopped the car.

"Oh no," he sighed upon recognizing the soldier. It was the same one who harassed him and Nabil the other day. And there was the older soldier too, the Iraqi.

The young soldier apparently recognized Hisham. Glaring at him, he yelled something indecipherable in Hebrew, peppering in the Arabic word t'hrid, incitement. "This again," Hisham murmured and smiled in exasperation. "Yes, yes…" he whispered, "I'm the teacher who incites all the students to be *shuhada*, martyrs."

"What are you talking about?" Hadil asked, baffled.

"I'll tell you later. Let's get through this damn checkpoint first."

The young soldier signaled him to roll down his window, and began to say things Hisham couldn't understand. He closely examined everyone in the car. Then he walked around to where Leila sat behind her mother, and fixed her with a long, dirty leer.

"Check out this *kussit*!" he shouted. This hot piece of ass.

A surge of rage and insult overwhelmed Hisham. He stormed out of the car, freed himself from the grip of the older soldier who was trying to hold him back, and marched around the car towards the younger man. "You animal!" he bellowed. "Have you no shame?! You vulgar dog!" The older soldier chased him, trying to stop him. The young soldier stepped back, terrified of Hisham. He raised his weapon and began to shout: "Halt! Halt!"

Hadil jumped out and hurried toward them, seeking to stand between the young soldier and Hisham. Then the soldier opened fire. Hisham froze. He watched as Hadil collapsed to the road, as if mown down by a scythe, and the other soldier, the Iraqi, opened his eyes wide in astonishment. The older soldier's left hand went to his neck, trying to check the injury. For a moment he struggled to stand, and then he slowly collapsed as if melting to the asphalt. Everything happened in a flash, Hisham would later recall when reliving the moment that ended life as he knew it. Leila's screams filled the air. Nadim gasped and sobbed in horror. The other soldiers rushed to the car. Thinking that Hisham had fired the shots, they pinned him to the ground. Hisham lay on his stomach with one cheek against the soil, seeing nothing but army boots and a crushed anthill, surrounded by crazed black ants running frantically in all directions.

CHAPTER 36
Tali

After breakfast, Tali joined her parents to visit Bracha-Bianca at her nursing home. She'd broken her pelvis and could no longer manage on her own anymore. The home was fairly close to Haifa, allowing Micha and his siblings to get there quickly in case of emergency. Many of its residents were from Eastern Europe, including Romania. Bracha-Bianca's Yiddish and Romanian, her children believed, would help her to fit in. They took turns visiting her every Saturday.

The home stood in the heart of a dense pine and cypress grove rich with green meadows and seasonal shrubbery.

"I don't like this place, to be honest," Micha said as he parked the car, "all this quiet. It's like a cemetery."

"I think it's pretty," said Rina.

"Me too," Tali seconded.

"Too beautiful," Micha sneered.

They headed to Bracha-Bianca's room. She was sitting on her bed, eyes fixed on the door, eagerly awaiting them. Like many residents, she lived from one Saturday to the next, her relatives' visit punctuating an otherwise dreary routine. Her thin hair, once black, was carefully combed back. Her red lipstick was painted on slightly over the lip line, and her cheeks were vividly rouged. She wore a long-sleeved dress under an unbuttoned vest. Kissing her on both cheeks, Tali got a sharp whiff of perfume.

"*Ce mai faci, mama*? How are you, mom?" Micha asked.

"*Bine, foarte bine, dragă*, sit, sit," she urged them. "Where's Itamar? Why he not come? He not want see grandmother?"

"You know how he is, Mom," said Micha in Romanian. "He got home very late last night and was still asleep when we left."

"Tali'le," Bracha-Bianca turned to Tali. "*Copilă mea*, my child, where friend? When marriage?"

"I don't know, Grandma. We'll see."

"Tali's going to America to study," Micha told his mother.

"To America," Bracha-Bianca repeated, her face crumpling. "You come see grandmother before go America, yes?" she begged in broken Hebrew.

Rina produced a colorfully-wrapped package from her bag. "I brought you a gift," she smiled at Bracha-Bianca. "It's a scarf." Rina opened it, pulled out the scarf, spread it lengthwise, and then wrapped it around her mother-in-law's shoulders. "You like it? You need it. It's still cold here at night. Spring is a little late." Then she took out a cake wrapped in foil and placed it on the small table. "I baked it for you. It's your favorite apple cake."

"*Merci, fata mea*, thank you, my girl. merci."

Micha suggested they step out for some fresh air. Bracha-Bianca liked the idea but refused to be wheeled out on a wheelchair. The physical therapist, she explained, told her she had to exercise her limbs.

"They're right, Mama," Micha encouraged her, "you need to be moving. You can't stay in bed all day." They helped her to hoist her heavy body from the bed onto the walker that stood next to it. They followed her as she dragged herself slowly to the yard, where they sat on the bench for an hour, with long silences interrupted by brief exchanges: How does she feel? Does she need anything?

How are they treating her at the nursing home? Does she take her medicine? Bracha-Bianca, in turn, wanted to hear about her children and grandchildren: their whereabouts, their health, their schooling. As the minutes slowly ticked away, Rina and Micha repeatedly checked their watches.

Suddenly Tali's phone rang. It was Yoav's sister Merav. Tali narrowed her eyes; it was not an expected call.

"Hi, Merav," she said, then her face darkened. She moved away from the bench and began to pace in a frenzy. Micha approached her followed by Rina.

"What's wrong?" he whispered with a sense of looming disaster. "What's wrong? Tell me!"

Tali looked at him transfixed and said, "Yoav was killed. He's dead." She stood there motionless. She dimly heard her father say, "Mama, we have to go home now."

"You just came," Bracha-Bianca complained in Romanian.

"Tali doesn't feel well," he said.

"What happened, *copilă mea*?" Bracha-Bianca asked with deep concern. Struggling to maintain his composure, Micha turned to his mother and said, "*Nimik, Mama, nu este Important, nu-ți fie frică*": nothing, Mom, nothing serious, don't worry now.

They thought the walk back to her room would never end. Bracha-Bianca inched forward with the aid of the walker. "I'm going to bring a wheelchair," Rina said. "You shouldn't," Micha replied hesitantly, which didn't stop her from rushing out to find one.

"*Bine, copilu meu*, my son, go to Tali. I hope she feels better," said Bracha-Bianca.

Some time later Tali's father would tell her how distressed he'd been that day at the nursing home. He could never forget the sight of his mother slowly moving with the walker. "I wanted to speed her up, get us out of that nursing home. Poor Mom. We just got there and already we were ditching her. But she could barely walk. My mind was jumping like crazy from you to her, you to her." Bracha-Bianca didn't protest their sudden departure again, however.

Grief, pain, hopelessness, exhaustion – all were mixed together. Yoav's parents' house swarmed with relatives, friends, and neighbors, most of whom Tali had never met. She went over to Nava, leaned down, and hugged her. Nava didn't respond. She sat motionless on the sofa, staring. Tali later learned that except for the ghastly scream that Nava let out when two military officers, a man and a woman, gave her the news, she had not stirred or spoken since. She had withdrawn into the dark realm that had begun to spread within her long ago, when Yoav's eldest brother died in his crib. Tali huddled with his sisters, Merav and Sivan, the three of them speechlessly seeking solace in each other's arms. Yoav's father Shaul was periodically overtaken by bitter, uncontrollable sobbing. The sight of the grown man weeping for his son touched every heart present, causing them to cry along with him.

CHAPTER 37
Hisham

The days following Hadil's death found Hisham lethargic and devoid of all vitality, yet he diligently attended to his parental duties. Numbly, mechanically, he drove the kids to school and the Scouts, washed their clothes, cooked their meals, did the shopping, and made himself available whenever they needed him. He felt as if a robot had taken over him, dwelling inside and actuating him without any desire or emotion that he could call his own. Hadil's parents and her aunt Maram made themselves available, and Hadil's sister Ranin went out of her way to help, stopping by almost daily, bringing her kids to keep Leila and Nadim company, and taking Nadim along on family activities.

Even a month into the death of his wife, when Hisham made his first visit to his family in Al-Jib, he was still possessed by a peculiar sense of self-alienation. But he thought it was time for the kids to rediscover the things they loved before the tragedy. They should move forward. It would take time, but it was the only choice. He tried to coax them into activities, even if they did them only halfheartedly at first. He wanted them to visit his parents with him, but only managed to convince Nadim - Leila refused. As they neared the checkpoint, Nadim froze.

"Don't worry," Hisham stroked his head. "It's fine,

don't be afraid."

Sitting with his parents and sister in the yard, Hisham thought about Leila. Since her mother's death, she locked herself in her room most of the time, stepping out only when absolutely necessary. Aside from school and meals, she kept entirely to herself. "You should go out," he urged her, "get together with friends, go to Scouts activities. I know how much you like it." But Leila stayed put. He begged her to share her feelings with him, but she was entirely closed off. Hisham vividly recalled her panic-stricken face, her screams of horror, and her violent trembling as she watched her mother lying dead on the asphalt and himself crushed under the soldiers' boots. Ever since that horrific day, she had crawled into her shell, and her silence thundered in Hisham's ears. It's not enough that she suffered from trauma, he thought, but her young soul seemed to bear a crushing guilt. Hisham wanted desperately to make her understand that no one, no one, was responsible for her mother's death except that Israeli soldier. He was the one who shot her. He was the one who killed her. He was to blame – he and no one else. Again and again Hisham relived each moment that led to Hadil's death. If only I knew, he murmured. If only I knew, I'd let the insult go. I'd let them trample my honor. Those Israelis... those savages. No values, no culture at all. How was I to know?

He took a sip of coffee and stared at his sister Siham, whose expression seemed particularly grim. Her desolate existence wasn't something he could contemplate right now. How to get his family back on track without Hadil? How to live without her? This won't be an entirely new experience, he chuckled mournfully to himself, I've been raising them almost alone for quite some time. "The wind does not blow at the ship's whims," he thought of a proverb. So whither does it blow? he wondered. Where shall it steer my life?

Hisham's mother looked at him and tenderly said,

"You've got to move on, my son. You need a woman. The children need a mother. Find yourself a good wife. Maybe we can find someone from the village for you, a relative. You have to start a new life. There's no choice – you've got to go on," she stressed as if to forestall any objections. "It's not good for you to be alone." Hisham gave her a thoughtful look. Before he had a chance to reply, his father, Marwan, seconded.

"She's right. You've got to move on. It's not good for you to be alone," he said, blowing streams of smoke from his nostrils. "Your grandfather, Mustafa, Allah have mercy on his soul, used to say, 'A home without a woman is like a body without a soul.'"

"You're right, you're right," Hisham nodded, as if submitting to their greater truth, "but we need time. The kids and I have to get over our loss first. Allah is gracious. There's a time for everything."

Marwan nodded in agreement but added, imploring: "Just don't wait too long. We're not saying you need to find a woman tomorrow. But you've got to move on, my son."

It seemed like there was nothing left to say. The heavy silence resumed, leaving Hisham to dwell once more on the memories of that cursed day. He'd been separated from the children, taken to a detention center near Ramallah, and placed in a small room. "Where are my kids?! I want to be with them!" he demanded, refusing to speak with his interrogators until the matter was taken care of. He kept yelling for his children until finally the interrogators asked for the number of a relative who could pick them up. He gave them the number for Hadil's sister Ranin. "She's on her way," they assured him. Only when they let him speak to Ranin and confirm that she'd taken Leila and Nadim back to Ramallah with her did he cooperate.

Dressed in civvies, the interrogators knew everything about him: his address, his occupation, his place of work, and details about his family. They knew about his brother Sharif and his political activities as a student at Bir Zeit. They went on and on, yelling at Hisham that he had attacked the soldier at the checkpoint, tried to snatch the gun from him and shoot him and the other soldiers. At one point Hisham was sure they would beat him, like the time twenty years ago, when he and his friends were pummeled by the men who'd grabbed them in a jeep. But the interrogators merely shouted, trying to extract a confession from him.

"Do you think I'm crazy?!" he said. "You think I'd do something like that to put my wife and kids at risk?! Like I want them killed?! What sort of person do you take me for?!" The interrogators gradually accepted his version of the story but still wanted to dispel certain doubts.

"You attacked the soldier," they insisted. "You tried to snatch his gun. That's what the soldier says." Hisham angrily shook his head in disbelief. "He's lying! I did not attack him, and I never went for his gun. All lies! All lies. I don't even know how to use a gun. Yes, I cursed him, but I didn't attack him! He was rude. Ask his friends, the other soldiers. He hurt my honor; he insulted me, insulted my daughter, insulted my wife. He shot her! He killed my wife..." Hisham broke into sobs, unable to control himself. "I cursed him, yes, I did... I curse him now! He killed my wife! I didn't attack him," Hisham repeated angrily. "What would you do if someone talked to your daughter like that, stepping on your honor?!"

He was released that evening, once the interrogators were completely satisfied that he was telling the truth. They told him he could file a complaint against the soldier with the Coordination and Liaison Administration, if he liked.

"What good would it do now?" Hisham replied sadly. "He destroyed my family. I lost my wife. My children lost their mother." He burst into tears again.

He went straight to Hadil's parents' house. He could

hear the wailing and screaming from outside. As soon as he entered, Aunt Maram rushed to him, hugged him, and burst out crying. Salwa and Ranin were sitting on the sofa, hugging and crying. Unaware of Hisham's presence, Salwa moaned: "We lost her, and we lost the children." She feared, it seemed, that placed under Hisham's sole custody Leila and Nadim would sever their ties with the Christian faith. Noticing Hisham, Hadil's father hushed her. Hisham ignored Salwa. He was looking for his children. They were sitting in a corner of the living room, attended by some young women he'd never seen before. The children were alarmingly quiet. He rushed to them and held them tight.

An hour later, Hisham's parents arrived with Siham, followed by Fuad, Afaf, and her husband. Missing were Sharif, who was still in no condition to leave home, and Abir, whose advanced pregnancy no longer enabled her to endure the torturous journey from her village near Bethlehem to Ramallah. Arij's parents were also there, as was Nabil, Hisham's cousin and childhood friend. Hisham's eyes kept roaming over the spacious but crowded living room as though in a fog, catching the faces of his Friends School colleagues Jawad and Anton, and Hadil's workmates, Riham and two others whose names he couldn't recall. Amer the taxi driver came in limping. Apparently, his cracked ribs hadn't healed yet, and he grimaced with pain at every step. People came in and out to offer their condolences. And there was Mandy, too. She shook Hisham's hands affectionately with tears in her bright blue eyes and a smile of profound sadness and compassion. She implored him to ask her for anything she could do to help.

Later that night the priest from the Church of Transfiguration stopped by. Salwa had already expressed her wish that Hadil's funeral be held in accordance with Greek Orthodox practice. "I want it to be like my father's funeral," she stated. The funeral was set for the following day, although at first Salwa tried to hold it off until Hadil's sister Mariam came from Santiago. Salim firmly objected.

"My dear, we can't wait," he said. "It would only prolong the children's suffering. It has to be tomorrow." He added that Arij would arrive from Amman by then, and that Mariam would make it to the ninth-day memorial. Salwa grudgingly relented.

All the while, Hisham lay low in the living room and said nothing. Only when he came back home did he suddenly feel that Hadil was being robbed from him all over again. The funeral, the ceremonies, the arrangements – everything was in Salwa's hands now, as if reclaiming Hadil back for herself and the Christian community, as if he, her husband, had merely been a temporary guardian. Late at night, Salwa and Maram went to the hospital morgue, washed Hadil's body, dressed her in her finest clothing, powdered her face, and drew lipstick on her lips. "She'll go to her grave as beautiful as she was in life," Salwa declared. They placed her in a casket and wanted to take her home.

"The weather can be quite warm these days," the morgue attendant said, focusing his gaze on them to drive home his meaning. "You'd better leave her here."

The next morning, Hadil's body was transferred from the Ramallah government hospital to her home in the al-Tira neighborhood. After a while, the funeral procession began, covering the short distance to The Church of Transfiguration. The casket was transported in a special municipal vehicle that was provided to Muslims and Christians alike. According to the religion of the deceased, sometimes it featured a large cross, and sometimes a large crescent, as if mocking the random meaninglessness of religious identity, especially in death.

The casket was placed in the church's consolation hall, whose thick curtains and dark-brown pews instilled a gloomy atmosphere. Hadil's face was visible, her eyes closed, her hands crossed over her chest. Her long hair was done up in a black crown that reminded Hisham of the saintly auras in all the icons on the church walls. Grieving relatives, friends, colleagues, and quite a few women – ones she'd helped at her center, he assumed – filed by to look at Hadil, wiping tears. Some bent to kiss her forehead, others to kiss the icon of the Virgin placed in her hands. Some shook Hisham's hands, hugged him, and whispered the customary platitudes: may her memory live forever, may the Lord repay your loss. Others noted the sacrifice Hadil had made for the cause, declaring: "She died on behalf of the nation." Hisham listened to the tributes and consolations with a frozen expression.

Later the casket was moved to the church's nave for the main funeral service. By then he was already able to recite the Trisagion. "Holy God, Holy and Mighty, Holy Immortal One, have mercy on us," he mechanically repeated the prayer, which was also printed on the ribbon of the bouquet placed next to Hadil's head. The priest read from Psalms: "There shall no evil befall thee, neither shall any plague come nigh thy dwelling." Hisham reflected on the words as Hadil reclined before him in the casket.

"No evil befall thee," he muttered sardonically. He approached the casket with the kids, his right arm around Leila's shoulders and his left hand on Nadim's. Examining Hadil's face, her cheeks, her lips, the hair on her head, different words rang in his ears – not from scripture, but from Lebanese poet Elia Abu Madi, and sung by Hisham's beloved Nazem al-Ghazali. He'd recited them to Hadil long ago on one of her birthdays. The funeral was imbued with an ancient mystical air: the shadows cast by the two chandeliers above the casket, the candles, the incense, the bearded clerics in black robes and conical hats flatly intoning psalms. Against their monotone, Hisham silently recited the poem:

My angel, what am I to gift you on this your holiday?
Roses?
But to me none are so pretty as that whose fragrance

your cheeks exude.

Or perhaps a ruby, burning like the blood of my heart?

But such crimson preciousness already dwells on your lips.

And maybe I shall give you my soul?

But this, your hands already hold hostage.

As the ceremony ended, the casket was again loaded onto the funeral car and made the short journey to the Christian cemetery, flanked by a procession of relatives and close friends. Only men were allowed to be present as the casket was lowered. Among them, Hisham was surprised to see Murad there. Murad approached him, offered his condolences, and urged Hisham to call if ever he needed anything. "Hadil was a special woman," he said. There was another brief religious ceremony, after which the family went back to Hadil's parents' house. In the evening the traditional mercy meal was held, signaling God's triumph over death.

Sitting in his parents' yard and compulsively reconstructing in his mind the episodes surrounding Hadil's death, Hisham suddenly heard Nadim laugh: a quick burst that died down immediately, as if apologizing for itself. It was the first time Hisham had heard his son laugh since Hadil's death. He was curious to know what had caused it, but didn't bother to find out. He recalled what Hadil had said about children's mental stamina just a few days before she was killed. Children are extremely adaptable, she said, and can find joy even in the harshest conditions.

CHAPTER 38
Tali

During the thirty day period between the funeral and the unveiling of Yoav's headstone, Tali shut herself up in the apartment, refusing all visits and her parents' pleas that she stay with them. "Just for a bit, Talush," her mother implored. "We'll go out, sit in a café, just you and me. It'll do you good." Tali declined. With the exception of her childhood friends Liat and Ronnie, she found all human company intolerable. With them at least she could be herself, let moods take her as they will. The three of them would sit together in comfortable silence for long stretches of time. When she wanted to share, they listened, and when she didn't, it was fine.

She would get especially angry when people who offered sympathies dwelt on the circumstances of Yoav's death. Random tragedy, she knew well, provoked speculation: if only Yoav had done this or that, and so on. People couldn't stomach the brute fact of shit simply happening.

"If I hear one more of those if-only speeches, I'm going to scream," she told Liat and Ronnie. "What fucking difference does it make that it was a stray bullet? Like it'd be less tragic if he was shot on purpose? I think of these stupid ideas enough by myself."

It was during the shiva, the seven days of mourning,

held at Yoav's parents' house, that she learned the identity of the Palestinian woman killed at the checkpoint. Yoav's relatives were passing around the newspaper story about the incident. Tali picked it up:

RESERVE SOLDIER AND PALESTINIAN WOMAN KILLED IN CHECKPOINT SHOOTING ACCIDENT

Reserve soldier Yoav Yarkoni, 30, was killed yesterday at the Fabric of Life checkpoint outside Ramallah. The cause of death was determined to be accidental, due to unintentional shooting by Yarkoni's shift partner. Also killed in the accident was Hadil Saada, 39, mother of two from Ramallah. Responding to the accident, the General Staff has launched…

Tali stifled a shriek. "It can't be… it can't be…" she shuddered. She grabbed her purse and fumbled for the business card Hadil had given her in Amman. She scrutinized the card. The name matched. "It's Hadil," she said to herself, shocked. She wanted to share it with someone, maybe Merav, but it wasn't the time or place. She remembered the way Hadil looked at her when she stormed out of the conference room back in Jordan, anxious for Yoav's safety, and Hadil's assurance in her last email: "I'm sure that in the end everything will turn out for the best."

Tali looked at Yoav's mother. Nava sat catatonically on the sofa, oblivious to everything around her. She had maintained this posture all through the shiva. Sometimes she gave the impression of listening to what people said, her eyes roving from one face to another. But they were empty, lifeless eyes. She'll never get over this, Tali thought, and she'll never stop blaming herself. Even before Yoav's death, Nava had very clearly been suffering from severe post-traumatic stress, consumed with the terror of losing another child. And now her worst fear had come to pass. She was well and truly gone.

The funeral and shiva were the first time Tali and

Yoav's respective parents met and quite obviously the last. Yoav's death had ended the relationship between the would-be in-laws before it began. He was gone, and Tali would go on with her life.

"So, you're flying out," Liat said in approval. It was evening, a few days before the unveiling of the headstone.

"Yes," Tali confirmed laconically.

"Why'd you pick NYU?"

"I've got history there," Tali said with an air of mystery.

Liat and Ronnie stared at her.

"Kidding," Tali smiled, "New York's the best choice academically."

"And you're going alone?" Ronnie asked before instantly realizing his gaffe.

Tali let it slide. "I already told them I'm coming. Everything's taken care of —visa, enrollment, curriculum, accommodation. The whole thing."

It was Galia Hoffman who pulled strings for Tali, telling her colleague at NYU's department of psychology about Tali's circumstances, and why she was forced to pick Boston over NYU before. She asked them to reconsider her candidacy. A few rules were stretched, and Tali was soon accepted to the doctoral program. "New York's a good place for new beginnings," Galia told Tali. "You're young, smart, and beautiful. You should have no problem fitting in. It's like I told you before," she added somewhat broodingly, "life doesn't always work out the way we plan it. The important thing is to do whatever you can with the hand you're dealt."

The unveiling of the headstone was set for 5 PM Monday, in the new military plot of Petah Tikva's Segula Cemetery. Tali was about to leave the apartment she'd shared with Yoav for two years, when she noticed a new email on her computer. It was from the head of the psychology department at Harvard.

Dear Ms. Nevo, it read, As you know, you had been placed on our waiting list. I'm glad to inform you that the

Harvard Department of Psychology can now offer you a spot in our PhD program. We apologize if this offer is overdue, and if you've already selected another institution. If, however, you still wish to enroll in our program, we'd be more than happy to have you. Please let me know your decision as soon as possible.

Tears burst into Tali's eyes. A car horn honked outside; Liat was there to pick her up. Tali couldn't take her eyes off the screen. The horn sounded again, more persistently. Tali heaved a long sigh, clicked Print, stuffed the printout into her bag, and ran downstairs.

As expected, the roads were congested. They drove in silence. Just before arriving at the cemetery, Tali's phone rang. It was Merav, Yoav's sister: "We're waiting for you in the military plot parking," she said. Tali took the printout from her bag, smoothed it out, and read it again. Tears rolled down her cheeks.

"What happened?" Liat whispered softly. As they parked and turned off the engine, Tali handed her the printout. Liat read it, then leaned across and hugged Tali. They got out and joined Yoav's extended family, which had gathered for the short stroll to Yoav's grave. There were Yoav's parents, his grandfather Shmuel, his grandmother Camilla in a wheelchair, uncles, aunts, nephews, friends. Tali approached Nava, Merav and Sivan, and silently embraced each of them in turn. She noticed a few of Yoav's army friends standing in a separate huddle, as if to avoid breaching the family's intimacy. They'd all been to the funeral as well. They briefly confided with Tali and Merav that they had little new information to tell about the ongoing inquiry. Amir, Yoav's company commander, said that Alon – the soldier who'd shot Yoav – was in a state of shock. It was clear to everyone that Alon's behavior had provoked the incident. Amir ruefully estimated that the upshot of the inquiry would be some tightening of conduct rules at checkpoints vis-à-vis local population, but little else.

"They'll say he panicked and lost control when the Palestinian charged at him. Alon probably wouldn't be penalized."

When everyone had gathered, they began the slow, quiet march to the newly marked grave. Chezi, Nava's older brother, handed out prayer booklets with ragged faux-leather covers and the title Elevation of the Soul in gilded letters framed with arabesques. Though not an observant Jew, he conducted the ceremony with skill. The mourners began to read out psalms from the Book of Psalms, with the verses' opening letters spelling out Yoav, son of Nava. "Blessed are those whose way is blameless, who walk in the law of the Lord," one of the mourners read out, followed by someone else reading the next verse, and so on. Yoav's father read out the kaddish in a cracked voice, tears trickling freely into his month-old beard. Nava reached out to brush her fingertips along the marble headstone, then ran them over the recessed letters of her son's name. Her face was frozen. Merav and Sivan wept. Tali stood next to them, likewise gazing at the headstone. Though freshly hewn, the stone gave her the eerie impression that the man underneath it had been dead for a long, long while, a permanent denizen of the cemetery. The headstone seemed to mark a brutal fait accompli: Yoav was dead, categorically and irrevocably, and there he lay. The glistening black letters spelled him out: Yoav Yarkoni, son of Nava and Shaul. Fell in action. Dates of birth and death, both Hebrew and Gregorian.

The ceremony was brief. In departing, each mourner placed a small stone on the grave. Tali waited for everyone to leave. "I need a minute alone," she told Liat. "Can you wait for me outside?"

Before she could speak to Yoav, she heard a female voice softly calling her name. She turned around and recognized the woman.

"I'm Einat," the woman said, extending her hand. "We met once."

"I remember," Tali replied, unable to suppress a tinge of jealousy as she sized up the well-dressed, remarkably attractive woman.

"Yes, we were close friends," said Einat. "But for the past couple of years we haven't been in touch. I found out from the TV - I couldn't believe it. And the way it happened... it's... I thought of visiting Yoav's family during the shiva, but I don't really know them. I met them once at our BA graduation ceremony. They probably don't remember me. Anyway, I felt I had to come, at least to this. I wanted to tell you how sad I was to hear it... and that I'm sorry for your loss. He talked about you with so much love. He was a special guy. I've always loved him."

"Thank you," Tali said sincerely. "Thank you for coming."

Einat smiled sadly, turned around, and walked away. Tali was finally alone, able to hear her own thoughts and feelings in front of the grave. But she couldn't get Einat out of her head. Suddenly her gut tightened. Einat said that she and Yoav hadn't been in touch for two years, but there was her email to Yoav: "I'd love to see you again before you disappear on me." And Yoav told her that he had spoken with Einat on the phone. Something didn't add up. And what did she mean by "I've always loved him"? Tali stared at the headstone as if to glean answers from it. The silence of Yoav's grave thundered against the distant voices of other mourners elsewhere in the cemetery. Tali placed her palm on the shining marble and sighed. Then she turned around and walked resolutely back towards the cemetery gate.

311

Made in the USA
Monee, IL
21 December 2021